Rushed

Relic

Brian Harmon

Rushed: Relic

ISBN: 1-945559-18-1
ISBN-13: 978-1-945559-18-1

This is book 9!
Want to start at the beginning?
Be sure to check out all the books in this series:

And don't miss these other great books by Brian Harmon:

The Temple of the Blind series:

Hands of the Architects trilogy:

For Guinevere

Chapter One

Eric closed the book and looked over the cover. *Reassembling the Ashes: A Collection of Historical Accounts of the Reconstruction of Creek Bend, Wisconsin After the Fire of 1881*, by local author Emanuel Voskstern. It was a fascinating read. Like anyone who grew up in Creek Bend, Eric had heard stories about the fire all his life, how it'd swept through the city, reducing buildings to smoldering ruins and killing dozens of people. He'd read plenty of books and articles by various local historians on the subject over the years—not to mention countless research papers written by his own students—but *this* book was different from most of what he'd seen. It focused less on the fire than on the things that were lost that fateful night. Voskstern wrote in fascinating detail about buildings and homes that would've been historical treasures if they were still standing today, like the opulent Allendar Mansion that now only existed in a handful of old photographs. And the Gudenhaus Inn that was said to have hosted celebrities, famous writers and powerful world leaders, including foreign dignitaries and presidents both former and future. And then there was the original courthouse and the train station, both of which were said to have been architectural works of art compared to anything standing in the city today. Irreplaceable records were also lost that night, burned to cinders, including, supposedly, documentation that would've connected a wealthy tycoon's socialite wife to a certain governor in a very scandalous way. Local businesses were wiped from the face of the earth, like the Achenbach Restaurant, said to have served the best fruit pies anyone had ever tasted and would ever taste again, given that the owner took every last secret recipe to his grave that night. And of course there was the immeasurable cost of all those human lives, including a talented poet whose work might've become the stuff of American Literature textbooks and a man who very likely would've become the next state senator and whose untimely death, for all anyone knew, could have altered the course of history for the entire country. There were even rumors of lost fortunes and incredible treasures buried forever in the infernal blaze. Voskstern had gone as far as to piece together a vision of what the city might look like today if not for that costly tragedy, although it could only be speculation, given that historians today couldn't agree on the exact locations of many of those lost buildings. The city had grown and evolved so much over the past one hundred thirty-seven years that no one was entirely sure anymore how the original streets were laid out.

It was a good book. He liked it. And it was signed, too.

All the books were signed. It was a book signing, after all.

He didn't usually come to these sorts of things. He wasn't a very social person. He preferred to spend his Saturday mornings at home. But when your wife was a talented and popular freelance cake decorator and caterer, you found yourself at a lot of different kinds of events. Karen knew both the author's daughter and Jess Levener, the bookshop owner, and so she'd been hired to provide refreshments. Naturally, she dragged him along to help carry things.

But it was over now. Voskstern had left. No one was browsing the shelves. Of Jess' two employees, Esther Liler had just left to take her lunch and Hellen Utelman was in the storeroom. The bookshop had fallen quiet.

Karen was gathering the last of the leftovers into the cooler to take home when Jess stepped into the office for a moment, leaving them alone in the shop for the first time since the doors opened. She glanced over at him, eyebrows raised, and whispered, "That was *weird*."

"Which thing are we talking about?" Eric whispered back as he rose from his chair and stretched his back. "The pervy old guy in the cowboy hat who came in groping at that girl young enough to be his granddaughter?"

She wrinkled her nose at the memory.

"Or that trashy woman who wanted poor Emanuel to sign

her chest so she could add him to her collection of 'celebrity tattoos'?"

"No, but *ew*."

"Or the super-creepy Easter Bunny?"

She glanced toward the corner of the room where the moth-eaten monstrosity was propped up behind a display of Easter decorations and holiday books. It was an old, homemade costume, a little piece of the building's history from long before Jess bought it and turned it into the adorable Tale As Old As Time Bookshop, and even back before it was a stuffy old place with the not-nearly-as-cute name of Muekler Books that reeked of cheap cigar smoke and was owned by that creepy old man with one blind eye. All around the abomination were pictures of children back in the late forties, when the place was still Gooden Books and Gifts. The thing was much newer in the photographs, but no less creepy. The children were sitting on its furry lap, posing for the camera. Most of them were smiling brightly, apparently unaware that the Easter Bunny shouldn't look like a vaguely bunny-shaped nightmare given unholy life by a deranged seamstress, but a few of them did look more appropriately uncertain about the horror on which they were perched. She shuddered and turned away from the probably evil rabbit. "Ugh. No. I meant the *book*. The whole fire thing."

"Ah," he said. "Yes."

Being the subject of the book at the center of the day's festivities, people had been talking about it nonstop. The fire on February seventeenth of eighteen eighty-one erupted out of nowhere in the middle of the night and spread across half the town in minutes, killing dozens of unfortunate citizens, many as they slept in their own beds. Authorities never determined what started it or even *where* it started, and it had long been said, often in dramatic, hushed tones, that the flames burned hotter than any natural fire and shrugged off all efforts to put it out. And some swore it had a mind of its own, even, by some reports, *defying the very wind.*

"It's so weird that *we know* what happened," she whispered, her gaze twitching toward the office door.

"You want to go around telling everybody what really started the fire?"

"No," she replied without hesitation. "Of course not."

Most people chalked it up to inadequate safety regulations of the time, but there were plenty of nuts clinging to wild conspiracy theories and ridiculous ideas ranging from government weapons testing to a crashed alien spaceship to a real-life, fire-breathing dragon slumbering somewhere beneath the city.

These things were *almost* as absurd as the truth.

"I'm just saying, it's weird that we *know* something like that and can't say anything."

It *was* weird. Everyone spoke of it with such awe. It was easy to tell that every one of them would've loved nothing more than to know the truth of how that fire started. But none of them would ever believe the truth if he told them. And he could hardly blame them. After all, a time-traveling genie wasn't even as believable as a fairytale dragon.

"Thanks you guys!" exclaimed Jess as she emerged from her office. She was an attractive and dainty woman in her early fifties with a cheerful and charming, girlish sort of energy. She practically *bounced* with every step she took. "Everything was *amazing*, Karen. Oh my god, I want that cupcake recipe!"

"I'll email it to you," she promised as she knotted the last of the trash bags.

Eric smiled as he closed the cooler. Karen had enough recipes to fill an entire shelf of cookbooks and she was always happy to share them. It didn't matter. The recipe was only half of it. The rest was talent and passion, and he didn't know anyone more talented and passionate in the kitchen than his wife. She cooked with love, as his grandmother used to say. And it shined in every bite.

"Are you sure you don't want me to leave you the rest of the leftovers?" asked Karen.

"Oh, *god no!*" gasped Jess. "I'd gain fifty pounds by tomorrow morning!"

"Good," said Eric, picking up the cooler. "More for me."

"*You* don't need all those either," said Karen.

"Yes I do."

Jess laughed. "Seriously, though, let's do it again next time, okay?"

"I'd love to," said Karen. "Just give me a call."

"I will! You guys take care!"

"You too," replied Eric.

They left through the back door, bidding farewell to Hellen on their way out and exiting into the narrow parking lot behind the building. "That was fun," said Karen as she carried the trash bags to the dumpster enclosure.

"It was alright," admitted Eric. As far as social gatherings went, he decided he liked book signings better than most. There wasn't a lot to do. He'd spent most of his time sitting in one of those cozy armchairs, reading, while Karen and Esther attended to the refreshments table. They'd really only needed him for a little heavy lifting. And Jess, Esther and Hellen were all delightfully sweet women to be around. But he still would've rather spent a cold, dreary Saturday like this one at home in his pajama pants.

He placed the cooler in the back of the SUV, then closed the liftgate and walked around to the driver's door, admiring the vehicle as he did so.

Two months ago, his familiar PT Cruiser was totaled. Then it was swallowed into another dimension...which wasn't even nearly the strangest part of that awful night. But the worst part about the whole ordeal was not knowing what, precisely, they should do about it. He was fairly certain that his insurance didn't cover anything that happened *off-world*. He and Karen had considered reporting it stolen. After all, it wasn't where he left it and he honestly had no idea where it might be... He didn't like it, but he didn't think he could afford to just let it go on a teacher's salary. But after a few days of deliberating about what they would tell the police, the entire situation bizarrely took care of itself in the form of a check from the insurance company. Someone out there, it seemed, had taken care of it for them.

They spent a few more days scratching their heads, wondering if it was really okay to take the money. It felt like a cruel trick.

The real world didn't work like this. But he *had* made a number of mysterious friends these past few years, like the otherworldly Lady of the Murk or the diminutive gas station attendant and his daughters.

In the end, they decided to be grateful for whatever help they were offered and used the money to put a down payment on a new vehicle. He'd even managed to convince Karen to make an upgrade and was now the proud owner of a brand-new Chevrolet Trailblazer.

The only downside was that it had significantly more cargo capacity than Karen's Subaru, and so she'd already begun commandeering it for her various catering jobs. It was probably only a matter of time before it became *her* Trailblazer.

He opened the door and peered into the empty cab. Then he glanced over to see what was taking Karen so long.

She was gone.

Frowning, he closed the door and walked around the front of the vehicle. "Karen?"

Tale As Old As Time was sandwiched between a CPA office and a dentist in a line of seven attached buildings. The parking lot was a narrow strip of asphalt between these buildings and the main warehouse of Stavard Distribution Services, just wide enough for a single row of parking spaces. There was a high fence blocking off one end of the lot, leaving only the one way to leave, and that was in the opposite direction she'd gone.

He called out to her again, a little louder this time.

A deep, primal sort of fear began to spread through him. And it wasn't an irrational kind of fear. He wasn't sure there was any such thing as irrational fear. Not for him. Because he knew things about this world that most people didn't. He knew that real things went bump in the night. He knew that monsters existed. He knew that terrible things happened *every day*. And he knew how easily people could vanish off the face of the earth in an instant.

"*Karen?*"

He picked up his pace, hurrying toward the enclosure where he last saw her, his stomach tightening into a burning knot. His vivid and rarely helpful imagination was already going to work, feeding him one nightmarish scenario after another.

Something wasn't right. He could feel it.

But then, as he circled around the enclosure, he found her. She was standing behind the wooden fencing, facing the building.

"Karen?"

She turned and looked at him as he approached. She had an odd, confused sort of expression on her pretty face. Her dark eyes looked strangely glazed.

"What're you doing?"

She blinked at him, then she turned and looked at the wall again. The buildings there weren't actually attached, he realized. There was a very narrow gap between the dentist office and the appliance shop on the end, barely wide enough for someone to sidle sideways into.

Except as he stepped around the corner of the enclosure, he saw that someone *was* standing there. A woman. And she wasn't standing sideways. She was facing straight ahead, seeming to defy the very physical space she was occupying.

Eric stopped and stared at her, confused. Everything about the scene baffled him.

Was that Jess? What was she doing out here?

No... That couldn't be Jess. First of all, her hair was the wrong color. It was a silvery sort of blonde instead of chestnut brown. And she wasn't dressed the same. Jess was wearing pants and a button-up shirt. This woman was wearing a sweater, a knee-length skirt and light, summery sandals in spite of the cold. Most of all, however, there was the way she was squeezed into that narrow space. Was it some kind of optical illusion? It was unnatural. She shouldn't fit there like that, yet somehow she did. His brain couldn't process what he was seeing. Her body and the space it occupied seemed to be two entirely different things.

The woman that wasn't Jess turned her eyes on Eric. They had a strange sort of shine to them, he realized, like the eyes of a wild animal.

"Eric...?" creaked Karen, her voice strangely small.

Then the thing launched itself from the alleyway, knocking Karen to the ground and lunging at him.

Four years ago, he might've stood there helpless, too flabbergasted to move, but this wasn't the first time he'd encountered something monstrous. His guard was up in an instant, his arms raised to defend himself, his feet shifting to brace against the assault.

The thing that wasn't Jess slammed against him. Sharp teeth tore into the sleeve of his jacket, tearing the fabric.

Did this thing always have a dog's muzzle? He was fairly sure it didn't. It wouldn't have looked like Jess if it looked like a snarling dog. But then where did all those teeth come from? They wouldn't have fit inside a human mouth.

He threw his weight forward, shoving the monster back, taking it by surprise.

It growled at him, a strange, monstrous noise that was neither human nor animal, because this thing was neither a woman nor a beast. It was something else entirely, something that he couldn't quite comprehend.

It seemed to size him up for a moment, shining, inhuman eyes filled with primal fury, then it turned and darted away on thin, furry legs that didn't look remotely human yet somehow still fit the sandals it was wearing.

As he watched, it bounded effortlessly up the wall, leapt over the chain link fence and vanished into the next lot, trailing a long tail behind it, no less.

He knelt over Karen. "You okay?"

She nodded, her wide eyes staring after the monstrous thing, still looking dazed. "She had really cute shoes..." she gasped.

Chapter Two

"It was Jess," explained Karen, confused. "She wanted me to follow her. It seemed important."

"It definitely wasn't Jess," said Eric. Without letting go of the steering wheel, he pushed up his sleeve and glanced at his forearm. The thing that wasn't Jess had left a few painful scrapes, but it'd hadn't drawn blood. The fabric had mostly protected him from its teeth. It was probably nothing he needed to worry about.

"I *know* it wasn't her," she snipped. "I mean, I know it *now*, obviously. And I kind of knew it then, too. There was something so...*wrong* about her."

"That she had a dog's face, maybe? Or was it the *tail* that tipped you off?" He pulled into their driveway and parked the Trailblazer, his head still spinning from the bizarre encounter behind the bookshop.

Karen shook her head and twisted a lock of hair around her finger. "She didn't look like that at first. Or...I didn't *notice* it at first? I don't know. It was so weird. Like I couldn't think straight. The whole thing sort of feels like a dream."

Nightmare was more like it. Whatever the thing was, it wasn't human. And it didn't act like most of the monsters he'd encountered in the past, either. This one was intelligent. Sneaky, even. *Calculating*. It made him shudder to think just how close he might've come to losing her back there.

"It was like I was hypnotized or something."

He glanced over at her. He didn't like to see her look frightened. She'd always been so guarded with her emotions. She hated for anyone to see when she was afraid or vulnerable, which wasn't surprising considering how mercilessly critical her parents had been when she was growing up. She never felt like she was allowed to cry or lose her temper, no matter what she might have been going through. Growing up for her meant never showing any signs of weakness. So when he saw even a hint of fear in her pretty features, he knew she was *really* scared.

The two of them sat there for a moment, the experience in the parking lot running over and over in their minds. It was happening again. *The weird.* It was calling out to him, beckoning him back into harm's way.

There was an uncomfortable knot somewhere deep in his belly that burned at the very thought. It felt as if a great weight were pressing against his chest, making it hard to breathe. It'd only been a few weeks ago that he went through that awful ordeal in Evancurt, after all. The events of that night had haunted him nonstop since he returned. He'd felt anxious and edgy at all hours of the day. *Jumpy*, even. He was zoning out in the middle of conversations. Even in the middle of class a few times. And sometimes, when he was alone, either at school or at home or even alone in the car, he found himself gripped by an intense and irrational fear that crowded every rational thought from his brain.

Now, as he sat there, his heart pounding in his chest, he wasn't sure he could do this again. With every fiber of his being he wanted to run inside, lock all the doors and hide his head under the covers until whatever was happening blew over.

But that wasn't how the weird worked. He didn't have the luxury of simply walking away. It never even gave him the courtesy of a warning.

He found his eyes drawn to the small, wooden orb hanging from the Trailblazer's rearview mirror. Given to him two years earlier by a self-proclaimed medium, the little ball of twigs and twine was supposed to dispel negative energy and encourage positive spirits. It used to live in his bedroom closet between episodes of weirdness, but after what happened in Evancurt, Karen decided that it should stay right here, ready and waiting for the unexpected in case it snatched him away again without giving him the chance to return home and properly prepare. But now he found that it had become a constant reminder that the weird could strike any time, any place.

And now, ready or not, it was happening again.

"That was really scary," said Isabelle, her voice rising from the cell phone in Karen's lap. "From what you guys are describing, it sounds like a skinwalker."

"Skinwalker?" said Eric. "What the hell is that?"

Karen frowned. "I've heard that before somewhere, I'm pretty sure."

"It's from Native American legends," she explained. "Especially Navajo. Supposedly it's an evil witch who can shapeshift into people and animals, especially dogs and coyotes."

"Witches again?" said Karen, concerned. Their last encounter with witches didn't go so well. Her husband was nearly murdered by a crazy woman with freaky yellow eyes and there was supposedly now a terrible curse hanging over everyone involved.

Was that what this was? Was this the beginning of the end? The inescapable consequences of their past actions finally catching up to them?

Eric and Karen exchanged an uneasy look at the thought.

"That's what the legends say," Isabelle replied. "But I don't think they're really witches. Not in any sense that we know them, anyway. I didn't sense any magic energy for one thing. In fact, I didn't sense any energy at all. Besides, it sounds more like a werewolf to me. Except with more *freedom*, I guess? Like, they don't need full moons and aren't allergic to silver or anything."

"Are werewolves something we have to worry about, too?" asked Karen, concerned.

"Not that I know of," she replied. "But I wouldn't exactly be surprised at this point."

"We're a long way from the Navajo nation," remarked Eric. That was in the American Southwest, nowhere near Wisconsin.

"That's true," said Isabelle. "And from what I know of them, they're not really seen all that far outside that region. It doesn't make sense for them to be here. But everything else about that encounter is pretty spot-on. I've even heard about them taking the shape of someone familiar and trying to lure you away somewhere."

"How do you know all this?" asked Karen.

"Same as always. Just stuff I've picked up from the trapped people."

Isabelle had been imprisoned in a strange state of being outside the regular flow of time for the past forty years, never physically aging. But thanks to a strange, psychic connection with her parents, she'd remained *aware* of the passage of time and the changes of the world around her. It was the same connection she shared with Eric after their fateful meeting several years ago, allowing her to peer into his mind whenever she wanted and follow along on his weird adventures, often offering him valuable information on the unusual things he encountered. She was even able to sense certain kinds of exotic energies in his immediate vicinity. The rest of her time was spent traveling around the world through what she described as a mysterious doorway that allowed her to pass from one "broken place" to the next. It was in these travels that she often ran across what she called "trapped people." They were people caught in the same timeless state as her, except each and every one of them had descended into an inevitable, crippling madness, their memories and their humanity steadily draining away, eventually leaving them little more than empty shells of their former selves. Whenever she found a trapped person, she immediately and involuntarily absorbed whatever knowledge and memories they had left. And it was surprising the things that some of them knew. It seemed that the vast majority of people who ended up trapped in the broken places were there precisely because they knew something they shouldn't know and were looking for something they shouldn't have been looking for. Most were self-proclaimed monster hunters, demon slayers and ghost investigators who found far more than they bargained for.

"Things I learn from the trapped people aren't always accurate," she said, "and usually it's pretty scant. But skinwalkers are different. For some reason, I've come across memories of them over and over again. They're never first-hand accounts. It's always 'a friend of a friend said this' kind of thing, but it's always the same stories over and over again, with seriously unsettling similarities."

Karen frowned. "Well that's kind of terrifying."

"Yeah…"

Eric opened the door and stepped out into the chilly afternoon air, his mind racing. There was a skinwalker on the loose in Creek Bend? What did it mean? Why was it here? And what nonsense was he going to have to deal with this time?

He had a bad feeling about this. His stomach had gone sour. He couldn't remember the last time he'd felt such sickening dread.

Karen hopped down, still holding her phone, and walked around the front of the Trailblazer. "By the way, are you still on that beach?"

"I am." This time, the mysterious door had taken Isabelle to a quiet beach house overlooking a vast expanse of water. She had no idea *where* in the world she was, but she could smell seawater, so it wasn't just a really big lake, she was on an eastern coast because the sun rose over the water in the morning and it was much farther south than Wisconsin because it was a lot warmer there. And there were no disturbing trapped people lingering there, which was always something of a relief. She'd been there for two months now and had still found no motivation to leave.

"Jealous," said Karen as she tightened her coat against the cold, March wind.

"It's a nice place if you have to be stuck somewhere," she admitted. But everyone who knew her knew that if she had any choice, she'd rather be in Wisconsin with them. Or else back home with her parents, of course.

Eric retrieved the cooler from the back of the SUV and followed Karen into the house, where he placed it on the kitchen table and immediately started the coffee pot. He had a feeling he still had a very long day ahead of him.

"Hi, Perri," said Karen.

"Hi!" chirped Perri. She'd appeared in the dining room doorway, wearing an oversized sweatshirt and yoga pants. Her feet were bare. Her long, blonde hair was tied up in a sloppy bun with escaped strands sticking out in every direction. Eric didn't think she could look any comfier. She looked as if she'd spent her day precisely as he would've preferred to. "How was the book signing?"

"It was fun," replied Karen as she shrugged out of her coat and hung it on the hook next to the door. "How was your day?"

"It was fine. I dusted and swept."

"I keep telling you, you don't have to do that. You're supposed to be getting rest."

"I wanted to help."

"You're already helpful. You don't need to push yourself."

"I'm not. Really. Besides, I'm feeling better."

"She's just restless," said Eric. He dropped his jacket over the back of the nearest chair, where it was immediately snatched away by Karen and hung properly beside hers. "She's always cooped up in the house. Let her help if she wants."

Perri gave him a shy smile and twiddled with the collar of her sweater.

Karen sighed and began unpacking the cooler. "I suppose…"

Perrine Roden had been living with them since Eric rescued her from Evancurt's nightmare machine. She'd spent forty-seven years alone inside that hellish contraption, trapped in a maddening void with nothing more than brief, psychic glances of the world outside. But although she admitted that it felt like a very long time passed in that place, she hadn't changed much mentally. She was still basically the very same twelve-year-old girl she was when the monstrous Walter Voltner put her there. Yet during that time her body had only physically aged about ten years, making her a fifty-nine-year-old woman with the mind of a twelve-year-old and the body of a twenty-two-year-old, meaning that as far as weirdness went, she fit right in.

When Eric first brought her home, Perri was exhausted and weak. She did little more than sleep for the first few days. And since then she'd been constantly ailing from some mild illness or another, very much as if her immune system had been sheltered for most of the past fifty years. She spent the vast majority of her time wrapped in a blanket on the couch, binge-watching Netflix and catching up on the world. Even now, she was nursing a cough and a runny nose.

Karen pretty much adopted her the moment she arrived and had taken it upon herself to nurse her back to health, but in the process, she'd become a little overprotective of the poor girl.

"Holly's on her way," reported Isabelle from Karen's phone on the table. "She'll be here in a few minutes. Hi, Perri!"

Perri's expression lit up at the sound of her voice. "Hi, Isabelle! I didn't know you were here." Then she frowned. "Or…wherever you are, I guess…?"

She liked Isabelle. They were a lot alike, after all. A *lot* alike. Both of them spent decades trapped by a madman inside an insane house where time didn't work right and doors didn't go where they were supposed to. Both of them had resisted the natural process of aging. Both of them were somehow connected with a monster named "Altrusk." And Isabelle was even able to detect some sort of psychic energy hanging over her that she suspected might be similar to what connected her to Eric.

They weren't exactly the same, of course. Isabelle hadn't aged at all in the almost four decades she'd been imprisoned. She still had the same thirteen-year-old body she had when she went missing in nineteen seventy-eight. And Isabelle had remained fully aware of the world as it went on without her, thanks to her psychic connections to her parents all those years. Perri, on the other hand, had not only missed most of the past half-century, but the forty-seven-year-old memories of those first twelve years of her life were as hazy as one might expect forty-seven-year-old memories to be. Her entire life up until a few short weeks ago had been reduced to little more than a distant gathering of vague and broken dream-like recollections.

It was a blessing as well as a curse, however, as she wasn't left particularly traumatized by the loss of the life she'd left behind in nineteen seventy-one. Naturally, she was saddened by the loss of her father and her caretaker, Bronwen, who was practically a mother to her, but in the distant sort of way one mourns loved ones they lost many years ago, rather than as a sudden and shocking tragedy. And she was proving to be something of a blank slate, too, absorbing the facts about this new and complex world she'd suddenly found herself in at an impressive rate. She didn't even sound like a girl fresh out of the sixties, although that was probably thanks in no small part to her mostly isolated childhood and the insistence of Bronwen that she learn to speak like a proper lady. Anyone who met her today would never guess that she was anything more unusual than a particularly timid and perhaps somewhat *sickly* young woman.

"Oh, and Paul's finishing up a job," Isabelle went on. "But he says he should be done in half an hour or so and not to die again."

"Oh," said Eric. "Well if *he* says not to, I guess I'll have to *try*."

"Not funny," said Karen.

"It was a little funny," said Isabelle.

But Karen didn't look at all amused. That business back in January had frightened her a lot. And Eric could hardly blame her. He would've been terrified, too, if he'd been in her place that night. Isabelle had been speaking to her, keeping her updated on the latest round of weirdness that had just sprung up on his way home, and then suddenly there was an accident and he fell unconscious, severing their psychic connection. For the next thirty or forty minutes she'd sat around waiting to see if he'd wake up, with nothing but the occasional flickering of fragmented dreams to let them know that he was even still alive.

"Wait…" said Perri, confused. "What's going on?"

"Weirdness," said Isabelle.

She turned and looked at Eric. "You mean like when you found me?"

Eric watched the coffee pot as it slowly filled, his thoughts still swirling in his head. "Something like that, I'm sure." He still had that sick feeling in his gut. He *really* didn't want to be doing this again.

"Karen was attacked by a skinwalker," explained Isabelle.

Perri gasped. "Oh no! Are you okay?"

"It didn't hurt me. Eric was there to save me."

"Thank goodness!" Then she frowned. "Uh… What is a…skin…?" She creased her brow, confused. "What did you call it?"

"Skinwalker," Isabelle said again.

"Oh…" Perri stood there a moment, still twiddling at the collar of her sweater, trying to decide if she should know what that was or not.

"Where have I heard that before?" said Karen, her pretty face scrunching up as she pondered the word. "That's going to drive me *nuts.*"

"It's a pretty widespread legend," offered Isabelle. "You can find stuff about them on the internet. And they've appeared in movies and on television. They were even in an episode of *Supernatural.*"

But Karen shook her head. She was fairly sure it wasn't just something she saw on television.

Perri turned to Eric and said, "What are you going to do?"

"Beats me." What he *wanted* to do was wrap himself in a blanket and hide under the bed for the next twenty-four hours or so, but that wasn't the correct answer. "Go out there and look around until something happens, I guess. The weird always finds me. Or I find it."

"I want to go with you."

He looked back at her, surprised.

"Absolutely not!" snapped Karen. "It's *way* too dangerous!"

Perri shrank a little at the outburst, but she didn't back down. "I *have* to help," she insisted. "He saved me from that machine. If it wasn't for him…"

"I know," said Karen, her tone softening. "But you're…"

"What? Just a kid?"

"That's not what I was going to say."

"Because I'm really not."

"I know."

"I'm apparently a grown woman now." She looked down at herself, at the body that still didn't seem like hers, and made a face at herself. "Period cramps and all," she added. Then she glanced over at Eric and blushed furiously. "Oh goodness… I'm sorry."

Eric rubbed his eyes. He already felt tired and the weirdness had barely begun. "You're fine."

"Hey," said Karen, "you don't want to hear about girl stuff, stop bringing them home like stray puppies."

"She's got a point there," said Isabelle.

"All I said was she's fine!"

He wasn't bothered by "girl stuff," as Karen put it. And right now, all he could think about was the unpleasant task before him and how things didn't end so well for him the last time the weird came knocking. Not a day had gone by since he brought Perri home from that nightmare that he didn't find his mind drifting back to those awful events…to those memories that were his but also weren't…and to how it all ended…

(Not even dead. Just…*gone*.)

"Besides," pushed Perri, "the ghost lady said he was going to need me! Remember? She said so." She looked over at Eric. "Didn't she?"

"Tessa *did* say I'd need you one day," admitted Eric. "But she never said *when* I'd need you. Or *how*. And I don't even know what's going on yet. You should stay here for now. If I *do* need you, I'll come back for you, okay?"

Perri frowned. "I guess…"

"It took me way too long to find you to let anything happen to you," he added, meeting her gaze for a moment and taking in those drastically different eyes. One was dark brown. The other was pale blue. "Heterochromia" was the scientific word for it. It suited her. That two-color gaze was as mysterious as she was.

From the other end of the house came the sound of the front door opening.

Perri turned and waved as Holly and Paige entered the living room and stepped into view.

"Hi, girls," called Karen. "Thanks for coming over so fast."

"Of course!" said Holly. "Hi Perri! How're you feeling?"

In a tone that was obviously aimed at Karen, she replied, "Fine, thank you."

Holly Shorring was a close family friend. She was also a witch. And she was a former stripper, which according to Karen was entirely Eric's fault for reasons he still couldn't seem to understand, no matter how hard he tried. Paige Mancott was also a witch, although she utilized an entirely different kind of magic from what Holly used, one with *voodoo* roots. They were sisters. All the members of their coven were sisters. That was just how things worked. (Except for the one boy in the family, Jude, who was obviously the *brother*.) The coven adopted Paige over a year ago, after that unpleasant business with the blood witches and the death of her mother, and she'd been living with Holly ever since, trying their best to teach each other their unique styles of magic.

The two had now grown quite close, and most people didn't know that they weren't actually sisters, though they looked nothing alike and had distinctly different styles. Holly was dressed in tight jeans, stylish boots and a warm, off-the-shoulder sweater, with her long, red curls tossed over one side, looking like she stepped right out of a magazine. Paige, on the other hand, was wearing much more comfortable-looking loose-fitting jeans with holes in the knees, her old, scuffed Converse sneakers and her familiar, Old Navy sweatshirt jacket with her long, blonde hair hanging loose about her shoulders and half-covering her face while she clutched her raggedy, stuffed bunny, Ghede, in the crook of her arm.

"So what're we doing?" asked Holly.

"Well…" said Karen, looking over at Eric. "We're not sure yet."

Eric poured himself a cup of coffee and sighed. "All we know is that there's a monster running around out there. I don't even know where to start. I mean, where do you go if you want to find a *skinwalker*?"

"Oh!" said Karen, finally remembering where she'd heard the word before. "I know where one is!"

Chapter Three

Eric slipped a portable charger and the old pocket watch he picked up in Hedge Lake into his front pants pocket with the little cloth pouch that Paige made for him a few months back. A mojo bag, she called it, which was some kind of voodoo protection charm. He didn't understand how such a thing worked, but he was happy to have any help he could get. Karen, Holly and Perri all had one, too, and like him they each carried it with them every time they left the house.

"You don't have to come with me," he said as he poured his coffee into a travel cup. Then he slipped back into his jacket and frowned at his torn sleeve. "If this really does have anything to do with that monster, I don't want you to get hurt."

"I'll be fine," insisted Karen. "I know better than to wander off by myself this time, don't I? And we'll have Holly, too."

"I won't let anything happen to her," promised Holly.

"I could help, too," pouted Perri. She was still standing in the doorway, watching them as they prepared to leave again.

"You'll get your chance," Eric assured her. "Besides, you're still sick."

She'd produced a tissue from somewhere inside her sweatshirt and was wiping at her nose. Now she hid it behind her back and blushed. "It's just some sniffles. I'm fine."

"We'll be back soon," promised Karen. "Stay here and help Paige with the divination spell, okay?"

She glanced over at the table and the big, silver bowl surrounded by candles. Paige already had four large pots of water on the stove. She didn't want to stay here, but at the same time, she was sort of curious about the divination spell. She'd heard about it, but she hadn't seen it yet. And she'd been fascinated by the idea of real magic since she was just a little girl, which was to say both a really long time ago and not very long ago at all...

Holly and Paige were two of the first people she met after she finally woke up in Eric and Karen's spare bedroom. They'd helped take care of her during those first few blurry days. Uncertain about taking her to a hospital, they'd instead sought the advice of their sister, Charlotte, who was sort of like the coven nurse, she guessed... Perri didn't really remember much about her. She recalled a heavyset woman with curly brown hair and a comforting smile that reminded her a little of Bronwen. She had a vague recollection of being given a series of injections. Vaccines, Karen had later explained to her. Immunity boosters. Vitamins. Tetanus. A flu shot.

She'd had lots of conversations with Holly and Paige. She'd heard all their stories. She knew they were capable of casting actual spells. But she still hadn't seen any of this magic with her own eyes. And she really wanted to.

She wiped at her nose again and said nothing more on the matter.

"Paige has really been improving with the divination spell," bragged Holly. It was easy to scoff at the idea of gleaning information about the impending future from nothing more than a bowl of steaming water, but Eric had seen it work on numerous occasions and had even glimpsed a glimmer of things to come, himself, while sitting in on the spell. "And her protection magic might be even more powerful than Del's blanket spell."

"Wow," said Eric. Delphinium's blanket spell was one of the most impressive things he'd ever witnessed. With it, she could cast protective magic over an entire city if she wanted to, powerful enough to repel anyone who might be trying to find the coven, provided that person wasn't another witch with knowledge of magic that, say, allowed them to teleport past such barriers...

Paige brushed back her blonde hair, embarrassed, and muttered, "It's not really *my* magic." It was taught to her by her mother, who learned it from *her* mother, who learned it from the powerful mage, Mambo Dee. And besides that, the actual source of the magic she used was a group of powerful spirits known as the loa, who granted her use of it in exchange for certain sacrificial offerings. (Not the kind that involved killing farm animals, thankfully.) "I'll ask the loa to protect the house while you're gone," she said. "And hopefully I'll be able to see something useful."

"You'll do great," Holly assured her.

Eric opened the door. "Don't let anyone stranger than my brother in the house."

"We won't," promised Perri.

"Help yourselves to cookies and cupcakes," said Karen.

Paige's eyes lit up. "Ooh! Yay!"

The three of them—four if you counted Isabelle—left the house and climbed into the Trailblazer.

"I called and talked to Del on my way over," said Holly as she buckled herself in. "She wanted me to keep her informed if anything was happening."

"Understandable," said Eric. "The whole karmic sin thing and all..."

"Exactly. But she says there's definitely no connection between that and whatever's happening here today. She's been keeping a close eye on that ever since we beat those blood witches and she can see a shadow looming on the horizon, but it's still pretty far off. She thinks it might be at least a year or two away yet. Maybe several."

"That's good to know," said Karen.

"*Very* good news," agreed Eric as he backed out of the driveway. That was one less thing to worry about today, at least.

"So where're we going?" asked Holly.

"The museum," replied Karen.

The Badernanter Historical Museum was located in the middle of town. Eric had been there lots of times. He enjoyed going there. It was always interesting. And it was always nice and quiet.

"What's at the museum?"

"The Monster of Creek Bend."

Holly looked understandably confused. "Creek Bend has a Monster?"

"That's what we're going to find out," said Eric. He didn't blame her for not knowing about it. She was still fairly new to Creek Bend. *He* hadn't even thought about the monster in years, he didn't think.

For as long as the museum had been standing, it'd been the home of something extraordinary. Some of the staff were quite proud of the Creek Bend Monster, also known as the Badernanter Monster, the Creek Bend Horror, the Creek Bend Mummy, the Creek Man and Joval's Monster. Others didn't like to speak of the thing and a few even considered it an embarrassment, a shameless hoax and a smear on the good reputation of the otherwise proud historical site. According to the stories, the thing was the mummified remains of a monster discovered by a man named Ezra Joval in the late eighteen hundreds and put on display as a means of attracting tourists. Most everyone who lived in Creek Bend had seen the thing at one time or another, and almost everyone agreed that it was obviously a hoax. But that didn't dissuade people from talking about it. Most agreed that, even as a hoax, it was a charming bit of local history. And it was a fun tale to tell the kids, if nothing else.

But what made the story suddenly and eerily relevant to Eric was the fact that Ezra Joval claimed the monster was the corpse of a *skinwalker* he'd discovered in the American Southwest. That made the Creek Bend Monster the key that connected their encounter behind the bookshop with the legends that were otherwise confined to the region surrounding the Navajo Nation. Given that the monster they saw fit the description of a real skinwalker as Isabelle knew them, and that there wasn't that much distance between the museum and the bookshop, all the pieces were definitely falling into place.

He'd seen the monster before, like almost everyone else who lived in Creek Bend, and it had never impressed him much. Even as a boy, he never really believed it was anything more than a very old and not even very well executed hoax. It certainly didn't look anything like the thing he and Karen encountered behind the bookshop. But Isabelle did say it was a shapeshifter so that didn't really disprove anything.

Everything's a thing, his brother, Paul, once said. And those words seemed truer every time the weird took hold of him. So maybe there was some truth behind the Creek Bend Monster after all.

Chapter Four

There was no one in sight when they stepped through the doors of the museum. The building was deathly quiet. It was perfectly normal to find it this way. The staff here was scant, consisting of only a handful of paid members with most of the day-to-day business handled by volunteers, so at any given time on any given day, the place might appear deserted. But given the circumstances of their visit, Eric's awful imagination took particular glee in immediately jumping to the morbid conclusion that they were going to find everyone here slaughtered by the dog-faced skinwalker woman.

They walked through the small lobby and past the stairs leading to the second floor where the library and Native American History exhibits were located. Eric spotted Emanuel Voskstern's *Reassembling the Ashes* on prominent display right next to the cash register in the museum's tiny gift shop. It was exactly the sort of place where a newly released book about local history by a local historian should be, yet it felt strangely ominous seeing it there.

The same felt true of the museum's many Easter decorations. All those pastel colors should have brightened the place up, but instead there was an eerie sort of contrast between the cheerful décor and the gloomy silence.

Directly ahead of them was a darkened doorway. The shadowy room on the other side was dedicated to the Fire of 1881. He'd walked through that exhibit more times than he could count, both before and after the weird began showing him the strange truth of the disaster. It used to be humbling, back before he knew the things he knew now. And it still was, but in a different and far more terrifying sort of way.

His stubborn imagination wouldn't stop insisting that something was desperately wrong here. This was where that monster behind the bookshop came from, after all. This was no longer a museum. It was a lair. A nest. A *feeding ground.* Any second now he'd see a crimson splatter of spilled blood. A trail of gore smeared across the glossy tiles leading off into a darkened room. The pale, motionless hand of a corpse sticking out from behind a display case.

He clenched his jaw and tried to force these thoughts from his head. What was wrong with him? Why did he feel so skittish? That hot, sickly feeling in his gut wouldn't go away. He had every reason to be afraid of the weird, but there was something different about this.

Was it because Karen had been involved? That was part of it, he was sure. That business in the bookshop's rear parking lot had given him a terrible fright. He couldn't stop thinking about what might've happened if he hadn't found her when he did. But it was more than that.

It was Evancurt.

The horrors of that place hadn't had time to fade yet. It was too soon. He was still lying awake at night, thinking about what happened there. He wasn't ready for more weirdness. He wasn't sure he could handle it.

But as he neared the darkened doorway, he realized that he could hear the soft murmur of voices from the other side. People were in there. And to the right, through a second and more brightly lit doorway, he caught sight of an elderly couple holding hands and strolling casually through the dairy farming exhibits. He heard the heavy clack of the main entrance door behind him and looked over his shoulder to see a tall woman in a long, expensive-looking coat march purposefully to the second-floor stairway, a large, heavy bag slung over one shoulder, looking as if she were here to do some serious research in the library. The clacking of her high heels echoed after her as she ascended the steps.

Definitely not as deserted as he first perceived. And yet that sour dread in his belly wouldn't ease up.

His betraying imagination, thwarted in its attempt to convince him that he'd entered a den of horror and bloodshed, decided instead to torment him with thoughts of how embarrassing it was going to be if someone overheard that he was here to look at the stupid fake mummy in the basement.

Why did his brain have to do these sorts of things to him? What did he ever do to *it*?

Karen led the way to the stairs leading down to the basement. That's where the monster had always been kept. For as long as the museum had been standing, the Creek Man had slumbered there.

He couldn't help wondering if he was only wasting his time here. After all, everyone knew the skinwalker corpse was a blatant hoax. The Creek Bend Monster was no more real than the ridiculous hodag. But who was he to say what could and couldn't be real?

Still, if the Creek Man had gotten up and walked away, wouldn't it have caused some kind of commotion? At the very least, it should've set off some alarms.

No matter how he rationalized it, he couldn't imagine the thing in the basement having anything to do with the monster that attacked them behind the bookshop.

As they approached the stairway, however, Holly tugged at his jacket sleeve. She was crowded close to him, her eyes sweeping across the room. She had an unsettled look on her face and was chewing on her fingernail, like she did when she was nervous.

"You okay?" he asked.

Those pretty eyes locked on his and stayed there. "There's magic here," she whispered.

He stared back at her, surprised.

Karen, too, had stopped. She'd just reached the stairs and placed her hand on the railing. "What kind of magic?" she whispered.

"I'm not sure. All magic has its own unique signature. This isn't something I've felt before. But it's definitely magic."

Eric glanced down at his phone.

I DON'T FEEL IT, reported Isabelle. BUT I'M NOT AS

SENSITIVE TO MAGIC AS SHE IS

Isabelle could detect all sorts of various energy types, while Holly could only sense magical energy, but where magic was concerned, Holly could detect far less of it from much farther away. And she could even sometimes identify the unique signature of the witch or coven responsible for the magic.

Karen crowded closer to them. "What about that magic background-checking thing of yours?" she whispered. "Can you feel anything with that?"

"That's not really a magic thing," replied Holly. In addition to being an actual witch with a formidable arsenal of real-life spells at her disposal, Holly had also been born with the impressive psychic ability to mentally background-check anyone she met. She could tell in an instant whether someone was dangerous or if they were hiding something. It was extremely useful, but it had nothing to do with the magic she was taught by Delphinium and her grandfather. "And no one's around right now. I can only read *people*, and only when they're physically close to me."

Karen pursed her lips and began twirling a lock of hair around her index finger. "Hmm…"

"Sorry."

"It's fine," she replied. "But why would there be magic in the museum? Is it the skinwalker?"

"Actually, a lot of museums give off small amounts of magic energy," said Holly. "There's a lot of old things from a lot of different places and times gathered in one place. Some of them are bound to have some kind of history with magic."

THAT'S TRUE, said Isabelle. IT'S THE SAME WITH OTHER KINDS OF ENERGY, TOO. THERE'RE LITTLE POCKETS OF WEAK SPIRITUAL ENERGY ALL AROUND YOU. I EVEN FELT SOMETHING GIVING OFF A LITTLE BIT OF PSYCHIC ENERGY A MINUTE AGO

Eric nodded. This wasn't entirely new information. She'd told him something similar about an antique shop he and Karen visited a couple years ago. In places with lots of old things gathered together, there's a high chance of encountering something that had absorbed exotic energy at some point in its past.

"Some of my sisters spend a lot of their free time visiting museums," explained Holly. "They study the old energy some of the artifacts give off. They've found stuff imbued with magic by witches who lived hundreds or even thousands of years ago."

"That's kind of cool," said Karen. "In a weird sort of way."

"I know, right? But this isn't like that." She turned and glanced around at her surroundings again. "What I'm feeling isn't just some residual magic. It's a lot more refined than that. It's *purposeful*. There's an active spell here. A *powerful* one."

Karen glanced around, too. She was still twirling her hair. Only Eric could see the worry buried deep in her expression. "Do you think we're in danger?"

"I can't really tell. Sorry."

Both of them turned and looked at Eric as if to say, "What now?"

"Let's see what's down there," he sighed.

"That's what we're here for," agreed Karen. Although he couldn't help but notice that she let *him* lead the way down the stairs this time.

That sour feeling in his belly still wouldn't let up. And his rogue imagination was delighted to offer up more new possibilities for what might be waiting for him at the bottom of these steps.

I FEEL IT NOW, reported Isabelle as he approached the bottom landing. Like always, her messages opened directly into the Messenger app, without him having to tap anything. As soon as he'd read it, another message replaced it: IT'S CLEARLY MAGICAL ENERGY, BUT IT'S UNIQUE AND VERY LO-CALIZED. Then: I COULDN'T FEEL IT AT ALL UNTIL JUST NOW. WHATEVER IT IS, YOU'RE DEFINITELY GETTING CLOSER TO IT

Holly and Karen both crowded him to read over his shoulder. "Purposeful," Holly said again.

SHE'S RIGHT. IT'S NOT JUST RADIATING FROM SOMETHING. THERE'S A KIND OF FLOW TO IT. IT REALLY FEELS LIKE IT'S DOING SOMETHING

"Be ready with that thrust of yours," said Eric.

A "thrust" was a magic spell utilized by Holly and most of her sisters that was essentially a violent projection of magical energy capable of inflicting physical damage on a target from a distance. Able to be used at a moment's notice, it was an extremely handy means of self-defense, especially when dealing with supernatural entities, but its drawback was that it was physically draining for her and therefore had a limited number of uses before it exhausted her and left her defenseless.

"Don't worry," she replied as she stepped through the doorway and into the next exhibit. "I'm ready for anyth—*oh my god!*"

Eric almost laughed, but managed to stifle himself. "Sorry. I probably should've warned you about this."

Through the doorway at the bottom of the stairs was the museum's taxidermy room. Game birds of all colors and sizes were posed in various display boxes, ducks and geese, pheasants and quail, some of them perched on branches, some of them sitting on nests. There were also great and majestic birds of prey. Eagles. Hawks. Owls. Most of them with their impressive wings outstretched. There was also a sizeable collection of mammals. There was a fox and a beaver. A pair of gray squirrels clung to the side of a fake tree. A badger stared back at them from a makeshift burrow in one corner. There were even fish. Huge, large-mouth bass, enormous catfish and a great, toothy pike all hovered motionless in a large display case, as if frozen in ice. And in the middle of it all stood a great, strutting deer with an enormous rack of antlers.

Holly hid her face behind her hands and squealed. "They're all looking at me!"

Eric chuckled. Personally, he kind of liked this room. This was the wildlife of Wisconsin, up-close and personal, practically at his fingertips. And it wasn't as if they were actively adding to the collection. These creatures were all antiques, hunted and mounted decades ago, long before the hunting of many of these species was banned, and for a few of them, before they went extinct. But he didn't blame her for being horrified. After all, they were essentially surrounded by glass-eyed *corpses*.

"Tell me when it's over!"

Holly was the sort of person you just automatically liked. People found her immediately endearing. And there was a reason for it. As odd as it sounded, in addition to her mental background-checking powers, she also had a more subconscious ability that made people like her more. She simply wanted to be liked (like anybody, really) and so she sort of reached inside the people around her and gave them a little nudge. But she didn't like to talk about that. It wasn't something she did on purpose and she hated the idea that she might be manipulating people, even unconsciously. And everyone who knew her had long suspected that, even more, she was afraid that it might be the only reason anyone actually liked her. A ridiculous idea, in his opinion, because he couldn't think of a single reason anyone *wouldn't* like her. She was kind, compassionate, loving and fiercely loyal. But he suspected it all went back to the fact that she was homeless for a while when she was young, back before Delphinium Thorngood took her in and gave her a home and a family. She even admitted to him once that after everything that'd happened, her biggest fear was finding herself all alone again.

"You can look now," said Karen as they passed through the last of the taxidermy and into a room filled with old farm machinery.

She peered through her open fingers. "That was icky," she pouted. "Is there anything else like that down here?"

"Only the monster," she assured her.

There were no signs pointing the way to the Creek Man's exhibit. There was only an unmarked hallway branching off the farm machinery room. And although it didn't have a "keep out" or "staff only" sign, there was something about such an empty and unassuming corridor that made a lot of visitors overlook it entirely. They simply never thought to explore farther. Maybe that was intentional. It certainly added another layer of mysteriousness to the room where the monster was kept. Or perhaps it was merely because there was some debate on whether or not the exhibit there should really be considered history. After all, not everyone thought that an obvious con artist like Ezra Joval deserved to be immortalized as part of the city's otherwise proud history.

It was strange how such a brightly lit hallway could look so dark and foreboding. Given the strange circumstances of their visit, it might as well have had that one flickering fluorescent light like that scene in every other horror movie.

Halfway through this hallway, Holly abruptly stopped and looked back the way they came.

"What's up?" whispered Karen.

Holly stood there a moment, her gaze sweeping through the empty hallway behind her and the silent machinery beyond. "I'm not sure..." she replied after a moment. "Something feels..." She shook her head. "Just my imagination, maybe? It felt like something was there. Like we were being watched."

Eric stepped past her and looked back out at the old machinery. There didn't appear to be anyone around. He glanced down at his phone.

THERE'S SOME MAGIC ENERGY SOMEWHERE IN FRONT OF YOU, she reported, BUT NOT NEARLY AS MUCH AS I'M FEELING FROM WHATEVER'S AT THE END OF THAT HALLWAY

"Maybe I'm just jumpy," said Holly, looking embarrassed.

"Let's not let our guard down either way," suggested Eric as he swept his gaze across the empty room. In his experience, there was *always* something to be concerned about.

Finally, they turned and continued into the next room. It was small, little more than a storage room, with only the one artifact taking up most of the floor.

"There he is," announced Karen. "Creek Bend's own monster."

The thing was laid out in a dusty, wooden box, like an open coffin, except it was twelve feet long and sealed with a fitted sheet of plexiglass. It was a hideous hodgepodge of a creature, with long, thin, hairy legs and arms, a great, barrel-like chest and a wolf-like head. It had hooved feet, huge hands with wicked-looking claws and a massive pair of deer antlers. (These necessitated three of the coffin's twelve feet.) The whole thing was little more than leathery skin and shedding fur wrapped around yellowed bones. It was wearing a ratty-looking patchwork of ancient-looking animal hides.

A shiny plaque on the side of the box identified the creature as "Yenaldlooshi: the skinwalker. Discovered by Ezra Joval in 1880 in an unknown cavern in what would later become New Mexico."

The walls of the room were adorned with framed newspaper articles about the monster's discovery and supposed eyewitness sightings of these creatures over the years, as well as old, blurry photographs of a gangly-looking man in an old fedora.

"That is *so* nasty..." grumbled Holly as she stared down at the monster in the case.

It was. And it was painfully obvious that the thing was a fake. The animal-hide clothing it was wrapped in was clearly there to hide the places where the so-called "monster" was wired together. It was nothing more than a carefully assembled collection of various animal parts. It wasn't even particularly good taxidermy.

And then there was the most important detail of all: the fact that it was *still here*, just as Eric remembered it. It hadn't gotten up and left. The dust inside the case hadn't been disturbed. It couldn't have been the thing that attacked them behind the bookshop.

It didn't even *look* like the thing that attacked them in the alley. The legs and arms were sort of the same, long and skinny, furry and animal-like, and the skeletal, wolf-like face was sort of similar to what he remembered when it had looked like a dog's face and not Jess' face. But that thing that came out of the narrow alley was much smaller than this, didn't look like a dried-up mummy and didn't have those horns.

Of course, it was supposedly a shapeshifter...but clearly the Creek Bend Monster hadn't left its display coffin. And that was a hard fact to dismiss.

He glanced over at Karen. She scrunched her mouth to one side in a look that said, "Okay...now what?"

And it was a good question.

Maybe Joval's hoax really was just a really big coincidence. Maybe the thing on display here had nothing to do with the thing that attacked them.

And now that he was thinking about it, it occurred to him that if skinwalkers were real, and if they were here in Creek Bend now, perhaps they'd been to Creek Bend before. The obvious fakery on display before them might have been inspired by the real thing. That would explain the coincidence. And it would mean that there was nothing to find here. It was a dead end.

But then...what was the source of the magic that Holly sensed? He glanced over at her. She was biting her nails again, her pretty eyes drifting around the room.

"Something's...not what it seems..." she said.

Karen looked up from the monster, her eyebrows raised. "What is it?"

"I'm not sure. But something in this room..." She closed her eyes and took a deep breath, then she lifted her hands and rubbed them together in front of her face. "Reveal," she whispered. And as she parted her hands, she pursed her lips and blew between her palms. A puff of visible steam poured out, as if they were standing in a freezer. At the same time, the entire room shuddered around them.

He'd seen this spell before. She used it to force a lingering spirit to reveal itself in a quiet basement on the outskirts of the city. It was how he came to meet the spirit named Tessa, whose ghastly bloody eyes were a drastic contrast to her kind and helpful nature.

On the other side of the room there was a loud thump and a rattle. Eric and Karen turned their gazes in that direction. There had never been a door there before, not in all the years they'd visited this museum, but there was suddenly one there now that looked like it had been there forever, a cloud of dust slowly settling around it.

"What's in there?" asked Holly, one last wisp of icy breath escaping her lips.

Chapter Five

"Okay, that was kind of freaky," said Karen, staring at the newly revealed door. "Is she always this scary when you guys do this stuff?"

Holly blinked and her expression melted into a childlike pout. "I'm not scary!" she whined.

Eric stepped up to the door. It looked less like a part of the building and more like one of the artifacts. It was handmade and very old. The wooden planks were rough and splintered. The oversized hinges and simple handle were badly rusted. The wooden frame was gray and worn with age.

"Smells like underground places," observed Karen.

"It does," he agreed. He wasn't sure how they didn't notice it before. It practically reeked of dank earth. He might as well be standing at the mouth of a cave or looking down the steps of an old root cellar. He placed his hand on the weathered surface of the door and examined the wall around it. This wasn't added later. It had been here since the concrete was poured. And it wasn't covered by anything. They just couldn't see it until Holly's spell revealed it to them. "Was this unseen?" he wondered.

I DIDN'T FEEL ANYTHING UNSEEN, replied Isabelle.

The "unseen" were places that, for reasons he still didn't understand, had become utterly undetectable to most people. They couldn't be seen. Noises produced within them couldn't be heard. Even the space these places occupied went completely unnoticed. Anyone standing inside the boundaries of an unseen location couldn't be seen or heard by those outside them. They didn't show up in pictures and videos. They disappeared from maps and records. The only thing that ever remained was vague knowledge that these places once existed and a stubborn certainty that they were now long gone. No matter how hard he tried, he couldn't wrap his head around how such a thing could possibly work, but he knew from experience that the unseen was real. He knew that there were nine such places right here in Creek Bend. The weird had dragged him through all of them at least once. And he also knew that these places gave off a specific kind of energy that Isabelle could sense when he was close to one. So if she said this door wasn't a tenth unseen, then he had very little reason not to take her word for it.

THAT WAS DEFINITELY MAGIC, explained Isabelle.

"Concealment magic," agreed Holly, who was reading over his shoulder. "Strong stuff, too."

WHEN HOLLY USED HER REVEAL SPELL, SOME OF THE MAGIC ENERGY I WAS FEELING DISAPPEARED

"Just some of it?"

VERY LITTLE OF IT, ACTUALLY. THE VAST MAJORITY OF IT IS COMING FROM SOMEWHERE ON THE OTHER SIDE OF THAT DOOR

He looked it over once more and then took hold of the handle. There was no lock. The only thing keeping anyone out was the magic spell that was hiding it.

"Funny thing about doors..." said a voice from behind them.

The three of them twirled around to find an elderly man and woman standing in the other doorway, watching them. The man appeared to be in his nineties. His head was mostly bald and wrinkled and peppered with liver spots. He was leaning on a cane and staring at them through thick glasses that magnified his pale eyes. The woman looked to be in her early eighties. Her hair was iron gray and cut short. There were deep wrinkles around her eyes and mouth and her body was very thin. She was fingering a silver cross that hung at the end of her necklace.

Holly stepped in front of Eric and Karen, shielding them.

"...not all of them can be closed again," the old man finished.

Eric felt his already-sour stomach twist at the realization that they'd been caught, yet he wasn't sure they'd actually done anything wrong. Nothing was broken or disturbed. There weren't any signs telling them not to enter the suspicious, secret door. And he wasn't aware of any rules that specifically stated that you couldn't dispel a magic barrier hiding a suspicious secret door. But you simply couldn't misbehave in a museum. Only criminals did things like that.

And yet neither of these people looked angry about the un-secreted door, or even the slightest bit surprised, for that matter. In fact, they were both *smiling*.

"Mr. Iverley..." said Karen, clearing her throat. "Mrs. Balm..."

Eric's eyes twitched back and forth between the two of them. "Iverley...?"

"He's the guy in charge of the museum?" said Karen, sounding as if he should already know this. And he supposed he probably should. "I've introduced you *at least* twice."

"Right," he said, feeling embarrassed. She'd provided catering to a number of the museum's many public events over the years. And she'd dragged him to most of them. "Him. I knew he looked familiar."

"You're so rude."

Mr. Iverley chuckled. He had a surprisingly charming smile, even though he was missing quite a few teeth in his old age. "It's good to see you again, Karen."

"You too," she replied.

"And you, too," he added. "Eric, was it?"

"That's right." Now he really did feel bad. The old man had actually remembered his name. Karen was right. He *was* rude.

"And Mrs. Balm," said Karen, turning her attention to the old woman. "How are you today?"

The old woman offered her own bright smile. "I'm still alive," she replied. "At my age, that's doing pretty fine, I think."

Karen gave a polite laugh, as if she hadn't heard that same response countless times before, then she elbowed Eric and said, "You remember Mrs. Balm, right?"

"I *do*," said Eric. And he did. "It's good to see you again."

"And this is my *assistant*," Karen went on, "Holly."

Holly glanced back at her, confused. She was holding her arm out, ready to use her thrust in case these people turned out to be hostile, but it wobbled somewhere between being aimed at the floor in front of her and at the two people who'd appeared silently in the doorway. "Um…hi?"

Karen had been introducing Holly as her assistant almost since she moved here. It was much better than saying, "This is the stripper my idiot husband dragged home for our eleventh wedding anniversary. Isn't he romantic?"

Mrs. Balm fixed her bright smile on Holly. "You're a witch," she said. It wasn't a question. There was no doubt in her voice.

Holly raised her arm again. "So are you," she said. Again, it wasn't a question.

Eric pointed at her. "Wait… Mrs. Balm really is a witch? I thought that was just a silly rumor."

Karen shrugged. She'd told him before that the cheerful old woman in charge of the museum's public events was into pagan stuff, but she didn't think she was an *actual* witch. She thought she was just a fan of that new-age, positive-energy-flow type stuff.

Mrs. Balm continued smiling. "I *am* a witch," she confirmed. "Just like my mother and her mother and hers before her."

"Huh," was all Eric had to say to that.

"The concealment spell hiding that door was yours," said Holly.

"That's right."

"And that was you watching us in the hallway a minute ago, too, wasn't it?" She was still holding out her arm, still ready to attack at any sign of aggression. Although neither of them looked in any way like they were about to start a fight.

"Also true," replied Mrs. Balm.

Karen stepped forward and pushed Holly's arm down. "Okay, take it easy," she said, grimacing. "Please don't start blowing things up inside the museum."

The old man straightened up a little, surprised. "Ah. Yes. As exciting as I'm sure that would be, not blowing up anything in the museum would be preferred, please."

"Yes," agreed Karen. "*Please.*"

"One time," grumbled Holly, not taking her eyes off the old witch. "I blew some stuff up *one time.* I said I was sorry."

"She *did* say she was sorry," said Eric. "And she cleaned the refrigerator for us."

"I did!"

"Whatever," said Karen. "Just take it easy."

Holly glanced over at Eric, uncertain, and he could hardly blame her. Not all witches were nice, after all.

"What do you feel?" he asked her.

She looked back at the old couple. "They...don't *feel* dangerous. I mean, I'm not getting any blood witch kind of vibes or anything... But I've been tricked before."

"Relax, dear," said Mrs. Balm. "I have no intention of picking a fight. Besides, I can already tell I wouldn't stand a chance against you."

Eric glanced down at his phone.

I'M NOT FEELING ANYTHING FROM THOSE TWO, reported Isabelle. THEY'RE NOT USING ANY MAGIC RIGHT NOW THAT I CAN FEEL

He looked back up at Holly and shrugged.

She crossed her arms and went back to chewing on her nails, her gaze twitching back and forth between the old man and the old woman.

"You're right," said Mrs. Balm. "We *were* watching you. I have to admit, I didn't expect you to sense us there. Very impressive."

Eric frowned. "So...when we were out there in the hallway...?"

"I thought you were going to walk right into us for a second there," chuckled Mr. Iverley.

"If you'd taken one more step," said Mrs. Balm, "you would've collided with me and broken the spell. You gave me quite a fright."

"Magic is fascinating, isn't it?" said Mr. Iverley. "I never get tired of Yolanda's spells." Again, he flashed that charming smile, this time with an almost *childlike* glee. "I feel like Harry Potter every time."

"It *does* delight him to no end," she agreed, still smiling her sweet smile.

"So you're *not* a witch, then?" Eric asked the old man.

"Unfortunately, no," he replied with a wistful sort of sigh.

"You wouldn't be very good at it anyway," Mrs. Balm assured him.

"I suppose not."

Eric and Karen exchanged a confused look. "Okay," he said. "But why were you spying on us?"

"We were observing, of course," replied Mrs. Balm.

"We wanted to see why you were here," said Mr. Iverley. "We had to make sure it was really you."

Eric looked back and forth between them. "You sound like you were expecting me."

"Does that surprise you?" wondered Mr. Iverley.

"Not very much," admitted Eric. Although he never knew where the weird might take him until he actually arrived, there was almost always someone there waiting for him.

"Did your magic show him to you?" asked Holly. That was, after all, how Delphinium found him three years ago.

"That's right," said Mrs. Balm. "You see, we're in a bit of trouble right now."

"And Yolanda and I aren't as young as we used to be," sighed Mr. Iverley.

"We needed help," she explained. "And when I used my mother's spell to ask for it, it told me that someone would come and that I should wait and watch for his arrival. That was three days ago. We'd grown impatient, but we had to be sure it was you before we could approach you."

"The fact that you were able to find that door settles it," said Mr. Iverley.

Eric glanced back at the old door.

Mr. Iverley's grin widened. "You've come to see *him*, haven't you?"

"Him?" asked Karen.

"Yenaldlooshi," said Mrs. Balm.

Holly frowned. "Yen…? What?"

"Yenaldlooshi," she repeated. "Our Creek Bend Monster. It's his *Navajo* name."

Eric had just read that name on the oversized coffin's plaque. It was quite a mouthful.

Mr. Iverley walked over to the monster's coffin, then leaned on his cane and peered down at the horned conglomeration of mummified animal parts lying inside with an expression that was strangely warm, as if the hideous mockery of nature held a wealth of fond memories for him. Then, without looking up, he asked, "What do you know about Ezra Joval?"

Eric cocked his head to one side, surprised by the question. "The guy who 'found' this thing?"

"He was supposedly some kind of *Indiana Jones* type adventurer, wasn't he?" volunteered Karen. "He traveled the world, bringing back stories, each one more outlandish than the next?"

"That's what he *claimed*, anyway," agreed Eric. "He was an attention-seeking con artist." He'd read about the man when he was a boy. His stories were thrilling back then. But they were downright nonsensical to think about as a mature adult. "He also claimed to have hunted some kind of sasquatch thing in the Canadian wilderness, a Satanist witch in the Louisiana Bayou and a vampire in the Rocky Mountains."

Holly glanced around the room. "Are…those things on display here, too?"

"No, he didn't bring back any of those," Mrs. Balm assured her.

"Oh." She went back to chewing on her nails again. "That's good."

Eric stared at the plaque, recalling all that he knew about Ezra Joval. He was like a character right out of some goofy old television show, always full of wild stories. He was constantly up to something, always trying to pull one over on someone, looking to con anyone out of a dollar. He also claimed to have banished a demon that was terrorizing a small town in Connecticut, conversed with a race of gods through an undiscovered spring on an oasis deep in the deserts of Mexico and found a vast network of underground tunnels he claimed was a sort of subterranean highway system connecting several ancient Native American *mega-cities* that were far more advanced than anyone had ever suspected.

"A professional hoaxer," said Karen.

Mr. Iverley chuckled. "Very true," he agreed. "But at the same time a complete load of crap."

Eric had been staring at Joval's monster, his thoughts swirling over the history of the man behind the beast, but at this he looked up, surprised.

With a great, satisfied grin, Mr. Iverley said, "The truth is that Ezra Joval was perhaps the greatest hero of his time."

"Seriously?" said Karen. It wasn't hard to see why she'd have her doubts. Joval was Creek Bend's most famous *town kook*. Everyone knew he was a liar and a con man. Most suspected that he suffered some form of undiagnosed mental illness.

"Most of those stories were exactly what everyone believes them to be," explained Mr. Iverley. "*Utter nonsense.* But not because Ezra was some kind of nutjob. It was because that was precisely the intention. People were *meant* to think he was a liar. He sacrificed his reputation to keep what he found a secret. He played the fool. He bore all the scorn and criticism. And all the while he was protecting the world from a terrible evil."

Eric looked down at the monster in the box, as did Karen and Holly. Surely he wasn't trying to say…

The old man chuckled again. "No. Not *that* thing. It's just as fake as everyone says."

"Oh…" said Holly, confused.

"But Ezra Joval really *did* find the Yenaldlooshi in those caverns all those years ago," Mr. Iverley continued. "And he brought it to Creek Bend in hopes of finding a way to seal it away." He looked up at them then, his charming smile gone and replaced with a look so serious that his next words gave them all chills: "Because Yenaldlooshi isn't just some moldy corpse. It's *alive*. Biding its time in a death-like sleep. It's an honest-to-God *boogeyman.* A *relic* of a dark and terrible age long forgotten. And an *absolute evil* that can never be destroyed."

Eric stared back at him, shocked.

Then the old man's smile reappeared. With a delighted twinkle in his eye, he said, "You wanna see him?"

Chapter Six

Mr. Iverley stepped past them, opened the mysterious door and gestured for them to follow, then he and Mrs. Balm set off through the narrow, gloomy corridor that lay waiting behind it.

Eric went next. He was reluctant. And really, didn't following a pair of overly friendly senior citizens into a dark, moldy tunnel hidden in the basement of a mostly deserted museum to some unknown, subterranean location where no one would likely be able to hear them screaming warrant at least a little bit of healthy cynicism? It sounded like the start of a bad horror movie. But no other options had presented themselves. He came here hoping to find answers to why there was a skinwalker loose on the streets of Creek Bend and these two seemed willing to give him some.

Karen followed close behind him. Her lovely face showed no sign of fear, as usual. She looked perfectly stoic. Curious, even. No one, not even Eric, would have known that she was the slightest bit nervous if not for the fact that he could feel how tightly she was clinging to his hand.

Holly took the rear with her cell phone clutched in one hand and her thrust ready at a moment's notice with the other.

"So you're telling us that you have the *real* Creek Bend Monster hidden in a secret passage under the museum?" asked Eric.

"We do," replied Mrs. Balm as she followed Mr. Iverley deeper into the dank passage. "Ezra Joval's house used to stand on this very property. It was right about where the patio and garden are now, where we hold our socials."

Eric's gaze washed over the old stone walls on either side of him. They were grimy and draped with cobwebs. The floor was packed earth. A single row of dull, yellow lights had been strung along the low, arched ceiling.

Was it odd that he seemed to find himself in a lot of tunnels like this? Why did the weird like tunnels so much?

"For over thirty years," she went on, sounding as if she were conducting an ordinary tour, "the Creek Man was on display right there in his living room. Ezra used to charge people a penny a piece for a look at it."

Eric recalled seeing an old photograph in the fake monster's exhibit room of Joval standing next to a hand-painted sign advertising just such a deal.

"But the thing on display was a fake," explained Mr. Iverley. "It was *always* a fake. The *real* relic was locked away in a hidden cellar under his house, where it remains to this day."

"Wait…" said Holly. "Why would he bother trying to make money passing off a fake skinwalker when he had a real one?"

"Because it was never about the money," he replied. "The real Yenaldlooshi was dangerous. Joval, himself, called it a 'curse on mankind' and swore he'd never let it see the light of day again. The fake you saw back there was a decoy. If anyone ever came looking for the real monster, they'd take one look at the phony thing and leave."

"Oh," said Holly, understanding. "Because why would he bother passing off a fake skinwalker when he had a real one?"

Mr. Iverley chuckled. "Exactly."

"The house, itself, was torn down in nineteen fifteen," Mrs. Balm informed them, "when Ezra entrusted the land and both monsters to his close friend and founder of this museum, William Badernanter, but the cellar and its contents remained. Except for the addition of this tunnel connecting it to the museum basement, the room you're about to see has remained undisturbed for almost a hundred and forty years."

"How many people know this is down here?" asked Karen.

"Including the three of you?" said Mr. Iverley. "Just five."

Six, thought Eric, glancing down at his phone. But they didn't need to know about Isabelle.

"Just the two of you?" said Karen, surprised. "No one else at the museum knows about it? Not even Edwin?" Edwin Muvens was the museum's head curator. If anyone should have access to a decades-old mummy, she would've thought it'd be him.

"The responsibility of watching over Yenaldlooshi was passed down to us by our predecessors," explained Mr. Iverley. "For me, it came with the job. When I took over for Old Man Grayfurs in 'eighty-three, he brought me down here and showed it to me. For Yolanda, it was passed down her family line. She took over for her mother, who took over for *her* mother, and so on."

"Always two of us," explained Mrs. Balm. "The one in charge of the museum to keep the cellar's existence a secret and a witch to monitor the spells. Ever since the day it was sealed away."

Ahead of them, the passage bent to the right. It was longer than Eric had expected. He decided he really didn't like it down here. It made him feel uneasy. Probably because of various past experiences with dark, underground places.

As they rounded the turn, Holly said, "There's really strong magic ahead of us."

"Binding spells," said Mr. Iverley. "And concealment charms."

"My great grandmother's magic," bragged Mrs. Balm. "Clarissa Crowlinger. She was the witch who helped Ezra bind the monster in the first place."

"With some potent Navajo hexes thrown in for good measure," Mr. Iverley added.

I FEEL IT, TOO, said Isabelle. IT'S STRONG. AND IT'S NOT LIKE ANYTHING I'VE EVER FELT BEFORE

Eric could see a door ahead of them. It wasn't like the one behind them. It looked more like a prison cell door, constructed of iron bars and bound with heavy chains. There was nothing but darkness beyond it.

The air was growing thicker. The atmosphere felt heavy. And there was a foul smell, too. It was a subtle stench, but it was there, a rotten sort of odor that made him think of dead things.

He could hardly blame Karen when she squeezed his hand a little tighter.

"Ezra Joval went down in history as a fraudster," said Mr. Iverley as he approached the barred doorway, "but history and reality often conflict. The real Joval was a *hero*." He stopped at the bars and turned his attention to a small switchbox mounted on the wall. "In the autumn of eighteen eighty, he wandered into a small town in what would become Northern New Mexico and found it under attack."

"According to the story my mother passed down to me," said Mrs. Balm, "Children were disappearing. Sometimes from their own beds. An illness was affecting people, driving many of them insane. Gravesites were dug up in the night. Pets and live-stock were found slaughtered each morning. And terrible screams and wailings haunted the late hours."

"The entire land had become cursed," said Mr. Iverley.

"My gosh..." sighed Holly.

Mr. Iverley nodded. "Joval felt that the universe brought him there to help those people, so he set off into the wilderness in search of the cause of all the misery. And he found it." He reached out and flipped the switch.

There was no lighting inside the room. Instead, four flood lights were mounted to the bars of the door and aimed inward. It was as if no one had dared to set foot inside the room since it was closed up, not even to illuminate it. The moment the old man turned them on, the darkness was washed away, revealing a space smaller than the room containing the fake skinwalker's exhibit.

Mr. Iverley and Mrs. Balm stepped aside, inviting them to look.

The space was crowded with things, all of them hoary with a thick layer of dust and cobwebs. There were old, wooden bar-rels in the corners, clay pots arranged on the floor and a strange, three-foot-tall, cylindrical column of tarnished copper. And at the center of it all stood a monstrous-looking box of iron plates and bars. It was considerably smaller than the coffin with the fake skinwalker, but infinitely more ominous, not leastwise be-cause of the heavy chains that had been threaded through the bars of the box and looped through iron rings mounted into the concrete walls and floor all around it and secured with very old and very formidable-looking padlocks. There were strange-looking strings of beads and eagle feathers hanging from the box and draped over the chains. And odd sigils were drawn on every flat surface.

It looked like the sort of thing that was made specifically to contain something you really, *really* didn't want to escape.

And inside the bound, iron cage, visible in the burning glare of the flood lights, was a skeletal-thin figure mostly wrapped in coarse fabric and dried animal skins so that its head and most of its torso couldn't be seen. It might've passed as human if not for the strange way the skull bulged against the wrappings and the unnatural, almost scaly texture of the flesh where it was visible.

"That thing is *way* scarier than the last one," said Holly, hugging herself against a chill.

Eric couldn't argue with that. The horned atrocity in the last room wasn't convincing at all, but this thing looked real. And it had an ominous aura about it that he didn't think could be faked.

It actually felt *evil*.

"White ash is the key," explained Mr. Iverley, waving a wrinkled hand at the dust that covered every surface. "A secret recipe. Crafted by the Navajo, packed into these oak barrels and loaded onto Joval's wagon along with the monster. It was what allowed him to transport Yenaldlooshi all the way from the desert."

"And a key component to the binding spells," added Mrs. Balm.

"Nobody really knows what happened during that journey into the cavern," Mr. Iverley told them. "The journals Joval left behind were fakes, just like the monster on exhibit. He didn't want anyone knowing anything about the real Yenaldlooshi, or the location of the cavern where he found it."

Eric understood that perfectly well. After all, he'd been to places like that. He wouldn't want anyone to go nosing around in the fissure he traveled on his first encounter with the weird. It was dangerous in there.

He stared at the eerie scene before him. That unpleasant

knot in his belly was only growing tighter and hotter the longer he looked at it.

What was the purpose of the copper column? Was it some sort of magic grounding rod, perhaps? Magic was such a weird thing. Sometimes it seemed utterly wild and untamable, and other times it seemed to adhere to its own scientific rules.

"It doesn't *look* alive," observed Karen. Back in that last room, when he revealed that the horned monster in the coffin was a fake and that the real one was elsewhere, he'd told them that it was still alive, but this thing didn't look like it'd been alive in a very long time.

"Not even a little bit," agreed Holly.

"Oh, he's alive alright," Mr. Iverley assured her. "You can feel it if you stay down here too long. At first you dismiss it as nothing more than your imagination, but after a while you know better."

"It watches you," said Mrs. Balm, crossing her arms as if suddenly cold. "And it moves. Just a little. Just enough so you can't entirely be sure. But it does."

"Sometimes you can even hear its heart beating," added Mr. Iverley.

Karen shuddered. "I'll take your word for it." She looked the monstrosity up and down once more, as if making sure it wasn't about to jump out of its cage at her, then turned her puzzled expression on Eric. "But if this guy's been locked up here all this time, then what about the one that attacked me earlier?"

Mrs. Balm stiffened. A horrified expression overtook her gentle features. "What?"

"Oh yeah," said Holly. "Skinwalker on the loose. Maybe we should've mentioned that sooner...?"

"That's why we came here," said Karen. "Because you're the only people we know who keeps one as a pet."

"Oh no..." sighed Mrs. Balm. She turned to Mr. Iverley. "If they're already here..."

"We thought they might come," Mr. Iverley reminded her.

"But not this soon! They'll be coming *here!*"

"The spells are still in place," he insisted. "They won't be able to find him."

"For now! It's only a matter of time!"

"What's going on?" demanded Eric.

Mr. Iverley turned his gaze on him. That charming smile was gone. He looked deathly serious. "As I've said before, we don't know much. We only have the information that Ezra Joval and Clarissa Crowlinger passed down along with the responsibility of guarding the chamber. According to this information, Yenaldlooshi isn't just any skinwalker. He's the *original*. There's an entire race of them, all descended from this one dominant specimen."

"Wait, so there's an *army* of these things out there?" gasped Karen.

"Jesus…" sighed Eric. Just the one was scary enough. The thought of a *horde* of those things was beyond terrifying.

"What you saw must've been a descendant," explained Mrs. Balm. "They're here to take Yenaldlooshi back."

"But why now?" wondered Karen. "I mean he's been here this whole time…"

"The directions that were passed down to us," Mr. Iverley went on, "warned us to never tamper with the room. That's why it's locked behind this door. Setting foot inside could affect and weaken the spells keeping it hidden."

"They said that if anything caused these spells to fail," said Mrs. Balm, "the Creek Man could begin to awaken and his children would likely be able to sense his presence."

Holly scrunched up her face, confused. "So…did something happen to do that?"

"Something did," she confirmed.

"There are three crucial elements to the spell that keeps Yenaldlooshi contained and concealed," explained Mr. Iverley. "There's the white ash. There's the continuous watch of a witch." He gestured at Mrs. Balm, who had already informed them that her family had been doing just that for four generations. "And finally there's the idol."

"Idol?" said Karen. "What, like that little golden statue from the beginning of *Raiders of the Lost Ark*?" Was Ezra Joval *actually*

Indiana Jones?

"More of a doll, really," explained Mrs. Balm. "Not nearly so impressive at a glance. Made of clay and straw. *Very* old."

Karen looked over at Eric. "Still seems a little cliché, doesn't it?"

"I don't know where it came from," Mrs. Balm went on, "and I can't begin to explain how it works, but the magic wouldn't be strong enough to bind Yenaldlooshi without it."

"So where is it?" asked Holly.

Mr. Iverley sighed. "It *was* sitting on the pedestal right in front of him."

Eric stared at the curious copper column. Was it more strange or less that it was a pedestal for a magic idol and not a grounding rod for magical energy? He didn't even know anymore.

"Three nights ago," said Mrs. Balm, "as I was getting ready to leave for the day, I felt a strange disruption in the magic. I came straight here and found it gone."

"Stolen?" said Karen, surprised.

"Vanished into thin air," said Mr. Iverley. "Right from under our noses. And without a trace. The door hadn't been forced. The spells hadn't been broken. There weren't even any footprints." And that *was* quite a trick, considering that the whole room was covered in that strange white ash.

"Who could've done something like that?" wondered Eric. The pedestal was too far from the bars for someone to simply reach through them.

"One of those other skinwalkers?" wondered Holly. She was gnawing at her nails again, trying to process everything. "But wait...how could the skinwalkers find Yenny...uh...*their king guy*...with those magic barriers in place?"

"They couldn't," replied Mrs. Balm. "It's not possible. If Yenaldlooshi couldn't get out, his descendants certainly wouldn't be strong enough to get in. Besides, if they knew where he was, they wouldn't be so sneaky about it. They'd be swarming this building, probably tearing themselves to pieces trying to force their way through the barrier."

Karen twirled another lock of her hair as she processed the idea of someone intentionally trying to awaken such a monster. What reason could there be? And what kind of person would even be capable? "Another witch, then?"

"I would've felt any magic that strong," she replied.

"Well *somebody* must've done it," reasoned Eric. "Because it doesn't sound like the sort of thing that just happens by accident."

"That's true," agreed Mr. Iverley.

"Did anyone see anyone suspicious before it was taken?" asked Karen.

Mrs. Balm fiddled with her necklace while she considered the question. "There was *one* gentleman who came to the museum the day it disappeared," she recalled. "He was dressed strangely. All black, head to foot. Spooky looking. I wouldn't have thought much about it, but he had a peculiar aura about him. Kind of gave me goosebumps."

"That does sound kind of suspicious," reasoned Karen.

She nodded. "He didn't stay long, though. As far as I know, he never even came downstairs."

"He could've still been involved somehow," said Karen. "It's not like we've never met any strange-looking people who were up to no good."

Eric nodded.

"We don't have a much time," warned Mr. Iverley. "Now that the magic's been disrupted, he's starting to stir. His children have already sensed that he's in Creek Bend and they're swarming here. It's only a matter of time until he wakes up."

"And what will it mean if he wakes up?" asked Karen, not sure if she wanted to hear the answer.

"It'll be bad," replied Mrs. Balm. "*Very* bad."

"Last time it started to wake up," agreed Mr. Iverley, "was the day Joval brought it to Creek Bend. And it ended with half the town burned to the ground."

Eric was staring at the vacant spot atop the copper pedestal, but at this he turned and looked at the old man, surprised. "Wait…"

"Exactly," he sighed. "The last time Yenaldlooshi started to wake up was in winter of eighteen eighty-one."

"That's…" began Karen, but she trailed off. The Fire of 1881?

"Wait…?" said Holly. The two of them looked at each other, confused.

"I know," said Mr. Iverley. "It's a lot to take in."

"It is," agreed Eric, but that wasn't what surprised them. After all, the three of them already knew what started that fire, and it wasn't an elder skinwalker. Was all of this somehow tied to that business with the jinn?

Again, he found his thoughts drifting back to Evancurt and how everything he'd done seemed to lead him there. All those ghostly messages he'd received over the years. Those strange encounters with Perri in the void. Dream Eric. *Altrusk*. All those things converged in those strange acres, as if it had all been leading him to that one, awful night from the very beginning.

Was *everything* connected?

"Time is running out," said Mrs. Balm. "We have to find the idol and get it back into the containment room as soon as possible."

"But how do we find it?" wondered Holly. "I mean, if we don't even know how it was stolen…?"

"How do we know it's even still in Creek Bend?" asked Karen.

"Or that whoever took it hasn't already destroyed it?" added Eric.

But Mrs. Balm shook her head. "It can't be destroyed. And it's still bound to the enchantments on this room. It can't have left the vicinity of Creek Bend. I'm sure of it."

"Okay then," said Eric. "But even if it hasn't left the city, that doesn't narrow it down a lot. Where do we even start?"

"We can't tell you that," lamented Mrs. Balm. "When I asked my magic what we should do, it showed me nothing except that I should expect *you* to arrive."

"Yeah, that's about the way it always goes down," he grumbled.

"It's how *we* found you," Holly reminded him.

"I'm afraid Yolanda and I won't be much help," Mr. Iverley sighed. "We're not as young as we used to be."

"But if you can bring the idol back here," said Mrs. Balm, "I have the spells that can put everything right again."

"We know it's a lot to ask," apologized Mr. Iverley.

"Don't worry about it," said Eric. "I've done this kind of thing before. Strangely enough."

As soon as these words were out of his mouth, however, he found himself frozen by the hair-raising sound of a low, menacing moan that seemed to reverberate from the very stone around them.

Everyone's terrified gaze turned to the rotting figure chained inside the iron cage.

"Well…" he said, his voice cracking a little, his mouth suddenly dry, "…not *exactly* like this…"

Chapter Seven

Eric, Karen and Holly each left the museum carrying an armload of bright-yellow drawstring pouches with the museum's name and address printed on them. Each one was filled with the same white ash that covered every surface of the real Yenaldlooshi's cramped prison.

"Anyone involved in this unpleasant business should have a bag on them at all times," Mr. Iverley had warned them. "Rub some on your skin to protect yourself."

Mrs. Balm had then placed her hand on her throat and slid it down to the middle of her bosom to demonstrate. "Best over your neck and chest, right here. Cover your throat and your heart."

"Use it on any weapons you have, too," instructed Mr. Iverley. "Rub it on blades. Dust any bullets before you load them into a gun. Even if all you have is a baseball bat, just make sure to dust it really good. It's the only way to hurt them."

"Sprinkle some all the way around the foundation of your house," added Mrs. Balm. "Wouldn't hurt to spread a little around inside, too, especially near any windows or doors."

Eric couldn't think of one good reason why throwing some ashes around would help them if they were attacked by one of those monsters. But logical thinking like that rarely helped anything when it came to the weird. He did, after all, prevent a cosmic conqueror worm from chewing a hole in the universe with a foul-mouthed medium's arts and crafts project.

They stashed most of the ash in the back of the Trailblazer, but heeding Mr. Iverley's warning, they each slipped a pouch into one of their jacket pockets, just in case.

"That was freaky," said Karen as she fastened her seat belt. "I can't believe that *thing* is real."

"We've seen stranger," said Isabelle, speaking through Karen's phone.

Eric plucked his travel cup from the cupholder and nodded.

"It was just…*creepy*," she went on. "I mean did you hear that *moan*?" She shivered at the very memory.

"It wasn't giving off any kind of energy that I could feel," reported Isabelle. "But then again, it was totally drenched in magic energy, so that could've just drowned it out."

"Not that it has to give off energy to be dangerous," added Eric as he sipped his coffee.

"That's true," she agreed.

"I never sensed anything suspicious about those two people, either," reported Holly from the back seat. "They just seemed kind of scared. And genuinely relieved that we were there to help."

"Pretty lucky, I think," said Isabelle. "I mean, a lot of times nobody tells us anything. They were actually pretty helpful."

Again, Eric nodded. Thanks to Mr. Iverley and Mrs. Balm, they knew what they were looking for and why the skinwalkers were in Creek Bend. They even knew how to defend themselves against the monsters.

"Never face a skinwalker alone," Mr. Iverley had warned. "Stay paired up. Don't get separated. If you're by yourself, they can get inside your head. People don't turn up dead when skinwalkers get them. They don't turn up *at all*."

Eric and Karen had glanced at each other at this. That was precisely what happened in that parking lot. She was caught off guard. She was confused and disoriented. Her head felt fuzzy, as if she'd been drugged. If Eric hadn't shown up when he did…

They don't turn up at all, he thought with a shiver. Then, on the heels of that, he found himself thinking, *Not even dead…just gone.*

He forced the thought away. That was another time and another place. It was another *life*. Those haunted words belonged in the past. He needed to stay focused on the present.

"Don't trust your eyes and ears around one," Mrs. Balm had added. "Above all, they're tricksters. If something doesn't seem right, it's probably not."

He took another sip from his coffee cup, then returned it to the cupholder. His stomach still felt sour.

"But why bring that monster to Creek Bend of all places?" asked Karen. "That's what I don't understand."

"I keep wondering that, too," said Eric. "I mean if I remember right, Joval wasn't from here, was he?"

It was generally thought that he came to Wisconsin randomly, hoping to find a bunch of gullible suckers to buy his ridiculous stories, far from his hometown where people knew better than to believe his lies. But if the Yenaldlooshi wasn't just an elaborate hoax made up by an attention-craving con man...if the story was *real*...

"Maybe it was just random," suggested Isabelle.

Eric frowned. "I don't know how much I believe in random chance anymore."

"I know what you mean," sighed Karen. "It's like these things are just *attracted* to you."

"What I want to know," said Isabelle, "is what those skinwalkers have to do with the jinn?"

"Exactly," said Karen. "We already know the jinn was what started the big fire. I mean, don't we? It traveled back in time after being summoned by those gray agents in nineteen sixty-two, which was why there were those weird reports of the fire behaving strangely and being so hard to fight. Because it was jinni fire. Right?"

"That's what I was told," replied Eric. Although it sounded about as far-fetched as things could get, it had actually made a certain amount of sense. He'd witnessed the power of the jinn's flames firsthand and it was much like those old stories about the inferno burning hotter than any normal fire and moving through the city as if it had a mind of its own. A jinn's fire seemed to be an extension of itself. And it explained why no one ever knew where or how the fire started. The only thing he never really understood was why it went back to eighteen eighty-one, specifically. A man he only knew by the silly moniker of "Steampunk Monk" once theorized that there must have been a reason why the jinn selected that year, that there must've been something in the city at that time, something that it was drawn to.

Could it have been drawn to Yenaldlooshi? They'd both been described as "godlike" after all. Maybe there was some kind of relation there.

But why travel all the way back to eighteen eighty-one if it'd been right here this whole time? Mr. Iverley told them that the monster began to stir the day Ezra Joval brought it here. Was it because that was the only night in all those years as Creek Bend's most well-kept secret that Yenaldlooshi actually began to wake up? Or was there something about Mrs. Balm's great grandmother's concealment spell that prevented even the jinn from reaching it in nineteen sixty-two?

The world was so much stranger than he ever imagined it to be, and it only kept getting stranger. He couldn't hope to ever comprehend it all.

Karen shook her head. "The whole thing's just crazy." She turned around in her seat, intending to ask Holly if she'd ever seen anything in any of her divination spells that might have pointed to any of this, but the thought was driven out of her head at the sight of Holly with her jacket open and her sweater pulled all the way down to her navel. She was rubbing ash from her pouch onto her chest and neck. "Oh! Look at you…"

Eric looked back over his shoulder.

"*Don't look!*" snapped Karen.

He quickly faced forward again, startled. "You *said* to look."

"I obviously wasn't talking to *you!*"

"*How was that obvious?*"

Holly looked up at her, confused, her sweater still pulled down. She didn't try to hide herself. "What? The lady in there said to put it here, right?"

"I don't think she meant to do it in front of everybody!" snapped Karen.

She scrunched up her pretty face. "I'm not in front of *anybody*. I'm *behind* you."

"You know what I mean!"

She glanced up at Eric, apparently not seeing the problem

here. "You can't see anything," she argued, looking down at herself. She was still wearing her bra. And even if she wasn't, she was only pulling it down in the middle. It was only a little extra cleavage.

"You can't see anything," agreed Eric as he reached for his coffee again.

"I told you not to look!"

"I wasn't *trying* to look. And I *wouldn't* have looked if you hadn't *said* to look."

"I told you I wasn't talking to you!"

"It's *fine*," insisted Holly. "He's already seen me naked anyway."

The look on Karen's face made her snap her mouth shut and yank her sweater back up.

Then Karen shot Eric a dirty look.

"Oh sure," he grumbled as he took another sip of his coffee. "It's all *my* fault." He dropped the cup back into the cupholder and shifted the Trailblazer into gear.

Holly's phone rang and she quickly fished it from her purse and answered it. "Hi Paige!" She glanced up at Karen and said, "Nope. *Perfect timing*, actually."

Karen turned around and leaned back in her seat, her lips pressed tightly together.

"Let me put you on speaker." Holly swiped at the screen and then held the phone out for everyone to hear. "How's the divination going? Do you have something for us?"

"Um… I think so. I mean, I got a lot of stuff, I guess, but…well, it's super *weird*."

"It's *always* weird," said Eric.

"Always," agreed Holly.

"Okay…but, like, I think my mind keeps wandering. I can't tell what I'm seeing and what my bored brain just decides to think about. I mean, I thought I saw a *smurf* once, so…"

Holly gave her head an indecisive sort of wobble. "That happens sometimes. Just tell me what you saw. We'll sort it out from there."

"Okay…well the first thing I keep seeing is smoke and fire.

Like, *lots* of smoke and fire."

"Fire of 1881," said Eric as he pulled out of the parking lot and headed back toward Main Street. "That keeps coming up today."

"And the jinn," agreed Isabelle.

"And I saw glass trees."

"Glass trees?" asked Holly, not sure if she'd heard correctly.

"Like, made of all sorts of colors of glass. A whole forest of them. Almost like a stained-glass picture or something?"

Eric tried to think if there were any churches or other buildings in town with ornate stained-glass windows, but he couldn't think of any off the top of his head, especially ones that specifically depicted trees.

"And I kept seeing a girl in a red coat," said Paige.

"God, no," groaned Eric.

Holly looked up at him, surprised.

"*No*. No more girls, please. Everywhere I go, there's always some *girl*."

"Well, you *do* like to collect them," accused Karen.

"It's true," agreed Isabelle.

"Shut up, you," grumbled Eric.

"Sorry," said Paige.

"We're just the messengers," said Holly.

He sighed. He found Isabelle on his first journey into the weird. Less than a year later, he found Holly and her sisters. Then Tessa. And Paige. And now Perri. Everyone was already giving him crap about it. Karen's best friend, Diane, had begun referring to them all as "Eric's harem," which never failed to make him feel like some kind of creep.

"What else do you have?" asked Holly.

"Dogs," said Paige. "I keep seeing dogs. Ugly ones. Not cute at all. Scary ones, even."

"Skinwalkers," said Eric, remembering the snarling, canine face of the monster behind the bookshop.

"No surprise there," agreed Holly. "What else?"

"A really long, dark hallway," said Paige. "That was super creepy."

"Hmm…" said Holly. "That tunnel under the museum, maybe?"

"Could be," agreed Eric.

"Probably," said Karen.

"And I saw a book."

"Book…" said Holly, thinking.

"A lot of random things," said Paige. "Animals, mostly. Deer and squirrels and rabbits."

"That was probably that creepy taxidermy room we had to walk through," reasoned Holly. She gave a visible shudder as she remembered having to walk back through there again on their way out. "*Twice.*"

"But also, like, hippos and flamingos. An alligator, I think. That sort of thing."

Holly frowned. "Wait, I didn't see any of those kinds of animals down there…"

"Because there weren't any," said Eric, confused.

Karen glanced over at him. "You planning a trip to the zoo today?"

"I hope not. That sounds like a terrible place to have to deal with the weird."

"Also lots of *rainbows.*"

Karen looked up through the windshield at the dreary sky, but it didn't look like a rainbow sort of day out there.

"And I keep seeing white people," added Paige.

Holly scrunched up her pretty features at this. "Huh?"

"I mean, not *white people* white people," she explained, flustered. "Like, people *painted* white or something. I just see these creepy, white silhouettes kind of glowing in the darkness. Or sometimes there'll be this really creepy, white face staring back at me with all-black eyes. It was really scary."

"White people…" sighed Holly. "What could that be…?"

Eric stopped at the light and switched his turn signal on. Why did magic have to be so cryptic? It was *magic*. It could see the future, but it couldn't give them a straight answer?

"I kept seeing, like, *sewers*, too," said Paige.

"Ew…" said Holly.

Karen wrinkled her nose. "Sewers?"

"Yeah. Like manhole covers and storm drains and stuff."

"Well that sounds awful," said Isabelle.

"I know, right?" agreed Paige. "Totally gross. Sorry."

"Is that where the idol's hidden?" wondered Karen. "In the city's sewers?"

"God, I hope not," grumbled Eric.

"Sorry," said Paige.

"Not your fault," he assured her. He couldn't decide if it made him feel better to have a heads-up that today's episode of *Eric in Weirdland* might involve sewer tunnels or if that was something he was better off not knowing about.

"I think I saw dice once," Paige went on.

"Dice?" Karen looked over at Eric. "What, are the bad guys going to challenge you to a game of Yahtzee or something?"

"That'd definitely be a change of pace."

"And, um…" Paige hesitated, embarrassed. "Is it…uh…weird that I keep seeing *boobs*?"

Holly sat up at this. "Boobs?"

Karen reached over and smacked Eric's shoulder. "Don't even think about it!"

"Ow! Don't think about *what*? I don't even know what she's talking about!"

"Yeah," Paige went on. "Just, like, *boobs*. Not, like, *women* with their boobs out, but just, like, *by themselves*. Just sort of…hanging there… Kind of right in my face… It was super weird. And seriously uncomfortable."

"If I find out you went to another strip club, you're a dead man," threatened Karen.

"I'm not in control of where the weird sends me!" returned Eric. "And you know I didn't *want* to go to that strip club."

"For what it's worth," said Holly, her voice cautiously timid, "I'm really glad he came to find me at the Dirty Bunny that night."

"No one's talking to you, Red," grumbled Karen. But she looked out her window and said nothing more on the matter. She was fully aware that if Eric hadn't gone into that building that night that Holly would've died.

The light finally changed and Eric pulled onto Main Street.

"Anything else?" asked Holly.

"Um...yeah. One more. There's this...uh... Thing? I don't...really know what it is, actually. But it's really *big*. It takes over the whole bowl and then we can't see anything. It's like an *eclipse*. And once it appears it won't go away until we stop and boil more water. It's really weird."

Again, Holly scrunched up her face. "That's a new one."

"Are we doing something wrong?"

"I'm not sure. Was that everything?"

"There were a few other things. Flickers, mostly. Flashes. I couldn't quite make them out. But I felt a lot of really *bad* emotions. Fear, mostly. I kept getting this really intense feeling of, like, impending doom. Like something was coming for me. Something really, *really* scary. I had to get up and check to make sure all the doors were locked."

"Probably not a bad idea," grumbled Eric.

Karen nodded.

"Oh, but *Perri* saw something," exclaimed Paige.

"Oh!" said Holly. "That's great!" She'd been working with Paige for months, teaching her how to use the divination spell, and she wanted to teach Perri to use it too. The more people you had, the more energy was available for the spell and the more information it would yield. But she hadn't actually begun training her yet. She hadn't expected her to be able to see anything.

"Except it wasn't in the water."

Holly's expression turned to puzzlement in the space of a single blink. "What?"

"Yeah, she wasn't even in the room. It was during one of those times when we'd walked away because the water was eclipsed. I went to use the bathroom and when I came out, she was just standing at the door, looking sort of frazzled. I guess it just sort of hit her."

"What did she see?" asked Eric.

"A lighthouse."

"Lighthouse?" said Karen, bewildered.

"There aren't any lighthouses in Creek Bend," said Eric.

"I know," said Paige. "It's weird, but she says she saw a lighthouse shining in the dark in the distance. And she said that something about it was *really* scary."

"Lighthouse..." muttered Eric. How far was this skinwalker business going to take him? Was he going to have to pursue the idol thief all over Wisconsin? Or even across the country?

Usually this sort of thing wasn't that drawn out.

From somewhere in the background, Perri's voice spoke up for the first time. "Don't forget to tell them about the cow."

"Oh, right," said Paige. "I forgot about that one."

"Cow?" said Holly, surprised.

"What about the cow?" asked Karen, sounding more concerned than the subject of cows typically warranted.

"Yeah, I saw a cow. And it was...uh...*dancing?*"

"A dancing cow?" Holly looked more confused than ever.

"I think it was wearing a tutu."

Karen and Eric both looked at each other, surprised. "Pottie!" gasped Karen.

Holly stared at them, her face awash with puzzlement. "Huh?"

Chapter Eight

Eric circled the block and pointed the Trailblazer back the way they came. Minutes later, he was pulling into the parking lot behind Ternheart Mercantile, where he chose a spot well away from the doors. (He was still in that new car stage where he'd rather walk a little farther than take any unnecessary risks of someone parking too close and dinging his doors.)

"That's Pottie?" asked Holly. She stared through the windshield at the forty-foot-tall mural painted on the back wall of the building. It depicted an almost disturbingly realistic cow standing upright and striking a ballet pose in a pink tutu and slippers.

"It used to be Pottle Dairy Distribution," explained Eric as he killed the engine and unbuckled his seatbelt. "So...Pottie the Cow."

Holly stared up at the bovine ballerina. "I guess that makes sense."

"If I remember right, recalled Karen, "she was painted by one of the Pottle family's sons way back in the sixties. The new owners had her fully restored when they took over the location in the early nineties and have kept her maintained ever since. I guess there're a lot of people in town who consider her one of Creek Bend's little treasures."

"Not all that unlike Joval's Monster," added Eric.

"True..."

The three of them stepped out of the vehicle and looked around. The streets were fairly quiet for a Saturday afternoon and there wasn't a soul in sight from back here.

"Don't forget the ash," Holly reminded them.

Eric reached for the pouch in his pocket. "Right..."

Karen made a face at the thought of rubbing ashes on her skin, and he could hardly blame her. It was cold and gritty against his fingers, somehow both coarse and slick at the same time. And it smelled funny.

He glanced around to make sure they were still alone and that no one was watching, then he lifted his chin and smeared the strange, grimy mixture onto his neck.

"Feels gross," observed Karen as she plunged her dirty hand down the front of her shirt.

"I know," he assured her. And he did. He knew very well how she must have felt. Karen didn't like messes. She was a very tidy person, used to keeping her workspace clean as she bustled about the kitchen every day. The idea of intentionally making herself dirty went against her instincts. And then there was the fact that they had no idea what this stuff really was. Mr. Iverley had simply called it "white ash" and described it as a secret Navajo recipe. They didn't know what might be mixed in with it or even what kind of ash it was. For all anyone knew, they could be smearing something truly grotesque on their skin right now.

"It's not *that* bad," reasoned Holly, tugging at her sweater and peering down at her own dusty chest. "You get used to it."

Karen closed the pouch and returned it to her pocket, then she dusted off her hand and grimaced. "If you say so. Let's get this over with so I can go home and have a shower."

"Sounds good to me," agreed Eric, already leading the way to the doors.

Ternheart Mercantile was one-part indoor craft fair, one-part antique mall and one-part overpriced gift shop consisting of five sprawling rooms all stuffed to bursting with all manner of merchandise. You could find homemade soap, candy and pre-serves, hand-crafted clothes, accessories and jewelry, herbs and spices, candles, flowers, novelty signs, wreaths, beauty products, dog treats, old-fashioned toys, holiday decorations and pretty much anything you could imagine hanging on a wall in your av-erage grandmother's house. It wasn't really his sort of thing, but Karen had dragged him here on more occasions than he could count. And he usually walked out loaded down like a pack mule.

Currently, there was an abundance of Easter-themed mer-chandise, especially near the doors and registers, along with a few remaining St. Patrick's Day leprechauns and shamrocks.

At least it wasn't crowded. There were only two employees that he could see and hardly anyone was browsing today.

"Not that I'm complaining," said Karen as she scanned the familiar labyrinth that stretched out before them, "but why are we here?"

"Because the Pottie cow said so?" guessed Holly.

She wrinkled her nose. "That's not a good name for her..."

"Not at all," agreed Eric.

Karen shook her head. "No, I mean *why*. There must be some reason that Paige saw that mural in the divination, right? Like, doesn't that mean Eric is supposed to come here?"

"That's usually how it works," said Holly. "The whole reason it's in the water is because it's a part of Eric's future. He's *meant* to come here for some reason. But it doesn't usually give him such a specific location to go to."

"That's right," he agreed. "Usually, I don't know where it is I'm supposed to go until I'm already there and I see the clue staring me in the face."

"Right. The clues are always so vague. We might not necessarily be in the right place. I mean, the cow was *outside*. It could just as easily have meant the parking lot. Or maybe there's some other place you can see the cow from."

"Well, maybe it's different this time because *Paige* was conducting the divination," suggested Karen.

"Maybe..." agreed Holly, though she didn't look very sure.

"She has some kind of relationship with those voodoo spirit things, doesn't she? Maybe one of *them* helped her."

"Literally anything's possible," said Eric, still looking around. "We just have to figure out if we're in the right place or not." As he was saying this, however, his cell phone chimed at the arrival of a new text message. He pulled it from his pocket and looked at the screen.

I FEEL SOMETHING, Isabelle informed him.

He raised an eyebrow and glanced up at Holly.

IT'S KIND OF FAINT, BUT THERE'S A STRANGE ENERGY LINGERING IN THAT PLACE

Holly crowded next to him and read the screen. "What kind of energy?"

NOT SURE, she replied.

Then: BUT IT'S SOMETHING FAMILIAR

He looked around. A familiar energy… She recognized spiritual and psychic energy when she felt them. She also knew magical energy when she felt it, despite the fact that it varied wildly from witch to witch and coven to coven. So it wouldn't be any of those. And they'd already established that Isabelle couldn't detect any kind of energy from the skinwalker he encountered behind the bookshop, so that wasn't it, either. But that didn't narrow it down much. There were other kinds of energy out there, things she felt far more rarely, like the odd energy given off by unseen places and even a distinctly chilling *hell energy*. And there were energies that she'd so far only *theorized* might exist.

DON'T GET CARELESS. PAUL IS ON HIS WAY OVER RIGHT NOW. HE SHOULD BE THERE IN A FEW MINUTES

"Right," he mumbled. He lowered the phone but kept it in his hand. If anything changed, he wanted her to be able to tell him as soon as possible. "Let's have a look around," he said, already setting off through the crowded displays."

"And we're looking for *what*, exactly?" asked Karen.

"I wish I knew," he replied. "Just…keep your eyes open for anything that seems out of place."

She glanced around at the countless things on display around them, bewildered. "Sure… Piece of cake…"

"You know what just keeps bugging me?" said Holly, "How did they get the doll thing out of that room? The concealment and containment magic was still intact when we arrived at the museum. I can't wrap my head around it."

"Is it possible the spell was broken when it was stolen and Mrs. Balm just cast another one?" asked Karen.

Holly shook her head. "No, fresh spells have a different feel to them than ones that've been there a while. You can tell the difference."

"Oh."

"Besides, it wasn't just *that* spell they got past. There was binding magic *heaped* on that room. Those locks were permanently frozen and those chains were impossible to break."

Eric nodded. "Yeah, they *really* didn't want that thing getting out."

THAT WASN'T THE SORT OF PLACE YOU PUT JUST ANY MONSTER, agreed Isabelle. THAT ROOM WAS DESIGNED FOR DRACULA-LEVEL BADDIES

"Lot of good it did them," grumbled Eric.

"They didn't even leave footprints," recalled Karen.

It was a hell of a mystery all right. Eric could only hope that since the divination pointed them to this place that they'd find at least *some* answers here.

He stalked past a rack of reusable shopping bags sewn together from recycled pet food bags and a huge display of intricately designed birdhouses, his eyes wide open for anything out of place...as if he'd really know if anything was out of place in this cramped labyrinth of artificial flowers, pottery, wildlife paintings and porch wreaths.

Lots of things in here had Wisconsin on them. There were cutting boards, signs and clocks all cut into the shape of the state. It was embroidered onto purses, pillows and potholders. And it was emblazoned on beer steins, coffee mugs and shot glasses.

He caught sight of more copies of Voskstern's *Reassembling the Ashes* on display with a number of other locally authored books. Was he going to see those *everywhere* he went today?

A large, hand-painted sign approximately the size of his front door informed him that all he needed was love and a kitten, but he really didn't think that was going to cover it for him today. Plus, the weird was no place for a kitten.

"Can't *you* do something?" asked Karen, turning her attention to Holly.

Holly blinked back at her, confused. "What?"

"Like back at the museum. You used a spell to reveal what they were hiding in the basement."

"That was different. It was *magic*. I could sense it as soon as we walked into the building. I can't sense anything here. Whatever Isabelle is feeling is something else."

"But I recognized that spell," Karen pushed. "You and Eric told me about it. You used it to make Tessa reveal herself for the first time. So it must work on spirits, too, right?"

"No. Tessa's a ghost, but she's also a *witch*, remember?"

She frowned. "Oh yeah… I keep forgetting you can be both."

"I didn't sense her spirit. I sensed the residual magic her spirit was clinging to."

"Oh."

"Sorry."

"It's fine," replied Karen. "It was just a thought."

As he neared the far wall, Eric glanced down at his phone.

SOMEWHERE TO THE LEFT, I THINK

He nodded and set off again, his gaze washing over the various things that were for sale all around him. There was a large selection of hand-carved, wooden statues of dachshunds in various sleeping positions. There were several cabinets full of extremely well-crafted dollhouse furniture. There was a large display of locally harvested honey and maple syrup. There was even a display of beautifully decorated, ornamental masks that he thought were almost as cool as they were creepy.

ARE YOU OKAY?

He looked down at the screen and raised an eyebrow. "Yeah. It's not like I haven't been here a million times."

YOU KNOW WHAT I MEAN

The problem with having someone inside your head was that you simply couldn't lie to them. Of course he knew what she meant. And of course she knew that he knew it.

YOU KEEP THINKING ABOUT WHAT HAPPENED THERE

It was true. Every time he had an idle moment, he found himself back in those frigid woods.

Evancurt…

Those memories weren't even his own, yet they haunted him in a way that very few of his real memories ever had.

"I'm fine," he muttered under his breath. And it wasn't a lie.

After all, he *was* fine. Much more so than the Eric who actually belonged to those memories. It was merely that there were a lot of emotions caught up in all that. He was still processing things. And this business with the skinwalkers had come too soon. He didn't feel like he'd been given enough time to properly process something as heavy as the concept of a time-torn version of himself being *wiped from existence.*

YOU'RE OKAY, Isabelle assured him. DON'T GET HUNG UP ON THE PAST

He nodded. She was right, of course. He needed to stay focused. This was the weird. He needed to stay on his toes. Anything could happen at any time.

"Eric?" called Karen. Her voice should have come from right behind him, but she sounded far away.

He looked around, confused. Where did they go? He was all alone.

"What are you doing?"

He turned and peered through a display of dangling wind chimes and a tiny rainforest of fake ferns and silk lilies to see Karen and Holly looking back at him from the next aisle over.

"I take my eyes off you for one second and you've already wandered off."

He looked back the way he came. Did he make a wrong turn? "I was talking to Isabelle," he said. It felt like a lame excuse, but it was also the only reason he could think of.

"You're hopeless, I swear." She pointed forward and said, "Meet us at the end of the aisle.

"Yeah…" he replied, still trying to figure out where he made the wrong turn.

SHE OBVIOUSLY WASN'T PAYING ATTENTION EITHER, said Isabelle. Then, right on the heels of that: DON'T TELL HER I SAID THAT

He nodded and looked back the way he came again. It wasn't all that strange, really. This place was a maze. It wasn't even the first time he'd gotten turned around in here. But it didn't seem like he had time to get lost. They must've split up almost as soon as they started walking.

Not that it mattered. He turned and continued on. They'd meet back up at the end of the aisle in just a minute. "Can you still feel that energy?"

I CAN

AND IT FEELS LIKE YOU'RE GETTING CLOSER TO IT

He looked up from the phone and glanced around, but there was nothing nearby that looked like it should be giving off strange energy.

Then again, he had no idea what something that gave off strange energy might look like...

And where was the end of the aisle? He didn't make another wrong turn, did he? He looked back the way he came, but he couldn't see Karen and Holly anywhere. Had he wandered into the next room this time? He didn't remember walking through the doorway.

Why was he so distracted?

He started to turn back and retrace his steps, but his cell phone chimed at him.

THE ENERGY IS STRONGER THERE, reported Isabelle. KEEP GOING

"Sure," he muttered, continuing on.

He walked past a display case containing a selection of stones and crystals. During that business with the blood witches and the karmic sin, he met a coven of witches who used just such things to amplify and direct their magical powers. "Could something like that be the source of the energy?" he wondered.

IT'S ALWAYS POSSIBLE, replied Isabelle. BUT I DON'T THINK SO. IT FEELS LIKE IT'S MOVING

He looked down at the screen, confused. "Moving?"

IT'S HARD TO TELL FOR SURE, THOUGH

Why would the energy be moving?

Before he could ponder the meaning of a moving energy source, his foot caught on something and he stumbled and fell. He threw his arm out to catch himself on a display stand, but only managed to clumsily slap his hand across it, dragging a tray full of handmade pendant necklaces off into the floor on top of him with a resounding crash.

The next moment, he was lying face-down on the concrete, covered in jewelry and feeling like an idiot.

What the hell was that?

He sat up and looked behind him, but there was nothing there. It appeared that he'd only tripped over his own foot.

Embarrassed, he began gathering up the jewelry, which turned out to be much harder than he thought it would be. In his rush to clean up his mess and escape before someone saw him, he was clumsy. He kept dropping things. And he had no idea how this stuff was arranged in the display case. He was just piling them on it, probably making an even worse mess.

He glanced up at the various ceiling-mounted security cameras. Someone better not put that on the internet. If he turned into one of those damned memes, he was going to be pissed.

How embarrassing...

He snatched up the last of the dropped pendants and stood up, dusting himself off. He felt bad. The display almost certainly looked a lot nicer than this before he came crashing through it. But on a positive note, no one seemed to be around to witness his grand blooper.

He should really try to put things back nicely and not look like a jerk, but he kind of just wanted to run away...

As he went to lay the last pendant atop the pile, however, he paused and stared at it. It was a small, silver ring, about the size of a dollar coin, with an arrangement of little crystals of various colors beaded through fine wire that was tied into the shape of a tree.

"Glass tree..." he sighed. Paige said she saw glass trees. She even described them as being different colors, like stained glass. He looked down at the pendants piled on the tray. All of them looked like that. And when he looked up, he realized that there were dozens more hanging from the netting strewn over the top of the booth. He was literally looking through a *forest of glass trees*.

"The Tree of Life," said a voice from behind him.

Chapter Nine

Eric jumped and turned to face the man who was standing there. He was tall, thin and pale, with long, black hair and strangely wide, excited-looking eyes. He was dressed in a full-length, black trench coat, black leather boots and a very long, brightly colored scarf more suited to the winter months than late March, even on a cold day like today. He seemed to be buzzing with energy, yet at the same time he looked extremely weary. There were dark shadows under those excited eyes and his lips, though pulled into an eager grin, were thin and colorless.

"It's really popular these days with the spiritual crowds," the wild-eyed stranger went on. "To different people it represents everything from health and wisdom to peace and tranquility to death and the afterlife."

Eric glanced around, confused. Where did this guy come from? No one was around a moment ago when he looked to see if anyone had witnessed his embarrassing spill.

"As a symbol, it's known all over the world in one form or another. It's been called the Sacred Tree, the Cosmic Tree, the World Tree, Yggdrasil and the Tree of Knowledge, just to name a few."

Was he trying to sell him one of these necklaces? Did he work here? What was happening.

His phone chimed an answer at him. He glanced down at it and read, ENERGY!

As in the strange energy she felt when he first entered the building? He closed his fist around the phone and looked up at the man again. Was it coming from *him*?

"Some think its origins are simultaneous with humanity's, that the first thing Adam beheld in the blinding light of his brand-new world was the gently swaying branches of the tree he was born under."

Eric did his best to keep a straight face. "Very interesting," he replied, though he was only being polite. He didn't care about the symbology of some silly jewelry. He was way too preoccupied with whatever this energy was that Isabelle was sensing.

"Isn't it?" The stranger flashed him a delighted smile that seemed to match those wide, wild eyes. "But not half as interesting as this lovely city of yours."

IT'S DEFINITELY COMING FROM HIM, texted Isabelle.

"It's a nice town," he agreed as he read the screen. "I'm rather fond of it." *And I'd very much prefer that it stay in one piece*, he thought, but didn't say aloud. What was going on here? Who was this man? Why was he giving off some sort of energy? And how was he involved with this skinwalker business?

He glanced down at the long coat and heavy, black boots. Was this the guy Mrs. Balm saw creeping around the museum the day the idol went missing? The one with the peculiar aura?

But she didn't say anything about an obnoxiously colorful scarf. That should've been something that stood out in her memory. Was it something he'd picked up in the time between then and now? He was no fashion expert, but it didn't look to him like it went with the rest of the outfit at all.

And looking at it now, he realized that it wasn't just a random pattern, either. There was a distinct order to the colors. It was a repeating rainbow pattern.

Rainbows... he thought, distracted. Another piece of the puzzle from Paige's divination.

His phone chimed in his hand again.

I'VE DEFINITELY FELT THAT KIND OF DARK ENERGY BEFORE

"But I'm not just talking about the local culture," the stranger went on. "I'm talking about the *crossroads* on which the city stands."

Eric struggled to maintain his poker face. Crossroads? That wasn't something an ordinary person would casually bring up to a stranger on the street. Only someone deeply knowledgeable about the weird would know that this city was sitting on a point in the universe where multiple worlds overlapped. An insane woman he knew only as Mistress Janet told him about it two summers ago while trying to seduce him because she believed that he had some sort of tremendous power inside him and that she could steal it if she could just get into his pants…which just sounded like the plot for a bad smut novel…

How this guy knew about it, he didn't yet know, but he wasn't going to let on that *he* knew what he was talking about.

But the stranger in the rainbow scarf tipped his head to one side, those wild eyes seemingly boring into his very soul. There was something unsettling about that expression, but he couldn't quite put his finger on it. "But you'll know all about that, won't you? After all, you're Eric Fortrell."

Eric blinked, surprised to hear his own name. That sour knot in his belly started to burn even hotter. "I'm sorry…do we know each other?"

"No," replied the stranger. "We've never met."

I'M PRETTY SURE HE'S NOT PRODUCING THE ENERGY, Isabelle informed him. Then: IT'S MORE LIKE HE'S SATURATED WITH IT, LIKE HE'S BEEN SOME-WHERE THAT'S FLOODED WITH THAT ENERGY

He clenched his jaw, biting back an urge to curse, and met the stranger's gaze again. *Just like the others*, he thought. He knew where this was going. He'd already guessed it for himself, after all. This guy knew about the crossroads under Creek Bend the same way Mistress Janet knew about them.

He was an agent.

He couldn't honestly say he was surprised. But he wasn't remotely happy about it. Like he didn't already have enough to deal with today. And he certainly didn't care for the thought of an agent already knowing his name before they'd even met.

The stranger offered him another shining smile. "But I know who you are," he said. "I know *all about you*."

Eric felt his heart drop into his belly with the sour knot. He had a bad feeling about this. *Karen*, he thought.

I SENT HER AND HOLLY BACK TO THE FRONT

OF THE STORE, Isabelle assured him.

"I know about the fissure," said the stranger. "I know about the nine hidden secrets. The witch wars. The fairy ring. The worm. The Black World machine." Those wild eyes seemed to light up a little brighter with each addition to his list.

He felt as if he should say something along the lines of, "I have no idea what you're talking about," or, "I think you have me confused with someone else," but his mouth had gone dry. He couldn't seem to unstick his tongue from the roof of his mouth. The fissure was the rift between two worlds that he traveled on his first journey into the weird. The "nine hidden secrets" obviously referred to the nine unseen structures scattered around the city. The "witch wars" was certainly a reference to the battles Holly and her sisters had engaged in against the phony Magic Man in Illinois and the blood witches the following year in Wisconsin. Then there was the Conqueror Worm business in Hedge Lake. The childlike fairies at Bellylaugh Playland. And finally the spirit-powered nightmare machine that was Evancurt. These were some of his many experiences with the weird, all summed up and neatly arranged for him.

This guy wasn't joking around. He knew exactly who he was talking to.

Had the mysterious organization been watching him from the start? It hadn't seemed as if the previous agents had any idea who he was, but perhaps that was all a mere ruse. Or maybe they'd all simply been lower-level agents who hadn't yet earned the proper security clearance yet.

He'd been involved in some way with the deaths of four agents in the past few years. If this guy knew about that, things were probably going to get a little awkward.

"I also know all about your lovely wife, Karen," he went on.

"Now hold on there," growled Eric. Again, that knot in his gut tightened.

"Your brother Paul. The witch, Holly Shorring."

"Watch it!" he warned

Again, that mad grin widened. "The girl you're talking to right now on that phone."

Eric shoved the phone into his pocket. "Who are you?" he demanded. He didn't expect an answer. Agents were members of a mysterious, unknown organization that made strange and unusual things their business. He'd met several of them in his weird adventures and none of them had ever shared their names. Instead, he'd given them silly nicknames like the Foggy Man, Pink Shirt, Mistress Janet and Steampunk Monk. He'd probably be calling this rainbow scarf guy "Skittles" or something the rest of the day.

But the stranger gave him an odd little bow and replied, "Wilford Lafayette. A pleasure to formally meet you."

Eric stared at him for a moment, surprised. "Oh…" was all he could think to say.

"Too much?" asked Wilford Lafayette, his expression drooping. He looked embarrassed. Those big, wide eyes were suddenly full of self-conscious doubt. "A bit of a mouthful? A little old-fashioned? You can just call me Will, if you want. Or Ford." Those wild eyes rolled thoughtfully across the ceiling as he considered the way it sounded. "I like Ford," he decided. "How do you feel about Ford?"

"Sure…" he replied, befuddled. "I just…wasn't expecting you to really tell me your name."

Wilford Lafayette—Ford for short—cocked his head again and flashed him a knowing grin. "The old 'company policy,' right? 'Share no names. Share no secrets. Leave no trace.'" He lifted his hands and waggled his fingers dramatically. "Ooooh. Scary."

Eric stared at him. He wasn't sure what was happening here. This guy was breaking all the rules. He didn't act like an agent. But then again, what did an agent act like? The Foggy Man, once they were finally face-to-face, was little more than a scared kid. The cowboy was a deranged psychopath who only wanted an excuse to murder people. Mistress Janet had a god complex. And Steampunk Monk had turned out to be an unexpectedly reasonable man who only seemed to be in it to further his own strange research.

"Well, in all fairness," said Ford, crossing his arms behind his back and grinning like a smug child, "I never said it was my *real* name."

"Ah," said Eric. That *did* make sense. Now he found himself wondering why the other agents hadn't simply made up fake names to share with people. Wouldn't that have been easier?

"Gotta follow the rules, after all." Then he slumped forward and wrinkled his nose into a spoiled sort of sneer. Those wild eyes wandered off into the distance. "So many stupid rules..." he grumbled. "I hate rules."

What was with this guy? Even for an agent, he was behaving weirdly. He was starting to think that this "Ford" wasn't firing on all cylinders.

The strange agent's expression abruptly changed again. That childish, pouting sneer vanished in an instant, replaced with a look of such intense seriousness that Eric had to make a conscious effort not to back away.

"I'm bored of this conversation. What do you say we skip ahead to business?"

He stared back at the man, meeting those strange, wide eyes and trying not to look as if he wanted to turn around and run away as fast as his legs could carry him. "What exactly *is* your business here? If you know so much about me, you could've killed me any time you wanted."

Ford flapped a dismissive hand at him. "I have no interest in killing you."

"Then why are you here?"

That great, disturbing smile reappeared. His teeth were very straight and very white. They almost didn't look real. "I'm here because of *this*," he replied, reaching into the trench coat and withdrawing a very familiar book.

Emanuel Voskstern's *Reassembling the Ashes*...

He stared at it for a moment. This all started after the book signing. And it kept showing up. Now even the agent had one? No wonder Paige saw a book in her divination.

He looked up and met the agent's gaze. "It's a good book. But what's so special about it that it brought *you* here?"

"Secrets," replied Ford, still grinning that disturbing grin.

Again, he looked down at the book. "What kinds of secrets?"

"*Big* secrets. *Profound* secrets."

"Such as…?"

That grin melted away and the man blinked, as if surprised. "Well they wouldn't be *secrets* anymore if I told you, would they?"

Eric stared at him, unamused.

"I'm betting you'll figure it out for yourself," said Ford, his grin reappearing. He slipped the book back into his coat. "Besides, *why* I came here isn't all that important right now. What's *really* important is what I found once I arrived." He turned and examined a large dollhouse filled with carefully crafted little furniture. "You see, now that I'm here, I've found that things are all messed up. Someone's been tampering with dangerous forces and something very *evil* slumbering beneath these streets is very close to waking up." He picked up a tiny bed and examined it more closely. "You already know about that, though, don't you?"

Eric said nothing.

He put the bed carefully back where he found it and turned to face him again. "Getting to the point, I need your help, Eric Fortrell."

"My help," he said, skeptical. "What exactly is it you want?"

For a moment, Ford only stood there, staring back at him with those big eyes as if he'd somehow gotten stuck like that. Then, just as suddenly, his face changed again. His lips stretched into a huge, delighted-looking smile.

This time, Eric *did* take a step backward. There was something deeply wrong with that face. Especially those wild eyes. There was something very close to madness there, if not already well past it.

"What *I* want?" chuckled Ford. "I want the same thing *you* want."

Eric squinted at the madman. Call him a pessimist, but he doubted that the two of them shared the same sorts of goals. "And what's that?"

"To save the city of Creek Bend from annihilation, of course."

Chapter Ten

"Annihilation…" breathed Eric. This had certainly escalated quickly.

The wild-eyed man in the colorful scarf sighed the word back at him, enunciating each syllable with dramatic emphasis: "*Annihilation.*"

"That's a big word. Not a lot of room for interpretation."

"There's nothing *to* interpret." Ford stepped closer to him, lowering his voice as if concerned about being overheard. "We're talking about the earth and sky torn apart. An apocalyptic *abyss* yawning open beneath our feet. Everything and everyone engulfed in an endless, black nightmare of nothingness."

"Poetic," grunted Eric.

"Thank you!" he replied, looking very proud of himself.

Eric ran his hand through his hair, frustrated. Was this guy really an agent? Because agents were terrifying people, most of whom had terrifying powers. And he was more and more certain that this guy was just *nuts*.

"Point is," said Ford, his expression turning serious again, "this town's gonna be screwed if we don't do something." He reached out and poked Eric in the chest. "You already know that. I already know you know it. Let's not waste time we don't have pretending you don't."

He had a point, Eric supposed. Mr. Iverley warned him that if Yenaldlooshi were to wake up, it would be a disaster. But Mr. Iverley had also been under the assumption that Yenaldlooshi caused the Fire of 1881 when it began to stir after first arriving in Creek Bend in the back of Ezra Joval's wagon. Eric knew, however, that the jinn was the real cause of the fire. At least, he *thought* the jinn was the cause…

But what if it wasn't the jinn? What if he'd been deceived?

It wouldn't be the first time an agent lied to him. And wouldn't it have made more sense that the fire was caused by a god-like monster that was actually *in* the city in eighteen eighty-one instead of a god-like monster that was summoned in nineteen sixty-two and then traveled *back in time* to eighteen eighty-one?

He was so confused…

"Here's the deal," said Ford. He plucked a mason jar candle off a display shelf and looked it over as if bored. "It's in the interest of…" Those wide eyes rolled up toward the ceiling again, as if he were searching for the right words. "…let's call them my *employers*…" he decided. He unscrewed the lid and smelled the candle, then made a face at it and put it back down. "They'd rather not let this city be wiped off the map," he finished.

"It's in their interest," scoffed Eric. "Sure." In his experience, the interests of agents were far removed from the interests of anyone else involved.

Ford swooped forward and slipped his arm around Eric's shoulders, as if they were old buddies. "Don't be like that!"

Eric stiffened. It took all his willpower not to yank himself free of the weirdo's grip and bolt for the nearest door.

"Sure, my people are a little…" He scrunched up his face, struggling with the words for a moment. Then he simply quit trying and let all the expression fall away. "Okay, most of them are evil bastards. *But…*" he held up his index finger as if to drive home the point, "…they're evil bastards who *don't want to see this town destroyed.*" Then he frowned and looked thoughtfully down at the floor. "I mean they probably have *evil reasons* for not wanting to see this town destroyed…seeing as how it's technically a vital strategic location in the greater cosmic order of the universe and all…"

Eric stared at the man, surprised.

"Plus all the potentially *weaponizable* resources accessible through the control of such a location…" He shook his head and blew a long breath through his pursed lips. "And then there's the fact that it's an *ideal* location for *all sorts* of *really questionable* cross-dimensional research…" He flapped his hand in that dismissive gesture again and said, "But even so. Today, we have a common goal."

"Right," said Eric. He already knew much of that. Mistress Janet told him about most of it. She even showed him the freakshow they'd assembled in the basement of the unseen psychiatric hospital with all those monsters they'd summoned from other worlds. It wasn't even all that far-fetched to imagine how someone with the right tools and knowledge could turn a dimensional crossroads into a weapon of unfathomable destruction. After all, wasn't that precisely what Evancurt was?

But if Creek Bend was so important to these people, why did they keep showing up and causing so much trouble? Why did the gray agents summon the jinn? Why did Mistress Janet want to rip a hole in it?

Ford gave his shoulders a hard squeeze. "Whatever the reasons, we're all on the same side today." Then he grinned a surprisingly annoying grin and added. "We're totally *besties!*"

"Please stop touching me."

Ford withdrew his hand and made a face at him. "That's not how besties talk to each other, Eric."

"Fine," said Eric. "We're on the same side."

Those wild eyes lit up again. "Fantastic!"

"So what do you know about the idol that was stolen three days ago?"

It was a risk, blurting that out. He knew it was. If it turned out that this guy was baiting him for information, then he was playing right into his trap. But Ford knew that the entire city was in danger. He knew about his past experiences with the weird. He was betting he already knew about the secret room at the end of the tunnel under the museum.

Ford grinned at him again. "I know that no human could have taken it from that impressive vault. No skinwalker, either." He turned and strolled away from him, suddenly interested in a display of potted succulents. "Only a god could've done something like that."

Eric pined for the days when gods were just the subjects of old myths and Rick Riordan books. Real gods were a pain in the ass. He'd much rather stick with just the one.

"I also know that, without the relic, the spells holding Yee Naaldlooshii will fail very soon."

Eric couldn't help but shudder. Something about the way *he* pronounced the monster's name was indescribably ominous. "Can you tell me how to find it?"

Ford smiled at him again. "No."

"No, you can't or no, you won't?" pressed Eric.

Again, the strange man with the wild eyes and the brightly colored scarf smiled. "Only Yee Naaldlooshii, himself, will be able to tell you that."

Again, Eric shuddered at the sound of that name. Was it only his stupid imagination? Why did it feel like somewhere deep, deep down in his most buried memories, he knew that name and was terrified of it? "Well that's a problem," he growled, "since we *really* don't want to wake him up."

Ford chuckled. "True. But he's *already* waking up, isn't he? Right now, his mind is in that twilight realm between sleep and awakening. If someone were to find a way to get *inside his mind* while he's in this state…"

"And how the hell do we do something like that?"

That knowing grin on his face was almost more than Eric could stand. "There exists a spell," he said, the words practically slithering from his lips. "It's a very *dangerous* spell. A very *forbidden* spell." He leaned a little closer and whispered, "But I can get it for you."

Eric ran his hand through his hair. Now they were talking *magic*? What the hell was happening here? How did he find himself conspiring with this lunatic?

"You don't have to," said Ford. "If you think it's too dangerous, you can just do it your way." He raised an eyebrow. "What *was* your way, exactly? Were you planning to just scour the entire city for it and hope you get lucky?"

His cell phone chimed in his pocket. He took it out and looked down at the screen.

I REALLY HATE TO SAY IT, BUT HE HAS A POINT

Ford chortled as if he, too, had read the text.

WE HAVE NO PLAN OF OUR OWN WHATSOEVER.

UNTIL WE DO, WE SHOULD AT LEAST CONSIDER IT
AS AN OPTION

"Fine," grumbled Eric as he slipped the phone back into his pocket. He really hated this. He didn't trust this guy as far as he could spit, but he had no idea what else to do. "Give me the spell."

"Well I don't have it *with* me," said Ford. "I'll have to retrieve it."

"And how long will that take?"

"Not long. In the meantime, there's something you're going to need before you can cast the spell."

"What's that?"

"Go to the parking lot behind Bender's Bar and Grille on Gillern Street," instructed Ford. "Wait there. Keep your eyes open. A skinwalker has been prowling that area. Track it down and capture it. You'll need it *alive*."

Eric gawked at him, horrified. "Are you out of your mind?"

"You'll do fine," Ford insisted. "They're not all that strong on their own. It's only when they attack in packs that they're really dangerous. As long as you don't let them get in your head, anyway."

He ran his hand through his hair again and sighed. A live skinwalker? How in the hell was he supposed to do that?

"Besides, you're Eric Fortrell. And Eric Fortrell is *special*. He has an important job to do. He's an integral part of the *machine*."

"What job?" demanded Eric. "What machine?" He hated that word. *Machine*. It reminded him of Evancurt...as if he needed any help remembering that awful place. "What are you talking about?"

Ford crowded closer again. That disturbing grin stretched a little wider. Up close like this, Eric thought it looked positively *crazed*. "Nothing," he replied. He crinkled up his nose and flashed him a smile that for some reason reminded him of the way his grandmother used to smile at him when he was little and did something that amused her. "Only a game," he said with another dismissive flap of his hand.

"I don't understand *anything* you're saying right now," Eric informed him.

He raised his index finger as if to make a point and laughed, "I know! Isn't it *fun?*"

Eric stared at the upraised finger as it drew closer to his face. There was something strangely mesmerizing about it. He found his gaze fixed on it. "No. It's not."

Ford pressed the tip of his finger against Eric's forehead. It felt oddly cold against his skin. "See you soon, *bestie.*"

Before he could react, the world around him swam out of focus and darkness enveloped him.

Chapter Eleven

How long had he been in this place? It felt like a very long time. He couldn't remember it ever *not* having felt like a very long time. It was as if this had always been his existence.

He was fairly sure he had a life before everything became darkness and haze, but that was a long, long time ago. He floated through this endless darkness, lost and alone, his head filled with half-conscious thoughts of dog-faced people, mummified monsters in glass-topped coffins and wild-eyed men in black trench coats and rainbow scarves.

Whatever world had come before this one had long ago vanished. He couldn't feel the ground beneath his feet. He wasn't even sure that *he* existed in this place. The only thing he knew for certain was that he wasn't dead. He'd *been* dead before, after all. More than once. And that was a different kind of empty floating sensation. Death was darker. Death was murkier. And although this hazy place was cold, death was *colder*. No, this place was somewhere *else*. Somewhere *within*, he thought…though he wasn't entirely sure what that meant.

Then something strange happened. For the first time in an endless age, a voice drifted through the silent haze. It was very faint at first, barely there at all, almost half-imagined. Then it came to him again, a little louder now, a little closer. He tried to look around for the source, but it was difficult to tell if he was even moving. He couldn't feel his body.

Did he even *have* a body?

The voice continued to draw closer.

No… *Voices*. Plural. Not just one, but two. A conversation? Idle chatter?

He tried to focus on these voices and the all-encompassing haze gradually began to part.

Someone was there. A shadow was emerging from the gloom. A face.

A *familiar* face.

She was sitting there, her arms propped on the table in front of her, relaxed, her gaze fixed on a large bowl of steaming water in front of her.

Perri?

She looked just the way she did when he last saw her, still dressed in the same sweatshirt and yoga pants, her hair still thrown back in that sloppy bun.

Perri. He remembered now. This was where he first met her. This was the timeless void the psychic parasite first plunged him into in the basement of that hospital in Illinois the same night he met Holly. And where Steampunk Monk's strange, psychic handgun sent him a year later. And where Ari, the old mambo's mysterious toll collector, sent him during his visit to Guinee a few months later.

He remembered it all so clearly now.

He tried to call out to her, but he couldn't find his voice. He couldn't even feel his own tongue. Did he have a mouth at all? It was as if he no longer existed in this world, as if he were nothing more than a suffering consciousness lost and adrift in the lonely miasma of this endless haze.

But although he couldn't speak, Perri suddenly gasped and sat up. She turned and looked directly at him, those starkly different eyes meeting his gaze, seemingly from across the very cosmos.

"Perri?" came a familiar voice from the clouds. It was Paige's voice, he realized. He couldn't see her from wherever he was. He could only see Perri. His entire perception of the world from this place was centered only on her. But they were both right there, sitting at the table together. "You okay?"

"Why are you here?" asked Perri.

"What?" said Paige.

"*How* are you here?" amended Perri.

"Are you...talking to someone?"

Eric tried to speak, but the words refused to form. He

didn't seem to have a body anymore. She seemed to be looking him directly in the eye, but it sounded like Paige wasn't able to see him at all. Only Perri knew he was there.

Was she really looking at him? Or was she only reacting to his presence? Did she even know it was him?

Was she even real? Or was this entire otherworldly experience nothing more than a queer dream?

He was so confused!

Perri stood up. She looked concerned. "Are you okay? Did something happen? Do you..." she trailed off, her eyes widening. Then she turned and looked behind her.

He followed her gaze into the vast, hazy darkness that loomed there. He didn't see anything at first, but then shapes began to materialize from the gloom. A dirt road stretched out before him. Rotting fences on either side separated it from dead and empty fields.

Something stood at the far end of that lonely road, he realized, way off in the distance. He couldn't see it from here, but he could feel it. As he settled his eyes on that distant point in the haze, a strange and ominous feeling settled over him.

Then a light blossomed in the distance, blinding and burning in the otherwise cold and smothering darkness. After ages of floating alone in the hazy blackness of the void, any light should have been welcome, but there was nothing comforting about this blazing beacon. Instead, it was as if some great and terrible thing had just opened a hellish, blazing eye and turned its hungry gaze on him, as if he were Frodo standing in the terrible glare of Sauron's all-seeing eye.

Something *terrible* was waiting at the source of that light.

"You're kind of freaking me out here," said Paige. "What are you looking at?"

Perri turned and looked at Eric. "The lighthouse..." she sighed.

"That again?" said Paige.

What was happening here? He didn't understand any of this.

Then Perri squinted at him. No...not at him, he realized.

Her gaze was fixed over his shoulder, at something *behind* him. "Who's that with you?"

He turned. Or…he *thought* he turned… He seemed to look the other way, but he had no sense of moving or even looking away from her. He simply found himself staring back the other way.

At first, there was nothing there but that endless darkness. But then he saw something. A shape was looming there. A person, he thought, barely visible through the haze, but he couldn't make out any details. A woman, perhaps?

He tried to call out to this person, to ask who was there, but his voice seemed to die away before it even passed his lips, and the person—if that was really what it was—faded back into the haze.

There was something familiar about this presence, he realized. He *almost* knew who it was. If only he could think clearly…

Then Perri's voice called out to him again, but from much farther away than before.

Again, he seemed to turn without turning, facing her, but without any sense of moving.

But Perri was gone. He was alone again in the void.

"Eric?" she called, her voice dwindling away.

He reached out, *really* reached out this time, he could feel his arm as he raised it and stretched it outward into the haze. "Where are you?"

Then the haze blew away. A blinding light washed over him. Someone knocked his hand aside.

"I'm right in front of you, dumbass! Now *wake up already!*"

Eric squeezed his eyes shut and then opened them again. His brother's hairy face was hovering over him. He let out a startled, "Whaaaa!" and covered his eyes.

Paul stood up, scowling. "You're not much to look at yourself, shithead."

"What the hell happened?" He looked around. He was sitting on a child-sized garden bench with one foot stuck in a decorative wheelbarrow and his aching head half inside an overturned picnic basket. The overhead lights felt as bright as the sun and his whole body ached. Paul, Karen and Holly were all standing over him.

"*You* tell *us*," said Paul. He held up his cell phone. "Isabelle told me to meet you here, but as soon as I walked in the door, she called me again, freaking out, saying you were in trouble."

"It was scary," said Isabelle through the phone's speaker. "I totally lost you."

Karen smacked his shoulder. "What are you doing going off on your own like that?"

He sat up, dislodging himself from the picnic basket, and rubbed at the spot on his forehead where Ford pressed his finger. He could still feel the strange coldness of whatever magic he used on him. "Where'd that guy go?"

"No idea," said Holly. "We never saw anybody."

"Must've slipped out another way," reasoned Paul as he glanced around. The place was huge. And its multiple rooms would've made it easy for someone to slip out unnoticed. "What did he look like?"

"Uh…" he rubbed at his eyes, trying to clear his head. "Tall guy. Thin. Black hair. Kind of pale. Dressed all in black. Except for this long, rainbow scarf."

Karen frowned. "What, like an emo Dr. Who?"

He gave his pounding head an indecisive wobble. "Yeah, sorta…"

"He has the same energy as all the others," said Isabelle. "He's definitely an agent."

"Them again?" said Paul, looking around.

"But there was also a lot of other really weird kinds of energy coming off him. He knows *way* too much about the weird. And about *you*. I mean he even knew about *me*."

"Yeah. I don't like it."

"At this point, we have to assume that our mystery organization knows about you and is watching everything you do."

"Well that's terrifying," said Karen.

And it was. None of the prior agents had seemed to have any knowledge of him until the weird forced their paths to cross. This guy was different. This guy was *dangerous*.

"Can you still feel him?" asked Eric.

"No. I can't feel any of that weird energy now. He's long gone."

Again, he rubbed at his forehead. "How long was I out?"

"Not even a minute, I don't think."

"Huh. Felt a lot longer than that…"

"You went to the psychic void again," she reminded him. "It *always* feels like eternity in there."

"Right…"

"I'm talking to Paige right now. That was no dream. Perri actually saw you while she was sitting at the table."

"Huh," he said again.

"Come on," said Paul, grabbing his arm and pulling him to his feet. "Get out of there."

Eric grunted as he stood up, then he wobbled a little on his feet.

"Easy there."

"Don't rush," agreed Holly.

"The hell did he do to me?" he grumbled.

"Can I help you with anything?" said a voice from behind them.

They all turned to find a small, bespectacled teenage girl standing there, her magnified eyes scanning the disheveled displays. According to her nametag, her name was Callie.

"Uh…?" said Eric.

"Oh, we're fine," replied Paul. "We're just taking our friend home." He tightened his grip on Eric's arm, as if he might fall over again if he didn't hold on tight, and added in a sad, embarrassed sort of whisper, "he's fallen off the wagon again."

Callie's eyes widened a little at this. "Oh…"

"Wha?" said Eric.

"Very disappointing," sighed Paul.

Holly took his other arm and gave his hand a sympathetic pat. "We're all here for you," she assured him.

"Huh?" What was happening? He met the girl's gaze, saw the pity in her eyes and felt his face flush red with embarrassment…which probably only made him look more drunk.

"We're so sorry," said Karen as Paul and Holly led him away.

"Oh, it's fine," replied Callie. "No trouble. I hope he gets better soon."

"Thank you. Us too."

"Let's get you home now," cooed Paul as the three of them ushered him through the doorway and back toward the front of the store.

Eric looked from one to the other, confused. "What just happened?"

Chapter Twelve

"Feeling better?" asked Paul as he pulled out of the parking lot of Ternheart Mercantile and pointed his aging pickup back toward Main Street.

Karen was taking Holly home in the Trailblazer to see if she could help Paige with her "eclipse" problem in the divination. And also because Karen had decided that catching a live skin-walker was "men's work," which didn't exactly surprise him.

"You mean besides being completely *humiliated*?" growled Eric from the passenger seat.

"Yeah. Besides that."

"Just *peachy*. Thanks."

Paul was grinning ear to ear, delighted with himself.

"Seriously, what the hell was that? Did you guys *rehearse* that?"

Paul chuckled.

"I thought it was clever," said Isabelle, who was still on Paul's speaker phone which was now resting in the cup holder. "They got you out of there without that girl suspecting anything weird."

"It *wasn't* clever," snapped Eric. "That girl was about the same age as my students. What if she recognized me? Do you know how fast they'd fire me if a rumor got spread around that I'm an alcoholic?"

"You'll be fine," insisted Paul.

He sighed and ran his hand through his hair. "Did you get a read on that guy?"

"He's definitely an agent," replied Isabelle. "That was the same energy I've felt from every agent you've encountered. But there was something else going on there, too. I felt a lot of other energies mixed in with it. I don't really understand it, but I think there's a lot more to this guy than just your average agent."

"Average," scoffed Eric.

"True," she agreed. "Poor choice of word."

And thinking back on it now, he was willing to bet that it was Ford who separated him from Karen and Holly. And he was probably the reason he tripped and fell into that Tree of Life pendant display, too. Had he messed with their minds somehow?

"But seriously, this guy's different. Be very careful around him."

"Count on it."

Paul turned off Main Street onto Seadel, then turned left onto Gillern Street and into the parking lot behind Bender's Bar and Grille. He chose a spot in the corner, facing out toward the street, and killed the engine. "Okay..." he said, scanning the street. "Now what do we do?"

"I guess we just wait," replied Eric.

Ford told him to come to Gillern Street and that was where they were. It wasn't a big street. From here, they could see pretty much all of it. The only other thing on this side of the street was a little nail salon, simply called Miss Mavis' Nails. Across from them was a single building containing several small businesses. There was an instrument store named Lullaby Music, a comic books and collectibles shop named Tubby's Secret Identity and a little dress shop named Bonnabel's that still bore the name of the old Hosh Shoe Store that was the property's original business over the door. Seadel Street and the river were on the right and Milwaukee Street and the busy Verti-Go gas station were on the left.

They sat there in silence for a while, watching, waiting.

"You sure this guy wasn't just trying to keep you busy?" wondered Paul after about five minutes had passed with no sign of any dog-faced women.

"No," replied Eric. "But it's the only lead we've got so far."

Another five minutes passed. Paul grew visibly more impatient the longer he sat there. And he kept glancing over at Eric.

"What's up?"

"Just been wondering how you're doing."

Eric glanced over at him. "What?"

"It's just…you've been a little weird lately."

"Of course I'm weird. There's another agent in town. And those skinwalker things."

"You know what I'm talking about. Even *before* today. That last weirdness… That *Evancurt* business. All those messed-up ghosts. You've been a little off ever since I picked you and Perri up that night."

"Have I?"

"You have. You've been kind of moody, for one thing. Kind of mopey, too. And sort of *jumpy*. It really messed with your head, didn't it?"

Eric sighed. He looked out at the passing traffic. "I guess it did."

"Not that I blame you. I mean, shit…" He shook his head. "You actually *remember* it, don't you? You remember *dying*."

Eric remembered *everything* that happened that night. Every excruciating detail. *Especially* how it ended. He wished he didn't. At the very least, he wished that the memories weren't so vivid, that he could pass the whole ordeal off as a particularly bad dream. And why *should* it be so clear in his memory? It wasn't even really *his* memory. That wasn't him. He'd spent the entire time lying face-down, unconscious in the dirt and snow. The him that set off into that nightmare and ultimately evaporated into the ether was nothing more than a time-torn spirit, a doppelganger from another timeline in which he never survived his first encounter with the weird.

That Eric, like him, awoke from a very extraordinary dream that he couldn't remember, but which filled him with an overwhelming urge to dress and rush out into the warm night. They were literally one person as they hurried out into the driveway and opened the driver's door of the now-gone silver PT Cruiser. But for reasons he still couldn't understand, that was where they split. One of them, the one who was here in this truck today, didn't sit down behind the wheel. He closed the door and went back inside. He returned to bed and to all the days that would follow. The other Eric, the one that would become Dream Eric, *didn't* stop there. He climbed into the vehicle, started the engine and followed the mad urge to drive that *this* Eric resisted that night and the next.

That other Eric never made it home. He died in the strange depths of the cathedral, where time and space were compacted by the weight of two worlds crushing down on each other. Two worlds...and two timelines.

That Eric became the dream that showed *this* Eric the way, and that was all. He never existed, because the *real* Eric never left that first night.

Or so he thought.

For three and a half years, that other Eric had existed inside him, a spirit, torn from its body and its own timeline by the powerful forces deep within the cathedral, then locked inside him, entwined with his own soul, with no idea what it was, how it came to be there or that it was ever anything else.

"It wasn't even death," he said at last. "Death is a *departure*. It's a journey. There's a *destination* waiting for you when you die. I know that now. I mean, I've seen *hundreds* of ghosts. I've actually *been* to Guinee. I've *seen* the other side. But what happened to me that night... Or...to that *other* me..." He shook his head. "That wasn't death. I didn't go anywhere. I just...stopped existing. Everything I ever was and ever would be... Gone. It all just...*ended*. *I* just ended."

"Holy shit..." uttered Paul.

"So yeah. I guess you could say it messed with my head a little."

It wasn't a fear of dying that had gripped him in that cold, Wisconsin forest that night. He'd come to realize that death, itself, didn't frighten him at all. He was afraid of a lot of other things. He was afraid of not being able to stop the people he cared about from dying. He was afraid of leaving Karen and the others behind while they still needed him. And after some of the things he'd encountered in his experiences with the weird, he was even afraid of the circumstances of his death, that his eventual demise was going to be horrible, gruesome, excruciating and perhaps even humiliatingly undignified. (He *had* nearly been killed by both monkeys and clowns on various occasions, after all.) But he wasn't afraid of death, itself. In fact, a part of him looked forward to the day he'd be reunited with his three departed grandparents. What he was scared of, it turned out, was *ending*. He was scared of his soul blowing away into the ether again and never being reunited with *anyone* he loved ever again.

He wanted to run away. He wanted to hide under a rock and never come out. But that skinwalker monster nearly took Karen. Running away wouldn't protect her. Running away wouldn't protect *anyone*. He had to stop what was happening in this city. Even if it meant risking that same, horrible fate again.

"Seriously, though," said Paul. He shifted in his seat, uncomfortable. "What're the odds of going out that way?"

Eric turned and squinted at him. "It literally happened to me."

"Okay, fine. What're the odds of it happening *again*?"

"Pretty high, actually. It wasn't just Dream Eric who ended in Evancurt. *Hundreds* of souls were absorbed by that machine over the years. And you can't tell me you don't remember what we did to those blood witches."

"They brought that on themselves. That old mambo broad told you so, remember? They committed a... What was it called again?"

"Karmic sin."

"Yeah, that. They committed a karmic sin. They were doomed from the moment they made that decision."

"I'm not arguing that," returned Eric. "But what we did to them... The spell we used... It didn't just kill them. It *erased* them. Their souls were *devoured*. They *ended*. Just like Dream Eric ended. And by doing that to them, we *also* committed a karmic sin."

Paul frowned. "Speak for yourself. I wasn't even there. You dumped me in that freezing-ass forest in Canada, remember?"

"You were there when we made our decision. You didn't object. None of us objected."

He looked the other way, uncomfortable. "Like we had any choice..." he grumbled.

"Doesn't matter. My point is, it's happened before. It happened to Dream Eric. It happened to countless spirits trapped in Evancurt. It happened to those blood witches. And it happened to that girl in Illinois, too."

"You don't know that. No one knows if that damned knife really cuts souls."

Didn't they? Hadn't he proved it on the roof of the bokor's apartment building in Chicago? He'd been over it so many times in his head since that morning. If Desmond Weizner's cursed dagger didn't pierce the yellow-eyed witch's soul, then why didn't the dark god summoned by their forbidden spell devour her along with the other blood witches? The only reason that made any sense was that her soul was already damaged beyond repair.

But he didn't say any of this. What happened in that Illinois field was too painful to speak about.

"And that wasn't your fault either," insisted Paul. "That girl was nuts. That's not going to happen to you."

Eric glanced over at him again. "It *did* happen to me," he repeated.

"No, it happened to...uh..." His face twisted up as he tried to muscle his way through the argument. "That was the *other* you," he decided. "Doesn't count."

"That makes no sense."

"It makes perfect sense. Shut up. My point is, it's not going to happen to you. I know it won't."

"How can you possibly know something like that?"

"Because the universe loves you, remember?"

Now it was Eric's turn to look confused. "What?"

"It's like all those things those witches are always saying about you. You're *special*. There's something about you. It's *why* all this crazy stuff keeps happening to you. And why you keep walking away from it, even when there's no conceivable way for you to survive. Even in Evancurt that night. Even when you *end* you still find a way to walk away. What was the name of that chubby woman who was in charge of those crystal witches?"

"Myra Tonnerby?"

"Yeah, her. She told you the universe was always going to

protect you. That it'd go out of its way to protect good people."

"She also betrayed an obscene amount of people who trusted her because she believed it was the only way to save her coven."

"She never said the universe loved *her*. She said it loved *you*. You're the kind of good person she was talking about, and she obviously wasn't."

Eric wasn't so sure about that.

"My point here is, I think she was right. The universe loves you. It's going to keep protecting you right up until you finish whatever it is you were put on this weird earth to do. So you might as well get out of your head about it."

"Huh," was the only response Eric could think of for that.

Paul shifted in his seat again and scratched at his beard. "Now *me*, on the other hand... I don't think the universe thinks all that much of me."

"You might be right about that," agreed Eric. The universe *did* seem to have something against poor Paul. He never seemed to catch a break when the weird came to town.

"Okay, *that* is one ugly ass dog," said Paul.

Eric had let himself get distracted and wasn't watching. Now he sat up, surprised. Across the street from them there was, indeed, a dog trotting up the sidewalk. Or something that sort of resembled a dog. If you didn't look too closely. To say the least, it was no best in show contender. It had a half-starved, diseased look about it, with long, bone-thin legs, mangy-looking fur and a weirdly proportioned head. In fact, the more he looked at the thing, the more deformed it looked. Even its tail was wrong. It was too long, too slender and too flexible, more like the tail of a rat than that of a dog.

"What did you say a skinwalker was supposed to look like again?" wondered Paul. "'Cause all I know about them is what I saw on that episode of *Supernatural*."

"It's whatever it *wants* to look like," replied Isabelle. "It's a shapeshifter."

Eric watched as it trotted along the far sidewalk, sniffing at the pavement. It didn't look anything like the thing that attacked them behind the bookshop. That thing had passed as human at first. Then, when he interrupted its hunt, it changed into that upright monstrosity with the thin, furry legs and great, toothy jaws. But the more he watched the unattractive creature, the more wrong it looked and the more convinced he became that it could be nothing other than one of those monsters.

"So they can turn into anything?" asked Paul.

"I don't know about *anything*," replied Isabelle. "I've heard of them taking the shapes of dogs, coyotes and wolves. And they can mimic people you know. I've also heard of them turning into crows. I don't think they can, like, turn into a *tree* or anything, though."

"And they can *hypnotize* people, too?"

"Something like that. It's like that first one got into Karen's head and made it hard for her to realize something was wrong. Don't underestimate them. They're dangerous."

"Right," said Eric.

"I've even heard that they can spit these sharp, bony projectiles," she recalled, "that can pierce your body like bullets while leaving no visible wound on your skin. It's like it just teleports directly inside you and the only way to get it out is to cut it out of you."

Paul frowned at the screen. "You're just making shit up now."

"Nope. That's what I heard."

He scratched at his beard and watched the creature through the windshield as it made its way slowly up the sidewalk.

"The biggest difference between what I've collected from the trapped people and what's going on now," said Isabelle, "is that all those people were passing through the same area around northern New Mexico at the time of their encounters. They were in skinwalker territory. These things are hundreds of miles from home. I keep wondering, did they sense Yenaldlooshi the moment the idol was taken outside the concealment spell and then run all the way to Creek Bend?"

"That was only three days ago," recalled Eric.

"That's quite a marathon," remarked Paul.

"I know, right?"

Eric found himself imagining a huge pack of coyote monsters sprinting across the country on their furry hind legs, darting across highways, cutting through farm fields and neighborhoods at supernatural speeds, all of them swarming to this unsuspecting little Wisconsin city. He couldn't help but shiver a little.

"It's creepy," agreed Isabelle. "These things aren't like most of the monsters you've encountered. They're clearly not bound by the same laws of nature. As humans, we may not even be capable of comprehending what they really are or what they can do."

The monster paused at the door of Bonnabel's and began sniffing at the threshold. It looked like it was searching for something. Was it looking for Yenaldlooshi? Was there a clue in there somewhere that might help them locate the missing idol?

"What could it want with a place like that?" wondered Paul.

"Maybe there's a nice mannequin in there he wants you to meet," offered Isabelle.

"Bite me, phone girl."

"Touchy much?"

"You only *sound* like a little girl. I can still tell you off."

"Rude."

"Settle down, children," grumbled Eric.

The monster didn't seem to find what it was looking for at Bonnabel's. It continued on toward the comic shop.

"Come on," he said, opening the door and quietly hopping down out of the cab. "Let's get this over with."

Chapter Thirteen

Before leaving Ternheart and parting ways with Karen and Holly, Eric had transferred several pouches of the white ash Mr. Iverley gave them from the Trailblazer to Paul's pickup truck. Although understandably reluctant, Paul had rubbed some of it on his neck and chest, just as Mrs. Balm had instructed everyone to do. They also powdered a length of rope from the back of Paul's truck with it. It was fairly clear that he hadn't really understood how a pile of ashes was going to make any difference against shapeshifting, dog-faced monsters, but he did everything Eric told him to do.

Eric was the expert on the weird, after all.

Now Paul took the powdered rope from the truck bed and followed Eric across the street. Ahead of them, the monster trotted past the next storefront, this time without pausing to sniff the door, then disappeared around the corner of the building.

Eric picked up his pace, desperate not to let the thing escape.

At least, he *hoped* that thing was a skinwalker and not just a particularly ugly stray dog. Ford sent them here with instructions to catch and contain a skinwalker that was prowling this area. As much as he didn't want to trust the wild-eyed weirdo, he didn't seem to have any other leads. He knew it to be a fact that Yenaldlooshi was already waking up. He'd heard the monster's unearthly groans with his own ears. Ford wasn't lying when he said that it was only a matter of hours before all hell broke loose. If this *was* what he needed to do to find the missing idol and he messed it up, there might not be enough time to find another one.

But he *really* didn't like this. His gaze kept drifting toward the crowded Verti-Go and the busy intersection between him and it. That was a lot of witnesses. If things went sideways, he was going to end up being the center of a whole lot of attention. And the two of them probably already looked pretty suspicious, snooping around with ashes smeared on their necks, carrying a dirty rope, probably looking for all the world like they were trying to put together a lynch mob.

God, I hope we don't get arrested today, he thought

"It'll be fine," Isabelle assured him.

Paul looked down at his phone. "Huh?"

"Wasn't talking to you, mannequin boy."

"That's it," he snapped. "Get out of my phone. Shoo." He disconnected the call and shoved it into his pocket.

"Will you two be quiet!" hissed Eric.

He reached the end of the building and peered around the corner.

The creature was nowhere to be seen. The only thing over here was a concrete stairwell descending into the earth, encircled by an iron railing. There was a door at the bottom, leading into what could only be a basement level. It was standing half-open. "Any idea what's down there?"

"Nope," replied Paul. "Never been here before."

"Think there's a skinwalker down there?"

"Or worse."

"Want to go first?"

"Want to kiss my ass?"

"A simple 'no' would've sufficed."

Paul grinned. "I know it would've."

Eric glanced over at the gas station one last time, wondering how many people might be looking back at him, and then started down the steps. "Careful," he whispered.

"So that thing where the universe protects you...?" Paul whispered back. "Do you think there's any kind of *proximity* to it?"

"What?"

"You know, like a *bubble*. Like it'll protect you and anything in, say, *a six-foot radius* of you?"

"How the hell should I know? What does it even matter?"

"Just trying to figure out whether it's safer to stand as *close* to you as possible or as *far away* as possible."

"Let's talk about it later," hissed Eric as he approached the suspicious doorway.

The lock didn't appear to be broken. It had simply been left open. Looking it over, he couldn't see any sign of an alarm on it.

"Sure. Later. As if *both* of us are guaranteed a later."

"Seriously not a good time!"

He shined his light through the opening, his eyes peeled for the reflection of predatory eyes. Inside was a long, mostly empty space with four cheap, metal folding tables set up, each one surrounded by matching folding chairs.

When nothing moved, he gripped the edge of the door and pulled it open. The hinges groaned and creaked. Between the light and the noise, there was no chance anything inside wouldn't know they were coming, so he located the light switch and turned it on, illuminating the space. There was a set of wooden stairs leading up to the first floor and a utility space in the far corner containing the building's electrical panels and furnace. Modern ductwork snaked across the bare joists overhead. There was a repurposed kitchen counter and sink along one wall, complete with cupboards, a microwave and a full-sized refrigerator. And there were several bookshelves scattered around the room, each one loaded with large books and brightly colored boxes.

"Ah!" said Paul. "I know what this place is. It's Tubby's nerd dungeon."

"'Nerd dungeon'?" asked Eric, bemused.

"*Dungeons and Dragons* parties," explained Paul. "Some of Kevin's friends used to come here and play."

"Oh." He glanced around the room again. "That makes sense. I guess." It explained the simplicity of the room.

The "Tubby" of "Tubby's Secret Identity" wasn't named for his figure. In fact, the old man was actually quite scrawny. His real name was Hermes Tubbard and he'd been Creek Bend's local "comic book guy" since before either of them were born.

"I prefer poker, myself, but to each his own."

Eric nodded. The idea of sitting around a table making up

fabulous adventures was lost on him, but then again, he supposed it would be. After all, his life was already full of fantastic adventures, terrifying monsters and real-life magic. "At least we know we're in the right place."

"We do?"

"Paige said she saw *dice* in the divination."

Paul nodded. "That fits."

"It does." He glanced up at the ceiling. The comic shop was right above them, but it was quiet up there right now. He heard no footsteps or voices. Unlike the door leading outside, the door at the top of the stairs appeared to be tightly closed.

"So…then where's the skinwalker?" asked Paul.

It was a good question. He was fairly sure the monster had come down here, but perhaps it had darted back behind the building instead. There didn't appear to be anything here. The room was empty.

But as he slowly walked around the first of the gaming tables, he thought he glimpsed something moving in the corner of his eye, a barely visible motion in the gloom beneath the stairs.

"Stay by the door," said Eric. "Don't let anything leave."

Paul obediently returned to the door and stood guard, clutching the powdered rope in front of him as if it were a shield.

Eric made his way toward the far end of the room, his hand shoved into his pocket, gripping the pouch of ash hidden there and hoping like hell that Mr. Iverley knew what he was talking about when he armed them with it. Because if he was wrong, or if this turned out to be something other than a skinwalker, he might as well have armed himself with a handful of kitty litter.

There weren't many places to hide in here. It was mostly empty space. But then again, he wasn't looking for a person. These skinwalkers were able to shrink down into much smaller canine shapes *and* could seemingly defy physical space, as that first one had demonstrated when he saw it standing in the too-narrow alleyway. So if there *was* one lurking in here, it could potentially be squeezed into almost any small gap.

He glanced into the far corner where the furnace stood like a silent sentinel in the shadows. At the same instant, something small ducked out of sight behind it.

CAREFUL

"I know," he breathed.

He crept forward, his eyes wide open, watching for something to dart from either side. But as he circled around behind the furnace, he found nothing.

He stopped, confused, and glanced around. Had he only imagined seeing something move back here? Or were skinwalkers even trickier than he thought? He turned and scanned the area. Isabelle did say that they were able to turn into crows. That was pretty small. A crow could fit into a lot more nooks and crannies than a dog or coyote. And if they could turn into a crow, then why not something even smaller? Could they turn into something as small as a rat? Or even a mouse? He ran his hand through his hair and stared back across the room. There were cabinet doors under the sink. Maybe it was hiding in one of those. Or maybe it had squeezed into the space behind the refrigerator. For all he knew, perhaps it was able to slip through the crack under the upstairs door and had escaped through the comic shop. If this thing really wanted to hide, would he really have any chance of finding it?

It was all so tiring. Why did the weird have to be so damned exhausting? He needed a break.

His gaze drifted toward the gaming tables. Maybe he should just sit down for a few minutes.

Maybe even put his head down and close his eyes.

That sounded good…

In fact, it sounded *really* good. His eyes were so heavy…

"Eric…"

Just a little catnap, maybe… Ten or fifteen minutes was all he needed… Maybe twenty…

"Eric…"

"Hmm?"

"Help me, Eric…"

He blinked, confused, and looked around. "Wha…?"

"Help me…"

He lifted his head and looked up at the ceiling above him.

There, wedged somehow into the space atop the ductwork, was Karen. Her lovely face was pressed against the space between the metal and the wooden joist, her eyes wide with fear and tear streaks on her face. She was reaching for him with one outstretched hand. "How'd you get up there?" he asked, confused.

His cell phone chimed in his pocket. A new text message from Isabelle, he was sure. But that didn't seem important right now. Right now he was trying to understand how Karen got up there in that little space.

"Help me..." she said again. Her voice sounded funny. It didn't sound like her at all. Was it because she was wedged in there so tightly? Was she hurt?

His cell phone chimed a second time. Then a third. Then again and again in rapid succession. The sound was disorienting.

He should've turned off the phone. Then he could get some rest.

"Take my hand..."

Yeah. That seemed like the thing he was supposed to do. He lifted his arm, dazed.

Karen was so pretty. He loved her so much. Although he wasn't sure he liked what she'd done with her hair. That silvery blonde color didn't suit her at all. It was all wrong like that.

But again, the only thing that mattered was taking her hand.

He reached up.

His fingertips brushed hers.

Then Paul shoved him aside and threw a handful of ash into Karen's face.

She let out a savage howl and began thrashing around.

"You okay?" gasped Paul.

Eric squeezed his eyes closed and shook his head. Already, that sleepy haziness was clearing. "Yeah. I think so." What the hell just happened? Why would he think for even a second that Karen would actually be in a place like that? It didn't even *look* like Karen.

The thing atop the ductwork was still thrashing and screaming in pain. The noise was deafening. It sounded as if the entire thing was going to break apart and come crashing to the floor.

So much for getting out of here unnoticed.

"Don't let it get away!" snapped Eric.

But Paul was already moving, keeping pace with the thing as it banged and rattled its way across the basement ceiling.

Then it dropped onto one of the gaming tables, overturning it and sending metal chairs clanging across the concrete.

Paul cursed and scrambled after it.

It didn't look like Karen anymore. Now it was only a half-human shape writhing on the floor, clawing at its face and occasionally lashing out at the air around it, blindly attempting to wound anyone who might get too close.

It wasn't even dressed like Karen. It was wearing nothing but a light, summery dress.

Paul was hovering over it, dodging those slashing claws, trying to figure out how to get ahold of it without getting his face torn off.

Eric, on the other hand, found that he felt considerably less fearful of the monster than he was *angry*. How dare this filthy creature pretend to be Karen? How could he have been fooled by such an obvious trick? He threw himself onto it, pinning down its legs and seizing one of its flailing arms in each hand.

The monster responded by contorting its face into something dog-like and snapping at him.

"Get over here with that rope!"

Paul darted forward, the rope already unrolled. "Hold it down!"

"I'm trying!" grunted Eric. "It's *strong*!"

"Put your weight into it!"

"My weight *is* in it!"

The skinwalker let out a wicked growl and wrenched one of its bony arms free. It slashed at Eric's sleeve, shredding the fabric and cutting into the flesh underneath.

Cursing, Paul seized its arm and shoved it back down, looping the rope around it.

"What's taking so long!" hissed Eric.

"You know," he grunted, "contrary to what the movies will have everyone believe, I don't find myself having to tie someone up all that often! I've never done this before! Cut me some slack!" He yanked the rope tight, wrenching another howl from the monster. "Shut up, damn you!"

"Make sure it's tight!"

"No shit!"

"I'm just saying! These things can change shape!"

"I'm fucking aware of that!" Paul looped the rope around the monster's legs and arms again and yanked it tight.

Again, the monster snarled. Its head was whipping back and forth, snapping its jaws, trying in vain to sink its teeth into someone's flesh.

They were making far too much noise for Eric's liking. He kept thinking that this thing's howls could probably be heard from across the street if anyone happened to be listening. And while it wasn't exactly the sound of someone screaming for help, it was bound to be the sort of noise that would turn a few curious heads. And God forbid anyone be walking by on the sidewalk right outside...

And he was absolutely right. Through the deafening cacophony of their fight, he never heard the door creak open. He never heard the approaching footsteps. He never even noticed that they were no longer alone in the room until his eyes fell on a pair of sneakers not five feet away.

Slowly, he and Paul both lifted their heads and looked at the eighteen-year-old girl who was standing there, dressed in faded blue jeans and a bright red jacket, staring down at them with an expression of utter bewilderment.

"*Dad? Uncle Eric?*"

Chapter Fourteen

Paul stared up at his daughter, his mouth agape. "Uh…"

"Heeeey…" said Eric, wincing. "Ally…"

"*What the hell are you two doing?*"

Suddenly, the creature beneath them twisted itself around. "Help me!" it cried, its voice suddenly much smaller than it was before. From beneath its long, silvery hair, the face of a young girl was staring up at her with wide, terrified eyes. "Please don't let them hurt me!"

Alena Fortrell—Ally to pretty much everyone she knew—blinked down at the girl, a horrified expression overtaking her fair features.

"Oh no you don't!" grunted Paul. He yanked the pouch of ash from his pocket and dumped the rest of it over the creature's head. In an instant, it let out another vicious snarl and unraveled its face into a monstrous conglomeration of jaws and teeth as it howled and thrashed in pain.

Ally let out a startled cry and took a step backward. "What the absolute *fuck*, Dad?"

The girl had her mother's beauty and biting sarcasm and her father's flair for imaginative language and total disregard for offending people, which had often made for some pretty memorable conversation in the Fortrell household.

"It's complicated?" tried Eric.

"*Complicated?*" She thrust a finger at the writhing thing beneath them. "What *is* that thing? And what the hell are you *doing* to it!"

"Just…give us a minute," grunted Paul. "We're kind of busy right now…"

The monster gave a strange lurch and twisted its body around farther than it had managed before, its teeth snapping closer than ever to Eric's face.

Ally uttered a very unladylike curse and backed up a few steps.

"Get ahold of it!" grunted Eric.

"I'm trying!" Paul grunted back. He seized two fistfuls of its silvery hair and yanked its head back. It let out a furious wail and snapped its frothing jaws. Then he shoved it back down again, slamming its head against the concrete and finally silencing it. "There," he gasped. "That'll shut it up for a while."

"Jesus Christ you guys!" gasped Ally.

"If you killed it," panted Eric, "you're catching the next one on your own."

"It'll be fine," he insisted, frowning down at the unconscious creature. "I mean, probably…"

"I knew you guys did some pretty weird shit in your spare time," said Ally, "But this is next-level freaky."

"What do you mean 'weird shit'?" said Eric. He looked over at Paul. "What've you been telling her."

Paul shrugged. "I don't know what she's talking about. Sometimes I have to take you to your AA meetings is all. And every now and then you fall off the wagon and I have to come get you 'cause you're running around naked in the trailer park. Shit like that. That's all."

Eric stared at him. "Is there anyone in this town who *doesn't* think I'm a raging alcoholic because of you?"

He seemed to consider the question very carefully. "I'm sure there has to be at least a *few*."

"What the hell *is* that?" demanded Ally.

Eric glanced up at her, then down at the creature again. It didn't look like Karen anymore. And it didn't look like a scared little girl, either. It didn't even look like the extremely ugly dog they followed here. It appeared to have been caught in mid-transformation as it struggled to free itself from the rope so that it looked particularly monstrous. It had a roughly humanoid shape, but twisted all out of proportion. One hand was small and almost human, but attached to a muscular arm covered in silvery, mottled fur. The other hand looked more like an elongated *talon* attached to a thin, hairless arm with pale, blotchy flesh. One of its legs was shriveled and dog-like, mostly hairless, ending in a knotted paw-like appendage with huge, jagged claws. The other leg had escaped the ropes and was sticking straight out, furry and deer-like, three feet long, bone-thin and ending in a twisted monkey-like foot with much smaller claws. Its torso was long and lean, bony, with a protruding spine and far too many ribs, swollen on one side of the belly and weirdly bloated where the hairy shoulder connected to it. Its neck was long and covered in silvery hair like a horse's mane. And its head was a nightmarish conglomeration of protruding jaws, bulging fangs, human nose and sunken, corpse-like eyes. And now that the struggle was over, he realized that it appeared to be female, with small, mal-formed breasts and no external genitals visible through the mat-ted fur covering its deformed crotch. And it smelled at least as foul as it looked. "It's a...uh..." He cleared his throat. He hated this part. There was just something about saying the names of the monsters aloud that always sounded crazy, even to his own ears. "Skinwalker."

She made a face at him. "What like on *Supernatural?*"

He wobbled his head a little as he knotted the rope tighter around those vicious claws. "Sure. Maybe?" Was that the univer-sal reference for a skinwalker? That one episode of *Supernatural?* Was he the only person who hadn't seen it?

"What're you doing here?" asked Paul.

"I was across the street at Mavis' salon." She held up her hand, revealing a shiny, pastel rainbow of nails, just in time for Easter. "When I came out, I saw you two creeping around and acting like a couple of weirdos, so I walked over here to see what was going on."

"Well there you go," said Paul, sitting up. "You saw. We were hunting skinwalkers. You can go home now."

"Like hell I will." She pointed at the monster. "Is that thing *real?* Like *really* real? And why the hell do you have it tied up?"

"Well we offered to let it ride shotgun," said Paul. "But it wanted to do it the hard way."

Eric sat up and clutched at his tattered sleeve. He was

bleeding, but only a little. Again, the jacket had probably saved him from some severe injuries. Both sleeves were now torn and tattered. "Like I said, it's complicated."

Ally nodded. "Uh huh. I'd say so."

"It's Eric's fault," said Paul as he bound the thing's loose leg and made sure it couldn't shrink out of its bindings when it awoke. "He's always getting himself into shit like this."

Eric nodded. "That's…yeah. That's pretty accurate."

"Does Mom know about this?"

"Nope," replied Paul. He raised an eyebrow at her. "And she doesn't *need* to know."

"Oh I'm *so* telling Mom."

"No you're not."

"I *totally* am."

Paul looked up at her, smirking. "Right. Like she's going to believe you."

Ally never took her eyes off her father. She simply lifted her phone and snapped a picture of the two of them sitting there like tired hunters, as if the unnatural beast were only a trussed-up deer.

He stared at the phone, his smirk vanishing. "Ah… Okay."

Eric's phone rang. He glanced at the screen, then accepted the call and lifted it to his ear. "Hey Holly."

"Holly?" said Ally, confused.

"Isabelle says you caught a skinwalker," said Holly.

"Yeah," said Eric. "Piece of cake. Thinking of taking it up as a hobby."

"That'd have to be more fun than stamp collecting, I'd think."

"Right? I'm thinking we could make a reality show out of it, like those alligator hunter guys."

"I'd watch it."

"What's Holly got to do with this?" asked Ally.

"Karen just wanted me to call and tell you you'd better not even think about bringing it back here."

He looked down at the monster. "Right…" It wasn't exactly a surprise that Karen didn't want this thing in her house, but what the hell else were they supposed to do with it?

"And I don't think it'd be a good idea to take it to the museum, either," added Holly. "Who knows what might happen if you got it too close to Yanni-What's-His-Name. It could wake him up faster."

"Or lure other skinwalkers there."

"Exactly," said Holly.

"Others?" said Ally, glancing around the room. "There's *more?*"

"So not home and not the museum," agreed Eric. But then, what was he supposed to do with the thing? He ran his hand through his hair and glanced around. For that matter, how were they supposed to even get it out of here? It was amazing that no one had shown up yet to see what all the noise was about. Well, no one *else*. "What about you?" he asked. "Have you tried another divination yet?"

"Divination?" asked Ally. She was becoming more confused with each passing second.

Paul put a finger to his mouth and hushed her. "Your uncle's working."

"What do you mean *working?*" she blurted, not hushing in the least. "He's an *English teacher!*"

"We tried once," replied Holly, "but Paige is right. There's some sort of *eclipse* in the water. We saw some dogs and some fire and then something big blocked our view. Sorry."

"It's okay. Any idea what could be interfering with the spell?"

"Spell?" said Ally. "Are you guys on some kind of drug?" Then she looked down at the unconscious skinwalker and added, "Am *I* on some kind of drug?"

"I really don't know," replied Holly. "It's not like anything I've ever seen before. It's not that we can't see what's there. It's like there's literally something in the way, blocking the view."

"Weird…" said Eric.

"It is. I called Del and told her about it. She's going to look into it and then get back to me."

"That's good. Thank you."

"You're welcome. Be careful out there!"

"Right."

"Oh, hold on. Karen wants to talk to you."

"Uh oh…"

There was a rustle on the line as the phone exchanged hands, then Karen's voice was shouting in his ear: "You got Ally mixed up in this *too* now?"

"Crap…" he sighed.

"What were you thinking?"

He glanced up at Ally. "It's not *my* fault she's out nosing around where she doesn't have any business."

She blinked at him, surprised. "Are you talking about *me* now?"

"Send her straight home."

"She says she's not leaving."

"I don't *care* what she says."

"I don't think I can make her. She's as stubborn as her father."

"That's true," agreed Paul.

"Who're you talking to?" demanded Ally.

"She's threatening to tell Monica."

"Monica already knows you two are weird. Tell her to get her butt home right now."

"Karen says you have to go home now."

She stared at him. "Aunt Karen knows about this, too?"

"You're in trouble now," chuckled Paul.

Ally shook her head. "Is the whole town in on this shit? How did she even know I was here?"

Her phone alerted her to a new text message: I TOLD HER

She stared at the screen, confused. "Uh…?"

I'M ISABELLE, BY THE WAY

"Okay, somebody just hacked my phone!"

KAREN SAYS GO HOME

"Karen doesn't get to tell me what to do!" she yelled at her phone.

"She says you don't get to tell her what to do," reported Eric.

"I *heard* what she said."

He looked over at Ally again. "She heard you."

"You're *really* in trouble now," said Paul.

"How am *I* in trouble? You two were the ones hog-tying that *thing* in some creepy basement like a couple of perverts!"

Eric frowned. "You see two guys tying up a *monster* and the first analogy that comes to mind is 'perverts'? Really?"

"She *is* her father's daughter," said Karen.

"Dirty minded girl," agreed Eric.

"Hey, I call it like I see it. I don't know what you're planning to do with that thing, but it looks kinky as shit."

"No getting kinky with the monsters," insisted Karen.

"Why would I be getting—?" He snapped his mouth shut and fought back an urge to curse. He really hated when she got under his skin like that.

"All I know," said Ally, "is that if either of you start taking off your pants, I'm totally calling the cops."

Eric squinted up at her and shook his head.

"You'd better not let anything happen to her," said Karen.

"I won't," sighed Eric.

"Be careful. Don't let that thing bite anybody or anything."

"We won't." He disconnected the call and glanced over at Ally again, his eyes drawn to her bright red jacket. The girl in the red coat... That was yet another of the divination's curious questions answered, he supposed. "You're in so much trouble right now."

"What did *I* do?"

"So what now?" asked Paul.

"Well we can't stay here," decided Eric. "It's amazing nobody's come downstairs already."

"Not *that* amazing," said Ally. "There's nobody up there. Tubby's has been closed the past few days."

"Oh..." said Eric. If he'd been paying attention as he walked by the door, he probably would've known that from the start and wouldn't have had to worry about all the noise they were making quite so much, but he'd been too pre-occupied with catching up to the skinwalker to even check for an open sign.

"I guess Tubby was in some kind of accident?" recalled Ally. "I don't really know the details. I only heard about it because of my friend, Danni. Her boyfriend's one of Tubby's loser gamer dorks."

"Well that simplifies things," said Paul.

Eric nodded. It *did* simplify things. Although the thought of something happening to the owner of this place was concerning. He couldn't help but wonder if the skinwalker had been involved in the accident in some way. Or perhaps Tubby's absence was merely the reason the monster chose this basement to squat in. "But we still can't stay here. That thing's going to wake up sometime and eventually someone's going to come to see what all the noise is about."

"Yeah, well we can't just walk out the door dragging a body, either," reasoned Paul. He glanced down at the hideous form of the unconscious skinwalker. "Not even one as ugly as this. That'll *definitely* draw the wrong kind of attention."

"Even if we *do* get it out of here without someone calling the cops on us," agreed Eric, "Where do we go with it?"

BACK TO THE UNSEEN MOTEL? suggested Isabelle. AGENTS APPARENTLY WON'T BE A PROBLEM

Ally pointed to his phone. "Is that the hacker?"

OR YOU MIGHT EVEN BE ABLE TO USE THE BUNGALOW

He shook his head. "No. I'd rather steer clear of anything related to the agents for a while."

"Agents?" said Ally. "What like the FBI? How much weird shit have you two been doing?"

Paul ignored her and looked up at Eric. "I think I know a place."

Chapter Fifteen

Eric did his best to clean up the game room under Tubby's Secret Identity. He put the table and chairs back where they belonged and swept up all the spilled ash, collecting as much of it as possible back into Paul's pouch. With any luck, the only thing missing was the empty trash can Paul stuffed the unconscious skinwalker into to carry it out of the building, and hopefully Tubby wouldn't report something like that to the police. Chances were good that some of the gas station's security cameras were pointed this way, after all, and it wouldn't take much investigating to spot three very suspicious people entering and leaving the property while the owner was away.

Fortunately, things were fairly quiet over there when they left. Traffic was light and there was no one standing out at the pumps at the Verti-Go, allowing him and Paul to make their way around the corner and back to the truck without attracting any unnecessary attention while Ally crossed the street to retrieve her own pickup from the nail salon parking lot.

The "place" Paul knew was north of the city limits, a few miles down Beer Road. (Which used to be *Bear Road*, but for the past twenty-five years or so someone had been painting over the A on the road sign until everyone simply gave up and started calling it Beer Road.) To get there, they had to cross a muddy ditch and follow a half-mile-long, washed-out driveway, at the end of which waited an open clearing with three mud-caked pickup trucks parked in front of an enormous *drainage pipe* protruding from the brushy hillside.

"I changed my mind," decided Eric as he stared up through the windshield at the big manhole cover dangling perilously by chains from the top of the concrete pipe with the words "The Man Hole" emblazoned across it. "I think I'd rather take my chances with the agents."

"Quit your bitching and help me with this," grumbled Paul. They hadn't dared put the trash can in the bed of the truck, in case the monster inside woke up and began thrashing around in the middle of traffic, so they'd made the drive with the ghastly package belted into the seat between them.

As the two of them wrestled the can out of the cab and onto the ground, Ally pulled up beside them in her Dakota. Regardless of what Karen said, she wasn't going to go home. She'd seen too much to simply let it go and forget about it. And in truth, he could hardly blame her. She'd stumbled into the wrong place at the wrong time and seen the "impossible" with her own eyes. Her perception thrown open to a world far bigger than she ever saw before, she couldn't possibly go back. In an instant, she knew the truth: that monsters were real. Some people would reject that kind of thing. They'd just rationalize it away and go back to the secure numbness of the world as they knew it before. But Ally was a Fortrell, after all. Like her father and her uncle and her brother, she was determined to see how deep the rabbit hole went.

He hoped she wasn't getting in over her head. The true world could be an ugly place. But truth be known, he was fairly sure she could handle this sort of thing. She didn't exactly play the role of the delicate flower, after all.

Besides, the "real" world could be pretty ugly, too. He glanced up at the dangling manhole cover. "Isn't that dangerous?" Those things were heavy as hell. If it fell, it could kill someone.

"Justin's good with a welder," replied Paul. "That thing ain't going anywhere."

Eric shook his head. "I can't believe you told your drinking buddies about the weird."

"I've known these guys forever," grunted Paul. "*You've* known these guys forever. They're trustworthy."

He supposed that was true. Justin was one of Paul's oldest friends. The two went all the way back to their grade school days. Eric could still remember him staying the night occasionally, back when he was still very young. He was a polite and friendly boy. But he had a very peculiar set of interests, as the sewer motif of his personal playhouse illustrated.

"And even if they weren't," Paul went on, "who'd believe anything they said? Especially *Greg*."

That was a fair point, too, he supposed. No one believed anything Greg said. He was a pathological liar with a flair for the extraordinary. According to him, he'd held every interesting job you could imagine, including serving in every branch of the military as well as working for the FBI, the CIA, the DEA and the DHS, among others. He was, at some point in time, a skydiving instructor, a sniper, a big game hunter, a licensed SCUBA diver, a treasure hunter, a South American jungle adventure guide, a famous producer of European adult movies and a much-feared member of a notorious underworld organization based somewhere in China or Russia, depending on the story he happened to be telling.

Paul grasped the plastic bin by its handles and picked it up. "Thanks. I think I can get it from here. Bitch is lighter than she looks."

"Maybe they're only as heavy as their smallest form," reasoned Eric.

"Maybe."

It sort of made sense, he supposed. If any sort of logic could be assigned to something as insanely unreal as a real-life skinwalker. It might even help explain why they could fit into such small spaces.

"Isn't that thing going to be seriously pissed when it wakes up?" asked Ally.

"Probably," replied Paul.

The three of them—four if you counted the thing in the trash can—made their way into the open drainage pipe, beneath the harsh row of flood lights to the strange, half-buried building's front door, which swung open as they approached, revealing the stout, pot-bellied form of Justin Teberly in his stained tank top and ever-present hunting cap. "Paul, my man! What's the big emergency?"

"You'll see," grunted Paul. "Hold that door open for us."

Before leaving Tubby's "nerd dungeon," Paul made a call to Justin, letting them know they were on their way. Eric knew he was right, that Justin was as trustworthy a person as they were going to find. But it still bothered him to know that he'd been running his mouth about the weird.

"Hey, Ally."

"Hi Justin."

"And Eric! I don't think you've ever been to my little man cave before, have you?"

"Can't say I have," he replied as he followed his brother through the doorway and glanced around.

"Paul!" exclaimed a tall, skinny man half-swallowed by the sagging cushions of an old, leather armchair. His legs were so long and the chair so broken down that his knees were almost as high as his chest. "How's it going, man?"

"Grab a beer, have a seat," grunted an extremely fat, surly-looking man with a thick, burly beard and a shiny bald head who appeared to be wedged into a much smaller armchair for some reason despite the fact that there were roomier places for a man his size to sit. His immense gut swelled over the arms like a great, bloated muffin top.

These men were Greg Laverson and Adam Winnards. They practically lived here and it was rare to ever see either one without a beer can attached to one hand or the other. In fact, in spite of the still fairly early hour, they both appeared to be well on their way to a hangover already.

"Gentlemen," greeted Paul.

Eric might not have been inside this building before, but he'd heard about it. The place was a veritable concrete bunker built into the hillside and designed with elements of a grand, metropolitan sewer system. It had great, stone archways, storm grate-covered windows and protruding lengths of pipes, some of which acted like decorative shelves while others were fitted with real water features. There was tattered and stained thrift store furniture arranged in front of an enormous and obviously quite expensive plasma television that was mounted right next to a huge, restaurant-sized refrigerator that Paul had told him once was constantly filled to bursting with beer. Next to it was one of those small ice cream freezers with the sliding glass tops, like you found in convenience stores, and a large steel drum cut open and tipped on its side like a barnyard watering trough filled to the brim with all kinds of junk food. There was also a pool table, a ping pong table, several old arcade machines, a pinball machine and an old Skee-Ball table lined up against the back wall. There was even a bar. This much of Justin's self-described "man cave" was almost enviable, but beyond that, the Man Hole went downhill at record speed. Seemingly decorated by a well-funded and utterly unsupervised pre-teen boy, the décor was sexist at best and utterly offensive at worst. Several two-dimensional silhouette cutouts of nude women in various, suggestive poses stood at strategic locations around the room so that you always seemed to be looking at one. There were three large paintings in bright, psychedelic colors on the walls, one depicting a woman's lips parted in an unnecessarily provocative manner, one of a woman's naked butt and one that was blatantly just a vagina. There was also not one but *four* separate pairs of huge, plastic breasts painted in bright, primary colors mounted on the walls. In the spaces between these pieces of perverted art were dozens of small, framed *Kama Sutra* illustrations. A huge, neon sign next to the refrigerator read, "SHOW US YOUR TITS," in blazing capital letters. In the back corner was a door labeled "Shack-Up Room" that Eric made a mental note to *never* visit. And in the very center of it all, right in the middle of the room, like a monument to the utter absurdity of all that surrounded it, stood a stripper pole.

The whole scene made his skin crawl.

"Sweet, Right?" boasted Justin, proud as could be. "Welcome to the *Man Hole*!"

"Terrible name," said Ally. "Seriously, the worst."

"It's a fine name," Justin insisted, deflating a little. The defensiveness in his voice said this wasn't the first time someone had called him out on it. Probably Ally.

"Really?" She cocked her head to one side and raised an eyebrow. "So how many guys have you had in your man hole?"

The face he made at this looked like he'd just bitten into a rotten apple. "That's not cool, man. Not cool."

In a deep, mocking voice, she said, "'Say, where were you last night, Bob?' 'Me? I was in *Justin's man hole*.' 'All us guys use *Justin's man hole* every chance we get.' 'You ain't lived 'til you've been in *Justin's man hole*.' 'Who *hasn't* been in Justin's man hole?'"

He stared at her, his entire face drooping into an exaggerated frown. "That is *not* okay."

"Ooh!" she exclaimed, her eyes widening with wicked delight. "I have a question! What's the most guys you've ever had in your *man hole* at one time?"

Justin shook his head. He looked utterly defeated. "You always were an *evil* little girl, weren't you?"

She flashed him a big smile at that. "Yes. I was."

"Don't listen to her," bellowed Greg. "She's just got a dirty mind."

"That's right," slurred Adam. "Gets it from her old man."

"That's right," agreed Greg.

"Yep."

"Yeah, everyone in town knows no one loves getting up in Justin's man hole like you two," jabbed Ally.

Both men groaned.

Eric glanced over at Paul. "God, she really is just like you, isn't she?"

Paul grinned. "Yep."

"Why would anyone want to be like *you*?"

His grin vanished. "Hey now."

"So what's in the can?" asked Justin. He, at least, seemed to still be mostly sober.

Greg and Adam rose from their seats, both of them with considerable effort, and walked over to see what was going on.

"Hope you guys are ready to sober up," said Paul. "Cause this is some seriously weird shit." Then he tipped the trash can over and spilled the skinwalker out onto the concrete floor, where it let out a weak snarl and strained against its bindings.

Justin and Greg cursed and jumped back.

Adam, however, let out a great, high-pitched scream and

backed away so quickly that he very nearly sent the whole of his tremendous bulk tumbling over the back of the sofa.

"Jesus, man," said Ally. "Get ahold of yourself."

He cleared his throat and rubbed the back of his neck, embarrassed. "That was...uh..." He glanced over at her, blushing bright red over that shaggy beard. "I... I wasn't expecting that," he finished lamely.

"Wuss."

Adam had an intimidating look about him at first glance, but beneath that he was the wimpiest guy Eric had ever met. There wasn't much he wasn't afraid of. Spiders and bugs freaked him out. He couldn't bear being outside in the summer with the mosquitos. He couldn't go fishing because he couldn't stomach handling the bait, or the fish for that matter. And he certainly wouldn't watch a horror movie. He'd even been known to faint at the sight of blood.

"That thing's *freaky*," grunted Greg.

Adam nodded, his eyes still wide with fright. "Freaky..." he agreed. "Yep..."

"Seriously, though," stammered Justin as he stared down at the twisted, half-human shape bound at his feet. "What *is* it?"

"Skinwalker," replied Paul. "We caught it over at Tubby's place."

"You *caught* it," said Justin, shaking his head. "Just like that, huh?"

"I'm pretty sure these two were about to go all *Deliverance* on it before I showed up," said Ally.

"Oh my god," gasped Eric.

"What? You put it in a dress and everything. Looked like some freaky-ass roleplay shit to me."

"We didn't put the dress on it! It was already wearing it when we got there!" He looked down at the creature.

"Why would a skinwalker be wearing a dress?" she pushed.

Paul looked up at Eric. "Yeah, why *is* it wearing a dress?"

"So it can pretend to be human, I guess. I don't know." Honestly, it was a good question. Both this one *and* the one behind the bookstore were wearing clothes that were different from what the person they were pretending to be was wearing. Were they just clothes that they stole from somewhere? "It doesn't matter," he decided, shaking his head.

"I'm more concerned about the fact that it's not wearing underwear," decided Ally. "One of you pervs didn't steal them, did you?"

"Knock it off," growled Eric.

"Whatever. Just know I'm *never* letting either of you watch my dog after this."

"Can we focus on the task at hand, please?"

"This is what you were telling us about, isn't it?" said Justin. "All those crazy stories. Monsters and ghosts and Men in Black type shit. This is like those pictures you showed us."

"You showed them pictures?" asked Eric.

"They wouldn't've believed me if I didn't have pictures," said Paul.

"That's kind of my point!"

"You guys take pictures, too?" said Ally.

"Quiet, you."

"Hell, I never believed you anyway," grunted Justin. "I thought it was all just drunken bullshit and Photoshop."

"Well, I can tell you they're right," said Greg, inflating at the prospect of sharing his immense knowledge of yet another fascinating subject. "That thing's definitely one of those skin-waltzers. I should know."

"Skin*walker*," said Ally, rolling her eyes.

"People call 'em by lots of names," he countered. "High up in the mountains in Kentucky, they called 'em by different names. I spent sixteen months in that area, you know, working as a guide for the feds, tracking down a large-scale meth operation."

"Meth," agreed Adam. "Big problem there."

"Right?"

"Skinwalkers are native to the Navajo territory, out west," said Ally. She glanced over at Eric. "Looked it up on my phone on the way over here."

"'Course they are," agreed Greg. He never stumbled in his endless storytelling. He was such a professional liar that it was difficult to tell if even *he* knew the difference between truth and fantasy anymore. "I was a Navajo shaman for three years back in the late nineties, you know."

Eric, for one, wasn't sure how he could've spent so many years away doing so many of the things he claimed to have done, when he'd spent almost his entire life guzzling beer and telling stories right here in Creek Bend.

"But there's other colonies of 'em out there," he went on. "They're just not as well documented."

"Not a lot of people up there," reasoned Adam.

"Exactly."

"Right," said Ally.

"Where did you get pictures?" asked Eric, ignoring the others. "Didn't you only have the ones of that little rhino thing that trapped you in that cabin?"

Paul nodded. "At the nudie camp, yeah. But I asked Karen to email me some of yours and she did."

"Why would she do that?"

"Why not? I risked my ass on some of those adventures of yours, too, you know."

He sighed and ran his hand through his hair. "Forget it."

"Is it dangerous?" asked Adam. He crept a little closer to the bound monster and nudged it with the edge of a push broom. "Can it get out of those ropes?"

"Where'd you even get that?" asked Ally, eying the broom.

"Aren't they supposed to be keeping a skinwalker in the museum here in town?" said Justin. He was slowly putting the pieces together. He was clearly the brains of these stooges.

"Funny you should mention that," grumbled Paul.

"Definitely related," agreed Eric.

Adam poked at the skinwalker's protruding teeth with the handle of the broom and the creature twitched. The motion wrenched another high-pitched scream from the fat man and he tripped over his own feet trying to back away.

"Seriously," said Ally, "can you *be* any more lame?"

Eric looked down at the bound skinwalker. It was starting to stir again. And he was sure it wasn't going to be happy once it was fully awake. "Look, the fact is that there are more of these things out there and they're *dangerous*. If we don't hurry, this city's going to be overrun. And *worse*."

"Worse?" squeaked Adam from his spot on the floor.

Paul nodded. "He's right. There's some seriously fucked-up shit going on around here. And we're going to need somewhere to keep this thing until we can figure out how to stop it."

Justin took off his hat and scratched his head. "Fucked up is right, man…"

Eric's phone alerted him to a new text message: HOLLY'S ON HER WAY OVER

"Does she know the way?"

Justin looked up, confused. "What?"

I GAVE HER DIRECTIONS

"Right." Even after all this time, he sometimes still forgot that Isabelle knew everything he knew, as soon as he knew it. Once he arrived somewhere, she was perfectly capable of telling someone else how to get there, meaning Paul and Holly could often be on their way to help him before he even thought about calling them.

"Who're you talking to?" asked Greg.

"That's the girl in his phone I was telling you about," explained Paul.

"No shit?" said Justin.

"The hacker?" asked Ally.

IF YOU'RE GOING TO INVOLVE THOSE THREE WEIRDOS, YOU SHOULD PROBABLY FILL THEM IN ON THINGS

"Yeah." He stuffed the phone back into his pocket and glanced around at them, sighing. "I know."

Chapter Sixteen

To the best of his ability and in the shortest amount of time possible, Eric explained the situation currently taking place in Creek Bend.

Greg, of course, had known about these things all along, but couldn't talk about it because most of it was classified.

Meanwhile, Paul and Justin dragged the struggling skinwalker across the floor and tied it to the stripper pole with a second rope freshly powdered with ash. And when they were done, they surveyed their work for a moment and then grabbed a third rope, just to be safe.

"Not what I intended the pole to be used for," grumbled Justin, "but glad it's coming in handy."

"Has the pole *ever* been used as it was intended?" asked Ally.

"A few times!" snapped Justin.

"Does your wife even count?" Paul wondered.

Eric had never met Justin's wife, but if the revolted looks that passed over everyone's faces were any indication, she wasn't someone he ever wanted to see using a stripper pole.

"Shut the hell up!" shouted Justin.

"So are we gonna have to cut this thing up or something?" asked Adam as he eyed the creature. He looked a little green at the thought. "Because I should probably mention that I failed biology class."

"I spent some time as a surgeon in the Gulf War," boasted Greg, who everyone knew had never been to any war and had never left the country, but somehow plowed on with impressive confidence. "But I'm a little rusty these days."

"Been a while," agreed Adam.

"Have to keep at it," said Greg. "Muscle memory. Big part of it."

"Definitely."

"No idea what we have to do yet," replied Eric. "Maybe Holly will have an idea when she gets here." *At the very least, she'll provide some much-needed brains*, he added in his head.

"I can't believe Holly's in on this, too," said Ally.

"In on it?" said Paul. "She's *part* of it. Where do you think Eric met her?"

"I thought she was Karen's assistant."

"That was *after* she came here. She's a witch Eric saved from some nutjob wizard guy."

"Witches!" slurred Greg. "I can tell you everything you need to know 'bout witches! Spent a winter studying the lost arts in the caverns hidden under Salem. Some fifteen years ago, that was!"

"Lotsa witches in Salem," agreed Adam. "Everyone knows that."

"Right?"

Paul frowned. "Except he wasn't a guy, was he? *She* was another witch...or something..."

"Don't hurt yourself," said Eric. "It's complicated."

"So you keep saying," said Ally.

Her phone chimed at her: WE'LL EXPLAIN EVERYTHING LATER. IT'D TAKE TOO LONG RIGHT NOW

She held the phone as far away as she could reach, as if the craziness might be somehow contagious, and said, "Maybe you could start with the hacker chick?"

I'M NOT A HACKER

There was a knock at the door and Justin shouted that it was open.

"Okay..." said Holly as she stepped inside, "...so I guess I see why we saw *sewers* in the divin—*oh my god there are boobs on the walls!*"

"Like 'em?" said Justin, looking excessively proud of himself.

"No! I don't!"

"Well this is officially the second grossest room I've ever been in," said Paige as she stepped in behind her, wrinkling her nose.

"Why is there a stripper pole?" asked Holly.

"Purely for fantasy," replied Ally.

"Shut it, Paula," snapped Justin.

"And didn't *you* used to be a stripper?" said Ally, squinting at her.

Justin, Greg and Adam all stopped what they were doing and turned to gawk at her.

Holly blushed and crossed her arms over her chest as if merely revealing that detail of her life could make the clothes she was wearing disappear. "Who told you that?"

"My *mom*."

She turned and glared at Paul. "Seriously?"

"Don't look at *me*. *I* don't tell Monica *shit*."

"Pretty sure Kevin told her," said Ally.

Paul chuckled. "Probably. He was pretty fascinated with that little fact."

"I'm *so* going to curse him next time I see him," grumbled Holly.

"Wait…" said Ally. "So my *brother* is in on this, too?"

"Most of it," said Paul. "Yeah."

She rolled her eyes and huffed. "Typical."

Holly fixed her attention on the creature tied to the pole. "So that's what a skinwalker looks like?"

"Sometimes," said Eric.

"It's really freaky," said Paige.

"It's not as scary as I expected," observed Holly.

"That's because it's not trying to bite your face off right now," explained Eric.

"Oh… Yeah, that'd probably do it."

Ally turned and looked at Justin, "Hey, that's right. You finally have a stripper in here and your pole has a skinwalker tied to it. What're the odds?"

"I don't do that anymore!" snapped Holly. Why are we talking about this?" She glanced around again, wrinkling her nose in disgust. "And what *is* this place?"

"This is Justin's man hole," said Ally.

Holly looked horrified. "Okay, that's just *ew*."

"*Very* ew," agreed Paige.

"Why would anyone name something that?" Holly asked. "I mean *gross*."

"Oh come on…" grumbled Justin.

"Can we get back on task here?" growled Eric.

But Ally was looking at Paige now, curious. "So is *she* a witch, too, then?"

"Uh huh," said Paige.

"Eric saved her from a *different* witch," explained Paul. "Make sure you don't touch the bunny."

Her eyes dropped to the raggedy rabbit the girl was clutching. "Okay… Why?"

"It eats people."

"Oh. Sorry I asked."

"He doesn't *eat* people…" clarified Paige.

"Yeah it's a lot worse than that," said Holly, who still remembered in hideous detail what happened to the last person who tried to lay a murderous hand on the granddaughter of the great Mambo Dee's apprentice.

Paige brushed a loose strand of unkempt blonde hair out of her face and squeezed the bunny a little tighter, embarrassed. "He only punishes people who try to hurt me."

"I don't think I'll take any chances," decided Ally. She turned and looked at Eric again. "So that woman who came to live with you guys a few weeks ago…"

"Perri," said Eric.

"Yeah, her. *Another* witch?"

"Nope," said Paul. "Psychic girl trapped in a timeless dimension for fifty years. She's actually twelve years old."

"Now you're just full of shit," she told him.

"Nope," said Eric. "That's about right."

"Pretty much sums it up," agreed Holly.

"Actually very well explained," added Paige.

SHE'S MORE LIKE ME THAN THEM, texted Isabelle.

Ally blinked down at her screen, bewildered.

"Don't get me started on psychics," grumbled Greg between swigs of beer.

Adam nodded agreement. "Psychics."

"So what's the plan?" asked Paul. "What do we do with this thing now that we have it?"

Eric turned his gaze back toward the monster. "I don't know. That crazy agent said he'd give us a spell, but I don't know how long it'll take or even how I'm supposed to get in touch with him again."

"*He* found *you* last time," Paul recalled.

"Right."

Holly stepped closer to the skinwalker and looked it over. The beast fixed her with a hateful glare and growled, but although Adam took a fearful step backward, she didn't seem the slightest bit fazed by the scary monster. "We can start by setting up some magic defenses in this...uh..." she glanced around at the obscene surroundings again, "...porn shop?"

"It's *art*," whined Justin.

"No it's not," said Paige and Ally almost at the same time.

"People just don't get art these days," sighed Greg.

Adam shook his head. "Don't get it," he agreed.

"Did you check the water again?" asked Eric.

"We did," said Holly, wrinkling her nose at the SHOW US YOUR TITS sign. "But it's the same as before."

"Eclipse," said Paige.

"Right. We still can't get past it. It's weird.

Eric's cell phone rang in his pocket. He pulled it out and looked at the screen, but there was no number displayed. He accepted the call, expecting it to be Isabelle, but the voice on the other end wasn't hers.

"A little birdie told me you caught yourself a skinwalker."

Eric frowned. "Ford?"

"Come have another chat with me. Just the two of us. We'll discuss that spell you need."

Why did that invitation sound a lot like, "Want some candy, little boy?" He glanced at Paul, then at Holly, uncertain. "Fine. Tell me where."

Chapter Seventeen

Holly loaned him her keys and he made his way back into the city, feeling a little like a canned sardine in the driver's seat of her tiny Prius.

Of all the places Ford could pick, why did it have to be this one? He'd really hoped to never come here again. And he hadn't been here since that business with Aiden Chadwick.

He stepped through the doors and looked around. Big Brooke Tavern wasn't very busy yet, but it would be picking up speed for the rest of the night. The place was pretty popular, after all. It wasn't really a restaurant, but it did offer a small menu of dining options—mostly burgers and wings—that was popular enough to fill the tables on weekends like these. And even though the place was technically a biker bar, right down to its Harley Davidson/God Bless America décor, it also attracted its fair share of casual diners.

The first time he was here, he entered by mistake through an unseen door at the back of the room and found himself unable to leave. The owner, a great, brutish-looking man named Leon Rufar, caught him trying to get out through the locked front doors and he distinctly remembered being quite sure that he was about to either be arrested or beaten senseless and thrown out with the garbage. It'd worked itself out, however, as Leon, unaware that his bar contained a secret floor and stairway and even an alleyway between his building and the next, had come to the conclusion that the whole thing was a simple misunderstanding and a coincidentally timed malfunction with the lock. But he wasn't able to make his escape before catching the hungry eye of Leon's wife and the bar's namesake, Big Brooke, who quickly made him feel so uncomfortable that he'd almost begun to prefer the thoughts of going to jail or getting his ass kicked by Leon.

He didn't see either of them, but he knew they were here. They ran the tavern with as little help as they could get by with. During the busy times, you could find a handful of people waiting tables and cleaning, and Eric was pretty sure there had to be at least one person in the kitchen making food, but any time the place was even a little bit quiet, you'd find just the two of them working there. A lot of people said that Leon was such a bear to work for that they couldn't keep a full crew if they wanted to. Others claimed that the two were just too cheap to pay wages. But Karen had told him once that it was simply the way they liked it. It was easier with just the two of them. No one for Brooke to be responsible for. Leon knew everything was getting done right. And he tended to believe Karen over anyone else. She was typically right about things like that.

He chose a seat at an empty table with his back to the bar and hoped no one noticed him.

"Can I get you something?" asked a young woman with bright purple hair and a surprising number of facial piercings.

He ordered a beer and she hurried off to get it for him. Then he turned his gaze toward the door and wondered how much longer he was going to have to wait for Ford. He *really* didn't want to be here any longer than necessary.

"Relax," he muttered to himself. There was no reason to feel awkward. It had been almost three years now. Nobody was even going to remember him.

But the thought had barely crossed his mind when a great shadow passed over him and he looked up to find a massive pair of freckled breasts practically bursting from a bright red corset top.

"Eric Fortrell!" bellowed Big Brooke Rufar.

He looked up at her beaming face, wide-eyed and blushing like a child.

Everyone in the tavern had stopped what they were doing to turn and look at him.

"I've got a bone to pick with you," she said.

At well over six feet tall, with broad shoulders and even broader hips, Big Brooke truly was bigger than life. But it wasn't just her size. Everything about her was big, from her great mane of badly dyed red hair to her vast amounts of exposed cleavage to her booming voice. She was loud, boisterous, flashy and flirty. She loved attention, especially from her male customers, and the more timid a man was toward her, the better she liked it.

The first time he met her, he remembered feeling as if she might eat him alive if he let his guard down for even a second, and there was something about those hungry eyes that made him feel that way again now.

She bent forward—much farther forward than he thought the situation really warranted—and fixed him with a piercing gaze that immediately made him look away. But when he did, he found that there was nowhere else for his eyes to go but to those huge, bulging breasts now jiggling directly in front of his face.

He felt himself blush even hotter and forced his eyes back up to meet her blazing gaze.

"You said you'd come back to see me again! What took you so long?"

He glanced quickly around the room. Everyone had already lost interest in Brooke's latest toy, a testament to just how often she did stuff like this.

"I really have meant to," he lied, smiling his best smile and trying not to sound like a frightened child. "But things have been just…*crazy*. Like you wouldn't believe." And that was certainly no lie.

"You here all alone today?" she purred, her gaze sweeping over the empty table. Then she leaned a little closer. "I can keep you company if you want."

He cleared his throat, uncomfortable, and leaned back a little. "Thanks," he replied, thankful to hear his voice remain even, "but I'm supposed to be meeting someone."

She pouted at him. "Don't tell me you've got a date." She leaned even closer, those huge breasts drifting ever nearer to his face. Her perfume filled the air around her, making him feel lightheaded. "I might get jealous."

"No." This time his voice didn't quite remain even. "It's business, actually. Just a little meeting." He didn't bother telling her he was married. He was fairly sure she already knew that. Not only was his wedding band perfectly visible, but she and Karen knew each other. She just liked to flirt. And it delighted her to see him squirm like this. If Karen were here right now, Brooke would probably still be flirting with him like this. And Karen would probably be finding the whole scene hilarious.

She leaned even closer.

Eric leaned back even more.

Was she *trying* to shove those things all the way into his face?

She bit her lip and giggled. "Well that's fine, I guess. How about after you're all done with *business*, I come back here and sit on your lap for a little while and you can tell me all about it?"

"Uh…?" He wasn't going to be able to lean back much farther…

"Let the poor man be, woman!" shouted Leon from behind the bar. "You're scarin' him."

There was a soft round of chuckling throughout the room at that, making Eric feel even more embarrassed.

"Fine, fine," she shouted back at him, straightening up again.

He glanced back at the bar and caught sight of a friendly smile shining through that burly beard.

"Good to see you again!" bellowed Leon.

"You too!" he shouted back, trying not to look too bewildered at the fact that they could still remember him after all this time.

His bumbling stupidity must've really left an impression that day.

The purple-haired barmaid appeared beside her and placed a mug in front of him with a friendly, "Here you go!"

"Thank you," said Eric.

"Thanks Mindy," said Brooke as the girl took off to deliver more drinks. Then she flashed him another hungry smile, shook her immense bosom at him and said, "Let me know if there's *anything* else I can get for you, okay sweetie?"

"Sure," said Eric, his voice cracking a little. Then he

watched as she turned her attention to a table of bikers who seemed a lot more eager for her attention than he was.

He took a gulp of his beer and then rubbed his eyes.

He didn't understand it. She blatantly flirted with every man she encountered, right in front of her husband. She never held back. The more uncomfortable someone looked, the more she poured it on. Yet Leon never seemed anything more than mildly annoyed by his wife's brazenness. It was no surprise, then, that there were a lot of wild rumors flying around about them. A lot of people were convinced that they were swingers, and that Brooke was fishing for new partners to play with. But again, he was inclined to believe Karen, who insisted Brooke was only having fun with all the local boys because it amused her and it was good for business. She would never actually cheat on Leon.

"Rough day?" said a familiar voice.

He opened his eyes to find Ford sitting across from him with a beer of his own and his annoyingly cheerful scarf. He was smiling that strangely disturbing smile again. "That's one way to put it."

"Well if anyone can handle it…" he began, raising his glass, "…it's Eric Fortrell." Then he took a long drink.

Eric leaned forward and glanced around to make sure no one was watching them. "Do you have the spell?" he asked in a hushed voice, and a powerful surrealness washed over him as he heard the words roll off his tongue. He felt like he was engaging in a drug deal. Crazily, he found himself wondering if this was how dark wizards in fairy tales got started down the path to the wicked side. What next? Mugging mages in dark alleys? Robbing a potion shop?

"Still working on it," replied Ford.

"Seriously? I don't know how long we can keep that thing tied up."

"Relax. It'll be here. Trust me."

Not a chance, thought Eric. Aloud, he said, "What're we doing here if you don't have the spell?"

He sat up and stared back at him, managing to look hurt. "Two besties can't just stop and have a beer together?"

Eric stared back at him, unamused.

Ford wrinkled his nose at him. "You should really lighten up. It's not like it's the end of the world."

"Isn't it?"

Again, the weirdo beamed at him. "Not with Eric Fortrell on the job."

"Can we cut to the point?" grumbled Eric. "I did what you said. I got the…" He glanced around, embarrassed. "…the *thing* you wanted."

"I know you did. I saw it all." He flashed him another huge smile and added, "I knew you could do it."

Eric stared at the stranger as he took another swig of beer. He saw them catch the skinwalker? Was he spying on them? Was it possible that he'd even set the whole terrifying ordeal up for him? He *did* know exactly where that monster was going to be. And if he was right about Ford having the ability to separate him from Karen and Holly back in Ternheart, then why not arrange a meeting with a skinwalker?

Ford belched and smacked his lips. "That's good stuff," he said. Then he turned his attention back to Eric. "Listen, I know you know how this stuff works. It's a big spell and big spells require big preparations. If you're not careful, you could end up worse than dead. And that's *not* just a figure of speech."

"I'm well aware of the concept of 'worse than death.'"

He smiled that slimy smile again. "I know you are. And that's why we have to make sure you're really ready for this. After all, you're my new favorite bestie. It'd be a shame if you ended up with your soul scattered across the nine hells."

Eric wondered if that was supposed to be a figure of speech or if "nine hells" was a real thing, but he decided he didn't want to know badly enough to ask.

"Spells have rules, you know. Sometimes you need more than just a pretty witch."

Eric watched as the agent took another swig. His mug was already nearly empty. Meanwhile, he'd barely touched his own. His stomach was too twisted up to enjoy it. "You mean like a prayer, a dance and a price, right?"

"Bingo!"

He'd learned during his weird travels that spells came in many forms. Sometimes they required magic words, like when Holly whispered, "reveal," to make the door to the relic chamber visible. A prayer. Sometimes they required a certain specific gesture or physical motion, like when Holly held her hands out to use her thrust. A dance. And sometimes magic came at a cost. A price. A *sacrifice*. Like when Paige offered her poetry to the loa in return for their protection. And sometimes they required more than one and even other components like an altar or specific times, dates and locations.

And sometimes there were even darker costs involved in spellcasting.

"But don't worry. I'm not going to send you scouring the globe looking for magic potion bottles and mystic lanterns."

He felt a chill creep down his back. It was scary how much this guy knew about his past. An eternally glowing lantern and a bottle of foul, reality-altering liquid were two of the components of the spell they used to defeat the blood witches that night under the supermoon.

And speaking of that night... "This spell," he whispered, leaning a little closer. "Earlier, you said it was dangerous. You called it a 'forbidden spell.' Tell me the truth. Am I going to regret this?"

That grin was maddening. There was a knowing twinkle in those wild eyes that looked dangerous as he whispered back, "Let's just say that using it isn't exactly a karmic sin."

That was probably good news. But it still bothered him just how much this guy knew about him and his past experiences with the weird.

"If you do it right..." he added, twisting up those grinning features into something that was supposed to look serious but didn't quite make it, "...and if you're strong enough...then everything should be fine. No lasting side effects." Those wide eyes swept across the ceiling above them, then slowly rolled back toward Eric again. "That being said..." He pulled his lips back in an exaggerated grimace, revealing those bright teeth. "Well, this *is* a spell that's going to send you deep into the psychic subconscious of Yee Naaldlooshii, where no human has ever dared to go before."

Eric couldn't completely suppress the shiver that name sent down his back. He also couldn't wrap his head around the fact that pronouncing it differently suddenly made it sound so much more terrifying. Why was "Yee Naaldlooshii" so much worse than "Yenaldlooshi"?

Ford flapped his hand at him, as if to dismiss the entire thing and said, "We can discuss the details once I have the spell in hand. For now, you only need to focus on the missing components."

"Right..." said Eric. As if he were supposed to just put the whole entering the monster's subconscious thing right out of his mind for now. "Fine. Then tell me what else I need for this spell."

Ford drained the last of his beer, making a show of enjoying it.

Eric didn't pretend to be waiting patiently.

"Two things," he said at last. "First, you're going to need something capable of aligning the magic and psychic flow in order to throw open the subconscious, making way for the connection."

"Oh crap," said Eric. "And here I *just* loaned mine to a friend."

Ford blinked those wild eyes at him, surprised for a moment. Then he threw back his head and cackled loudly enough to draw curious looks from around the room, which in turn made Eric shrink in his seat, embarrassed. "Touché, bestie," he chuckled. Then he leaned forward, his expression intense again, and said, "Don't worry about the details. You already have what you need."

Now it was Eric's turn to blink in surprise. "I do?"

"That pretty little witch of yours," explained Ford. "Holly, I believe her name was?"

Eric had to bite his tongue. It bugged him the way this guy threw the names of people he cared about at him. He couldn't help taking it as a threat.

"She's not only very skilled at utilizing magic, she's also a psychic conduit, isn't she?"

Eric frowned. Was he talking about the way she mentally background-checked people when she met them? And the way she unconsciously manipulated people into liking her? Thinking about it now, it made sense. She was capable of using magic *and* getting inside a person's head. It almost seemed *too* logical for the weird.

"*But...*" said Ford, thrusting a pale finger at him, "...she's not going to be able to handle casting the spell *and* holding open the door. You're going to need someone else there, too."

"A second witch?"

Ford grinned. "Right now, I'm betting you're thinking of that other little witch of yours, aren't you? The Mancott girl."

Eric glared at him. He *really* wished this guy would stop doing that.

"There's no way she'll be up to a spell like this one. You'll want someone much more experienced. Preferably someone who's familiar with Yee Naaldlooshii."

Eric frowned again. "You mean Mrs. Balm?"

Ford gave him an exaggerated shrug, as if the thought had never occurred to him before. "Sure. She'll do."

Eric sighed. He really hated this guy, but at least he didn't have to run all over the entire Midwest trying to gather spell components again. "So we take Holly and Mrs. Balm to the museum with this spell... Then what?"

Ford raised both his hands. "Don't go getting ahead of me here," he warned. "I said you were going inside Yee Naaldlooshii's mind. I never said you were taking the direct flight there."

He stared at him, confused.

"If you go entering his thoughts directly, you'll be driven mad at the first glimpse of whatever's going on in there. The human brain just can't handle it."

"So how do we do it?" asked Eric.

But Ford didn't answer him. He sat there for a moment, his

eyes distant, his expression slackening. Gone was that creepy perpetual grin. No trace of that crazy energy remained in those odd eyes. He suddenly looked empty.

In fact, he looked positively *dead*.

Eric sat up, his heart racing. What just happened? Did the strange weirdo have some sort of stroke right in front of him?

Should he call out for help?

He didn't know what to do.

Then, just as suddenly, Ford snapped out of it and turned those crazed eyes on him again. "Sorry about that!"

"What the hell was that?" gasped Eric.

Ford withdrew a small, leather-bound book from the pocket of his trench coat and laid it on the table between them. The cover was tattered and worn and there were lengths of twine knotted around the cover and between the pages. "There you go. Told you it was on its way."

Eric stared at the ominous little book for a moment, then glanced up at his companion, uncertain.

"Go on. A gift from me to you. Because we're *besties*."

Eric hesitated. "What is it?"

"It's exactly what I promised."

"So…the spell."

"Right."

"I thought you said you didn't have it yet."

"I didn't."

Eric squinted at him. "You didn't have it when you sat down, but you have it *now*?"

"It just arrived," explained Ford, his grin widening. He was enjoying himself. He liked this game. "Special delivery. I told you I was working on it."

Scowling again, Eric picked up the book and opened it. The twine was knotted in such a way that it allowed only three pages to be viewed. A small scrap of cloth covered the page facing the first. And what little he could see was utterly beyond his ability to read. It didn't even look like language. It almost looked as if someone had simply splashed ink onto the pages and smeared it around. It was difficult to tell if there was more white space or ink on the dingy paper. "I can't read this."

"Well of course you can't. Give it to your witches. It'll sort itself out."

"If you say so." He pulled back the corner of the cloth, revealing a portion of the page hidden beneath.

"Ah, don't go letting your curiosity get the better of you," warned the agent, his lips still curled into that maddening grin. "There are things written in that book that shouldn't be seen with mortal eyes."

Eric withdrew his hand and looked up, his eyebrow raised. He couldn't tell if the weirdo was joking or not.

"I expect that's why it was hidden away so well."

His eyes narrowed at this. "Hidden where?"

"Best you don't know," replied Ford, and left it at that.

Eric sighed and closed the book. "Fine. So what am I supposed to do with it? You said I'm supposed to go inside Yenaldlooshi's mind, then you said doing that would drive me crazy."

"Yes. Definitely keep that spell away from him."

"So what am I supposed to do?"

"Try to keep up," replied Ford. "What do you think that skinwalker you and your brother caught was for? Every skinwalker possesses a psychic link to the original. You'll be riding *that* mind into Yee Naaldlooshii's head and using it as a buffer." Then he leaned back in his seat and looked up at the ceiling again. "Of course, there's no guarantee you won't still go mad… But I'd say it's a fair improvement."

"Fantastic," grumbled Eric.

"Don't worry," laughed Ford. "You've got this!" Then he leaned forward in his seat, his expression turning serious, those wide eyes practically gleaming in the fluorescent glow of the bar lights. "*I believe in you!*" he gasped.

"Sure." He propped his elbows on the table and rested his face in his hands. He needed a moment. This was all entirely too much.

Why did the weird always have to be so frustratingly difficult?

He lifted his head and looked across the table again, but Ford was gone. Only his empty beer mug remained. "Right…" he muttered, picking up his own beer. "Guess we're done here."

THERE'S SOMETHING SERIOUSLY WRONG WITH THAT GUY, texted Isabelle.

"You think?"

NO, SERIOUSLY

HE KNOWS AN AWFUL LOT ABOUT THE WEIRD, EVEN FOR AN AGENT

Eric looked out across the bar. She was right. He wasn't like the other agents.

AND HE KNOWS WAY TOO MUCH ABOUT YOU

Also true. And not just his background. He knew where and when to find him when he wanted to talk. He knew what he'd been doing. He admitted to spying on him when he and Paul were catching the skinwalker. He even had his cell phone number.

The only other agent who seemed to know so much about him was Pink Shirt, and that was only because he was using his aura plasma to spy on him.

Was Ford doing something similar?

Or worse, did Ford have that same horrifying power? Because he desperately hoped to never encounter aura plasma ever again. He'd personally witnessed it melting a train and really didn't want to see what it could do to a human being.

He glanced down at the ominous little book, then tucked it into his pocket and rubbed at his eyes, exhausted. When he opened them again, Mindy was standing next to him with her bright purple hair and multiple piercings.

"Your friend leave already?" she asked.

"Yeah," he replied. "He's a real busy guy, apparently."

"You know you've got to pay for both of those drinks, right?"

Eric blinked up at her. "Huh?"

Chapter Eighteen

"Can you read it?" asked Eric.

Mrs. Balm studied the page. "I've never seen anything like this before," she replied.

"So you can't?"

"I didn't say that."

He looked up from the strange markings, an eyebrow raised.

After begrudgingly paying for the drinks, he left Big Brooke Tavern and contacted Mrs. Balm at the museum, asking if she could join them at the Man Hole. She was willing enough to lend them her many years of experience as a witch, but was reluctant to leave Yenaldlooshi unattended. Apparently, he was getting more and more "restless" as the night went on. He wasn't sure what that meant, exactly, but it sounded terrifying. Paul immediately volunteered to go to the museum and stand watch over the monster for her, which seemed surprising at first, until Eric remembered how much Paul hated being around when magic was taking place. Then Justin drove him to the museum and brought Mrs. Balm back, along with Mr. Iverley, who wanted to see the spell in action. But Paul hadn't been there ten minutes before he called and informed Eric with no shortage of overly descriptive expletives that the thing in the box behind the iron bars was "creepy as all kinds of fucking shit" and that they'd better wrap this spell business up fast.

"It's strange," said Mrs. Balm as she turned the one unbound page back and forth, examining both sides, "but I feel like I know what it says."

Holly nodded. "I couldn't begin to tell you exactly what's written there...like, I don't think there *are* any actual words...but when I look at it, I just sort of *understand* it. I know how the spell works. I know what to do."

"It transcends language altogether," marveled Mrs. Balm. "This is *very* old magic. My family had a book like this once. It was where my great grandmother, Clarissa, took the spell that originally bound Yenaldlooshi, but that book was stolen a very long time ago."

"Oh no!" gasped Holly.

Mrs. Balm nodded. "It was devastating. A young witch my mother had put her trust in betrayed her and disappeared with it. Fortunately, we had copies of the important spells, like the one to re-seal Yenaldlooshi. But the betrayal nearly killed my poor mother. She never really recovered from the depression."

"That's terrible," said Paige.

"Yes. But that was the past and this is the present. This book is far older than the one my family lost. In fact, it's older than anything I've ever seen before. And very, *very* potent. Where in the world did you get it?"

"From a friend," he replied. "Or so he keeps insisting. How dangerous is it?"

"Very," said both Holly and Mrs. Balm almost in unison.

"It's practically *radiating* an ominous feeling," said Mrs. Balm. "There's a very distinct and very insistent *warning* interwoven through the message." She looked up at him. "Are you *sure* you want to go through with this?"

"Of course I don't want to go through with it," he replied without hesitation. "If anybody has another plan, I'm all ears."

But of course, no one did.

Mrs. Balm turned her gaze on the monstrosity tied to Justin's stripper pole. Somehow it had managed to contort itself back into a mostly human form within its bindings, though one arm was still twisted at an impossible angle. It might've passed for a real woman except for the wicked claws extending from its fingers and toes that were far less exaggerated nails than jagged bones protruding directly from the skin. And then there was the great mass of bristling teeth that filled its bulging mouth. It stared back at them with a look of such scathing hatred that it was difficult to meet its beastly gaze for very long. "It's like a nightmare."

"The monster?" interjected Ally. "Or Justin's porn palace?"

She glanced around the room, disgusted. "Yes, well…"

"It's pretty neck-and-neck, I think," agreed Paige.

Holly nodded.

Justin didn't argue with any of them. He was slouched in the armchair across from Adam, still moping about the scolding the old woman gave him when he first brought her inside.

"Some people just aren't capable of appreciating art," Greg assured him.

"Closed-minded," agreed Adam.

"Take Banksy, for example. Good friend of mine. Can't really talk about him though."

"Big secret," said Adam, nodding.

"Whatever, losers," said Ally.

"Evil girl," grumbled Greg.

"Demonic," agreed Adam.

"Somebody ought to tie *her* to a stripper pole," decided Greg.

"Leave her there," agreed Adam.

Mrs. Balm cast her gaze across the room. "Enjoying yourself, Mr. Iverley?"

The old man was closely examining of one of the brightly colored pairs of plastic breasts mounted on the wall. He was reaching up, about to touch the shiny surface, but at the sound of his name, he snatched his hand back and turned to face her. "Hm?"

She glanced over at Holly and said, "I swear, there's no such thing as men. Just various stages of *boys*."

Holly nodded.

"So you guys are seriously going to cast a *spell* on that thing?" said Ally. "Like an *actual* magic spell?"

"That's the one and only plan," sighed Eric.

"I still don't know why it has to be you," said Holly. "If something happens to you, what are we supposed to do? We *need* you. Not just today, but when the karmic sin catches up to us. Del says you're our only hope."

"Delphinium exaggerates," insisted Eric.

"No, she really doesn't."

"I don't know about any of that stuff," said Ally, "but I'm pretty sure Aunt Karen will be pissed if we let anything happen to him." She cocked a thumb toward the second-hand furniture gathered in front of the enormous television, where Justin, Greg and Adam were sitting. "Why can't we send one of those idiots? No loss there."

"*I* don't wanna do it!" squealed Adam.

"Don't be a pussy," she told him.

"She's part devil," decided Greg. "I'm sure of it."

"Satanic," grumbled Adam.

Eric shook his head. "No, it should be me," though it was almost painful to hear himself say it. He really didn't want to. "People keep telling me the universe is protecting me. What if that means I'm the only one who *can* do these things?"

"Or…" countered Holly, "…what if the universe just expects you to know when to let someone else handle something as dangerous as this? Remember what Del told you. You'll be fine as long as you don't do anything to go against who you are. That means you can't take unnecessary risks thinking that you'll just keep being fine anyway."

"I remember." After their first meeting in that Illinois farmhouse, Delphinium Thorngood had informed him that she'd inquired about his future in the water divination and discovered that he would always come home safe. But that didn't mean he could afford to be careless. The catch was that he'd return safe only as long as he remained true to who he was. Taking unnecessary risks just because he was under the impression that he'd always be fine was a good way to undermine the prediction. If, by letting himself think that he was charmed, he did something stupid that he wouldn't have done otherwise, like playing a round of Russian Roulette, for example, would likely not end well for him.

I THINK IT HAS TO BE ERIC, texted Isabelle. HE'S THE ONLY ONE HERE WHO HAS ANY EXPERIENCE WITH THE PSYCHIC REALM

Holly read the message over his shoulder and pouted. "I

still don't like it."

Eric didn't like it either, but it was the only option that made sense. He turned his attention to the pissed-off skinwalker. "What do we need?"

"Nothing," replied Mrs. Balm. "We have Holly to open the psychic channel. And we have...Paige, was it?"

Paige brushed aside her bangs and nodded.

"Paige will monitor the spell and make sure nothing goes wrong. And I'll be the one actually conducting the spell. We'll get you inside and the rest will be up to you."

He nodded. "Alright. Let's get this over with, then. Tell me what to do."

"Sit down right here," she instructed, pointing at the floor directly in front of the skinwalker. "As close as you can get to...uh...*her?*"

The thought of getting that close to the thing again made his skin crawl, but he did as he was told, settling himself onto the floor and crossing his legs under him. It wasn't as easy as it was back when he was a schoolboy, but he managed it without too much grunting and complaining.

"You'll need to make eye contact," explained Mrs. Balm.

That wasn't going to be a problem. Already, the hideous she-creature was staring him down with those hateful, predatory eyes. It growled at him, parting those bulging lips a little and revealing some of the great mass of teeth hidden within.

"Paige?"

"I'm ready," replied Paige. She was removing a bowl of steaming water from the microwave. It was a much smaller bowl than they usually worked with, but since it was only her, Holly had assured her it would work fine.

"Focus only on Eric and the skinwalker. Feel the emotions. Monitor what he's feeling. Let us know if you sense any overwhelming fear or panic. If he's in danger, we'll need to know."

Paige looked nervous, but she nodded, blew her hair out of her eyes and sat down at the bar, ready to do her part.

Then Holly seated herself on the floor behind him and surprised him by slipping her arms around him.

"Whoa! Hold on!"

"No, she's right," said Mrs. Balm. "She needs to be in physical contact with you. The closer the better."

"Seriously?"

"It's fine," said Holly as she pressed her body against his back and hugged him tighter. "I don't mind."

He minded. What was "fine" for her clearly wasn't the same as what was "fine" for him. This wasn't what he signed up for.

He felt her face press against the back of his neck. The smell of her perfume and shampoo filled his nose. He felt her breath against his skin and watched as a lock of long, red hair slipped over his shoulder. She grasped the front of his shirt and squeezed him tight, mashing her chest against him.

It was entirely too stuffy in this room.

"So…*that's* how magic works?" said Justin. "Because I pictured it a little different…"

"I changed my mind," decided Adam as he watched the two of them from the depths of his sunken armchair. "I'll do it if Eric really doesn't wanna."

"Uh, yeah, me too?" agreed Greg.

"Right about now, I think I'd be more afraid of Aunt Karen than that skinwalker," observed Ally.

"Shut it," grumbled Eric. Then he glanced down at his phone in his lap.

I DIDN'T SAY ANYTHING

Keep it that way, he thought at her.

"I mean, that's pretty much how magic worked back when I was studying as a priest down in the Amazon," boasted Greg. "Except *I* required *three* women. Virgin Brazilian priestesses."

"Virgins," agreed Adam, swallowing hard. "Very important."

"Right?"

There was a sound of a cell phone camera firing behind him. "Hey, Uncle Eric, when you're done with whatever this is you're doing, there's some stuff I've been wanting for my birthday I want to show you."

Eric tried to ignore everyone. He *especially* tried to ignore the adorable redhead who had inexplicably ended up wrapped around his body in a cringingly intimate way. He tried to focus only on those monstrous eyes.

The monster unfurled more of those hideous teeth and growled again.

"Holly will be the one opening the way into the skinwalker's mind and holding it open," explained Mrs. Balm. "Without her, you could be trapped there forever."

"On second thought…" whimpered Adam, scrunching up his hairy face, "…I'm good."

Greg watched the two of them with a distracted expression on his face. "I'm still on the fence," he decided.

"Let's get this over with," said Eric.

"I'm ready," sighed Holly. How could she sound so relaxed? This was awkward as hell.

"Everyone be very quiet," instructed Mrs. Balm. Then she glanced across the room. "Mr. Iverley?"

"Hm?"

"What are you doing?"

The old man was standing in front of the giant, colorful vagina painting, staring at it, his arms crossed behind his back as if it were an ordinary piece in a gallery. "Oh, just reminiscing a little."

"*Please* try to focus."

"Sorry."

Mrs. Balm rolled her eyes.

Ally's phone buzzed with an incoming text. "Dad says hurry the fuck up."

"Really?" grumbled Eric. "Language?"

"I'm just passing along the message." She pointed at her screen. "See? He says it right here. 'Fuck.'"

"I'm sorry," he said, glancing up at Mrs. Balm.

"I'm not that easily offended," she assured him.

Then Ally's phone buzzed at her again. "Now he says the fucking monster keeps fucking moaning at him."

"Thanks," snapped Eric. "Tell him we're working on it."

"I'll send him that pic I just took so he can see how busy

you are."

"Can we just do this already?" he growled.

Chapter Nineteen

Eric never knew eye contact could be so…*menacing.*

The skinwalker stared back at him with such seething hatred that he could practically feel it radiating from the beast like a raging fever. This thing *loathed* him with every ounce of its monstrous being.

But he supposed it could be worse. Although the creature was in human form, it was no longer trying to pass itself off as a woman. He wasn't sure he could do this if those eyes were frightened and pleading. Or worse, if it had decided to mimic Karen again. There was no way he could focus through a distraction like that.

"This spell is mostly mental," explained Mrs. Balm. "It's almost like hypnosis. You're locking eyes and opening gateways between your souls."

"That thing actually has a soul?" asked Ally, surprised.

"Every creature has a soul," she replied. "Thinking otherwise is just plain arrogant. Even the evil things like this one that crawl out of the shadows have something resembling a soul."

"Huh."

Eric was worried at first that the skinwalker would realize what they were doing and simply refuse to cooperate. From the sound of it, all it really had to do was look away. But it stared right back at him with those furious, beastly eyes and held its gaze, unflinching. Did skinwalkers regard eye contact as a sign of aggression? Was he currently engaged in a battle of wills?

Mrs. Balm hovered over him. He could see her swaying slowly back and forth in his peripheral vision, making subtle gestures at the monster with one hand while she clasped the ominous little spell book against her chest with the other. Every now and then she hummed to herself, though not anything that resembled a tune. It sounded more like muffled words uttered under her breath. And the sound of it was indescribably creepy, like a haunting melody that you could almost remember, but not quite. It made him think of all the frightful places he'd been, from the maddening depths of the cathedral to the haunted shores of the Hedge Lake Triangle to the churning waves of death, itself.

"How do we know it's working?" wondered Justin. "His eyes gonna start glowing or something?"

"Quiet please," hissed Mrs. Balm.

"Gotta be quiet," grunted Greg.

"Quiet," agreed Adam, nodding.

"Gotta concentrate," said Greg.

"Takes focus," agreed Adam.

"Don't make me send you two to the Shack-Up Room," said Ally.

Was this working? Eric couldn't tell. Nothing was happening. He was just sitting there, staring into the freaky eyes of a monster woman while a bunch of idiots talked nonsense and a cute stripper clung to him like he was a teddy bear.

"Let your energy align with the skinwalker's," instructed Mrs. Balm.

Right. As if Eric had any idea whatsoever how to do that. He didn't even know he *had* energy, much less how to use it or to tell when it was "aligned" with anything.

"Right now, it's like you're towering over it," she explained. "You're looking down on it. You need to relax and let yourself slowly sink down to its level."

Again…he had no idea how to do that.

"Relax…" she said again.

Relax. That, at least, he could understand. He took a deep breath and then let it out slowly, never taking his eyes off the monster's.

They were such strange eyes. They were almost human, but not quite. At first he thought it was only the way the light reflected off them like the eyeshine of a wild animal. But there was something wrong with the iris. It wasn't round, he realized. It was wavy. Wrinkled. It was as if everything inside the sclera were a flowing curtain slowly fluttering in a softly rippling current. And there was a strange depth to the pupil at the very center, as if there were nothing but vast, empty space behind them.

And did they keep changing colors?

"Can you feel where he is?" asked Mrs. Balm, her voice sounding strangely distant, as if she were speaking in another room somewhere.

"I can," replied Holly. He could feel her lips brushing the back of his neck as she spoke, and yet she, too, sounded much farther away.

Had his heart been beating this fast the entire time? He didn't think it had.

"Be ready to open the pathway," said Mrs. Balm.

"I'm ready," Holly assured her.

I don't want to do this... The thought seemed to bubble up from somewhere deep inside him. *Don't make me do this...*

He *had* to do this. There was no other choice. But it felt like something inside him was squirming with fear.

Please...

"This is really starting to freak me out," said Adam from that same faraway place, though Eric wasn't entirely sure why *he* should be feeling freaked out. He wasn't the one staring into these horrible eyes.

"You get used to this sort of thing after a while," boasted Greg, yet it didn't sound like he was used to *anything*. His voice wavered with frightened uncertainty.

Was something happening out there? He didn't dare avert his eyes to check.

"He's getting close," said Paige.

"I feel it," sighed Holly.

"Almost there," agreed Mrs. Balm. Their voices were barely audible now. Why was everyone so far away? Somewhere, he thought he heard Justin curse. Was that Ally's voice? He felt like he was drifting away on a gentle current. It was strangely comfortable. And yet, somewhere deep down, it was profoundly terrifying. A voice somewhere inside him was screaming at him to stay alert, to not give in to the lull.

But he couldn't help it.

Darkness fell.

The night was hot and long. Hours unfolded, stretching into days and weeks, perhaps even months. Or perhaps not at all. Time had no meaning in these sweltering, sunless depths. There were no clocks here, only the endless, rhythmic beating of his restless heart.

And he wasn't alone in this place. Strange, twisted shapes writhed in the darkness all around him, sometimes scurrying right over him.

What is this place? he wondered to himself, and somehow, the darkness around him flickered. He wasn't sure how something could flicker without light, but this strange darkness did just that. It was as if it were a shining candle and he'd whispered the words directly into the flame instead of merely thinking them inside his head, making it dance against his passing breath. Except there was no flame. There was no light of any kind. There was only the endless march of meaningless time.

No… There was something else, he realized. There was *hunger.* Like a deep, throbbing ache deep inside him that wouldn't stop. It dragged on, hour after hour, day after day, insatiable and maddening.

What was happening to him?

Then a blinding light washed over him. He blinked and shielded his eyes. What happened? Where was he?

Slowly, the light gave way to shapes and he found himself peering up at a blazing sky. A hot, dry wind blew across his face.

What was he doing in the desert?

And why did everything have such a bizarre hue of colors. The more his eyes adjusted to the light, the more wrong everything looked. The sky had a sickly green tint to it. And the soil had a strangely bloody look about it.

He was down inside a gaping hole, crawling out onto the blistering rocks. Around him, those strange, twisted shapes were emerging as well.

The day was drawing to an end, he realized. Darkness was

coming. Soon it would be time to feed.

Except, he didn't know what that meant. Feed on what? Where? There was nothing but rocky desert floor as far as he could see. He couldn't imagine a place farther from the nearest IHOP. And yet that insatiable hunger was impossible to ignore. He was *excited* to feed. It'd been so long…

But he didn't feed on anything. Just as suddenly as he'd found himself in that blinding, off-colored desert, he found himself swallowed again by that endless, stifling darkness. But this time, he was aware of sounds. *Terrible* sounds. Tortured screams echoed in the depths below him. Tormented howls of pain and suffering, as if he were crouched at the very edge of hell, itself.

His heart was racing.

Was that fear? Or was it *exhilaration*?

In that strange, lightless flickering, he glimpsed a moonlit desert alive with racing shadows. Suddenly, he was running through the scrub under a blanket of blazing stars shining in a rainbow of colors like he'd never seen before while strange structures stood silhouetted against the horizon ahead of him.

Was this the same planet? Had he traveled to a different world?

No… The moon was a sickly shade of yellow, but it still wore the same face he'd always known.

This was his world. This was how *they* saw it. Those monstrous shapes running alongside him. How many were there? He tried to count them, but they blurred together and slid in and out of the background as they ran.

Darkness again.

Why did the taste of blood fill his mouth?

What was happening to him? What was this dark place? And who was he?

What was he?

"Stay with us, Eric," said a voice through the darkness. It was a soft voice. A pretty voice. Comforting and warm. A *familiar* voice.

Again, the world flickered.

Eric? He knew that name. And he knew the name belonging to the voice that whispered into his ear. It was Holly.

"Please don't leave us," she whispered.

Eric squeezed his eyes shut. When he opened them, he was still in that endless darkness, utterly blind. But he discovered that he didn't need light to see. He breathed in the hot, foul air and found that he could *smell* it. The earthy pungency of putrid dirt and mud painted a pattern of grooves against the sharp, bitter tang of minerals in the raw stone. Burning ammonia drizzled through the cracks and crevices, painting an acrid portrait of the gaping hole over which he was crouched. A festering haze reeking of blood and filth revealed a gaping chasm that seemed to plunge forever into the bottomless earth. And all the way down, foul-smelling, inhuman shapes crawled and groped their way across the walls of the chasm, dragging their repugnant forms through the myriad of offensive odors.

This was where they came from, he realized. This was the lair of the skinwalkers.

This was how they saw their sunless world.

And he was one of them.

"Please, Eric."

The world flickered again. The scene changed. He was racing across a country highway in a greenish rain, with harsh headlights glaring in the distance. Miles stretched out both behind him and in front of him. His legs and feet ached from the long journey, yet he pushed on. Only one thought filled his muddled brain: *Father...*

For the first time in an eternity, he'd called out to them, faintly, but unmistakably. Father was still alive.

Then, inexplicably, he found himself staring down at his own face. Except for some reason he looked monstrous. Even though they were his own, his features looked alien. His skin was covered in great, ugly blotches and tinted a ghastly grayish purple color that he was having a hard time comprehending for some reason, as if he'd never seen that particular color before.

Eric—the Eric down on the floor—was reaching up toward him, his eyes dazed.

Just a little closer...

Then Paul was there. He, too, looked monstrous.

He threw something in his face. (In *her* face?)

Pain blinded him.

The world flickered back into darkness.

Father... he thought, though the word sounded strangely alien, even inside his own head, as if he were thinking it in some strange language that he'd never heard before.

Now his body was bound to a pole with burning rope. His skin felt like it was on fire. Strange, monstrous shapes were gathered around him, staring at him, planning to do awful things to him. (To *her*.)

Help me, father.

Now he was staring back into his own eyes, except they looked ugly and twisted and evil. No wonder there was such seething hatred in her gaze. He was a monster. He'd captured her and bound her and now he was digging around inside her head before he killed her.

Help me, father! Don't let them kill me.

She could hear him. Somewhere in this land of monsters, father was calling out to her. She turned to face the calling voice and saw him there. He was bound with iron and foul magic, but he was growing stronger. He was waking up. He was calling...

She reached out for him, desperate and afraid.

Then everything changed again.

He was back in the bottomless chasm, surrounded by darkness and the overwhelming stench of rancid blood. The shadowy, crawling things scurried around him, worshiping him.

They were his children. And this was his kingdom. His domain. As it had been for ages untold...until the day *he* appeared.

He opened his eyes to see a man in an old, dusty fedora bending over him. He was wielding a strange little doll made of clay and straw and a bag of burning white dust.

Then there was terrible pain.

His body was on fire, yet he found himself living through a nightmare that he could not awaken from.

He remembered being dragged from his home of darkness and blood, barely conscious, seething with fury but unable to move or even cry out. He remembered traveling a vast distance as his children pursued him to foreign lands where the ground was cold and green and the scent of water made the air taste heavy. He remembered approaching a place that smelled of lots of people…and of something else, as well…something he hadn't felt since…

New memories flashed through his head then. A vast, lifeless desert the color of blood beneath a blinding, churning sky where strange creatures soared on leathery wings and painted streaks of fire with their flaming tails.

He was running, fleeing through this blistering wasteland with all his might.

They were coming for him. For what he had stolen from them.

Booming voices carried through the parched air in voices he didn't recognize, but filled him with unspeakable dread.

Then more images flickered and flashed through his head. Memories, he realized. Of deep, terrible places illuminated by the glow of molten rock and heavy with the stench of poisonous smoke. Of his lungs burning with the blistering fumes. Of his hands and feet sizzling against the scorching stone.

Then he saw *them*. Towering figures silhouetted against rivers of fire. Darkness and blaze. Ichor and smoke.

So enormous. So powerful. So *arrogant* that they never anticipated that someone would dare try to steal their treasure, much less actually succeed.

They couldn't have it. It was his now. He'd never give it back.

He raced across the burning wasteland.

Then the memory faded away and he was alone again, far from that long-ago place and trapped in this endless sleep, a prisoner of the thief and his burning ash.

Outside, his children were fighting. He could sense them. They didn't yet know where he was hidden, but they would tear this infested city apart and spill every drop of blood from any human who stood in their way to find him.

They were closing in.

He could smell his captors' fear as they drew nearer.

They'd almost won.

Then the jinn came, bringing with it its hellfire and destruction. The city burned. The people burned. His *children* burned. And when the fires had died down, the thief and the witch put him in the iron box and sealed him away where he couldn't sate his maddening hunger.

For many years he remained there, sleeping, waiting, sometimes listening to the human things that came to watch him from behind the iron bars.

Then, one day, he opened his eyes to see a strange, luminescent shape standing outside the bars, looking in.

It wasn't the witch or the old man. In fact, it wasn't human at all. It was something else. Something far older. Something with far more power.

It didn't speak. It didn't move. It only hovered there, staring back at him for some time. Then, somehow, it was hovering right before him, peering deep into his withered eyes.

"Look at you…" sighed a strange voice. "Look at how you've grown…" Then the shape twisted and churned through the darkness, little more than a writhing mass of glowing gas floating on the air, and snatched the foul doll off its pedestal. Then, before it left, it said something he didn't understand: "Are you in there, Eric? Are you looking at me? Are you looking for *this?* Come and get it. I'll leave it where all the other forgotten things have gone."

Somewhere in the distance, he could hear voices.

Something was happening.

Was someone screaming?

He tried to open his eyes and found himself looking out over the empty pedestal.

Paul was standing there, staring back at him between the harsh shine of the powerful flood lights, his eyes wide with mounting terror.

That's right… Paul was with Yenaldlooshi right now.

Paul…

Eric awoke with a start.

"Oh thank god!" gasped Holly, still clinging to him.

"Eric!" cried Mrs. Balm. She was leaning over him, looking closely at his face.

"What happened?" Glancing around, he saw that several of the Man Hole's lights were out. One of Justin's colorful, plastic busts had fallen off the wall, along with several of the framed *Kama Sutra* pages. And one of the wooden silhouettes had fallen over as well.

"The skinwalker suddenly freaked out," said Holly. "It started screaming and thrashing around. I've never heard anything like it before."

Eric stared at the monster. It was right where he left it, but it was no longer glaring at him with that furious look in its eyes. It wasn't going to be glaring at *anything* anymore. Its eyes were empty and glazed. Its jaw had gone slack, unfurling those monstrous, bulging teeth. Dark blood was oozing from its nose.

It was dead.

Holly was still clinging to him, as if afraid he'd plunge back into that monstrous world if she dared to loosen her grip. She was breathing hard. He could feel it, both her breath on the back of his neck and her heaving chest against his back. He could even feel her heart pounding through her breast. He'd frightened her. A lot. "You weren't answering us," she muttered. "You just sort of... *went away.*"

"You started making these really freaky growling noises," said Ally. "I think Adam wet himself."

"Monster girl..." grumbled Adam.

"She-beast," agreed Greg.

Mrs. Balm was clutching at her cross again. "We didn't think you were going to make it back for a minute there."

He looked down at his phone.

I SAW IT ALL, reported Isabelle. THAT WAS SUPER FREAKY

He ran his hand through his hair. It certainly was.

YOU ACTUALLY TRAVELED THROUGH THEIR MEMORIES. YOU SAW WHAT THEY'VE SEEN

He shivered at the thought of any of that being real. Especially those strange memories of that burning red wasteland and those blistering caverns. And yet, it had certainly *felt* real. He'd even experienced their acute sense of smell, so sensitive that he could piece together a view of that pitch-black hellscape in his mind.

I WONDER HOW LONG AGO THOSE THINGS HAPPENED

Eric decided he didn't feel like thinking about it too much right now.

"That was quite a show," said Mr. Iverley. "Very entertaining. Very *scary*."

You don't know the half of it, he thought, recalling the view of his own face as a monstrous, discolored abomination staring back at him. He actually saw himself as that skinwalker had seen him. He *became* the skinwalker. He became the *monster*.

"This is definitely a powerful book," decided Mrs. Balm. "Very dangerous. I'm not sure what we should do with it once this is over."

"I'll ask my sister," decided Holly. "Del can find a safe place for it."

Eric glanced back over his shoulder at her. "Can I get up now?"

"Oh!" She let go of him and scooted backward, blushing a little. "Sorry!"

"It's fine," he grunted as he stood up and stretched.

"Is little miss stripper *always* that clingy?" asked Ally.

"I was just distracted!" snapped Holly. "*You* try holding open a psychic pathway for that long. It's *exhausting*."

"Whatever you say."

Eric's phone rang. No number appeared on the screen. "Hello?"

"Are you still sane?" asked Ford.

"More or less," grumbled Eric. He didn't bother asking him how he knew that they were done. He wasn't exactly trying to hide the fact that he was watching them.

"Excellent! I knew you could do it! Did you find what you were looking for?"

"Not exactly. I saw *something* take the idol. It said it was taking it to where all the forgotten things have gone. But I have no idea what that means."

"All the forgotten things…" pondered Ford.

"Do you know what it was talking about?"

"I might have an idea. But to get there you're going to need the right tool."

"What kind of tool?"

"A compass. A very special one that's calibrated specifically to point you to the hidden doorway."

"Okay…" He had a special compass already, but it didn't actually *point* to anything. It just told him how far he'd traveled outside the borders of this world.

"I happen to know there's one hidden somewhere in this city, but that's all I can say about it."

"All you *can* say or all you *will* say?"

Ford chuckled. "It doesn't really matter, does it? You don't need me for this. Just have those little witches of yours look for it."

Before he could respond, the call ended.

Eric looked down at the phone, frustrated.

I DON'T LIKE HIM

"Hey, guys?" said Ally. "Dad just sent me a video that you guys should probably see."

She held the phone out as everyone gathered to watch. The screen showed a familiar image of the chamber at the end of the museum's secret passage. Paul's cell phone was aimed between the chained bars, allowing a grainy view of the box on the other side and something *squirming* inside it.

Horrible noises rose from the speakers of the phone as the monster in the box groaned.

Then it let out a terrible, blood-curdling howl and all of them heard a single word carried on the ghastly voice: "FOR-TRELL!"

Eric felt a chill race down his spine at the sound of his own name.

"That is *seriously* fucked up," said Ally.

"Come on," grumbled Eric. "At least *pretend* like you care about offending people." He glanced over at Mrs. Balm, embarrassed. "I'm really sorry about her."

But Mrs. Balm merely shook her head. "No, she's right. That *is* fucking terrifying."

Chapter Twenty

"Ezra Joval definitely wasn't lying about finding Yenaldlooshi in a cave in the desert," said Eric as he sat slumped in the kitchen chair.

The Man Hole wasn't a suitable place to conduct another divination session. There was no stove for boiling water, first of all, only the very small microwave, and no table big enough for everyone to sit around, except maybe the pool table. And, as Holly had put it, the place was just "way too *icky*" to spend another minute in. So while Mr. Iverley and Mrs. Balm returned to the museum to resume their watch over Yenaldlooshi, Eric, Paul and the girls all returned to Eric's house and gathered around the dining room table, instead.

Eric wasn't entirely confident about leaving Justin, Greg and Adam to dispose of the dead skinwalker, but Paul insisted they were up to the task and he supposed that was good enough for him. After all, he didn't think he wanted to know any more details than absolutely necessary.

"Do we have more spell candles?" asked Paige. She was bustling about the kitchen, boiling more water, preparing for another divination session.

"Check the bottom shelf in the pantry," replied Karen. "Left side. There should be a whole basket full of candles in there."

"I saw glimpses of where it came from," Eric continued. He shook his head at the foul memory. "Just a gaping crack in the rocks somewhere in the middle of the desert, probably barely visible from outside. But inside it drops into a vertical cavern that just goes on forever straight down. It's hot as hell in there. And you can't imagine the *smell*."

"I doubt it's just a cave," said Isabelle, her voice rising from

Eric's phone, which sat charging on the windowsill by the table. "I'm guessing the cavern entrance is a portal. That place is either a part of some neighboring dimension or a pocket *between* worlds."

"You could tell me it came straight from hell and I'd believe it," grumbled Paul, grimacing at the memory of the squirming, moaning monstrosity locked up inside that dusty cell. "I'll be having nightmares about that thing for *months*."

"We really have to smear this gross stuff on our skin?" asked Perri. She was standing at the counter, peering into one of the bright yellow drawstring pouches, uncertain.

"It's supposed to protect us from skinwalkers," explained Holly as she prepared the table for the spell. "The lady at the museum said to especially cover your heart and throat with it."

"Seriously?" The thought clearly made her skin crawl. She wrinkled her nose and peered into the pouch again.

"I'm pretty sure I even *saw* him once," recalled Eric. "Joval. As Yenaldlooshi must've seen him." He kept remembering the sweat-slicked face of the man in the beat-up fedora, as if he truly *was* a real-life Indiana Jones. "I still don't know how he did it, but it looked like he used white ash and the stolen idol."

"Which makes sense that it's so important to containing him," reasoned Isabelle.

"Are we really sure that this Ford guy wasn't the one who stole the doll?" asked Karen. She poured a cup of coffee and handed it to Paul.

"Seems like the sort of thing those freaks would do," he agreed. "Thanks."

"You're welcome."

"I don't know," said Eric. "The thing I saw during that spell didn't look anything like an agent. It didn't even really seem to have a body. It was just a glowing shape in the darkness. Even Yenaldlooshi seemed to acknowledge that it was something old and powerful."

"That guy *did* say that only a god could've taken the idol," recalled Isabelle.

"He did," agreed Eric. "Besides, why steal it then help me

find it?"

"Well," said Isabelle, "most of the agents you've encountered have had a pretty twisted sense of logic."

"They *did* summon a genie once and burned half the town to ash," recalled Holly.

"It smells funny," said Perri, still making faces at the contents of the yellow pouch.

"It's just ashes," insisted Holly.

"And don't forget that crazy woman who tried to summon a titan and tear a dimensional hole in the city," added Isabelle.

"Ashes of *what?*" asked Perri.

"I don't know," said Holly. "Mr. Iverley said it was some kind of secret recipe or something."

"What is it with those agents, anyway?" asked Paul. "Why're they all so weird? Remember that steampunk freak we ran into last time they were in town? The one with all those crazy drugs. Gave me a puking hangover, struck Kevin blind for the rest of the day and made the girls high as shit."

"I was *not* high," Karen informed him. She scowled at him as she handed a coffee cup to Eric. "I was just...*unfocused.*"

"You made a pillow fort in my living room," said Diane, picking up two more steaming mugs and passing one to Holly. "And then you demanded tea and yelled at us to call you 'Princess Kay.'"

"I don't remember any such thing," huffed Karen.

"If you say so." Diane Shucker was one of Karen's oldest friends, going all the way back to their days as college roommates. She was also one of the few people in Creek Bend who knew about Eric's weird adventures. Between the skinwalker attack, the monster at the museum and the run-in with that weirdo agent, Karen had decided that the situation called for all hands on deck. Specifically, she wanted some extra company for herself and Perri while Holly and Paige were off casting protection spells on Justin Teberly's sexist playhouse.

Karen sat down next to Ally and handed her a cup. "How're you handling all this?"

Ally had been sitting quietly the whole time, slouched in her chair, her arms crossed, listening to the inconceivable amount of crazy that was going on around her and trying to keep up with it all. "I'm fine," she replied, though she sounded a little guarded, like she didn't trust what was going on here. And Eric could hardly blame her for that. But she saw that skinwalker with her own eyes. It wasn't human. She saw its face transform from that frightened girl into that hideous monster. She heard the inhuman noises it made. She saw its alien eyes and those monstrous teeth. That was no trick. And then there was *magic?* Spells? Genies and titans? Agents with terrible powers? Little girls trapped in time-less, psychic realms. It all seemed so *insane.* "How long have you guys been doing this?"

"About four years now," replied Karen.

"And everyone here just *goes with it?*"

"We don't really have a choice," said Isabelle. "If Eric doesn't do these things, people die."

"No shit?"

"Some of us wouldn't be here today if not for him," said Holly. "*I* certainly wouldn't. And neither would Paige."

"Me, too," said Perri.

Ally's gaze drifted to her uncle as she sipped her coffee, looking very much as if she thought everyone must be either pulling a prank on her or else utterly out of their minds. This *was* Uncle Eric they were talking about, after all.

"Aren't there usually *two* agents?" asked Diane.

"Not always," replied Eric. The first one he ever met was working alone. "But it never hurts to be aware that there might be another one creeping around."

"These?" asked Paige, returning from the pantry with a basket of tea candles. "Which color?"

"It doesn't really matter," replied Holly. "The candles aren't important for the spell to work. They just set the mood and help us gauge the energy flow."

Perri started to dip her finger into the ash, but grimaced and pulled her hand back. "I mean...it's not...you know...*people* ashes or anything, is it?"

Holly looked back at her, a horrified grimace painted across her face. "What? *No!* Oh my god, why would you even think something like that?"

She shrugged, embarrassed.

"Seems like a valid question to me," said Paul. "It *does* look like something someone poured out of an urn."

"Please stop!" squealed Holly.

"What I don't get is how this skinwalker business connects back to the big fire," said Diane.

"At this point, I really think *everything's* connected," sighed Eric.

"My money's still on that agent," decided Paul. "Those guys have all sorts of powers. I wouldn't be surprised if they had somebody who could steal an artifact out from under a bunch of magic barriers."

"True," agreed Eric. "The guy was going on about how the organization he works for doesn't want this city wrecked and it sort of made sense, except…"

"Except for if they like it so much, why do they keep trying to destroy it?" asked Karen.

"Exactly."

She shook her head. "I don't know. Maybe he *wants* to wake up Yenaldlooshi."

"Scary," said Paige. She was standing over the stove again, waiting for the water to boil.

"Hard to tell what those freaks are up to," said Paul. "They're all a bunch of lunatics."

"I'm more interested in that lighthouse," said Isabelle. "That seems like it's probably important."

"Yeah," said Paige. "That didn't come from the divination spell. Perri saw that on her own, while we were waiting for more water to boil."

"I saw it, too," said Eric. "When Ford knocked me out. For a little while I was back in the psychic void again. I still don't really understand it."

"It's the psychic connection you share," said Isabelle. "Ours broke up when you went there, so I couldn't follow you, but after we reconnected, I could tell it was the same sort of thing you two shared back when she was still trapped in the void."

"It *did* feel like that," said Perri. She didn't remember much about her time in that empty place. It was literally a whole lot of nothing. A long, maddening loneliness that stretched on and on and on. Almost half a century of utter, soul-swallowing *emptiness*. But every now and then, dreams would pierce that emptiness. Dreams of *hope*. Dreams of the man she somehow knew would eventually find her and take her away from the loneliness. And then they were more than just dreams. Somehow, he came to her in the void. He drifted alongside her, so close she could almost touch him. She was able to call out to him, to beg him to save her. And then, just a few weeks ago now, he came to her one last time, wrapped his arms around her and dragged her back to the world of the living, where she discovered that she'd skipped half a century, her high school years and several bra cup sizes.

"I thought that happened before because we both happened to be caught in the same kind of psychic mindset," said Eric.

"Me, too," said Isabelle. "And that's kind of what happened today. That agent sent you to another of those weird mental states and you connected to her again, except this time she wasn't in the void. She was sitting at the table with Paige."

"It was kind of creepy," recalled Paige. "She just sort of looked up and started talking to someone who wasn't there."

Eric nodded. That was exactly how he remembered it, too, except he hadn't been able to see Paige at the time, only Perri and her immediate surroundings. Everything else was lost in that strange, hazy nothingness.

"It must be like it is with you and me," reasoned Isabelle. "You made a connection with her while she was in the void and it just stuck."

He frowned. "But we can only connect like that when I get clobbered by a psychic attack? Because I'm really hoping that stops happening to me."

"Maybe. I don't know. We may never know exactly how it works. But on the bright side, if we ever get disconnected like that, she might be able to see where you are, which is more than I can do. When your consciousness shifts into that other state, I can't follow you. It's a different kind of timelessness."

"There're different kinds of timelessness?" asked Karen.

"Apparently," replied Isabelle.

"Huh."

"So we're just sitting around here waiting on water to boil?" asked Paul.

"I'm going as fast as I can!" promised Paige as she peered into the steaming pots in front of her.

"You're fine," Karen assured her. "It takes time. Watched pots, you know."

"We should be out there looking for that doll," decided Paul.

"We don't even know where to start," countered Eric. "That's why we're here."

"We start with that agent," he pushed. "My money's on *that guy*. And we know all the places agents have used in the past. Like those unseen places. What about that asylum? They were hiding *monsters* in the basement last time."

"That doesn't exactly narrow it down," replied Eric. "Don't forget how big that building is. And the idol's only about the size of Paige's bunny."

"And if you start poking around in there, he'll know," added Isabelle. "We've seen before that they have some sort of alarm system in place, because every time you go into one, it's usually not long before an agent shows up."

"That's right," agreed Karen. "If that agent *did* hide the idol in one of those places, he could easily just sneak in and move it before you found it. Even if he didn't, it could take all day to search them all. How many are there again?"

"Nine, that we know of," said Isabelle. "Plus, there's no guarantee you'll be able to get to all of them. They don't always cooperate."

Eric nodded. Sometimes he had a hard time making himself see those places, even when he knew exactly where they were. And then there was the schoolhouse, which he didn't think was even possible to enter without a special shard of glass from some kind of magic looking glass to reveal the way. "We could end up wasting a lot of time."

"And that's *also* assuming this guy would even use an unseen location," Karen went on. "He could just as easily be using the Gardenhour facilities. It seems like they have some sort of history."

Again, he nodded. Back in 'sixty-two, the gray agents used two of Gardenhour's buildings in their scheme to summon the jinn. And the organization still had access to them just a couple years ago, when Mistress Janet was conducting her insane experiments.

"And then there's that bungalow," said Isabelle. "It's pretty well hidden. There's a good chance that any agents in town could be using it as a base of operations."

"You're talking about that place where we found Tessa," said Holly. "Just outside of town, near that Top-Down Bar. Where that sex-obsessed woman showed up and rubbed her fake boobs all over Eric."

"Oh my god!" gasped Ally.

Karen shot Eric a dirty look. "There is absolutely no more fraternizing with slutty agents."

"There was no 'fraternizing,'" grumbled Eric. "We've been over this. Isabelle vouched for me."

"I did," agreed Isabelle.

"Is this like how you and Holly weren't getting way too cozy during that spell?" asked Ally.

"Cozy *how*?" demanded Karen.

"I was holding open the psychic door," said Holly. "It was right there in the spell."

Ally showed Karen her phone. She looked at it, then glared at Eric. "Am I going to have to find you a chaperone?"

Diane peered over her shoulder at the screen and laughed. "Nice!"

"It was the only thing keeping him from getting trapped inside that skinwalker's head forever!" exclaimed Holly.

"If you say so," said Ally, laying her phone back down in front of her.

"It's true," said Isabelle. "That was the only way to make

sure Eric came back. I mean, I assume everyone *wanted* him back."

Karen didn't argue with this, but she also didn't agree with it. She picked up her coffee and continued to stare at her husband.

"I say we get out there and start looking," decided Paul, standing up and taking another swig from his coffee.

"Just slow down," said Diane. "Don't go doing anything stupid."

"Once the water boils we might be able to narrow down where you should look," said Holly.

"It's almost there," promised Paige. "Just a few more minutes."

"*Or*," pressed Paul, "we can get out there and start looking and you can give us a call as soon as you know something. We'll start with that bungalow. If there's nothing there, we'll start checking out those unseen places."

"Why're you so eager to rush off into enemy territory?" asked Diane.

Paul glanced around the room, a timid sort of look on his hairy face. "I don't like when they do magic. Me and magic don't go well together."

"Ah. I see." He *did* have a history of bad luck when it came to magic.

"Nobody's going to hex you," grumbled Holly.

"Not on purpose," added Paige.

Everyone glanced over at her.

"What? I'm still learning some of this stuff."

"It's just divination," said Diane. "How bad can you possibly mess it up?"

"Well, I *have* seen the water *explode* before," said Holly.

"Oh…"

Paul pointed at her. "See there?"

"It was just that once, though. And no one got hurt or anything."

"You can call and tell us what you find out," he decided.

But Eric didn't get up. Sitting around *did* make him feel anxious, but so did the idea of leaving the house. He still wasn't ready for this. His thoughts kept drifting back to Evancurt…and to how he technically never made it out of those woods.

Karen was still staring at him. She could see the indecision on his face. "I think everyone should just stay put for now," she decided.

Eric nodded again. He glanced over at Holly. "Did you hear back from Delphinium?"

"I did. She tried the divination and saw the same thing we did. She says it's something specific to this area. That Yoshi-whatsit thing…"

"Yenaldlooshi," said Karen.

"Yeah, him. And she also said it's not so much blocking our divination as our *future*."

Eric considered this. "So the thing eclipsing the divination is something that's going to happen to…*cut off our future?*"

"Um… That sounds exceptionally bad when you put it like that, but…pretty much. Yeah."

"Something like letting an ancient, mummified god wake up and stomp Creek Bend into oblivion, I'm guessing," said Isabelle.

"Then we should *definitely* be doing something," decided Paul.

"Calm down," said Karen.

"Any tips on getting around it?" asked Eric.

"She said to try focusing on the past, rather than the future," replied Holly, "so we're going to try that."

"What good will the *past* do?" wondered Diane. "Don't we need to know what's going to happen *next?*"

"The past can tell a surprising amount about the future," explained Holly. "After all, the future *started* in the past."

"If you say so…" she replied, trying to decide if she understood that.

Paul gulped down the last of his coffee and placed the empty mug on the counter. "That's it. I can't just sit here. I've got to do something."

"Good idea," said Karen, standing up. "Here." She plucked two of the bright yellow pouches off the counter and handed them to him. "Mrs. Balm said to scatter this stuff around the foundation of the house to help keep skinwalkers away. That should keep you entertained for a while."

Paul scowled at the pouches.

"She said inside, too," Holly reminded her. "Around the windows and doors."

Karen made a face at the idea of intentionally making a mess inside.

"Better safe than sorry," said Eric.

"Fine," she sighed. She picked up a third pouch and added it to the first two that Paul was holding. Then she added a fourth pouch. "And rub a little extra on yourself, too, so you don't get eaten while you're out there."

Paul glanced over at Eric, bewildered.

"But *outside*," she added. "I don't want any more cremated people on my floors than absolutely necessary."

"Oh gosh..." squealed Perri.

"It's not people!" huffed Holly.

"You don't know what it is," Diane reminded her.

Chapter Twenty-One

Divination wasn't the most thrilling form of magic that Eric had encountered in all his weird travels. It was essentially just everyone sitting around and staring into a bowl of steaming water while waiting for vague images and thoughts to pop into their heads. It was a long and painfully dull process that Eric simply didn't have the patience for today. He kept glancing around at the six women crowded around him. Only the two witches, Holly and Paige, seemed to have the focus necessary to keep their gazes fixed on the water. Karen and Diane were looking at him or at each other more often than the bowl. Perri seemed to fall somewhere in the middle. She was trying. He could tell. But nothing was coming to her, so she ended up watching Holly and Paige as much as the water. Ally barely looked at the water at all, her gaze slid from one person to the next, still processing the idea that these people surrounding her were so much more than she ever expected.

Or perhaps she was just sitting there wondering if her Aunt Karen had started mixing some happy new ingredients into her baking.

A few details had trickled out almost immediately. Holly and Paige both saw dogs, of course. And they saw fire and smoke. They saw the book.

Why did the book keep coming up? Eric had grabbed his copy of *Reassembling the Ashes* and flipped through it again. Ford told him there were secrets inside, but he still had no idea what he was talking about. Was there some kind of hidden code in the book? Did one of the pictures reveal some important clue that he hadn't yet noticed?

What was he missing?

"White faces again," said Paige.

"I saw that, too," said Holly. "It was creepy."

"What does it mean?" asked Karen.

Holly shook her head. "I'm not sure... It was just a bunch of ghostly, white faces in the dark. *So* creepy."

"Yeah, no thanks," muttered Diane. "You have fun with whatever *that* freakiness is. I'll be staying here where the wine is." Then she glanced over at Karen. "There *is* wine, right?"

"There's wine," Karen assured her.

"Nice."

Silence fell over the kitchen again. Holly and Paige watched the water. Eric took another sip of his coffee and glanced at the candles. It was difficult to tell if you weren't paying attention, but the flames were burning hotter than they were when they were first lit and the wax dripped down the sides a little faster than normal. Something about the magic energy caused them to flare up. The more witches were gathered around, the hotter the candles burned. The entire coven could burn through an entire twelve-hour candle in a single sitting if the energy flowed well.

He wondered if it was just the strange properties of magic that affected the candles or if the spell was doing something to the physical world, such as causing a change in air pressure or increasing the ratio of oxygen. He also wondered if it was weird that after all this time, he still found himself trying to find logical explanations to things that, by their very nature, defied all logic. It seemed like maybe he should've given up thinking like that by now.

"So..." said Ally, "...you guys really just sit around staring at a bowl full of water for hours on end?"

"It's not *that* many hours..." said Paige.

"Only when Eric needs us," clarified Holly.

Ally stared at the bowl, uncertain. "And you actually *see* things in there?"

"Sometimes," replied Paige. "Usually it's less *seeing* things and more just sort of *perceiving* them."

"So you stare at the water until you start *imagining* seeing things."

Paige blinked across the bowl at her. "Maybe?"

"It's complicated," said Eric.

"So you keep saying."

"You'll get used to it," said Diane.

"If you say so."

Holly shook her head. "I keep seeing the colors gray and yellow…"

"That's not vague at all," said Diane.

"A bridge, maybe?" said Paige. "And a well?"

Ally sat up and looked into the bowl, confused. There was nothing in there.

"How much of this stuff usually turns out to be real?" asked Diane.

"It depends," replied Holly. "Sometimes nothing. Sometimes most of it. But when we're looking for Eric, pretty much all of it turns out to be relevant in some way. Even things we dismiss as nonsense. It's kind of weird."

Eric stared at the water. Karen had told him before that she believed a higher power was steering his life toward some far greater purpose. She said it was the only explanation for why the weird kept reaching out to him like it did. And between the mysterious gas station attendant and the Lady of the Murk who guided his time-torn other self through Evancurt's doomsday machine, he had little reason to doubt her. It made sense, then, that Holly's divination spell would prove more accurate when aimed at him. Or as much sense as any of the weird ever made, he supposed.

"I still can't see anything…" pouted Perri.

"It takes time," Holly assured her. "You have to train yourself a little to keep focused on it."

"If you say so."

"Anyone can do it. Just be patient."

Diane stood up. "I don't know about anyone else, but I'll be much more patient with a glass of that wine. Anyone else want some?"

"A little early for me," said Karen.

"I need to keep my head clear," said Holly.

"I don't even know if I *can*," said Perri.

Diane shook her finger at her. "That's a good question, isn't it?"

"She's the oldest one here," said Isabelle.

"*And* the youngest," said Karen.

Perri propped her elbows on the table and rested her chin in her hands. "I'm so messed up..." she pouted.

"You're wonderful," said Karen. "Don't let anyone tell you otherwise."

"You're sweet," she replied, her voice muffled through her smushed lips.

"Bargaining," said Holly.

Karen leaned forward, frowning. "How do you see 'bargaining'? That seems like an awfully specific idea."

"It's just the word," she explained. "Bargaining. It keeps popping into my mind."

"Huh. Okay."

Paige leaned closer. "I just saw Eric at a tea party."

He frowned. "Tea party? Really?"

"I mean, I'm pretty sure."

"I feel like I'm not going to have time for a tea party."

"That really doesn't seem like you," said Karen.

"It really doesn't," he agreed.

Perri lowered her hands and leaned forward, squinting into the water.

"Did you see something?" asked Holly.

"I'm not sure... It wasn't very clear."

"Most of the time it's not," said Paige. "Just say what you see."

She shook her head. "I'm not sure..." she said again. She leaned a little closer. "Probably nothing, but it sort of looked like... I don't know. Like a *frozen flower*?"

Diane sat down with her glass of wine, nodding. "That sounds like it's about the right level of weird, doesn't it?"

"Makes as much sense as Eric at a tea party," agreed Isabelle.

Eric nodded.

"I see a black map," said Holly. Then she frowned and

pushed her mouth to one side as she pondered the thought. "Do maps come in black? Wouldn't that be hard to read?"

Eric leaned back and closed his eyes. He hated this part. Gray and yellow? White people and tea parties? Frozen flowers and black maps? What did it all mean? Why did it all have to be so damned cryptic? It was exhausting.

Holly leaned forward. "There's something there…" she said. "Way down deep. Can you see it?"

Paige leaned forward too, as did Perri, curious.

"It looks like a road…" said Holly. "And an old build-ing…"

"Oh yeah…" said Paige. "A church, maybe?"

Perri made a face at the empty bowl and glanced up at Holly and then at Paige, as if to see if they were playing a joke on her. Clearly, she couldn't see anything.

But Holly only nodded. "I think you're right. I feel like there's something there…"

Paige nodded back. "There in the doorway… There's some-thing…" Then she sat up, surprised.

Holly blinked and sat up, too.

"What happened?" asked Karen.

"Eclipse," said Paige.

"I guess that's all we're going to get for now," said Holly.

"It won't just go away if you wait?" asked Diane.

Paige shook her head. "Every time we've had to boil more water and start all over."

Holly leaned back, a befuddled look on her face. "I guess we weren't focusing hard enough on the past?"

Perri leaned over the bowl, frowning. "I can't even see the thing blocking us from seeing…" she muttered.

Paige stood up. "I'll start some more water."

"I'll let Paul know it's safe to come back in," said Isabelle.

Eric glanced down at his phone, then back at the empty chair behind him. "Oh yeah… Forgot about him." He'd had plenty of time to finish spreading the ash. He'd be out there somewhere, putzing around, waiting for the magic to be over.

Karen turned and looked at him. "So that didn't tell us *any-*

thing about where the idol is or where you're supposed to go next."

Eric was lifting his mug to his lips for another sip, but at this he lowered it again and furrowed his brow. She was right.

"Didn't Holly say something about a church?" asked Diane. "Right before the…uh…eclipse or whatever?"

"I only barely saw enough to see that it was a church before it got blocked out," recalled Holly. "I couldn't tell you where it was."

"Wasn't it next to a dirt road?" asked Paige.

"And it was pretty run-down," said Holly. "Like it didn't look like it was still in use."

Karen thought hard for a moment. "I can't think of any churches in that kind of shape around here."

Eric couldn't think of any, either. In fact, the only run-down church that came to mind at all at the moment was Father Billy's, and that was way out in the woods, deep in the fissure he explored on his first outing into the weird. And there was no road leading there.

The door clicked open and Paul's head appeared. He'd overdone it a little with the ash because his beard had gone white with it.

"Magic's done," said Diane as she sipped her wine. "You can come back in, you big wuss."

Paul stepped inside and closed the door behind him. "It's not my fault magic hates me," he grumbled.

"Don't make a mess in my house," Karen told him.

"You're the one who told me to put the ash on," he reminded her.

"*Everyone* needs to put some of that stuff on," said Eric. "Even if you don't leave the house."

Diane wrinkled her nose at him. "I thought the house was protected by magic or whatever."

"Better safe than sorry," he pressed. "Until this skinwalker business is over."

"Fine," she sighed.

Perri leaned closer to the bowl, still squinting at it.

Diane gestured at Eric with her wine glass. "This better not just be an elaborate plan to get your harem girls to shower together again, like with that steampunk monk business."

Karen shot him a dirty look. "You perv."

"I just told you they should take a shower to get that guy's freaky-ass drug dust off them. I never told you to put them in there *together*."

"But you sure liked the mental image," said Isabelle.

"*I did not!*"

"He *totally* did."

He reached over and disconnected the call.

RUDE, she texted.

"Just make sure everyone puts the ash on," he grumbled. "Trust me, it won't be nearly as amusing when you're the one being dragged off to hell."

"I said fine," sighed Diane. Then she turned and faced Paul. "Hey, Big Brave Man. Do you know of any dilapidated churches around here?"

He looked up, surprised. "Not around here," he replied.

"Well, damn," she said. "Then what are we supposed to do now?"

"Um…hey guys…" said Perri. She was still leaning over the bowl, staring into it. "Is the water supposed to be doing that?"

Everyone turned to find that the water in the bowl was swirling around, as if it were being stirred by some invisible force.

"Whoa…" said Paige. "I've never seen it do that before."

Holly leaned closer, her eyes narrowed. "What…?"

It was swirling so quickly that the middle had begun to bow inward, turning it into a small whirlpool.

"That doesn't seem right," said Diane.

"I've got a *super* bad feeling right now," said Paige.

Eric jumped to his feet. "Get back!" But before anyone could react, the water lurched from the bowl like a living thing and threw itself at his face.

He dove to the floor and the water instead sailed over him and struck Paul, who was knocked back against the door with all the force of a firehose.

"Holy shit!" exclaimed Ally.

"What the hell was that?" gasped Diane.

"Is he okay?" worried Holly.

Eric scurried across the floor, where Paul was coughing and gagging. "*Paul?*"

He replied with a series of angry and very vulgar curses.

"He'll be fine," sighed Eric. He sat up and ran his hand through his hair, wondering how many of these frights his poor heart had left in it.

"*Right ub by fucking dose!*" coughed Paul.

"Did anyone else see that, though?" asked Paige.

Holly turned and looked at her. "Yeah. It flashed through my mind at the exact moment the water blew out of the bowl. It was a parking lot, wasn't it?"

"There was a sign," agreed Paige, "but it was too quick for me to read."

"A *big* sign," agreed Holly. "And a soccer field?"

"Playground equipment?" said Paige.

"Is it time for recess?" asked Diane. She was dabbing at the fresh wine stain on her shirt.

"A park," said Eric.

"Furnanter," coughed Paul as he righted himself and wiped his dripping beard with his jacket sleeve. "It was Furnanter Park."

"Well there you go," said Diane. "I guess you know where to go next after all."

"Yippee…" groaned Paul. "Can't wait…"

Chapter Twenty-Two

"Fucking magic," grumbled Paul as he shifted the old pickup into gear, his grimy face freshly powdered with ash. "I *told* you it doesn't like me."

"You *did* tell me that," sighed Eric. "You going to live?"

"I'm fine. A little curse water up my nose won't kill me. Probably."

"It's not curse water."

"Last I checked, *regular* water didn't fly across the room at someone's face on its own."

That was true, he supposed.

While he and Paul went out to Furnanter Park to see if they could puzzle out just why the divination literally threw the location in their faces, Holly and the others would be attempting another round of divination.

Paul wasn't wrong. There was something peculiar about what happened back there. It was like when the water exploded the night he first met Holly, splashing the ceiling and showering everyone at the table with hot water. And it didn't happen by chance. Sissy Dodd made it happen. She was interfering with the spell all along, and when it started getting too close to the truth she was hiding, she blasted it back at them, ending the session. But what happened this time was different. The water didn't just explode. It moved on its own, first swirling around the bowl and then literally *leaping* out of it, throwing itself purposefully into Paul's face. Something was manipulating it with far more skill than Sissy had demonstrated. It even delivered a message to them, flashing an image of Furnanter Park through their minds as it flew across the kitchen. And then there was the odd fact that it didn't happen during the actual divination. Unable to see past the mysterious "eclipse" in the water, Holly and Paige had already stopped, meaning there shouldn't have been any energy flowing through the water. According to Holly, the energy used for the divination spell came from those using it, not from the water. Whatever—or *whoever*—caused it to happen, did so using their own power.

But Holly insisted that she'd know if another witch was interfering with the spell. Back in Illinois, Sissy was able to hide her identity because she used the same magic as her sisters. That wouldn't work again. After being away from the rest of her coven for so long and studying on her own, Holly's magic had changed enough that she could tell the difference between hers and her sisters, making her absolutely certain that the only magic at work in the divination was Paige's and her own.

But then what made the water move? Who sent the message that pointed them to Furnanter Park?

His phone rang, distracting him from his endlessly circling thoughts. He pulled it from his pocket, glanced at the screen, then accepted the call and held it to his ear. "Hello?"

"Hey there, Chosen One."

"Please don't call me that."

Poppy Underweir laughed. She had a lovely laugh, infectious even. She always seemed to be in a good mood, which he'd always found impressive, considering the unfair hand life had dealt her, taking her mother and her legs when she was only eight and forcing her to spend the *next* eight years of her life in the care of her violent, alcoholic stepfather. Although she preferred to dress all black and gloomy, she was actually one of the warmest and most easy-going people he'd ever known. Although she wasn't at all shy about poking fun at people. "Heard you were getting into trouble again."

"Well, you know how much I love trouble."

"You're pretty hopeless like that."

"I know."

"We've been looking into the water for you, trying to navigate around that eclipse thing Holly was talking about, and we thought you ought to hear what we saw. Unless you'd rather just wing it, of course. I mean, I wouldn't want to spoil any surprises for you."

"Tempting," he replied. "But I think you'd better just let me know."

"If you say so."

"I'm no fun, I know."

"No fun at all. First, about the eclipse itself... Whatever that darkness is, we got a *really* bad feeling when we tried to force our way through it. Seriously bad vibes. Reminded me a little of that time you encountered that rat demon. But *way* worse."

Eric frowned. That was a little concerning. If he remembered right, the rat demon had scared Delphinium a lot that day. Her only advice at the time was to get out of that building and run as far away as possible, but of course he wasn't able to do that. It was full of children.

That was a year and a half ago. The rat demon was sealed away now. But the real enemy had turned out to be not the demon at all, but a freaking *clown*, of all things, who was actually some sort of ancient remnant of some long-dead universe. And in the end, it was the clown that got away. It was still out there somewhere, probably still terrifying innocent people, like most clowns.

He often wondered where the creepy freak was now...

"You're going to have to be especially careful with this one," said Poppy. "When we look into the next few hours, things start to get hazy. There're some dangerous uncertainties in your path."

"In other words," said Cierra from somewhere in the background, "don't get cocky."

"I'll be sure to keep my guard up," he promised.

"Yeah, Cierra says hi, by the way," said Poppy. "Siena and Alicia are here, too." Cierra Lennenston, Siena Lowe and Alicia Vaine were all sisters of Delphinium Thorngood's coven of witches, just like Holly and Paige. He met each of them the same night he met Holly and Poppy. "We're on Eric Watch today."

"Thanks," said Eric.

"Our pleasure," replied Poppy.

"So what did you see in the water?"

"A lot of what Holly said she and Paige saw, for starters. Lots of dogs. Or...dog-like things, I guess."

"Skinwalkers," agreed Eric, nodding.

"And lots of fire. Like an entire city in flames."

Was that the past or the future? He couldn't help but wonder.

"And we saw a dark doorway. Old. Filled with cobwebs. Super creepy."

A dark, cobweb-filled doorway... That was new. But perhaps it was only a reference to the door Holly revealed with her magic in the museum's basement. He didn't recall seeing any cobwebs, but the visions in the water divination weren't always exact, literal snapshots of the future. Sometimes it took some creative liberties.

Paul pulled through the front gates of the park and made his way up the winding drive, past the pavilions and the playgrounds and the baseball and soccer fields. There was no one else here today. Furnanter was deserted. And there was so far no indication of why they were sent here. Nothing seemed out of place. There certainly didn't seem to be any skinwalkers prowling around.

"Siena says she saw a black key," said Poppy. "And Cierra saw a dark cemetery, I think."

"Dark and *dead*," Cierra called out from the background. "Not just a cemetery full of the dead. *Everything* was dead. Not a single sign of life. Not so much as a blade of grass."

"That's not unsettling at all," said Eric.

"I know, right?" said Poppy. "What else was there? Um... As usual, Alicia can't see anything but you."

"*Oh my god will you please stop?*" squealed Alicia from somewhere in the background.

"A raging fire, a dark doorway, a black key and a dead cemetery," listed Eric, eager to put the conversation back on track. Why did everyone think it was so amusing that the poor girl had a crush on him? She was probably well over it by now anyway.

"And I did too see something," huffed Alicia. "I saw stairs."

"That's right," said Poppy. "Stairs."

"Lots of stairs," said Alicia. "Like, *lots* of lots."

This left Eric scratching his head. Stairs? That seemed like something so common…yet "lots of stairs" seemed oddly specific.

"I don't know. Maybe you're going to get a lot of cardio today."

"That sounds fun."

"I know, right? I'm more of an elevator person, myself."

"I'll bet you are."

When he reached the parking lot farthest from the entrance, Paul nosed into a corner spot and killed the engine.

"Tell him about the bell," said Siena.

"A bell?" asked Eric.

"Yeah, that was a weird one…" said Poppy. "We didn't exactly *see* a bell… We *heard* it."

Eric sat up and ran his hand through his hair, confused. "How do you *hear* something in the water divination? I thought it was all *visual*."

"It *is*," said Poppy. "Sometimes we *infer* sounds from the things the water shows us, but this was an *actual* auditory kind of thing. We *heard* it. We *all* did. It was like a really *big* bell. Deep and clanging, but way off in the distance. And hearing it gave us all the most terrible feeling of absolute *dread*…"

"*Super* eerie," said Alicia.

Eric scratched at his ash-covered neck. What could the sound of a ringing bell possibly mean? That wasn't like any of the other images the divinations had offered him. But then again, what did *any* of it mean? A cobweb-filled doorway? An extra-dead cemetery? A black key? Was that anything like the *black map* that Holly saw?

"I think that's all," said Poppy. "We'll let you see what you can do with that and give you a call if anything else comes up."

"Thanks a lot."

"No problem. You be careful out there."

Eric assured her that he would and disconnected the call.

"More good news?" asked Paul.

"More *weird* news."

THIS "ECLIPSE" THING IS KIND OF UNSETTLING, texted Isabelle.

He looked out at the silent park spread out before them. "I know what you mean."

IS YENALDLOOSHI REALLY THAT DANGEROUS?

"Seems like it."

I CAN'T WRAP MY HEAD AROUND HOW EZRA JOVAL EVER CAPTURED HIM IN THE FIRST PLACE

He nodded. The way everyone talked about the museum's well-hidden relic, it was some kind of dormant god with the power to wipe Creek Bend off the face of the earth. But if that was the case, then how did one man ever manage to snatch it from the depths of its monster-infested lair, transport it hundreds of miles and seal it away in some dank cellar?

"So now what?" asked Paul.

It was a good question. Furnanter was a pretty big park. There was a lot of space to cover. And the clock was ticking.

"I mean, I think this is the place." He gestured toward the far side of the field in front of them, where a large, wooden sign stood marking the start of a hiking trail. "I definitely saw *that* while that curse water was cleaning out my sinuses."

"Sounds like we should check it out, then."

"Yeah. Let's get it over with." Paul opened the door and hopped out of the truck. Then he reached under the seat, withdrew a handgun and tucked it into his waistband under his shirt. "Just in case this is one of those 'guns simplify things' kinds of things."

"Suit yourself," said Eric. He stepped out into the cold, gloomy day and looked out at the dark opening in the trees behind the sign. "Back into the woods..." he sighed. "Why is it always the woods? I *hate* the woods."

"We don't *know* that's where we gotta go," reasoned Paul. "I also saw the park entrance. Maybe we're supposed to be back there somewhere?"

Eric shook his head. That wasn't how the weird usually worked. Somehow, he always seemed to end up exactly where he needed to be. Sometimes it felt as if the weird had him on a leash, dragging him along against his will.

And as he set off toward the trail, his phone chimed in his hand.

THERE'S SOMETHING OUT THERE, warned Isabelle.

"Of course there is," he groaned.

Chapter Twenty-Three

Eric had been in these woods before. Years ago. Long before his experiences with the weird convinced him beyond any doubt that he was definitely not a nature person. The wooden sign that Paul glimpsed in his "curse water" vision was a historical marker. This narrow trail was the only remaining path leading to the site of the old Weeldel Textile Mill. Back during the time that Ezra Joval first drove his wagon into town, this would've been a thriving hub of activity and a staple of Creek Bend's local economy. But that was a long time ago. Today, it was little more than a few crumbling foundations almost entirely reclaimed by nature.

THERE'S A REALLY HEAVY SPIRITUAL ENERGY AROUND THAT PLACE, reported Isabelle.

Because of course there was. It wouldn't be the weird if it didn't drag him kicking and screaming through some nightmarish, ghost-infested nightmare of a place at least once. And this area *was* rumored to be haunted, he recalled, like any place abandoned and left to the elements for any length of time. He'd heard countless stories about horrific accidents and gruesome deaths that supposedly occurred at the mill, leading to all manner of blood-curdling specters wandering these quiet woods at night.

Back in the normal life he had before the weird turned his world upside-down, he never believed any of that nonsense. These days, however, he just simply assumed *everything* was dangerously haunted.

IT'S ALMOST OVERWHELMING, Isabelle went on.

"You mean like Hedge Lake?" worried Eric. As soon as he crossed into that haunted area, she'd very nearly passed out from the intense levels of spiritual energy. And she remained ill the entire time he was there.

NOT QUITE THAT HEAVY, she assured him.

"Well that's good." He was already dealing with skinwalkers and a mentally unbalanced agent. The last thing he needed was another Hedge Lake Triangle.

AND IT'S NOT NEARLY AS WIDESPREAD, she added. THIS IS DEFINITELY CONCENTRATED IN A MUCH SMALLER AREA

He frowned at the narrow path before him. The old mill attracted a lot of curious visitors. It was a popular location for amateur ghost hunters and had more than its fair share of thrill-seeking kids looking to prove their bravery.

STILL MAKES ME FEEL YUCKY, THOUGH

"Well, I have no intention of sticking around here long," promised Eric. The forest was eerily quiet around them. The gloom was much deeper beneath the naked canopy. It felt colder than it did before they entered it. That much was probably natural, but there was also a strange heaviness to the air, too. It was almost stale. It had been a long time since he last walked this trail, but he didn't remember it feeling like this. Was it only in his head? Was he only imagining it because Isabelle had confirmed that these woods were haunted?

He wanted to blame it all on his nerves and his overactive imagination. After all, even if there *was* spiritual energy flooding this area, he didn't have the ability to feel it. Only Isabelle could tell him it was there. But his time in Evancurt had taught him, among other things, that he didn't always need Isabelle to tell him when he shouldn't be somewhere.

Finally, the trees parted to reveal the few remaining walls of the old mill.

Near it stood the weathered foundation and partially intact chimney of an old house. According to a large, covered signboard, the house was where three generations of the Weeldle family lived during that time period when the mill was still functioning. And there were other, even less intact foundations scattered throughout the surrounding woods.

There was something a little sad about such a setting. It was a humbling reminder of the constant and unstoppable march of time. And since it was located well away from the rest of the park features, it was especially prone to littering and vandalism. Empty cans and fast-food wrappers marred the surrounding woods and most of the walls were covered in graffiti.

"There's nothing here," observed Paul.

NO, THERE'S DEFINITELY SOMETHING THERE, countered Isabelle.

Paul frowned at Eric's cell phone screen, then turned and scanned his surroundings again. "Well, I don't see anything."

Neither did Eric. He stepped through a gap in the old wall where the concrete had long ago broken apart and looked around.

"Think there's another skinwalker out here?" wondered Paul.

NOT SKINWALKERS, insisted Isabelle. THERE'S A REALLY STRONG SPIRIT PRESENCE. AND IT FEELS EXTREMELY BAD

"Bad how?" asked Eric.

I'M NOT SURE I CAN EXPLAIN IT. THERE'S JUST SOMETHING ABOUT THAT PLACE THAT FEELS WAY OFF

He glanced around, uncertain.

IT'S LIKE I CAN FEEL ANGER, she continued. OR MAYBE IT'S MORE LIKE DESPERATION?

Eric's eyes scanned the empty walls. Many years ago, this space was filled with noisy machinery and busy mill workers, a great many of which, as he recalled, were only children. He couldn't say how many of those awful stories about gruesome accidents were true and how many were merely the morbid imaginings of the many paranormal enthusiasts who liked to talk about such things, but if even one child had died here, it more than earned its reputation as a place of terrible tragedy, as far as he was concerned.

I DON'T UNDERSTAND IT, BUT I'M CERTAIN THERE'S SOMETHING REALLY AWFUL IN THAT PLACE

PLEASE BE CAREFUL

"Yeah," promised Eric. "Count on it."

Everything recognizable about the old mill was gone now. Even the floor was gone, replaced with over a hundred years of undergrowth and towering trees. There was something oddly creepy about it all, even without the odd abundance of spiritual energy that Isabelle had sensed upon their approach. But no one seemed to be here. And he certainly didn't see anything that looked like a compass. Unless, of course, a compass looked like a weed. Or a chunk of concrete. Or that McDonald's soft drink cup that someone had left wedged in the fork of a tree.

Why were they here? Why did the water show them this place? Was someone trying to deceive them? Were they letting themselves be drawn *away* from what they were supposed to be doing?

"Hey…" said Paul.

Eric looked up to find him staring past him, into the trees that crowded the surrounding walls. He turned to follow his gaze, but there didn't seem to be anything out there.

"Thought I saw someone…" muttered Paul.

Eric looked on a moment longer. He didn't dismiss it as a trick of the shadows or overactive imagination. It was far better, in his experience, to assume that there *was* something there and he just wasn't seeing it. It could very well be staring back at them right now, hidden in the shadows or rendered invisible by some strange magic. It could even be standing behind some mysterious gateway between dimensions.

He'd seen a lot of weird stuff.

But still nothing moved.

"Guess not…" said Paul. Though like Eric, he didn't take his eyes off the place where he thought he saw movement.

"Don't let your guard down," warned Eric. He turned around to scan the area behind them and glimpsed someone peering back at him from directly over Paul's shoulder, visible for only a split second before ducking out of sight behind him. "Look out!" he gasped, shoving him aside.

Paul stumbled a few steps and twirled around, startled. "*What?*" he gasped. "*Where?*"

But there was no one there. The two of them were alone.

Eric stood there a moment, puzzled.

"What did you see?"

What *did* he see? The more he focused on the memory, the more *wrong* it looked. It had appeared to be a human face, but the eyes staring back at him through tangles of dirty, black hair were dingy and yellow and the flesh of the exposed cheek was pale and waxy.

I DON'T LIKE THIS

He turned and scanned his surroundings again. Out in the woods, something ducked behind a tree. Then, as he watched the tree, something darted past a gap in the foundation in the corner of his eye.

Paul saw something too, because he cursed and pulled out his gun.

Something cold touched the back of Eric's neck. He cried out, revolted, and twirled around. "Isabelle?" he gasped.

THE SPIRIT ENERGY IN THAT PLACE IS SWELL-ING REALLY FAST, reported Isabelle. I'VE NEVER FELT ANYTHING LIKE IT BEFORE. IT FEELS LIKE MY HEAD'S IN A VISE

"Hang in there."

I'M TRYING

Then: BUT IT HURTS

Paul jumped backward, clutching at his elbow. "Something touched me!"

At the same time, Eric felt something tug on the back of his jacket. He spun around, but again nothing was there.

"What are they?" asked Paul.

"How the hell should I know?"

"You've never seen anything like this before?"

"There's a lot of weird stuff out there, you know! There's always something new! Every time!"

Paul slapped at the back of his head and twirled around, jabbing his gun at the empty space behind him. "Maybe we should get out of here and think this through better!"

That didn't seem like a bad idea at the moment. But there

was also the undeniable fact that the clock was ticking. Like always, the weird was rushing him, dragging him along. If there really was something here that they needed, they might not have time to come back later.

He made his way through the dense trees and brush that crowded the old production floor as barely seen things moved in the corners of his eyes, peering around trunks and through doorways and over walls.

He could hear things now, too. Footsteps danced through the underbrush. Murmuring voices carried across the breeze. And somewhere in the distance, he was sure he could hear someone crying.

"I really don't like it here," grumbled Paul.

IT'S GETTING WORSE

Eric frowned at his cellphone screen, concerned. "Are you okay?"

IT'S MAKING MY HEAD POUND

"Trust me, we're not planning on sticking around much longer."

IT ALMOST FEELS LIKE SOMETHING IN THAT AREA IS MAGNIFYING THE SPIRIT ENERGY

"What could do something like that?"

I DON'T KNOW

GETTING HARD TO THINK

HURRY PLEASE

"Right." He lowered the phone and glanced around. Things were still moving around him. It seemed like everywhere except wherever he was looking was *alive*. "But where do I go? What am I even looking for?"

He wasn't expecting an answer. The weird wasn't usually so generous. But a broken voice suddenly came to him through the ghostly murmuring and weeping. "…house…" it sighed. "…fireplace…"

Fireplace? Eric didn't waste time. He exited the mill ruins and hurried over to the crumbling remains of the old house and the jutting form of the chimney.

Like the mill, the house was little more than a few crumbling walls utterly open to the elements. The fireplace was half-hidden beneath a thorny thicket of wild raspberry bushes.

Ignoring the swelling sounds of murmured voices and the eerie, distant shrieking that the weeping had turned into, he settled down onto his knees and reached inside, clawing at the dry weeds and cold soil, determined to dig up whatever was buried there.

"I think it's starting to get serious out here," said Paul. He was standing over him, still clutching his gun, and trying to follow all the things that were darting out of sight quicker than his eyes could follow.

"I know it is," grunted Eric. "Check around the outside. See if you can find any loose bricks or anything."

"What're we even looking for?"

"No idea."

"Then how do we know if we've found it?"

"You'll know it."

"If you say so."

"Just keep looking."

"I *am* looking!"

Eric withdrew his hands, shaking them. All he was doing was tearing up his fingers. If there was something there, he was going to need a shovel to find it.

Instead, he scanned the interior of the fireplace. Everything looked solid, but he leaned inside and ran his hands around it to be sure, examining it more closely while Paul searched the outer bricks for a hiding spot.

Frustrated, he craned his neck and looked up at the flu. Maybe in the chimney? He twisted around and tried to peer up into the shadows, but he couldn't see anything.

"There's nothing out here," reported Paul.

Grunting, he wormed his hand up into the narrow opening. This wasn't an ideal situation. He hoped to hell something nasty didn't have a nest up there. He grimaced at the terrible thought and forced himself to reach a little higher.

Something was there. His fingers closed around cold metal. Was this what he came for? Was this the compass Ford told him about? He wriggled it back and forth, grunting at the uncomfortable angle. The stone scraped at his arm. The hard, uneven earth beneath him hurt his knees. "Come on…" he growled.

Finally, the thing came loose. He twisted his wrist, turning the object vertically so that it wouldn't catch again, and started to pull it out.

Then cold, bony fingers closed around his forearm.

Chapter Twenty-Four

Eric uttered a startled cry as something inside the chimney yanked on his arm, pulling him deeper into the unknown darkness.

"What is it?" cried Paul.

"Something's got me!" he grunted.

"Get out of there!"

"Oh, why the hell didn't *I* think of that?" He strained against the unyielding stone as the thing inside continued to pull him upward. It felt like a hand, though no person should have been able to fit inside such a small space. Hard, bony fingers were digging into the flesh of his wrist. Was it another skinwalker? Had he inadvertently stuck his hand into one of their impossible hiding spots? Or was this something else?

There was always something new to curdle his blood, after all.

He planted his free hand against the outside of the fireplace and struggled to pull himself free, but the thing in the chimney had a grip like a machine.

This wasn't good. Was it going to break his arm? Or worse, relieve him of it altogether?

"Let go of me..." he groaned, his heart thudding in his breast.

His awful imagination gleefully offered a third and far more gruesome possibility, that he was about to find himself dragged all the way up into the narrow chimney, one splintered bone and twisted, ruptured organ at a time, until he was nothing more than a pool of dripping gore.

Up until now, his cries had been relatively manly, he thought, but the one that escaped him now was little more than a terrified, girlish *squeal*.

He lowered his head and pulled as hard as he could against the thing inside, but it refused to yield. "Help me!"

"I gotcha!" grunted Paul, already reaching in and taking hold of his arm.

It hurt. The more he struggled, the more his arm was raked across the stone and the more those bony fingers dug into his flesh.

Was it only his imagination again, or could he feel warm blood oozing down his arm inside his sleeve?

"Get me out of here!"

"I'm trying!"

The thing gripping his arm yanked upward again, twisting it and forcing another painful cry from him.

"Hold on!" shouted Paul.

"Holding on isn't exactly the problem here!" snapped Eric.

"You know what the hell I mean!"

Again, the thing in the chimney jerked upward on his arm, wrenching a series of bitter curses from him this time.

"Why the hell would you stick your hand up there in the first place?"

"Ow! Goddammit! Like you never stuck anything anywhere questionable! *Ow!*"

"Why? What've you heard?"

"*Ouch!*" He lowered his head again, grimacing at the pain, and coughed as a puff of smoke billowed up into his face. "Wha...?"

Directly beneath his head, in the loose dirt he'd dug up when he first knelt down to search the fireplace, something was smoldering. Small ribbons of smoke were rising out of it. Then a flame flickered up before his startled eyes. An alarming warmth was quickly replacing the cold. A fresh well of panic broke open somewhere inside him. "*Get me out of here!*" he coughed.

Paul cursed and yanked harder on his arm.

"*Now!*"

"*I'm trying!*"

The flame grew bigger and hotter. Eric tried to blow the fire out, but that only seemed to make the flames flare up even hotter. He craned his head back, wincing at the heat that stung his eyes. *"This is getting serious!"*

"Really?" snapped Paul. *"I didn't notice!"*

He coughed again. The heat was getting intense. The flames were only inches away and as long as the thing in the chimney was holding onto him, he couldn't pull his head back any farther. Forget losing an arm or being dragged up the chimney, he was going to get *roasted alive!* *"Help me!"*

"I'm trying!" Paul stood up and looked around for something—*anything*—he could use as a tool, but there was nothing to be found but broken bricks and concrete. If he had all night, he might be able to chip away the stone and slowly dismantle the fireplace, but time was rapidly running out and an icy panic was quickly taking over. *"What do I do?"*

"I'm burning up in here!"

But all Paul seemed able to do was utter the same foul word over and over again.

The flames were still growing. The heat licked at his face, burning his eyes. The skin on his cheek was beginning to burn. He twisted his head the other way, but it only shifted the pain from one side of his face to the other. *"GET ME OUT OF HERE RIGHT NOW!"* he screamed.

"I got an idea! Just hold on!"

"NOW!"

But before Paul could do anything, a strange, alien-sounding voice called out through the chaos, speaking in a language that was less words than noise. A second later, a hard gust of wind blew over him, blasting away the flames as if they were nothing more than a birthday candle. At the same time, the thing in the chimney let go of Eric's hand and he yanked his arm free, withdrawing the hidden object with it.

He threw himself backward and out of the fireplace before something else could grab him. He landed hard on his butt on the cold ground, then scrambled backward a few feet more, just for good measure.

"You okay?" asked Paul.

"I think so..." The lower half of his face was stinging and

he was scraped and bruised all up and down his arm. And he wasn't entirely sure yet if he still had eyebrows. But he was alive. And that was all that mattered. Even better, he had what he came for.

At least…he *hoped* this was what he came for. He held up the object he'd just risked his life to retrieve as he rubbed his battered arm and examined it. It looked sort of like an inside-out kitchen whisk. It was a short, metal rod with stiff, wire bristles protruding from one end and curving backward over his hand. Threaded through the other end were three small, wire rings.

A cold hand fell on his shoulder and he looked up to find a familiar, naked woman kneeling beside him, her bloody eyes fixed on his.

"It was you," he breathed. *Tessa* was the source of the strange voice and the mysterious wind that set him free.

Those bloody sclera used to be startling to behold, but he found that he'd grown used to them. Tessa was a ghost and a witch whose ever-naked form still bore the frightful markings of her untimely murder, but more than anything else, she was a friend. She'd helped him on many occasions. She'd even looked after him during those strange hours in Evancurt, when he had no one else. He no longer felt anything but warm feelings for those eyes. Instead, he now found himself far more unsettled by the terrified look on her face as she stared back at him. She looked as if she'd just had a terrible fright.

"Thank you!" he gasped.

When she spoke, the movement of her lips didn't line up with the voice that met his ears. The sound was distorted, almost warbling. It passed through his brain in a strange and uncomfortable way. But that was normal for Tessa. As odd as it sounded, it was just the way she spoke. "You have to get out of here," she warned him. "I don't know how long I can hold them back."

"What?"

But she was already gone. Faded away as if she were never there.

Eric sat there for a moment longer, blinking at the place where she was just kneeling. "Okay then…" he sighed.

"That was Tessa…" realized Paul. He'd never seen her before. He'd only heard stories.

"Yeah." It must've been her who told him to check the fireplace, too. "She saved my ass again." He was starting to lose track of just how much he owed her. He reached up and rubbed at his stinging cheek. "That one was a little close for comfort, though." Then he turned and looked at Paul. "What the hell are you *doing*?"

Paul was standing there, staring at the place where a bruised and naked woman had been kneeling just a few seconds before, looking dazed. But for some reason, he was also holding open the fly of his pants. Now he glanced down, distracted. "Uh…"

Eric's eyes narrowed. "Tell me right now that you weren't about to piss on me."

Paul managed to look offended. "You were *on fire*!"

"And *that* was your plan?"

"I didn't hear *you* coming up with any better ideas!"

"No! That is not okay!"

"Better than getting your face burned off!"

"Not by much!" He rose to his feet, still clutching his arm. "Ouch… Dammit."

"What if Tessa had taken another thirty seconds to get here?"

"We're not debating this!"

"Fine," grumbled Paul, zipping himself back up. "Be an ungrateful ass. See if I ever offer to piss on you again."

Before Eric could tell him that he was perfectly fine with that, something inside the fireplace let out a blood-curdling shriek and a great gust of cold, putrid-smelling air belched outward.

Paul let out a terrified jumble of half-coherent curses and quickly backed away.

All around them, that creepy murmuring was filling the forest again.

Eric stuffed the strange metal object into his jacket pocket and scrambled to his feet. "Yeah, time to go," he decided. But when the two of them turned, they found the doorway they entered through blocked by a gruesomely emaciated man covered in blotches and oozing sores. His filthy, pale flesh was stretched tight over his bones. His pelvis bulged from his hips. The shadows between his ribs were cavernous. His cheekbones were jagged spikes against the contours of his withered face and yellowed eyes stared back from the depths of his sunken sockets. In sharp contrast to the rest of his body, his belly was bloated and swollen.

Eric had seen that kind of swelling in books. A distended belly was a common symptom of extreme malnourishment in impoverished parts of the world. Was this the ghost of a man who had starved to death in life?

But as he stood staring at the gruesome apparition, it slowly opened its mouth, stretching and extending its chin well beyond its natural limits, all the way to the top of its bulging belly, revealing row after row of long, needle-like teeth.

"Like you said!" gasped Paul. "Time to go!"

The two of them turned and ran for the doorway on the other side, but a figure appeared there, too, blocking their path again.

This time it was a woman. Her skin was covered in the same kinds of blotches and festering sores. Her black hair was filthy and matted. Her eyes were a monstrous shade of yellow. Her naked breasts hung deflated and flat above the deformed swell of her great, bloated belly.

She, too, unhinged her jaw and revealed her countless teeth.

"Are these things skinwalkers, too?" gasped Paul as the two of them turned and fled again.

"I don't think so."

The wall on this side had mostly collapsed, leaving plenty of room for them to escape the ruins, but as soon as they were outside the house, another skin-and-bones form stepped from behind a tree, again blocking their path.

This one was a man with a great, mangy beard that squirmed with foul, unseen things. Behind him appeared a much younger woman with black stains oozing down both legs. Both of them were naked and filthy, with distended bellies and yawning, nightmare maws.

All around them, the forest was alive with them. Dozens of them. Hundreds, perhaps. They crept out from behind every tree and every wall.

"Isabelle?" squealed Eric.

DON KNO W, texted Isabelle.

CANT THNK

HED HRTS

Eric cursed. This was bad. They needed to get the hell out of here. But they were surrounded. There was no way out.

"Okay then!" growled Paul. He jabbed his gun at one of them and fired off three shots.

The results were pretty much exactly what Eric expected: absolutely nothing. The monstrous figure didn't even flinch.

"You didn't really think that was going to do anything, did you?" asked Eric.

"Okay, then what do we do?"

"Why don't you try pissing on them? See if that works."

"Don't be a dick. What do we do?"

But he didn't know. There were so many of them. Ghoulish, starved things with yellow eyes and monstrous, bottomless gullets were closing in on them from every side.

They didn't move like human beings. Most of them crawled on all fours like wild animals, their bony arms and legs twisted in unnatural ways. Some of them even seemed to *slither*. They inched forward, slowly, but determinedly, their huge, drooling jaws still gaping wide.

"*Eric!*"

"*I don't know!*" gasped Eric.

"*Well think of something!*"

"*Isabelle!*"

But Isabelle wasn't answering. Had the overwhelming haunted energy of this place become too much for her?

Like just before the ghostly wind set him free of the man-eating fireplace, a strange, alien voice passed through the forest like an ominous fog. All around them, the gloom deepened. The temperature dropped. And the hair on the back of Eric's neck stood up.

The monstrous spirits surrounding them felt it too. They scattered like cockroaches in the light.

Was that Tessa again? Was that some sort of spell?

"Run for the truck!" shouted Paul, who wasted no time bolting for the trail back to the park.

But as soon as Eric turned to follow him, something seized the back of his jacket and yanked him back. He turned to find a ghastly woman with a great, festering gash on her forehead thrusting those wide, drooling jaws at him.

He tried to pull away from her, but her grip was as monstrous as her face. He only succeeded in dragging her along the forest floor as he backed away.

"Get off me!" he growled.

Again, that alien voice drifted over him.

Was it a voice? The words were like nothing he'd ever heard before. It was less a language than a string of strange and unnerving noises, like old, rusty gears creaking and grinding together, a raspy sort of stuttering hisses and groans.

And then the ghoulish woman clinging to his jacket let out a terrible wail and came apart before his eyes, her body literally breaking into pieces and dissolving into a strange cloud of smoke and brackish blood.

He staggered backward, horrified.

All around him, invisible things cried out in fury.

"Go!" hissed Tessa's warbling voice.

Eric didn't hang around to find out what happened next. He turned and raced down the path after Paul, who was already well ahead of him. "Wait for me!" he shouted after him.

"Nope!" Paul shouted back.

"I said wait up!"

But he wasn't stopping. He ran on, never slowing down. "I'll meet you at the truck!"

"Just stop!"

"The universe loves you!" Paul shouted without looking back. "You'll be fine!"

"Get back here before I kick your ass!"

"Eric…"

He stopped and looked back the way he came. What was that voice just now? That wasn't Tessa. It wasn't warbled or distorted. It didn't sound ghostly at all. It was perfectly clear. It sounded as if someone had called out from right behind him. But where did it come from?

He turned to run again, but again the voice called out to him, soft and feminine: "This way, Eric…"

Again, he turned and looked back.

"Over here…"

He couldn't say for certain where the voice was coming from, or even if it was coming from any one direction at all, and yet he found his attention drawn to a point in the forest about forty yards away, where the shadows were deeper than the rest of the area around it.

He looked back in the direction Paul had been running, but he was already out of sight. Then he turned and looked back the way he came. There was no sign of the monstrous, starving specters, either. He seemed to be alone.

"Please hurry…"

There was something almost overwhelmingly sincere about the mysterious voice. It pulled at him, drawing him toward it.

His choice couldn't be clearer. He could continue back along the path and join Paul in the safety of the truck, or he could follow this mysterious, ghostly voice deeper into the same woods where he'd literally *just* escaped being devoured by a terrifying pack of ghoulish spirits.

One choice was clearly the right one and the other was clearly the stupidest thing he could imagine. Only an idiot could mess this up.

And so, cursing bitterly, Eric set off into the forest.

Chapter Twenty-Five

Why?

He kept asking himself this question as he plowed through the dense underbrush. Naked branches clawed at his exposed face and pulled at his hair. Thorns snatched at his pants legs and weeds tangled around his feet.

He couldn't think of a single reason why he should still be out here. All he had to do was keep following the trail back to the park. He would've been back at Paul's truck by now, giving him a piece of his mind for running off and leaving him back there, but instead he was getting himself lost.

Furnanter Park was located on the very western city limits of Creek Bend and blended into miles of wild forest. It was hardly the untamed wilderness. Chances were good that he'd eventually stumble across a road or a stream or a farm field, but he could lose valuable hours wandering in circles out here. And that was assuming that there wasn't something out here waiting to eat him, like the idiot he was.

Why was that mysterious voice so compelling? Why did he feel the need to follow it? He couldn't even explain it to himself.

His cell phone chimed in his pocket.

THAT'S A LOT BETTER, texted Isabelle.

"You okay?"

I THINK SO

"Does that mean the spirit energy's back to normal?"

IT'S GOING DOWN AS YOU GET FARTHER AWAY

"That's probably good." He glanced around, but there was nothing out here. To the casual observer, he probably would've looked hopelessly lost. "You going to tell me how stupid it is that I'm still out here?"

IF YOU THOUGHT THAT VOICE WAS IMPORTANT

ENOUGH TO FOLLOW, THEN I TRUST YOU

"Huh. Wish *I* had that much confidence in me."

WELL, YOU DID ALMOST GET EATEN BY THAT SKINWALKER BECAUSE IT PRETENDED TO BE KAREN

"Don't remind me…"

His foot caught on a root, tripping him. He stumbled and fell to his knees. Instead of standing back up, he rolled over and sat down on the cold forest floor.

Yeah. He could use a break.

THAT THING YOU FOUND

He looked at the screen, then reached into his jacket pocket and withdrew the object he found in the chimney. "Any idea what it is?"

NO, BUT IT'S STRANGE. IT'S GIVING OFF A REALLY FAMILIAR ENERGY, BUT I CAN'T QUITE PLACE IT.

He turned it over in his hand, examining it.

BUT I THINK I'VE HEARD OF GHOSTS LIKE THAT BEFORE

He raised an eyebrow.

THEY'RE CALLED PRETA. STARVED SPIRITS. SAID TO BE HORRIBLY CURSED. DRIVEN BY AN INSATIABLE APPETITE FOR FLESH AND BLOOD. YOU'RE LUCKY TESSA WAS THERE

"I usually am." He turned the device over and over in his hand, trying to work out what it was. There didn't seem to be an on switch of any kind. If it was the compass Ford told him to retrieve, then he had no idea how to read it. There was no needle or arrow. In fact, it had no moving parts at all. Finally, he gave up and stood up again. "What the hell am I doing out here?"

She didn't answer him. She was inside his head. She knew when he was being rhetorical. Instead, she said THE SPIRITUAL ENERGY IS ALMOST ENTIRELY GONE NOW. IT DOESN'T SEEM LIKE THE STARVED SPIRITS WERE ABLE TO FOLLOW YOU

He pushed on, inexplicably wandering deeper into the woods. Why did he feel so compelled to keep moving forward?

What could he possibly find out here?

THAT AREA WAS CHARGED WITH SPIRITUAL ENERGY. AT FIRST I THOUGHT IT WAS THAT DEVICE RAMPING UP THE ACTIVITY, BUT I THINK IT WAS THE SPIRITS, THEMSELVES, THAT WERE DOING THAT. I THINK SOMEONE MUST'VE PUT THEM THERE. LIKE, AS A TRAP. PROBABLY THE SAME PERSON WHO PUT THE DEVICE IN THE CHIMNEY

"Why would someone do that?" he wondered. Then he cocked his head to one side, confused. "*How* could someone do that?"

I HAVE NO IDEA, BUT IT'S A SCARY THOUGHT. IT SUGGESTS THAT WE'RE DEALING WITH SOMEONE WITH A LOT OF SUPERNATURAL POWER

"What else is new?" he grumbled.

TRUE

He ducked under a low branch and stumbled over another root.

He was surprised that Paul hadn't called him yet. He must've realized by now that something had happened. But when he glanced down at the phone again, he realized that there was a good reason for that. He had no service.

That was odd. It might look like the wilderness out here, but he still hadn't left the city limits. He should still have a signal. Unless…

He stopped walking and reached into his front pants pocket for the *other* compass. The one he brought home from Hedge Lake.

It looked like an ordinary old pocket watch because that was what it obviously used to be. But someone had removed the face and somehow modified the inner workings so that instead of recording the time, it recorded one's distance from the "real" world. When he was in his home dimension, the hands were completely stopped. But when he left that world and wandered into other realms, the wheels began to turn and the hands slowly began to move. The faster they moved, the farther away he was.

Right now, the second hand was slowly making its way

around the tiny, crowded gears.

"Where am I?" He raised his phone and looked at the screen. "Do you feel any kind of energy?"

But Isabelle didn't answer.

"Isabelle?"

He turned and looked back the way he came, cursing under his breath.

Again, he had two options: go back and try to find Isabelle and his cell signal or continue onward *alone*.

Obviously, there was only one *logical* answer.

So naturally, he returned the compass and the phone to his pockets and continued onward.

What the hell is wrong with me?

The landscape around him was starting to change. Great, knotty roots were breaking through the ground now, forcing him to move more carefully.

These whole woods seemed weirdly familiar. He stopped and turned all the way around, taking it all in. Maybe it was only his imagination. He'd been in a lot of woods these past few years. Almost any forest would probably look familiar by now. And he almost always encountered something terrifying in the woods, so he was practically conditioned to expect that his life was in danger every time he found himself surrounded by trees.

He started forward again, his eyes peeled for anything that might enjoy the taste of fat, stupid English teacher.

Then, finally, he caught sight of something in the trees ahead of him.

Something…yellow?

He walked toward it, squinting through the foliage at the brightly colored shape looming ahead of him.

Then, all at once, everything clicked into place.

It should've been obvious from the beginning where he was going. He arrived here through a forest. He lost contact with Isabelle before arriving. And according to the watch, he'd somehow slipped outside of his own dimension. It was just like the last time he was here.

In fact, this was where that very watch was given to him!

He pushed his way through the last of the forest, his gaze fixed on the bright and cheerful-looking house. The siding was bright yellow. The door was varnished pine. The shutters were an almost-yellow shade of orange. The foundation and chimney were built from yellow bricks. Even the shingles on the roof had a gold tint.

And surrounding the house, in stark contrast, was a strange collection of colorless concrete yard ornaments. A menagerie of animals was spread out before him, deer and birds, squirrels and cats, badgers and bears, cows and pigs, alligators and toads, turtles and puppies. There was even the top half of a big hippopotamus head protruding from the weedy lawn as if it were the surface of a muddy river. There were bird baths and windmills, little bridges with no water running beneath them, wishing wells, mushrooms, fountains, miniature castles and a small army of angels and chubby little cherubs. There were also fairy tale creatures like pixies, gnomes and dragons, and quite a few cartoon characters mixed into the mess.

There was no theme or organization to them. They seemed utterly random. And they filled the entire yard, surrounding the house like an army, leaving no room to even push a lawnmower.

As far as he could tell, everything was exactly as it had been last time he was here. Nothing seemed to have moved since then. Even the woods surrounding the curious yard appeared exactly the same, as far as he was able to tell. Except of course that all of this was in Northern Michigan last time he was here…

How did an entire yard move?

He pushed the thought from his head as he stepped from the forest. Looking for logic was pointless. Logic didn't matter much when it came to the weird.

The first time he was here, he entered the yard from behind the house and approached the back door. He never walked around. This time, he was closer to the front, and he found that there was no driveway leading up to it. The only way here seemed to be on foot through the woods. And somehow that didn't surprise him.

This was Cordelia's house.

And he was fairly sure you didn't get to Cordelia's yellow house by car.

He felt rather stupid. Holly had told him she saw the colors yellow and gray in the divination spell. Paige had even glimpsed a smurf in the water, doubtlessly the very one that his gaze fell on now, standing right between a trio of singing, sunglasses-clad frogs and a miniature Easter Island head. This was probably where most of the random things she saw in the water came from.

He didn't waste time lingering. Like the first time he was here, he made his way straight for the nearest door.

Was this the front door he was approaching this time? He thought last time that he walked up to the back door, but since there was no driveway, he wasn't entirely sure *which* side was the front.

He stepped up onto the porch and reached out to knock, but like last time, the door clicked open before his knuckles could fall upon the varnished pine.

"Cordelia?" he said, lowering his hand and taking a step back.

Cordelia was a petite and very plain-looking woman with big, inquisitive sort of eyes and very long black hair that trailed all the way down to the tops of her knees in frizzy curls. She spoke with a very small and strangely airy voice that seemed to carry an ageless wisdom.

Or maybe that part was just the way he remembered her. His first visit here had been quite strange. Looking back, it felt like a very *spiritual* sort of experience. She was very otherworldly. He couldn't help wondering what she might reveal to him today.

But when the door opened, it wasn't Cordelia who was standing there to greet him.

Chapter Twenty-Six

"Hi there!" said the familiar little girl.

"You..." said Eric, surprised.

"Me," she replied, beaming up at him with her big, green eyes.

"Nadia."

"You remembered!"

He did. She wasn't an easy person to forget. When he last saw her, she was in the back of a mysterious, white limousine belonging to an enigmatic and diminutive gas station attendant who once helped him locate a profound secret in the depths of an otherworldly cathedral. He no longer remembered what that profound secret was, though. Not consciously, anyway. His human brain wasn't able to handle such information. It would've killed him. So the little man suppressed it for him, driving it deep down into his subconscious mind, where he only recalled it in his unremembered dreams.

Nadia was the gas station attendant's daughter. She and her sister, Maxie, drove him and many of the witches all over the Midwest that night, leapfrogging the many miles between stops on strange, otherworldly "fringe roads" and seeking out seven mysterious *mages* in order to unlock an ancient and terrible curse to stop an evil coven of blood witches.

Because...why not?

Nadia was wearing faded blue jeans and sneakers under a long, flowing top that fit more like a dress than a shirt. It was a dark red color, with a yellow and white flower pattern. Her long, brown hair was pushed back under a bright pink hairband. She looked for all the world like an ordinary nine-year-old girl. But there was nothing ordinary about her. For one thing, she hadn't aged a day in the sixteen months since he last saw her. She should be ten or eleven by now. But only her clothes had changed since then.

"What are you doing here?" he asked.

"I'm here a lot," she replied. "This is my sister's house."

"You're sister?" He remembered the large woman who sat behind the limousine's wheel that night.

"No, not Maxie," she said, as if reading his mind. "My *other* sister."

"Cordelia's your sister?"

"Yep!"

He ran his hand through his hair, confused. The lady of the strange, yellow house was another of the gas station attendant's daughters?

She wrinkled her nose and puckered her lips in a thoughtful sort of expression and said, "Everyone always calls her by a different name, though. She chooses it based on who she's talking to when she introduces herself."

He nodded. Oddly enough, he remembered suspecting as much. Cordelia was the name of King Lear's good daughter. To Eric, who'd studied Shakespeare in college, and had taken a particular interest in that play's theme of madness and betrayal, the name had developed a sort of synonymy with goodness. Cordelia was kind, loving and loyal. She was trustworthy. He remembered distinctly thinking when the lady of the yellow house introduced herself as Cordelia that she must've plucked it from his very subconscious, specifically for him.

But he never thought any more about it until now.

"She's not here right now, but she'll be back soon. She said you should wait for her."

"Oh."

She stepped aside, pulling the door wide open. "Come on in. Take a break."

He stepped through the doorway and into a gloomy little entry space that opened onto a long, dark hallway to the left and a very small kitchen straight ahead.

Like last time he was here, he was struck by the lack of decoration. For someone who seemed practically obsessed with collecting every yard ornament she'd ever seen, Cordelia—or whatever her name really was—had surprisingly little interest in wall hangings, knickknacks, houseplants, rugs or even throw pillows. The kitchen was meticulously clean—every surface positively shined—but it was utterly stark, consisting of only a small amount of counter space, a sink, a gas stove and a refrigerator, all of which looked fresh out of the nineteen fifties. There was no microwave or toaster, no knife block or cutting board. There wasn't even a coffee pot. There was only an old-style teapot sitting on one of the stove burners.

He stepped through the little kitchen and into an eerily familiar living room. This area, too, was utterly bare but for a black leather couch with a bright red afghan draped over the back, a well-worn armchair and a curious-looking clock resting on the mantle of the fireplace. The walls were covered in very dark, unadorned wood paneling and the floors were an equally dark, stained hardwood that was nothing at all like the sunny hues outside.

It felt weird, being back here again. He hadn't realized until just now how much this place had felt like a dream. A part of him, it seemed, hadn't been convinced that his first visit here was real. And yet here he was again.

Nothing had changed the slightest bit.

"Have a seat," invited Nadia.

He glanced back at her, bewildered. Not everything was the same, he reminded himself. She wasn't here last time. And then there was the notable absence of Cordelia, herself.

He sat down on the couch, in the exact same place he sat last time he was here, and that surreal feeling only intensified as he found himself looking at the room from the very same vantage point.

It was as if he'd traveled through time.

"You want a Coke?"

He turned and looked up at her again. She was dressed differently than she was the last time he saw her, but her face was the same. And he could even remember her offering him a Coke the first time he met her, exactly as her father had done the first time he met *him*.

She raised her eyebrows at him, reminding him that she'd asked him a question.

"Oh, uh… No. But thank you."

She flashed him a pretty smile and then plopped herself down in the chair across from him. "She should be home any minute now."

He nodded, still feeling dazed.

"By the way, how did everything work out with your car insurance?"

"Insurance?" For a moment, he didn't understand the question. It seemed to come out of left field. Then it occurred to him. The mysterious check that paid for the PT Cruiser that was swallowed along with the rest of Evancurt. "Wait…that was you?"

"Yep."

He sat there, blinking at her, bemused. "I, uh… Yeah. Everything worked out fine. We bought a new vehicle. Trailblazer."

"Great."

He shook his head, "But how…?"

"Well it didn't seem right for you to just lose out on it. I mean, you kind of saved a lot of people that night. Both living *and* dead. The least I could do was take care of that much. And you can probably guess that my dad has a *lot* of connections."

"I'll bet he does…"

"Anyway, I'm glad that worked out for you."

"Yeah. Thanks."

"It's no problem." She flashed him another of those sweet smiles. "It's what I do. I help."

"So you've said."

"Which reminds, me," she added, tipping her head to one side. "There's one other thing I can help with, too, while we have a minute."

"What's that?"

"You keep thinking about her."

He frowned, confused. "I keep thinking about *who*?"

"The other Karen who belonged to the other you," she replied.

He stared at her, surprised in spite of himself.

"You keep thinking that if there was a version of you out there who left on the wrong day and never made it home, then there's a version of Karen out there who's been all alone since that day and has no idea what ever became of her husband."

He wasn't sure what to say. He did, indeed, keep thinking about that. It was just one of many things that still haunted him about the events of that awful night two months ago, but it was probably the most disturbing of all his recurring thoughts. He couldn't bear to speak it aloud. He hadn't even talked to Isabelle about it.

"Those two timelines converged the moment you reached the bottom of the cathedral and lived," she explained. "Because everything was compressed together, you both essentially reached for the jar at the same time. In that one instant when you chose *not* to open it, your timeline, *this* timeline, became dominant and the other ceased to exist. Only the other Eric remained of it, and only because his spirit attached itself to your body. There *is* no other Karen. And there never was. So you don't have to worry about her."

He rubbed at the back of his neck. "I...*think* I see."

She smiled at him. "It's complicated, but that's how it works."

"Huh." He looked out the windows at the gray day beyond. He trusted her. He didn't think she'd lie to him just to make him feel better. Somehow, he simply knew that about her.

"And don't worry about any more timelines, either," she added. "There was no version of you who ever left on the second night. Or any other night. You either left the first night or you waited for the third."

"Oh. Okay."

"Hope that was helpful!" she chirped, beaming at him.

"Yeah. It definitely was."

Then she hopped up out of the chair. "Oh good, you're home!"

Eric stood up, too, surprised to see Cordelia strolling through the kitchen doorway, her long, frizzy hair trailing behind her. She was wearing the same kind of dress as the last time he saw her, long and simple, light and airy, but this one was brown with dark green patterns instead of the pale green one she was wearing last time. She wore gold flip-flops with little plastic flowers on the straps. Her jewelry was exactly the same, though. Jingling ring bracelets dangling from both her wrists and a large pendant on a thick gold chain around her slender neck.

"It's good to see you again," she said. Even for such a small woman, her voice seemed so wispy and soft, with such a fragile quality. And yet he knew somehow that there was nothing fragile about her. She was like the gas station attendant. Slight, but profound. And like him, she knew things.

Thinking about it like this, he wondered if he should've guessed all along that she must be his daughter.

"You too," replied Eric.

She strolled right up to him, within inches of his face, as if she meant to kiss him, then stopped and stood there, looking up into his eyes, studying him. "I wish it could be under better circumstances."

"Yeah…"

"Did you find what you were looking for?" asked Nadia.

Cordelia didn't take her eyes off Eric. "Unfortunately," she replied.

"Then she *does* have it."

"Yes."

Eric glanced back and forth between the two of them. "Who has what?" he asked, confused.

But Cordelia didn't answer him. She stood there, staring at him, studying his eyes. She even leaned a little closer.

"Um…?"

"I see you," she sighed.

He wanted to ask her how in the world she could ever *miss* him from this distance, but something about those three words sent a wicked chill racing down his back. A strange, involuntary panic raced through his body, an almost irresistible urge to turn and flee through the nearest door. An unexplainable dread filled him.

Don't make me go! he suddenly thought, though he wasn't sure why he would think such a thing. Then, just as quickly as it came over him, the feeling simply vanished again.

"Hm," said Cordelia, as if she found him incredibly interesting. Then she leaned back again and smiled at him. "Please sit down. We don't have much time."

Chapter Twenty-Seven

"This is how it always is, isn't it?" said Cordelia as she settled into the chair. "Never time for a proper talk. Always in a *rush*. Always running out of time. It's almost as if the universe has to exhaust every other possibility of salvation before it's allowed to summon you."

Eric sat back down on the couch across from her. "Yeah, I've noticed that, too."

She smiled her kind smile and said, "First thing's first: you'll need to be careful. Things will be different from now on."

"Different how?"

"You've drawn a lot of attention to yourself. *Dangerous* attention. Dark things are starting to turn their gazes toward you. Things much bigger than you've dealt with until now. *Godlike* things."

Again with the gods. Why was everyone so hung up on that?

"So…does that mean I messed up?"

Cordelia's smile was sweet and reassuring. "Not at all. It was inevitable."

"You weren't going to be able to fly under the radar forever," agreed Nadia. She was lying on her belly on the floor in the corner of the room and playing with a small, metal box.

That was good to know, he supposed. After all, it wasn't as if he had any idea what the hell he was doing.

"You have far too big a role to play in the events that are unfolding in the universe right now to remain unnoticed," said Cordelia.

He stared at her. "What kinds of events?"

Her eyes gleamed as she replied, "*Profound* ones."

"Ah…"

"We can't tell you everything," said Nadia. She gave the box a gentle twist and transformed it from a cube to a sphere. It appeared to be some sort of complex puzzle box. He wasn't sure where she got it from. He didn't remember seeing it lying around and it was too big to fit in her pockets. "It's like I told you last time we talked. It could really mess things up."

"Right. I remember now." That night in the limousine, while Maxie drove them around the fringe roads, crashing over other-dimensional potholes the size of football fields. She teased him with hints of a greater destiny but warned him that knowing too much about it could doom him to failure. This was the same thing.

"Until recently," explained Cordelia, "there was a second consciousness sleeping within you."

He nodded. Dream Eric. Before he was set free of this mortal shell and off into the hellish acres of Evancurt to his untimely doom.

"That consciousness was helping to shield you from those who would seek to destroy you."

He frowned. "I thought it was what was *attracting* things to me?" That was what Tessa had told him, anyway, after he learned the truth about his time-torn other self.

"It was. It attracted *spirits* to you. But there are things out there beyond the physical and the spiritual. And that surrounding spiritual energy helped to conceal the *other* energies that are attached to you."

He considered this for a moment. He didn't know anything about any *other* energies. Isabelle had never mentioned any other energies. But maybe she couldn't feel them because they were always present. Like the way you tended to get used to a constant smell and stopped noticing it. And now that he was thinking about it, his very connection with Isabelle might give off a certain amount of psychic energy. He was essentially *possessed* by the spirit of that other him. There probably was a certain amount of spiritual energy surrounding him that whole time. But now... "But now I'm all alone," he realized.

"Well..." she said, tilting her head to one side and smiling her mysterious smile again, "...I wouldn't say *alone*."

He supposed she was right. He still had Tessa. She assured him that night that she wouldn't leave him now that his other self had departed. And indeed she was there in the ruins of that old house when he needed her most, just before he came here. So there was still spiritual energy around him. He was still being *haunted*.

"But the other you was a particularly special sort of bond," explained Cordelia.

"A perfect fit," agreed Nadia.

"I guess it would be," he replied. It was *him* after all.

"Moving forward, I'm afraid you'll find yourself in more danger than ever before. Every decision you've made in regard to this business will eventually come back to you in some way, large or small."

"Okay..." He ran his hand through his hair as he processed this. "And I'm guessing you can't give me any details about any of that, either."

"Unfortunately, no."

"Right... So what *are* you allowed to tell me?"

"Everything is changing," replied Nadia. She rolled onto her back and held the metal ball above her small face, peering at it. "The cycle is broken for the first time in eons. The rules have been discarded. The agreement is forfeit. The peace between the Three Powers is breaking down." She pulled a tiny lever and six small, metal arms snapped up from the top of the ball. "Everything's kind of a mess right now."

He shook his head. "Am I supposed to know what any of that means?"

"No," said Cordelia.

"Just checking."

"You're just one of many pieces in another machine," said Nadia. She gripped two of the metal arms and pulled them apart. Slowly, the ball unwound itself into a saucer.

"Gears turning inside a dusty prophecy," sighed Cordelia.

Eric looked back and forth between the two of them, concerned. "You mean like Evancurt?"

"No," said Cordelia. "Nothing so simple."

"Oh…" Evancurt? *Simple*? It ran by luring, trapping and devouring *ghosts*, was built across multiple *dimensions* and simultaneously utilized drastically different and often directly opposing *laws of nature*. How much more complicated could a machine get?

Cordelia smiled her sweet smile. "It's not important," she assured him. "It's not for you to worry about."

"If you say so… What can you tell me about what's happening *today*?" he pressed. "In Creek Bend?"

"Creek Bend is like you," said Nadia. "It's another component in the machine. But like any component in a machine, it can fail." As if to demonstrate, she pushed a small panel on the side of the saucer and the whole thing snapped itself back into a cube again.

"Events are in motion right now," said Cordelia, "that threaten to tear the city—and the machine—apart at its seams."

Eric ran his hand through his hair again. Why did everyone keep talking about machines. Ford said something about that, too, now that he was thinking about it. "You mean the *skinwalkers*."

"They *are* a part of it," replied Cordelia. "But not the whole of it."

"They're just littler pieces in a *smaller* machine," said Nadia. She sat up, crossed her legs beneath her, and gave the puzzle box another twist.

"Is *everything* a machine?" he asked, staring at the curious little box.

"In a manner of speaking," affirmed Cordelia.

He nodded as if he understood.

"Creek Bend is built upon a location of extreme significance in the universe," she went on. "Places like that are dangerous. Places like that *attract things*."

"Things like skinwalkers?"

"All sorts of things," said Nadia, not looking up from her box.

"Take a closer look at the past," advised Cordelia.

"Turn back the pages," agreed Nadia.

"Find what's been lost and make sure what's sleeping doesn't wake up."

"You're definitely gonna wanna hit the snooze button," said Nadia.

He looked back and forth between the two of them, bewildered. "Uh…?"

"The answers will come," promised Cordelia. Her smile was kind and convincing. "In time." She turned and looked over her shoulder at the clock on the fireplace mantle. "But not now. It's time for you to go."

"Oh…" He nodded. "Yeah. Okay."

She stood up and he followed her lead.

"Listen carefully," she said, fixing him with her mysterious gaze again. "You're dealing with a very dangerous enemy today. He's very powerful and very unpredictable. I can't begin to guess at what his goals might be, but you're going to have to be especially careful in these next few hours."

"You're talking about the one who stole the idol and set all this weirdness in motion."

"Yes."

"You know who it is?"

"I know *of* him. I can't tell you where he is right now or even where he came from."

"He kind of exists outside of our range of vision," explained Nadia.

"He's been around a *very* long time," Cordelia went on. "He only turns up every now and then, but he almost always leaves a path of tragedy and chaos in his wake."

"Total menace," said Nadia as she folded the mysterious puzzle box into a star shape.

"Not only has he stolen the object keeping Yee Naaldlooshii bound…" Cordelia informed him, speaking the monster's name in that strange way that kept making him shiver, "…but he's hidden it in the one place you can't reach."

He frowned. "I saw him when we used that spell. He said he was taking it to where 'all the lost things went' or something."

"Inside those forsaken acres," she sighed.

235

Eric didn't understand what she was talking about, but he reached into his coat pocket and withdrew the object he took from the ruined fireplace. "I have this."

"That will lead you to the hidden entrance," she explained, "but to get inside, you'll need the key."

He frowned. "He didn't say anything about a key," he muttered. Then he shook his head. "Okay... Well then, where *is* the key?"

"It *was* hidden safely away in Creek Bend, within easy reach."

"Was?"

"It was stolen," explained Nadia. "Just like the idol."

"So it's gone?"

"No, not gone," replied Cordelia. "I've found where it was taken. But it's in a very dangerous place."

"Of course it is," sighed Eric.

"Come with me." She turned and walked back toward the kitchen.

He followed her.

"Bye!" Nadia called after him. "Good luck!"

He glanced back at her as he left the room. What was he getting himself into now?

Cordelia walked through the kitchen, then turned and stepped into the darkened hallway. "Stay close to me. You don't want to get lost in here."

He didn't pay much attention to this part of the house when he first arrived. His gaze had been drawn toward the living room, where he spent all his time when he was last here. But now it occurred to him that this hallway was a lot longer than it should've been. *Impossibly long*, given the dimensions of the house on the outside. But then again, "impossible" just didn't seem to have the same kind of weight as it used to...

"I don't know what game our enemy is playing," said Cordelia, "but it's a dangerous one. He didn't just steal the key. He took it somewhere even *I* can't get it."

"And where's that?"

"He offered it as a gift. To *her*."

"Her who?"

Another hallway intersected the one they were in and Cordelia turned and followed it to the right, leading him deeper into what was starting to resemble a sprawling hotel rather than a quaint little house. "She's never claimed a name in any modern language," she explained. "In the distant past, when people still knew how to reach her, some referred to her as 'the Barterer' or 'the Dealing Woman.' Others called her 'the Woman of the Hoard,' but she's no woman. She's very ancient, very clever and very powerful. You won't take it from her. Your only option will be to find your way through her city and bargain with her for it."

Why was it so dark in here? The lights in the ceiling weren't very bright and they were located entirely too far apart. The weird always made him feel like he was inside a horror movie, but this seemed particularly unnecessary. "Why do I get the feeling it won't be nearly as easy as you make it sound?"

"I don't expect it to be easy at all." Again, the hallway intersected and again, Cordelia turned. "Her realm is a very dangerous place to be. I'm not sending you to haggle with some used car salesman. She's cunning and ruthless. And she won't let such a treasure go for nothing. She *always* wins." She turned and looked at him, her eyes disturbingly sad. "There's no way around it. I'm afraid I'll be sending you to make a deal with the devil."

"Oh…"

"That probably sounds like I'm being melodramatic," sighed Cordelia.

"No, I'd say that fits in just right with today's events," said Eric. He'd already joined forces with an agent and took part in the casting of a forbidden spell. Why *not* add dealing with a devil to the mix?

Besides, wasn't "bargaining" one of the words Holly saw in the divination? And so was an endless hallway, now that he was thinking about it. He looked back and forth. Although there were intersections here and there, he hadn't seen a single dead end. Each new hallway he passed seemed to go on forever. And the farther they went, the more distance there was between the doors, too. He thought at the time that maybe what Paige saw in the water was referring to the secret tunnel in the museum's basement, but once again he found himself looking at exactly what was revealed.

"You can't be fully prepared to face her," warned Cordelia, "but I can give you some general rules to guide you. First, don't forget that she has you at a disadvantage. She knows you need the key. She won't give it up unless she benefits more than you do. You can't beat her. You're going to be the loser in this, no matter what you do. You can only reduce the cost of the trade as much as possible."

"So...pretty much just try to come back with my soul?"

"That would be preferable, certainly."

He ran his hand through his hair. He said that more in jest than anything, but now he was seriously wondering if this Woman of the Hoard might actually deal in souls. "But what can I possibly have that she'd even want?"

"You *don't* have anything like that."

"Oh..."

"But you might be able to *get* something like that."

Why was that bad feeling he had about this whole situation only getting worse?

"Offer her the Skies of Esepthal."

Eric canted his head to one side, confused. "What?"

"Don't concern yourself with what it is. Not today. It's like the gentleman at the museum warned you about opening doors. If all goes well, you'll have to find out in time, but there's no reason to concern yourself yet with things you can't control. It would only be cruel."

He ran his hand through his hair. "If you say so." *Skies of Esepthal...* he thought, committing the name to memory. "But how do I even know I can trust this...whatever she is?"

"Well, that's the second rule. She won't lie to you. She doesn't deal like that. She doesn't have to."

"Well that should make it a *little* easier," he reasoned.

"I wouldn't necessarily say *that*," she replied. "you'll still need to be very careful."

He nodded. "Count on it."

"The third rule…" she went on. "And this is *very* important. No matter what she offers you, *don't* be tempted to bargain for anything else."

"Why would I?"

"Don't get cocky. She's *very* clever. She knows your innermost desires, perhaps even better than you do. Above all, she's a temptress."

He nodded. "All right. Noted."

Finally, she stopped and turned to face a door.

It didn't seem to be a particularly special door. It looked just like all the others. He wasn't sure how she could even tell them apart.

"This is it. You'll be on your own from here."

"All right then. Let's get it over with."

She gave him another of those kind smiles and then pushed open the door. A set of dark stairs waited on the other side to carry him deeper into the darkness.

He stepped through the doorway and stared down into the gloom, his heart swelling with dread at the task before him.

"One last thing," said Cordelia.

He paused and looked back over his shoulder.

"About the things that dwell in the city."

"Yes?"

"Whatever you do…don't look them in the eyes."

As he stood there, letting those ominous words circle around in his head, the mysterious Cordelia closed the door between them.

Chapter Twenty-Eight

Eric descended the dark steps, his heart pounding with grim anticipation. What had he gotten himself into now? The compass was supposed to be the last thing he needed. But now not only did he have to find a *key* in order to *reach* the place where the thief hid the idol, but he was going to have to do some heavy haggling with what sounded like the sketchiest shopkeeper in the universe.

Why couldn't it ever just be easy?

The stairs descended through the darkness, gently curving, winding farther and farther downward, illuminated by the dingy light trickling through narrow, vertical shafts cut through the sloped ceiling twelve feet above him. He looked up into the dreary glow each time he passed beneath one and felt again and again as if he were looking up through a manhole from the depths of some vast sewer system.

And for all he knew, that was precisely what this was. Cordelia did say it was a city, after all.

But if that was the case, shouldn't he be going *up* instead of *down*?

Ahead of him, the steps leveled off into a landing from which two more staircases branched off, one straight ahead, the other to the left, both of them continuing downward. The latter was considerably brighter, so he chose that way and continued on.

A moment later, he stepped out of the darkness and into an eerie twilight. He peered up at a hazy, orange-tinted sky framed by rocky earth and high stone walls.

That definitely wasn't the sky he left behind in Creek Bend. Not only was it the wrong color, it seemed to be missing both clouds and a sun. The air was a little colder, too. He could faintly see his breath when he exhaled. And it *smelled* different. There was an unusual staleness to it. It tasted bland. It tasted *sterile*.

He withdrew the old pocket watch and confirmed with little surprise that the wheels were turning even faster now than they were in the woods approaching Cordelia's house.

This was yet another world, one even farther from home.

He pulled out his phone and looked at it. He didn't expect to have a signal, but he was hoping that Isabelle would at least be able to get through. He already knew, however, that she couldn't, because she would've contacted him as soon as they were reconnected, if only to let him know she was there again. And he quickly realized that even if she *were* able to connect with him, she couldn't talk to him if she wanted to. The battery had gone dead.

When did that happen? It was working fine until he approached Cordelia's house.

He pulled out his portable charger, feeling rather proud of himself for being prepared this time, only to discover that it, too, was dead.

He frowned at the two devices. He was sure the portable was fully charged. Did he grab a dead one by mistake?

No. Something else had happened. He looked at his watch and found that even *that* battery was dead. Something had drained every bit of electrical power he had on him.

Was it those starved spirits? All those old ghost hunting shows he used to watch talked about how spirits could drain batteries in order to manifest themselves. Was that what happened? Had they drained all but a little bit of his phone battery so that he and Isabelle used the last of it in the woods before he reached Cordelia's house?

But he didn't recall noticing that the battery was low while talking to Isabelle. He felt like he wouldn't have overlooked something like that. Not on a day when he really needed it.

Perhaps it was something about *this* place, instead. Maybe there was something about this world that sapped away electrical energy. Evancurt was like that, he recalled. That was why there were no phones or vehicles.

Whatever the reason, he didn't like it. Without his phone, he was alone. Just like in Evancurt.

The very thought was enough to tighten his gut into a steaming knot.

"Okay, take it easy," he muttered to himself as he turned and surveyed the queer city. "I mean, there's probably a Starbucks around here somewhere, right? They're everywhere else."

Cracking jokes wasn't nearly as fun without Isabelle to tell him he wasn't that funny.

He returned the useless phone and charger to his pants pockets and looked around. He was standing on a circular patio-like area paved with cobblestones. From here, several stone archways led down into even more underground stairwells like the one he'd just exited. Several more sets of stairs also led down, but remained above ground, hugging a sloping hillside crowded with stone walls. Still other stairs waited to carry him *upward*.

He stood there a moment, unsure where to go. This was a confusing configuration. It didn't make sense. And Cordelia didn't give him any directions for *how* to get to wherever this so-called "Woman of the Hoard" was waiting, only how to deal with her once he arrived.

What was he supposed to do?

He turned his attention to the steepest of the stairways leading up. Maybe if he just found a higher vantage point, the way forward would be clear.

But after he made his way up and finally laid eyes on the greater city, he realized that he would have no such luck. Sprawled out below him was an absurd labyrinth of stairways, all of them winding around, climbing over or carving through a dizzying landscape of steep mountain slopes, deep gorges and sheer cliff faces.

"What the hell...?" he grumbled. Who would even come up with something like this? It made no sense. He couldn't even see any buildings. There were no doorways or windows, only those arched tunnel openings. Every surface was either a stairway or a stairway landing transitioning to more stairways.

"Stairs..." he grumbled. Poppy did tell him they saw stairs

in the divination. Alicia even specified that there were *lots* of them.

This had to be the absolute *least* handicap-accessible city in the known universe. If the people who lived here didn't have buns of steel, they weren't even trying.

If anyone had ever lived here. Cordelia had called it a city, but the lack of any visible dwellings seemed to suggest that it was something else. He didn't see anything here *except* stairs.

But *something* had to be here. Cordelia told him so. She'd warned him not to look them in the eyes, which was a surprisingly creepy thought, even after the day he'd already had.

He glanced around once more, then continued upward.

How did he end up in a place like this, anyway? When he woke up this morning, all he was supposed to have to do was help Karen with the book signing. Now he was wandering around in an entirely different universe where there was ten thousand ways to travel up and down the mountainsides but not a single bench on which to sit and rest.

He was getting really sick of the weird. He just wanted to be normal again. He missed being normal.

The stairs leveled out onto another cobblestone-paved landing. On his left was a sheer drop overlooking a sprawling expanse of the city. In front of him and on his right were three more sets of stairs, two of them continuing upward and one descending back down into the mountainside through another of those gloomy tunnels.

It would help if he knew where the hell he was supposed to be.

If the Woman of the Hoard lived here, then where was she? He stepped closer to the ledge and peered out over the city. He had a good view from up here. If there was something here, he should be able to see it.

And then he *did* see something. A little farther along the ridge, at the top of the highest peak, a large number of winding stairs appeared to converge on a single, large opening near the hazy peak of the mountain.

Could he see *windows* carved into the rock face?

An actual building after all?

He scanned the whole scene again, his thoughts churning. Maybe it wasn't a city after all. Maybe it was a literal labyrinth. Was this whole place nothing more than an elaborate maze ingeniously designed to confuse and slow down anyone seeking to deal with the Woman of the Hoard?

He couldn't decide if that was a brilliant deduction or the most ridiculous thought ever. But the more he thought about it, the more convinced he became that this was the only explanation that made any sense. Why else would someone go to the trouble of building something like this?

The only thing missing was a fearsome minotaur to guard the whole thing.

And yet, as he peered down over the edge of the cliff at the lowest levels of the city, he caught sight of something moving down there. A dark and shadowy shape was slowly making its way up a stairway. (And really, what else would it be doing, except maybe making its way *down* a stairway?) He couldn't tell what the thing was from this distance, but although it seemed to have a mostly human shape, he was quite sure it *wasn't* human. Even from here, he could tell that there was something dreadfully *wrong* about it.

And now that he'd seen one, he found that he could see another. Farther off to his right, about halfway up the mountain slope, another was slowly descending.

Then he spotted another.

And another.

How many of them were there?

(Don't look them in the eyes.)

A shiver raced down his back and he turned and scanned the area around him, half-convinced that he was going to find one creeping up behind him.

But he was still alone. For now.

He glanced up at the opening in the mountain top, then selected the stairs that seemed to be pointed in that direction and began to climb.

He didn't like this. Just what had he gotten himself into?

The steps leveled off again a short distance up the mountain, this time offering him two choices. He could continue up to his right or he could travel straight ahead, but down again, both of them cutting through those creepy, poorly lit tunnels.

He ran his hand through his hair, frustrated. This could take all day.

Was that the plan? Was this what the idol thief intended? For him to waste the next few precious hours lost in this vertical labyrinth while Yenaldlooshi finished waking up?

What if it was waking up *right now*? What if he returned from this place only to find the entire city in ruins?

No... He didn't have time to waste thinking about it. He set off down the steps in front of him. It opened up again at the bottom and he could see the cobblestones glowing in the orange twilight.

But as he neared the bottom, a shadowy form stepped into his path.

He froze, his heart stuttering in his chest. Then he quickly scurried back up the way he came before the thing could see him, cursing under his breath the whole way.

What *were* those things?

He crouched down and risked a look back.

He could see its shadow at the very bottom of the steps. It seemed to be just standing there. Had it heard him? Did it know he was there?

A tense few seconds passed, then the shadow, and presumably the thing attached to it, turned and shuffled off in the other direction.

His heart still pounding, he headed back up to the previous landing and took the stairs leading higher into the mountain.

He didn't like this. It was bad enough being lost in a labyrinth. But to have to dodge monsters as well? The odds of him ever finding his way to that highest peak were getting slimmer and slimmer.

He made his way through the next passage and found himself at the base of a tall, winding staircase with no monsters in sight.

But he glanced back the way he came. Even if he did succeed here, how in the world was he supposed to find his way
back? Cordelia never explained that part to him. He wasn't sure
he could find that first staircase again already, much less by the
time he'd gotten himself utterly lost. And even if he did, was he
capable of finding his way back through that endless maze of
hallways inside the yellow house?

Would that door even open for him?

He sighed. One thing at a time. That was the only way to
get through this sort of thing. He turned, his legs already aching,
and continued up the endless steps.

Chapter Twenty-Nine

Eric stopped climbing and looked around. He was gasping for breath, his feet and sides aching, his thighs and butt burning, his heart pounding like a bass drum. These last stairs had seemed to go on and on, winding higher and higher into the strange landscape, never branching or leveling off. And now he stood looking out over the eerie city from a towering vantage point that revealed more of it than he'd yet seen. It seemed to go on forever, stretching past the surrounding mountain valley, to every horizon, even farther than he first realized.

And he could reach none of it from here.

After all that, the stairs had simply ended. Before him was a sheer three-hundred-foot drop and nothing more.

He swallowed hard, wheezing, sweat dripping down his face. "Well, shit," he gasped.

Then he turned, defeated, and made his way back down again.

Chapter Thirty

Eric sat down on the cold stone, gasping and wheezing as if he'd just finished a marathon and wondering, not for the first time, just what the hell the universe was thinking when it chose *him* for these things.

He was breathing hard. His body hurt. He was sweating profusely in spite of the chill in the air. Even his head was spinning. He felt dizzy from the exertion.

And all he'd done was make his way up to that pointless dead end and back!

In all his weird travels, he'd found himself in many perilous situations, a great many of which were, in all honesty, *stupid* ways to die. At various points along the way, he was attacked by angry apes, narrowly avoided being gored by the alien equivalent of a buffalo, was nearly eaten by a giant fish *and* a giant frog and came unsettlingly close to being strangled by an irritable tree, just to name a few. And at this rate he wouldn't be surprised if he simply dropped dead from heart failure while trying to navigate a labyrinth of *stairways* because he was too lazy to ever get his stupid ass in shape no matter how many times he found himself in situations like these.

Seriously, shouldn't the universe's "chosen one" at least be someone with a *gym membership*?

He leaned forward, propped his elbows on his knees and rubbed his weary eyes.

Did Cordelia really expect him to be able to handle this?

He lowered his hands and opened his eyes to find a pair of withered black legs standing there in front of him.

He felt the blood drain from his face. Stark terror filled every nerve ending in his body.

He lifted his head, his horrified gaze sliding up the strange body that stood before him, following legs at least as high as his whole body was tall to the matching, withered torso of a towering, shadowy figure bending over him, staring down at him, its head drawing closer and closer.

Don't look them in the eyes!

He forced his eyes shut and lowered his head.

That was close!

And yet…what did it matter? It was right there in front of him. It was looking right at him. It didn't need to make eye contact to rip his head off. (Or however these things usually dealt with trespassers.) It was only a matter of seconds before he felt those long, black hands seize him.

But those very seconds passed and the monster didn't move.

His head bowed as far as possible, he dared to crack one eye open, just a little, just enough to see what it was doing.

Those legs were still there. It wasn't moving.

It seemed to be just standing there, staring down at him, studying him.

What was happening? Was it playing with him? Was it confused?

His heart racing, his body trembling with fear, he glanced around at what little he could see from this limited perspective.

The monster was standing on the landing while he sat on the lowest steps. Behind him was nothing but the exhausting climb back up to that dead end. Ahead of him were two more stairways, but he wasn't going to be able to get to either of them without pushing past the monster.

What was the thing doing, anyway? He could see its shadow moving. It still seemed to be bending over him, studying him. Any second now it would grow bored of whatever it was doing and finish him off. He was sure of it.

And yet it continued to do nothing.

He lifted his head a little, risking a better look around, and peered to his right. Beyond the steps was a steep, rocky slope.

He tried to remember what the landscape over there looked like the first time he came through here, but he couldn't quite recall. A lot of the landscape here was comprised of vertical cliff faces. If he weren't careful, he could end up a broken heap at the bottom of one of them.

But long, icy fingers raked down the side of his face and he discovered how quickly he could stop worrying about such things.

He launched himself to his feet, bolted over the low wall and tried to run, but his feet stumbled over the loose rocks and uneven surface. He slipped and staggered, narrowly missing an open hole that must've led down to one of those tunnels.

It wasn't wide enough for him to go tumbling down, he didn't think, but a broken leg certainly wasn't out of the question.

Sure that the monster must be right on his heels, he forced himself to go on. He could see another stairway up ahead, carved into the mountainside. If he could reach that, he could make a run for it.

But the slope grew too steep and treacherous. His foot went out from under him. He fell. He rolled. Rocks clawed at him as he slid down the mountainside, catching at him, knocking him around.

Then the ground disappeared altogether. He was falling.

A fresh surge of panic filled him.

This was it.

This was the stupid way he was going to die.

Then, much sooner than he expected, he hit the ground. Hard, sharp edges hit him like blunted axe blades, digging into his ribs, shoulder and spine. A hard blow to the back of his head sent the spinning world around him out of focus and a dizzying display of colorful stars darting through his vision.

He slid for some distance down the hard stone steps, feeling every rise and run along the way until at last he came to a stop and lay there, groaning, unable to breathe, his body racked with pain and a drizzle of gravel and rocks raining down around him.

Okay…so he was still alive. If not, he was fairly sure it wouldn't hurt this much.

That didn't go nearly as he'd hoped it would. Something

almost certainly had to be broken.

Time crawled by. Then, finally, he regained his breath and scanned his surroundings. He was alone again. Whatever the tall, black figure was, it didn't seem to have followed him. It probably knew better.

Grunting with pain, he forced himself to sit up and took a quick assessment of the damage.

He could still feel his legs. That was good. He didn't seem to be bleeding profusely. Also good. And none of his limbs were bent at a weird angle. This was going *much* better than he expected.

He rose to his feet, wincing at sharp pains in his back and shoulder. His sides hurt when he took a breath.

Broken ribs?

Even if they *were* broken, there wasn't much he could do about it. He was just going to have to carry on until he found his way out of this new nightmare.

He looked back and forth, gathering his bearings, for all that was worth, and set off hobbling down the steps, hopefully in the direction he wanted to go.

He was limping a little, but he didn't seem to be hurt that bad. As he carried on, his joints loosened up. His breathing became easier. His muscles continued to ache, but that wasn't really surprising. They were aching *before* he decided to body surf the mountainside.

All things considered, he was doing okay.

Until he reached the bottom of the steps and another towering black figure stepped from a tunnel opening and turned to face him.

He averted his eyes and turned around, only to find that another one was making its way down the steps from above.

Cursing, he covered his eyes and carefully surveyed the ground around him. Going off-road definitely wasn't an option this time. There was a sheer wall on one side and a deadly drop on the other.

The monsters closed in on either side of him. He could see their shadows as they approached, their long, upper bodies stretched forward, their arms seeming to float at their sides, looking at him.

"Don't look them in the eyes…" he muttered.

Maybe that's all there was to it?

With no other choices available to him, he took a shaky, aching breath and continued down the steps, toward the first of the two monsters.

His heart was pounding with terror, yet as he walked around the creature, it didn't attempt to grab him. It only stopped and turned with him, following him. Step by step, he continued on his way, unimpeded.

They really weren't going to do anything to him as long he didn't look them in the eyes? Was that really the only thing that made them dangerous? It seemed ridiculous, but he was in no condition to complain. Although he did wish he knew this fact *before* he fell down the mountain.

And they were still creepy as all kinds of hell.

He dared a look back, careful to shield his eyes with his hand lest he be too tempted to look up, and saw both pairs of withered, black feet following him down the steps.

"Okay…" he muttered, facing forward again. "This is how it's going to go, I guess…"

Chapter Thirty-One

Hours seemed to pass. He wasn't sure how many. That strange, twilight glow never changed. He had no sense of time whatsoever.

Was this one of those places where time didn't pass the same as it did in the real world? He hoped so, because Yenaldlooshi wasn't going to be asleep much longer.

He wandered up and down the endless stairways, choosing directions as they seemed to make sense when possible, completely at random when not. Several times, he found himself at dead ends and forced to backtrack, always having to slink back past the towering black figures that had followed him there.

He was picking up more of them as he went. There were at least eight of them back there now. Maybe ten. It was hard to count something you couldn't really look at.

They never made any attempt to attack or grab him. They didn't even block his path. Whenever he was forced to move toward them, they always stepped aside, always made room.

They *seemed* perfectly harmless. But he knew better.

He carried on and on, forcing his gaze down to the ground in front of him, lest he make eye-contact and find out what made these things so fearsome that Cordelia had made it a point to warn him. He wasn't sure what exactly would happen. Maybe these things were like Karen's Great Aunt Veronica and would talk his ear off about their most recent batch of health issues if he showed even the slightest sign that he had an idle moment. He'd made that mistake before and if what these things intended to do to him was *half* as unpleasant as the gritty details about Aunt Vera's irritable bowel syndrome, then he *really* didn't want to take any chances.

He wasn't sure how much time had passed, only that his

legs and body were nearing their limit. He was exhausted. He was bruised and scraped. He was starting to think this awful ordeal would never end.

Then, at some point, he stepped out of a darkened tunnel and peered up the steps ahead of him to see the opening in the highest mountain looming directly over him.

Finally!

He picked up his pace and climbed faster. But just because the ending was in sight didn't mean it was easy. It was at least another three hundred steps, and his aching legs made it feel like three *thousand*.

But eventually he found his way to the opening in the mountain. It was much bigger up close, at least as large as an airplane hangar. And the inside was so vast that the ring of windows circling the room did very little to illuminate what awaited him inside.

As he entered the deep gloom, he risked another look back to see what the monsters behind him were doing, but they had stopped some distance back without him realizing it. They were now only a crowd of thin, black figures watching him, the features of their mysterious faces too distant to allow eye contact.

Somehow, having lost his creepy entourage didn't fill him with much relief. After all, what were *they* afraid of?

He turned his attention to the darkness in front of him and walked forward.

The floor was different in here. It wasn't made of the same rough cobblestone as outside. In fact, it wasn't stone at all. It was soft soil. And the deeper into the darkness he went, the muddier it became.

It smelled awful in here. Swamp-like. Like rotten vegetation and dank, moldy places. And like something else, too, something musky. Something *sweaty*.

Something was dripping from the ceiling, creating a slow pitter and plink of rain on the surface of the puddles around him.

He could feel cold water seeping through his shoes and into his socks.

Something was moving in the darkness ahead of him.

No...*several* somethings. Barely visible things wriggled in the darkness all around him, squirming and burbling in the mud. A long, wet, squelching noise originated from somewhere ahead of him.

He wasn't alone here. This whole room was alive.

And it was watching him.

He stopped walking and listened to the awful sounds around him. Seconds passed with nothing happening. Then, just as he was about to call out, a strange, whispery voice spoke up in the darkness: "What do you want?"

Eric suppressed a hard shiver. Good. It seemed that they were getting right down to business. "I was told you have something I need."

Silence followed this.

"It's a key," he explained. "Am I in the right place? Are you the one who has it?"

"I have *lots* of keys," replied the mysterious voice.

All around him, those wet, squelching, bubbling noises rose up again. At the same time, he heard small, metal things clinking and clanking together in the darkness. It did, indeed, sound like lots of keys jangling together.

"Keys to all sorts of things."

"It's a special key," explained Eric. "It's..." He tried to remember what the thing in Yenaldlooshi's memory said. "It's for the place where all the forgotten things have gone," he finished. "The place where I need to go."

"Is that so?"

Eric stared into the darkness. "Somehow, I think you already knew all this."

"Perhaps I did. Perhaps I didn't. What would you give me to tell you?"

"Nothing," he quickly replied. "I'm only here for the key. Nothing else."

"Fine..." The darkness churned before his eyes. Something was moving in the mud. Cold water flooded over the tops of his shoes. He shivered, but not because of the chill. It felt as if something in that darkness was looking very closely at him, *ap-*

praising him. "For the key, then…"

"I've been warned about you," he said, trying to keep his voice even. "I know how you do things. I'm willing to deal, but I won't pay just any price."

The very darkness seemed to shudder with a menacing laugh. "Is that so?"

"I know you won't take less than the key is worth to you. I know that you'll come out the winner in any deal we make. I'll accept that. But that also means that if I walk out of here without the key, *you* lose, too, because that key is worth less than whatever you would've settled for. So how about we skip the part where you try to screw me over and start bargaining reasonably?"

"Clever boy…" sighed the voice in the darkness. This time, it sounded like it came from right behind him. "So tell me, what do you think is a fair price for the key to saving everyone you love?"

He took a breath, steeling himself against the terrible aura he felt emanating from whatever this thing was. Woman of the Hoard? Cordelia was right. This *thing* was no woman, not by any stretch of the imagination. Forcing his voice to remain even, he said, "The Skies of Esepthal," just as Cordelia had instructed.

That strange, monstrous presence shifted and circled around him. He looked back over his shoulder and caught sight of a strange, slithery shape silhouetted against the hazy orange glare of the open doorway.

"Is that all?" whispered the terrible voice of the monstrous Woman of the Hoard.

Eric furrowed his brow. "Isn't that enough?"

"For everyone you love?"

"It's a fair price. More than fair. You know it."

"Is it?"

"Yes." But of course he knew no such thing for certain. He only had Cordelia's word that the Skies of Esepthal…whatever the hell that was…was worth anything at all, much less the key to saving Creek Bend and everyone in it.

What was he supposed to do if she refused to trade for it? It was the only bargaining chip he had.

"It should be worth more than that to *you*." It slithered around him again. Something slimy brushed his cheek in the darkness, making him cringe. "Isn't that worth, say…*your life*?"

"No."

"Really? All their lives aren't worth yours?"

"No, because they'll need me again. And I think you know that, too."

"You mean that little *karmic sin* you're carrying around inside you?"

"If I die today, I can't save them when the time comes to pay for that sin. They won't have a chance."

"And you really think you can overturn karmic retribution?"

"I have to believe I can."

"Interesting." Again, the thing squirmed and slithered through the darkness, splashing cold water over his feet and kicking up more of that foul stench. "So let's assume you *can* save them. What about after? If you're still alive when the dust settles and they no longer need you to save them, would it be worth your life *then*?"

This was a creepy conversation. And he thought door-to-door salesmen were pushy. "I can't know that now. They may *always* need me."

"That's an arrogant assumption."

"It's arrogant to assume I can make things so I *won't* always be needed."

Again, that creepy laugh rolled through the room. "Well then, what about *another* life?"

"*Another* life? As in *someone else's* life?"

"Why not?"

"That's not mine to give."

"Any life is yours to give, just as any life is yours to take, as long as you're willing."

He shook his head. "That's awful. Why are we discussing this? I only want a key. Why are you talking about lives? You could ask for anything." He glanced around. "How about a lamp for this place? It's a freaking *dungeon* in here."

But the Woman of the Hoard didn't seem to be listening.

"You act as if you've never traded a life for your own."

He clenched his jaw. "That's not the same. My hand was forced."

"Do you really believe that?"

"It wasn't my choice."

"And that makes it different?"

He wasn't entirely sure how to reply to that. Sure, he'd made choices that cost others their lives, but it was those same people who forced him to make those choices. The foggy man. Pink Shirt and the cowboy. Sissy Dodd. Fettarsetter. The blood witches.

God, the list just went on and on, didn't it?

But he didn't make those decisions. *They* forced them on him.

Didn't they?

"Interesting…" sighed the voice. "Then tell me *this*. Would you trade the life of someone who is destined to cause you nothing but misery?"

"What?"

"Someone who will stand in your way. Someone who will take something precious from you. Someone who will only force your hand in the end anyway."

He stared into the darkness, uncertain.

"I see a man with the image of a spider on his left hand. A man who has done terrible things already. A man whose actions will bring you and countless others nothing but pain." Something in the darkness slithered closer. "Tell me… Is *his* life worth the lives of those you're trying to save today?"

Eric clenched his fists. "No. I won't deal in lives. That's final."

The thing in the darkness shifted and churned. Something heavy squelched through the mud. "Pity. I thought you needed this key."

Eric stared at the ever-shifting shape in the darkness. "I made my offer. The Skies of Esepthal." (Whatever that meant.)

"Not enough," hissed the Woman of the Hoard.

He stared at the wriggling shapes in the darkness for a moment. "Fine. I guess I'll just have to find another way then." He turned and walked back toward the doorway, but something sharp jabbed into his back and he froze. Suddenly, there was a monstrous face looming beside him, a face so terrible he couldn't quite seem to process exactly what he was looking at.

"And what makes you think I won't just take your life anyway?"

Eric found himself staring into a pair of strange, muddy eyes. Was he supposed to be looking at those? Cordelia never specified whether he should look into *her* eyes. He was just going to have to assume that, since he wasn't dead yet, it was okay.

"Do you have an answer for *that?*"

The pain in his back intensified as something pressed harder into his skin.

"Answer quickly."

"You can't kill me," replied Eric through clenched teeth. "You wouldn't have tried to trade the key for it if you could just take it."

"But I *can* take it. *Easily.*" As if to demonstrate, she pressed the sharp thing even harder into him. He could feel warm blood trickling down his back.

"Exactly," grunted Eric.

This seemed to catch her off guard. "What?"

"If you can just take it, then it has no value for you. And if it has no value, then you get nothing. Just like if I walk out that door right now, you're left with only the key and you lose."

Everything was silent for a moment.

Eric held his breath and clenched his jaw against the pain in his back.

Then the sharp thing vanished and the thing in the shadows laughed. "I think I like you."

He turned to face it again.

"Fine. Bring me the Skies of Esepthal. If you can."

"I can," he insisted, confident. After all, Cordelia wouldn't have told him to bargain with it if he couldn't…right? "But first I have to finish my work in Creek Bend."

Something squirmed in the darkness at his feet and he

looked down to see a small, wooden box being pushed up out of the mud.

"Do not forget your promise," she hissed.

"I won't." Although he couldn't help but wonder if he'd regret waiting to meet the man with the spider on his left hand... Would there come a day when he sorely wished he'd accepted that offer? "I'm not sure how long it'll take me, though."

"I am patient."

He bent down and picked up the box. It was heavier than he thought a key should be. And much bigger. Whatever was rattling around inside was much more than just a housekey. "Okay, then," he said, turning away. "I'll be going."

"Are you sure there's nothing else you need?"

"Yep. I got what I came for." He picked up his pace. Cordelia warned him not to make any more deals. The sooner he left, the better.

"Not even a cure for your karmic sin?"

He paused. He couldn't help it.

"I can do that."

"No. We'll handle it on our own."

"I can give back lives as well as take them, you know."

He glanced back over his shoulder. "What?"

"That girl...the one who died in your arms..."

Sylvia Dodd... Sissy Dodd's innocent alternate personality...

"I could give her back to you, you know. Stitch her soul back together. I can even separate her from the wicked one. You could give her back to her sisters and finally be free of all that guilt."

Eric turned to face the doorway again. This was just cruel. Bring back poor, innocent Sylvia Dodd? He could have hope that they'd find a way to save everyone from the karmic sin...but bringing Sylvia back was something they simply weren't ever going to be able to do.

"Or perhaps..." sighed the voice, "...you'd like me to set free the little girl inside your head."

He tightened his grip on the box. "That's not fair..."

"Everyone has things they want. You're no different."

He stared into the light of the open doorway, clutching the box. Set Isabelle free at last? Let her finally return home to her parents?

And poor Sylvia...

"I could give you both of them, you know. I'll only charge you one more favor."

He turned to face the darkness. He could see her there, a monstrous, looming form in the shadows. "No," he said, the word tearing at his heart like thorns. "I'm only here for the key. That's my final answer."

"Have it your way," sighed the voice. Then something cold and slimy shot out of the darkness and pierced his chest.

He let out a startled gasp.

"But if you ever change your mind, you know where to find me."

Then the darkness became absolute.

Chapter Thirty-Two

He drifted through the cold darkness, lost and confused. A very long time seemed to pass, with nothing but brief, dream-like fragments of thoughts and memories to break up the maddening emptiness, and even those were few and far between.

His only clear awareness was that he'd been here before. But that awareness was as much as his scattered mind was able to process. He couldn't begin to remember *when* he'd been here before, or where, or how he came to be there, much less how to escape.

Sometimes, he only floated there, hovering in the emptiness, only half-conscious, like that cozy dreamlike place his mind went just before he fell asleep at night. Other times he found himself seized by the icy grip of sheer terror. And still other times he found himself slowly spiraling into the black depths of lonely, agonizing despair.

Occasionally, voices drifted to him through this darkness. They were familiar voices, though he couldn't make out what they were saying. They seemed very distant from this place. And they didn't seem to be talking to him. It was little more than random snippets of casual conversation carried across the endless nothingness. Whenever he tried to focus on them, they withdrew back into silence and his thoughts broke apart again, plunging him back into confusing darkness.

But the worst, by far, was the monsters.

He couldn't see them. Nor could he hear them. But they were there. He could *feel* them. They swam the blackness of the abyss all around him, massive, unthinkable things passing through the void. They were pure nightmare, darker and more terrible than anything ever imagined. He knew, somehow, that the mere sight of one would drive him utterly and irreversibly insane. And he was floating through their world like a tiny speck of plankton tossed upon the waves churned up by the passing of a pod of great whales, merely waiting for the inevitable moment when he'd eventually be sucked in and swallowed whole. But day after day seemed to pass in the monstrous emptiness and nothing ate him.

Then something changed. He realized he wasn't floating anymore. He was standing, though he couldn't remember there being a point in which his feet touched the ground. There was no transition between the two states.

He turned, searching his surroundings, trying to remember if this, too, was somewhere he'd been before. His senses seemed to have returned. For the first time in a while, he could think. Though he couldn't quite recall what he was doing the last time he was able to think.

Confused, he chose a direction at random and began to walk.

There were more voices in this place. He could hear a conversation. He tried to follow the sound of the words, but he couldn't tell which direction it was coming from. In fact, the very *concept* of direction seemed to escape him here. He couldn't discern forward or left from back or right or even up from down.

Then someone was standing in front of him. Someone he knew. A woman. She had her back turned to him. Her blonde hair was tied into a messy bun. She was wearing an oversized sweatshirt.

Perri...

His heart leapt in his chest. Perri was here. That murmuring conversation was everyone back in his kitchen. Was he home? Had he finally found his way back from this endless darkness?

He reached out to her, tried to lay his hand on her shoulder, but although he seemed to be standing right behind her, he found that he couldn't reach her from here.

But he didn't need to reach her. She gasped and turned around, those strikingly different-colored eyes fixing on his. "Eric!"

He was still reaching out for her, his hand floating in the

empty space between them that seemed so strangely to be both mere inches and endless lightyears.

All around him, he could hear voices muttering in surprise.

"Where are you?" she asked. "What's happening?"

He opened his mouth to speak, but no words would come.

What was this place? What was happening? Even the voices were asking questions. They wanted to know what she was seeing.

Perri reached out to him then. And although he couldn't seem to reach her, he discovered that *she* could somehow reach *him*. Her slender fingers enlaced in his, latching onto him.

And then, in an instant, he seemed to fall. He clung to her hand, never letting go, and yet he plunged through this empty, timeless space, hurdling through a bottomless abyss.

And then, without any transition at all, he was sitting in a tiny chair at a tiny table in a tiny little house, with a little girl's tea set spread out before him.

Tea party… he thought, his mind finally clearing. Paige said she saw him sitting at a tea party.

He turned and looked around. He knew this place. This was where he first heard Perrine's name. And where he had his first glimpse of her. This was the treehouse back in Evancurt. But it wasn't old and rotten. It was bright and new. There was warm sunlight shining through the window and door. This wasn't the treehouse as it'd been in January. This was the treehouse as it was in that strange flashback he experienced. This was the treehouse as Perri had known it.

"What just happened…?" said a small voice.

The seat across from him was empty when he turned away, but when he turned back again, he found that Perri was now sitting there. Except she, too, wasn't the Perri he knew. The girl sitting there was only about twelve. This was the Perri who entered the Evancurt machine, before she was plunged into the void for nearly half a century. This was the Perri *she* still thought she was, he realized. This was who Perri still was in her own mind. She was even wearing the same dress she was wearing when he took her from that timeless place, except that it actually fit her again.

She looked down at herself, confused. "What's going on?"

Before he could begin to tell her that he had no idea what was happening, a telephone rang.

Both of them turned to find that the cup and saucer at the place beside them had turned into an old-fashioned office phone with a blinking red light.

He glanced at Perri, then reached out and pressed the button.

"Well, this is new," said Isabelle from the phone's speaker.

"What's happening?" Eric asked her.

"I have no idea. You were out in the woods after you escaped those starved spirits. Then you just sort of disappeared. You know you scare the hell out of me when you do that, right?"

"Sorry," he said, although he didn't think it was his fault. It wasn't like he had the option to just mute himself whenever he felt like being alone. "How long have I been gone?"

"About an hour."

"Is that all?"

"It's long enough to have all of us worried sick! What happened to you? And where *are* we?"

He looked around at the treehouse again. His head was much clearer. All that floating business he'd experienced suddenly felt like nothing more than a brief dream. And yet, he must still be asleep. He couldn't really be back in the treehouse in Evancurt. That treehouse was half a century old and falling apart. And he didn't think it existed anymore. It was gone. *All* of Evancurt was gone.

But it felt so real... He could see the leaves of the forest swaying outside the window, the mottled sunlight dancing across the dusty glass. He could feel the breeze blowing in from the open doorway overlooking the porch. It smelled like summer.

He shook his head. Everything was coming back to him now. "Wait! *The key!*" He was holding it in his hands when the Woman of the Hoard lashed out at him and sent him hurdling through the universe.

"Don't freak out," said Isabelle. "I'm sure it'll be wherever your body is when you wake up."

"My body?" He was probing at the place on his chest where the monstrous woman pierced him, but he still seemed to be intact. In fact, he was better than before, he realized. His body didn't ache anymore. His injuries had vanished. His feet were even dry.

"Well, think about it. This can't be real. I'm still trying to catch up with what's going on in your head, but a lot happened while you were gone, didn't it? Wait…that Cordelia lady is those limo girls' sister? That's kinda crazy."

Perri pressed her hands to her chest and frowned. "Aw, I was just getting used to those…" Then she glanced up at Eric, blushed and dropped her hands to her lap, embarrassed.

Eric squeezed his eyes shut and ran his hand through his hair. Why were they here? What happened to him back in the Woman of the Hoard's reeking lair?

"So there's a whole city of just stairways? That's a real thing? Not just some weird metaphor?"

"It's just…weird that they're gone…is all…" muttered Perri.

"Uh huh."

"Who's the Woman of the Hoard?" asked Isabelle.

"I mean, not *totally* gone," Perri went on. "I still have *some*. I was *starting* to…uh…grow…" She cleared her throat, blushing brighter than ever, and looked away.

Eric turned his full attention to the telephone. "What's going on?" he asked.

But Isabelle didn't seem to be paying attention. "She really said she could free me?"

Eric stared at the phone, his heart sinking. "I…don't know if she was telling the truth about that. Cordelia told me not to make another bargain. She said I couldn't trust her."

Perri looked back and forth between him and the phone, confused. "What's going on?"

"I understand," said Isabelle. "I can see it. It's all coming together."

"That was hard," he assured her.

"I know. I can tell. You did the right thing. We can talk about it later."

"Yes."

"Huh?" said Perri.

"What is this place?" asked Eric. "Why are we here?"

"Right!" said Isabelle. "Um, if I were going to guess, I'd say we're all inside the psychic void."

"You mean that place I was stuck in for all those years?" said Perri.

"Some variation of it, anyway," confirmed Isabelle.

Perri glanced around, worried. "We're not going to be stuck here for another fifty years, are we?"

"No. We're not *really* here," Isabelle explained. "It's just a sort of mental projection. A memory made physical. This place is familiar to all of us in some way. You and Eric were both here. And I've pretty much been everywhere Eric's been because I see through his mind. He and I have had a psychic connection ever since the day we met. And I could tell that you two had something similar from the moment you first woke up in his and Karen's spare bedroom."

"We do?" asked Perri.

"I've been thinking that it might explain why she's been catching up so fast. At first I thought maybe you were just really smart, and I still think you are, but I think it's really that you're subconsciously tuned into his brain. It's a lot like how I absorbed some of his talents. Like I used to be terrible at spelling and grammar stuff, but I hardly ever misspell anything when I text him. It's like I downloaded all his English teacher knowledge.

"Huh…" said Eric. "Wish it was that easy to pass it on to my actual students."

Perri looked over at Eric. "If that's true, then why can't I read his mind like you can?"

"Your connection to him isn't *exactly* like mine is. They seem to work differently."

"So if this is all just a mental projection," wondered Eric, "then why are you still just a phone?"

"Perri must be the one who constructed this place," reasoned Isabelle. "She took all the darkness and emptiness and timelessness of the void and turned it into something real and familiar."

"*I* did that?" asked Perri. She picked up the teacup in front of her and turned it over, examining it.

"You did. But you have no idea what I look like."

"Oh yeah…" She put the teacup back down and pointed at the phone. "That's the phone from my dad's office, though," she realized.

"Yeah. That's probably about as familiar as I'm going to be to you. Physically, anyway."

Eric nodded. Was it weird that some of that actually sort of made sense? Or had he gone mad after all?

"So…I can set up mental tea parties now?" She picked up the teapot and peered inside. It was empty. She couldn't decide if it made more or less sense that there was no tea at this tea party.

"I'm not sure how it works," said Isabelle. "Just a theory here, but I think maybe it takes all three of us. You provide the mental constructions and I provide the communication channel. And Eric's the link between us. But I can't be sure of anything."

"That's confusing," said Perri.

"It is," agreed Isabelle. "And I don't know if we'll be able to just do this whenever we want, either. So far, this sort of thing only happens when Eric's consciousness is attacked."

Perri looked at him. "Is that what happened?"

Eric shrugged. If Isabelle didn't understand what was going on here, he didn't have a chance at understanding it.

"The last time you two connected like this," recalled Isabelle, "was when that weirdo agent knocked you out at Ternheart."

Eric nodded. "And that was a lot like those times Steampunk Monk whammied me with those freaky concoctions of his."

It happened twice. The first time, the strangely dressed man hit him with a foul-smelling liquid in a squirt bottle and sent him fleeing through the city's riverfront properties while suffering nightmarish LSD-like hallucinations. Paintings came alive in the art gallery. Monstrous machines chased him. He even had a run-in with a pack of corn creeps! The second time, Steampunk Monk took out a rusty old handgun, put it to his own head and somehow sent him spiraling into a second nightmare, this one of the city in fiery ruins.

"Right," agreed Isabelle. "And that was one of the times you saw Perri, remember?"

That was true. The second time. Just before he awoke. He was drifting in the void, lost, and she called out to him, begging him to find her and save her.

It also happened when he was attacked by that psychic parasite in Illinois, and again when he 'died' and went to Guinee to talk to Ari, the toll collector, to seek entrance to Mambo Dee's hidden realm.

He considered all this. "So...this is a *subconscious* place?"

"Looks that way."

"Huh." He looked down at his hands. "I *feel* awake." He ran his hand through his hair again and tried to think back. "I don't remember anything after she jabbed me in the chest." It was like a dream. It faded away like smoke.

"The weirdest part about all this," said Isabelle, "is that while I'm here, I can't seem to talk to anyone else. I've been trying to call Karen to let her know you're okay, but I can't reach her phone. I can still sense my parents, the same way I can sense you, but I can't communicate with anyone but you right now."

Eric frowned at the phone. "Okay..."

"It might mean that *I'm* in an unconscious state right now, too. That we're all basically *dreaming* this."

"Wait..." said Perri, concerned. "So what happened to the me who was back in the kitchen just now? Did I pass out? Everyone'll be worried!"

Around them, the treehouse seemed to let out a long groan.

"What was that?" asked Perri.

"The projection's weakening," realized Isabelle. "When you started worrying about what was happening in the kitchen, you started to wake yourself up."

She looked around, her mismatched eyes widening. "What

do I do?"

There was another groan, louder this time, and accompanied by a loud crack from somewhere beneath their feet.

"Relax!" gasped Isabelle. "Don't think about things outside of the projection!"

"I can't help it!"

The treehouse began to lean to one side. Eric grabbed the table, his own eyes wide with panic. "What happens to me if she wakes up?"

"I don't know!" gasped Isabelle.

"I'm sorry!" squealed Perri.

With another loud crack, the floor dropped out from under them.

Perri screamed.

Eric cursed and braced himself.

But the treehouse never hit the ground. Instead, the world dissolved around him and he found himself plummeting through the endless darkness that brought him there.

Chapter Thirty-Three

When he opened his eyes, Eric was lying on the cold ground, surrounded by trees.

What just happened? Why was he in the woods again?

He lifted his head and looked down at himself. He was clutching a familiar, muddy box against the breast of his grimy jacket. "Ah..." was all he could manage to utter. The box with the key, still reeking of the swampy muck that covered the floor of the Woman of the Hoard's lair. Isabelle was right. He hadn't lost it after all.

But that didn't explain where the hell he was.

He sat up, groaning. His head was pounding and his feet were cold and wet again. He could barely see straight. Why was everything so hazy? And why did his body hurt so bad? He felt as if he'd fallen down a flight of stairs.

"Oh yeah..." he muttered. "That happened, too, didn't it?"

Groaning at the aching in his legs, still clutching the muddy box against his chest, he managed to stand up with the aid of a nearby tree trunk. But standing was only the first obstacle. Now that he was on his feet, he found he wasn't quite ready to use them. He leaned against the tree and groaned.

This happened when Ford sent him to the void, too, he recalled. It took a little while to get his bearings. But this felt considerably worse. Was it because he was a lot more tired now? That first time was still early in the day. He'd been through a lot since then.

"Eric!"

He looked up, squinting out at the woods in front of him, but no one was there.

"Eric! Hey!"

"Wha...?" He turned, swaying on his feet, staggering like a

drunk, and looked out the other way.

"Over here!"

Finally, he turned his gaze toward the top of a nearby hill. Paul was there, gesturing impatiently for him to follow.

"Hurry up!" he shouted. "This way!"

Paul… That's right. He was in Furnanter Park with Paul before Cordelia summoned him off the trail. The Woman of the Hoard must have returned him to where he started once she was done with him.

He let go of the tree and stumbled forward a little bit. It felt like the ground was tilted funny. He tucked the box under one arm and squeezed his eyes closed again. "Feel funny…" he mumbled, his voice slurred. He felt drunk.

"My truck's parked over this way," said Paul. "Hurry up. They're coming."

"Who's coming?" He turned and looked back the other way, but he couldn't see anything. They seemed to be alone out here. But then again, he couldn't think clearly. He rubbed his eyes, confused, and then blinked out at the forest again.

Something was moving out there, he realized. Something *big*. A shadowy, canine-like shape crept through the underbrush with the silent stealth of a skilled predator.

Skinwalkers? Here?

"Not good…" he mumbled. Paul was right. It was time to get the hell out of the woods.

"Move it!" shouted Paul.

"Stop yellin' at me…" He shook his head and started up the hill after him, cursing at the branches that kept clawing at his face as he pushed his way through the dense brush and jabbing branches. Why was it so hard to think? And how was Paul able to maneuver through all this foliage? His own feet kept getting tangled up. And all the while he was clinging to the muddy box, trying to keep from dropping it.

When he reached the top of the hill, he glanced back again. The thing in the underbrush was definitely following him. It wasn't even trying to hide. Its hungry gaze was fixed on him.

"Right over here!" called Paul. He'd made his way down the

other side of the hill now and was standing at the edge of a stagnant-looking stream, motioning for him to hurry, as if he needed any more encouragement. "We have to cross!"

Eric hurried after him. Halfway down, he stumbled over a rock and would've fallen if he didn't happen to catch hold of a strong branch. He looked back up the hill as he righted himself and this time he saw *two* shapes stalking through the underbrush.

He cursed and hurried on down the hill.

"I'm parked just on the other side!" shouted Paul as he splashed into the water.

Eric realized that he could see civilization now. There was a fenced-in lot just beyond the trees on the other side of the stream. And a large building beyond that.

He *knew* that building. That was Delbenton Lumber Company. But that wasn't near Furnanter... That was all the way over on the opposite side of town. How did he get here?

"Don't stop!" insisted Paul.

But Eric *did* stop. He looked down at the water. It was filthy with litter and there was a foul smell wafting up from the ditch. Paul was only up to his knees where he was standing, but it looked much deeper beyond that.

And it was *March*! That water was going to be freezing!

He looked up the stream and then down it, but saw no better options for crossing.

"Hurry!" shouted Paul. "They're right behind you!"

He looked back up the hill. There were three of them now. They weren't even trying to hide. They were making their way down the hill toward him, all of them crouched down, teeth bared.

They were definitely skinwalkers. They looked just like the one they followed into Tubby's basement, before it climbed up onto the ductwork and pretended to be Karen.

"Get in the water!"

Eric clutched the box with one arm and ran his other hand through his hair. "Okay!" he shouted. "Just..."

"Just *what*? Don't be stupid! Hurry up!"

He started to step forward, but again he hesitated. He

wasn't sure why. Paul was absolutely right. He had to cross the water. There was no other way. Yet he found himself hesitating, the muddy toe of his shoe hovering over the oil-slicked surface. He shook his head and withdrew his foot. "Hold on..." he muttered. "Just a minute..."

"We don't *have* a minute!" said Paul.

"Just...my phone... Don't want to get it wet..." He shifted the box to his other arm and then fished his phone from his pocket.

"Forget the damn phone! *Get in the water!*"

"Oh yeah..." he grumbled, looking at the screen. "It's dead... I forgot..."

Everything felt so wonky. His head was still swimming. Why was it so hard to think straight? It didn't take this long to get over it when Ford did this to him. Was it because the Woman of the Hoard was a lot stronger?

"*Just get in the water!*"

"Other thing..." grumbled Eric, shaking his head.

"*What* other thing?"

He could hear them moving down the hill behind him. They were getting closer with each passing second. They were almost upon him. "In here," he said, reaching into his jacket pocket this time and rummaging around in it.

"*They're right behind you!*" shrieked Paul.

"They're in front of me, too," said Eric. He withdrew his hand from his pocket and threw a handful of ash into Paul's face.

The reaction was immediate. Paul let out a monstrous howl of pain. He threw himself into the water. As he thrashed and flailed, his familiar features snapped and twisted, distorting into something inhuman.

That was never Paul. It looked like Paul. It sounded like Paul. But there was something wrong with him, something he almost didn't notice between that queer eternity he spent floating in the psychic void and the skinwalkers' strange magic.

But he figured it out. And looking back now, he couldn't understand why he didn't notice that it wasn't Paul right away. His hair was the wrong color. He wasn't dressed like Paul. And he didn't even have a beard. And then there was the fact that he had a *tail*...

He plunged his hand back into his jacket pocket and withdrew the pouch of ash as he twirled around to face the three monsters behind him.

They were right there. Just one more second and they would've had him, but as soon as he thrust the pouch at them they lurched backward as if he were swinging a burning torch.

They didn't like the ash. That was why Not-Paul wanted him to jump in the water, he realized. It wanted him to wash off the ash he'd rubbed on his throat and chest back in Ternheart's parking lot.

And yet knowing that wasn't going to help him much at the moment. He might be holding them off, but there were four of them surrounding him now, all of them snarling and snapping, watching for any opportunity to take him down and drag him away.

He only had the one pouch of ash and he'd already used a good portion of it. He was going to have to use the rest of it wisely if he wanted to get out of these woods alive.

He clutched the muddy box under his arm and waved the pouch in front of him. They really didn't want to come near this stuff. They grew more agitated with each passing second.

He had one idea. Hoping like hell that it worked, he poured the ash over his own head, then he squatted down and smeared it over his skin and clothes, protecting every inch of his body.

The skinwalkers howled with rage.

"Didn't count on that, did you?" he taunted. And it might've been one of his better moments of bravado if not for the fact that the cloud of ash made him cough as he said it.

The monsters didn't look all that impressed, either. With an odd and disorienting sort of motion, one of them stood up on its hairy hind legs and bared a troublingly vicious set of jagged teeth at him. He couldn't quite wrap his head around it. It wasn't exactly as if it had just stood up. It didn't even have the same shape it did before. Its torso and arms didn't look nearly so human a moment ago. And it didn't have such long fingers and toes. But at the same time, the change was so fluid that it appeared deceptively natural. He wondered whether it was their curious physiology that allowed them to change like that or if it was some kind of magic, but it was hard to concentrate on such unimportant things when his attention was fixed on the broken branch it was holding in those monkey-like hands.

He cursed. A problem solver. Great. Just what he needed.

The other two skinwalkers rose onto their hind legs as well, transforming from four-legged monsters to two-legged monsters with the same strangely elastic motion. One snatched a large rock off the ground and raised it over its head, threatening him. The other one lurched away a few steps and ripped up a chunk of a broken log roughly the size of a traffic barrel.

He took a step backward, his eyes flitting from one monster to the next.

This was bad. The ash might keep them from pouncing on him, but it wasn't going to stop them from simply bludgeoning him to death with whatever they could find lying around. And there was no way he was going to be able to take on all of them.

Then an awful, gurgling imitation of Paul's voice from the middle of the rancid stream behind him said, "Get in the water, Eric."

Chapter Thirty-Four

The thing in the water definitely wasn't Paul. Never mind the silvery-blond hair or the missing beard. It wasn't even remotely human. It was long and lean, its body rippling with powerful muscle, its alien eyes shining in that weird, animal-like way.

And in case being a literal *monster* wasn't bad enough, it was now brandishing a broken beer bottle.

Eric turned in a circle, his gaze shifting from one beast to the next. These were definitely not good odds. He was going to have a hard time staying optimistic about this.

And to make matters worse, he saw that only the one that was pretending to be Paul was wearing clothes. The other three were naked, which was unfortunate because this new upright position they'd assumed spared no details about skinwalker anatomy.

Two things were clear. First, these three were all definitely *male*. And second, if he survived this, the mental images he was going to take away were going to haunt him for a very long time.

"Okay…" he gasped, turning around again, trying to keep all four in sight. "Let's just take it down a notch, okay? You guys wanna play a little fetch or something?"

They crept closer, makeshift weapons raised.

He wished he'd had enough sense to bring more than one bag of ash. "You know what? You guys let me go right now…Petco gift cards all around. What do you say?"

The one that wasn't Paul snarled at him.

"Whoa there…" He lifted the mostly empty pouch and shook it, letting the last of it drizzle down around him. "Bad doggies!"

The one with the rock lurched forward and started to throw it.

"*No!*" he shouted at it. He thrust the empty pouch toward it, threatening it, and the thing jumped backward, shielding itself with the rock instead. "*Bad! No!*"

Deep down, he knew he was only pissing these things off worse, but he couldn't seem to help himself. He was too afraid right now to think of any other way to handle this situation.

He needed to do something. Eventually one of them was going to stop being skittish and just take a swing at him. And all it was going to take was one good blow to the head and it would be over.

He kept turning, his gaze darting from one to the next, sizing them all up. The one with the rock seemed more twitchy than the others. It kept lifting it, as if to throw it, but then hiding behind it whenever he moved the pouch toward it.

"Put it down, Eric," snarled Fake Paul.

"Not a chance, Cujo."

The monster splashed toward him.

Time was up. It was now or never. He made his decision and charged the rock-wielding skinwalker as if he meant to shove the empty, ash-covered pouch into its face. The thing reacted just as he hoped it would. It reeled backward with a terrified yelp, opening a way for him to slip through and run for it.

In a good book, the hero of the story would make a daring and clever call like this and escape the monsters' trap. This would probably be followed by an exciting chase scene with lots of close calls and heart-pounding action, but eventually he'd find the perfect opportunity to get away, probably via some death-defying, action-movie-worthy stunt that left his pursuers seething in frustration while he fled to safety.

Apparently, whoever was writing *his* book was too lazy for any of that, because instead the skinwalker with the rotten log lurched forward on its freakishly long legs and struck him in the back of his head, sending him sprawling face-first into the dirt where he lay dazed and reeling in pain.

If the log had been any less rotten, it might've caved his skull in, bringing his role in all this weird nonsense to a very anti-climactic end, but instead his head had proved to be harder and the log exploded into splinters on contact.

It still hurt like hell, though. And the worst of it hadn't even begun yet. He needed to be back on his feet and running, but it was a struggle just to push himself up onto his hands and knees.

The skinwalkers closed in around him. He could see them through the tears of pain that had sprung to his eyes. He could hear their strange, snarling voices.

Something struck him across his back, wrenching a painful cry from him.

The tree branch.

He dug his fingers into the earth and tried to crawl away, but again the branch came down on him.

Next would be the rock. Or maybe the broken bottle.

He couldn't get away!

Something struck his right shoulder. Then his lower back. His buttock. His left side. A blind panic gripped him. There was nothing he could do. He was going to die here.

Unable to escape, he curled himself into a ball as the monsters closed in around him and waited for the end.

But the end didn't come as quickly as he expected. The blows to his back stopped and the snarls of the monsters changed.

Confused and still dazed from the initial blow to his head, he dared a peek between his arms.

The monsters had all moved to one side of him and were backing into the stagnant water of the drainage ditch. They were snarling and growling and glaring at something behind him.

Something else was growling, too, he realized. There was a low, menacing sound that seemed to roll through the air like ominous thunder. He could almost feel it reverberating through the earth beneath him. The sound of it sent an icy shiver crawling up his back and made the hairs on his arms tingle.

Very slowly, he lowered his arms and lifted his head off the ground. He turned, blinking back tears of pain, wondering what manner of monstrosity could frighten away a pack of savage skinwalkers, half-convinced that whatever he saw when he looked back was going to be the last thing he ever saw in this world.

The beast was crouched just a few yards from where he was lying, its hackles raised, its yellow eyes blazing. But it didn't attack him. Nor would it. He *knew* this beast. He stared at it for a moment. Then he blinked hard, squeezing his eyes closed for a moment, trying to clear his vision and his head.

It was only a cat, after all. *His* cat. The same great, grouchy Maine Coon he'd brought home from Hedge Lake two years ago.

It was only Spooky.

And yet, he'd never heard Spooky make such a terrifying noise before. In fact, he'd never heard *any* cat growl like that before. It was much more like the sort of noise he'd expect to hear from some great, menacing, three-headed beast crouched at the gates of hell.

But then again, even as he lay there, he realized that the sound the cat was making wasn't what he thought he heard when he first turned to face it. It was just a very angry cat growling at a pack of stupid dogs.

Had he only imagined the hellish sound in that moment when blind panic still gripped him?

He glanced back at the skinwalkers, but they had already reached the far side of the stream. Once again running on four legs instead of two, the pack fled off into the forest.

He rolled onto his back and groaned.

That really sucked.

"Thanks, buddy," he said.

But Spooky wasn't paying him any attention. Now that the skinwalkers had left, he was just sitting there, his hackles lowered, bathing himself as if nothing strange had happened.

He didn't waste any energy wondering where he came from. Spooky had always had a curious way of showing up in unexpected places. He'd always known that there was something peculiar about the animal. It didn't seem to be just a cat at all. And while he was wandering those haunted acres of Evancurt, one of the spirits there confirmed that Spooky wasn't a cat at all, that he was something else entirely, though she either wouldn't or couldn't tell him what.

He sat up and rubbed at the back of his head.

This sort of thing happened to him a lot more than was strictly normal.

As the real Paul reminded him earlier in the day, a witch named Myra Tonnerby once told him that nothing could ever really happen to him because the universe loved exceptionally good people and would go out of its way to protect them. He, for one, didn't think he could be described as "exceptionally good" by any stretch of the imagination. "Not a total jackass," maybe, but certainly not "exceptionally good." Just ask any of his students. Yet time and time again, something always seemed to snatch him out of harm's way.

Maybe Myra had it wrong. Maybe it wasn't "exceptionally good" people the universe loved. Maybe it was cranky people. Socially standoffish people. Maybe it, too, hated teenagers with their noses perpetually stuck in their cell phones and found in him a kindred spirit of some sort. Or maybe what it really loved was stupid and clumsy people. Maybe he *amused* the universe. Maybe it found him entertaining.

He picked up the pouch of ash and shook the last of it into his open hand.

That wasn't going to be enough to protect him if Spooky ran off and those skinwalkers came back. He was going to need to find his way home.

He heard the rumble of an approaching engine and looked up to see a pickup truck lumbering through the trees.

There was a bridge over there, he realized. That was good information to have. That was his way out of these monster-infested woods, at least.

But as he watched, he realized that he recognized the truck. It lumbered to a stop and someone jumped out. A moment later, Paul was rushing toward him, pushing through the naked under-brush. He ran up to him and knelt in front of him, his eyes wide open. "You okay?"

Eric stared up at his brother. Dark hair and beard. Human eyes. No tail. He was dressed in his usual work clothes.

He reached up and slapped him. The ash in his hand exploded into a white puff, painting the side of his face.

Paul stood there, his eyes squeezed shut. "What was that for?" he coughed.

"Just checking."

Chapter Thirty-Five

Eric eased himself onto Justin's old couch, groaning at the pain in his back and legs. Between his world record-worthy step count in Stairway City, his less-than-graceful tumble down the mountainside and getting his ass beat handedly by that pack of skinwalkers, he really wasn't feeling as perky as he was before he set off for Furnanter.

"Take it easy," said Holly. "I've got some Ibuprofen in my purse. Get him something to drink."

"Sure," said Paige, hurrying over to the refrigerator.

"I'm getting too old for this," he grumbled.

"You know you're the youngest guy in the room, right?" asked Paul.

He rubbed at the back of his neck. "Are you counting all the centuries I've spent floating around in that damned psychic void?"

"He's got a point," said Isabelle. She was speaking through Paul's phone while Eric's was charging. "It's like an eternity in there and he's practically got a membership card to that place."

"Poor guy," said Holly as she shook out two tablets for him.

"I'm fine," he assured her. And he was, all things considered. Even better, thanks to Isabelle letting Paul know where he was as soon as he caught sight of the lumber yard, he didn't even have to hike out of those damned woods. And of course, thanks to Spooky, who simply sauntered back into the woods after Paul arrived. "Could've been worse. Paul could've been there to 'help.'"

"Don't start with me," snapped Paul.

Holly looked back and forth between them, confused. "Huh?"

Paul turned and faced her, determined to make his point. "Okay, say you're *literally on fire* and someone offers to piss on you. What d'you do?"

She looked horrified. "Ewwwww."

"What the hell is *wrong* with you?" snapped Ally.

"Come on! I'm just saying it's a viable, last-ditch strategy! That's all!"

"Is there anything in here except beer?" asked Paige.

"Maybe in the back," replied Justin.

"Beer sounds perfect," said Eric. "Bring me one of those."

She looked up. "Am I allowed to do that?"

"You're not *drinking* it," said Ally.

"Just checking..." she muttered.

Eric glanced over at the stripper pole. The skinwalker was gone. All that remained were several loops of cut rope and a pile of scattered ashes that trailed off toward the doorway. He didn't ask what they did with the corpse. They probably dragged it out into the woods and buried it. He decided he didn't want to hear about it.

"So that's a real thing?" said Justin. "A psychic void?"

"Everything's a thing," said Paul and Eric together.

"Pscyhic void," slurred Greg from his worn-out chair. "Those'll add some years to you. I know all about it."

"Make you old," agreed Adam.

"Would you two idiots shut up?" grumbled Ally.

"Witch," hissed Greg.

"*Wicked* witch," agreed Adam.

"Watch it," said Holly, shooting them a dirty look.

They both shrank deeper into their chairs, mumbling apologies.

"So what's with the box?" asked Ally. It was sitting on the coffee table in front of everyone, still unopened.

"It's *supposed* to have a key inside it," explained Eric as Paige handed him the beer. He thanked her and then added, "And if it doesn't I'm going to be *pissed*."

"So we're going to open it and see?" pressed Ally.

"Won't do us much good leaving it in there," reasoned Justin.

"It's not going to melt our faces off like *Raiders of the Lost Ark* or anything, is it?"

Eric shrugged. "I mean, *probably* not."

"You need to be careful though," said Isabelle. "That thing's giving off the same kind of energy as that compass you found at the mill."

Eric sat up a little straighter. "Oh yeah. That thing." He reached into his jacket pocket, relieved to find that he hadn't lost or broken it during all the excitement between then and now. "Almost forgot about that."

"And I finally figured out where I know that energy from," she added.

Eric glanced over at the phone. "Where?"

"Evancurt."

"What's that?" asked Justin, noticing the looks on everyone's faces.

"What does that box have to do with Evancurt?" asked Holly.

"I don't know," replied Isabelle. "But that's the same energy I felt draining out of the forest when Eric woke up in those woods that night. I'm sure of it."

It wasn't surprising that she hadn't recognized it right away. Isabelle wasn't there for most of what happened in Evancurt. For that matter, *he* wasn't there for most of it, since the vast majority of his memories of that night weren't his own.

He shook his head. "Evancurt is gone. The Lady of the Murk told me it was disappearing from this world forever. She said no trace of its existence would remain."

"Did you hit your head or something?" asked Ally.

He glanced up at her. "Quite a few times, yeah."

"Just asking…"

"I don't know anything about how that sort of thing works," said Isabelle. "But that is *definitely* the same energy."

He frowned at the box.

"So…do we open it or not?" asked Holly.

"I think you still have to open it," said Isabelle. "I mean,

Cordelia sent you to get it. It must be important, right? Just...you know. Be careful."

He looked over at Paul, who only shrugged.

"You're in charge," he reminded him.

"Okay then..." He grasped the latch on the box and snapped it open. Then, with a grunt of effort, he lifted the lid and peered inside.

Evancurt was a lot of things. Eric had spent a lot of sleepless nights and restless days these past few weeks thinking about the memories he'd inherited of that awful place. It was a ghost town swallowed by a haunted forest. It was a doomsday machine built by mad scientists. It was a prison for lost and confused spirits unable to tear themselves away from the tragedies of their own deaths. And above all, it was a morbid stage on which godlike beings played godlike games with human souls.

Before he looked into the box, he couldn't fathom what all of that could possibly have to do with whatever came out of the mud in the Woman of the Hoard's shadowy lair. But now, as he gazed upon the revealed secret lying within...he was even more confused.

Inside the box was a strange metal object. It was roughly ten inches long, comprised of a subtly curving shaft, about an inch and a half in diameter, covered in an odd, crisscrossing pattern of small, protruding knobs of various sizes and a flared, disk-like head, about the diameter of a baseball, with a series of grooves that curved around the outer rim and spiraled inward toward the center. It appeared to be comprised of two different kinds of metal, one a dark, reddish brass-like color and the other a much lighter silver. Unlike the box it came from, it was clean and shiny, seemingly brand new.

Holly leaned in for a closer look. "What is it?"

"I have no idea." Carefully, he reached in and grasped the object, lifting it out for a better look. It was heavy for its size, but beyond that, removing it from the box gleaned no additional details.

"It looks like some sort of device, doesn't it?" said Justin.

Eric wasn't sure what it looked like. He wasn't even sure

what kind of metal this was. It wasn't brass and silver. The coloring wasn't quite right. There was no visible tarnish. And although it was comprised of various individual pieces, he couldn't discern whether any of those pieces actually moved. He couldn't make out any wheels or hinges anywhere. It didn't seem to turn or fold or flex.

It looked a lot more complicated than the compass, though.

"Are you sure it's the same kind of energy?" asked Eric, looking at the phone again.

"Positive. It took me a while to finally remember, but it's definitely the same thing I felt that night. And I can feel it even more now that you've taken it out of the box. That thing feels just like Evancurt did."

Eric turned the object over in his hands. "But what does this thing have to do with that place? Do you think it came from there? Is it a part of that machine?"

"I don't understand it," replied Isabelle. "I'm just telling you they feel the same."

He turned the object around again, this time with the flattened head straight up, and examined it. There were tiny little details in those spiraling grooves. Working parts maybe? He couldn't tell. He brought it closer to his face, trying to make them out.

"It looks like a flower," observed Holly.

Eric glanced up at her, then looked down at the object again. Holding it as he was, almost as if he were smelling it, it *did* look like a flower. That odd, spiraling pattern on its head resembled folded petals. Those odd knobs on the stem could have been thorns.

"A frozen flower!" exclaimed Paige. "That's what Perri saw in the divination!"

Eric nodded. She was right. It was a cold, hard flower, literally plucked from the earth, no less.

"Looks like some kind of steampunk dildo to me," announced Ally.

Eric sighed. "*Seriously* inappropriate."

"What? It looks like a dildo."

287

"Oh gosh…" sighed Holly.

"Ew…" said Paige, wrinkling her nose.

Eric turned and glared at Paul.

He shrugged. "Well it *does* sort of look like a dildo."

"No it doesn't!"

"That's just 'cause your holding it wrong," he pressed. "Turn it around."

Ally gestured at it. "See, the little end goes in the—"

"*Can we focus here?*" snapped Eric.

She crossed her arms over her chest and turned away. "Sounds to me like someone's already got one in there."

Paul snorted.

"So what now?" asked Holly. "We've cast the spell. We've found the compass and the key."

"Dildo," said Ally.

"*Key,*" returned Holly, glaring at her.

"Agree to disagree."

"What do we do with them?" she finished, rolling her eyes.

Eric looked down at the compass next to him. "Cordelia said I'd need the compass to find the doorway and the key to open it. We should have everything we need."

"So we use the compass first," reasoned Paul, picking it up off the couch and turning it in his hands. "How does it work?"

"No idea."

Ally felt her phone vibrate and pulled it out. "Aunt Karen wants to know what's up. You want me to tell her about your dildo?"

"Please stop!" cried Holly.

"She said to keep her updated, so…" She turned away from them and started tapping away at the screen.

Then Holly's phone rang, too. She frowned at the screen, then accepted the call and held it to her ear. "Hello?" She listened for a few seconds, then turned and held it out to Eric. "It's for you."

He glanced around, uncertain, then took it from her. "Yes?"

"Excellent job!" said the voice on the other end.

"Ford."

"I gotta say, I didn't expect you to wrap it up so fast! You even have the key! I'm *super* impressed, bestie."

"I see you're still watching everything I do."

"Of course I am! It's so entertaining watching you work. I'm thinking about becoming partners on a full-time basis."

"Yeah, that's a hard pass for me."

Ford laughed. "Don't be like that! We were *made* to work together. We're practically soul mates!"

"Do you *want* something?" snapped Eric. "Because I've had a really long day and I'm getting *really* grumpy."

"You're no fun."

"I'm usually not."

"Be nice or I won't tell you how to use the compass."

Eric sighed. "You can tell me?"

"Of course I can. It's not as hard as it seems. Its function becomes apparent when you get close to its programmed target."

"So I just have to get close to it?"

"Exactly. After that, it'll be nothing to find the pucker point."

He frowned. "What the hell is a *pucker point?*"

"It's the lock that matches that key, of course," replied Ford.

"So the 'pucker point' is the keyhole?" He looked down at the strange device. "I find that and just insert this into it?"

Ally and Paul both looked at each other, "Dildo."

"Stop it!" snapped Holly.

"Majorly immature," said Paige.

"Don't try too hard to understand it," said Ford. "Black World tech is extremely advanced. *And* a lot of it works on completely alien physics."

Black World tech? He'd heard that before, hadn't he? The Lady of the Murk said something about Evancurt being a "remnant of the Black World." And just today Ford referred to Evancurt as a "Black World machine." Did that mean that these two devices and that awful machine were from the same world? Were they the same kind of otherworldly technology?

"But it's a big world out there," Ford went on. "I can get

you close enough to the entrance to work it out, but you've got to do one last thing for me."

Eric sighed. Not another task. He just wanted to get this over with and go home. "And what is that?"

"Tell me you had fun playing with me today."

He blinked. "What?"

"You heard me."

"You've got to be joking."

"What's he saying?" whispered Holly.

"I *do* love my jokes," said Ford. "But I'm serious. I want to hear you say it."

He sat there, his jaw clenched. What kind of nonsense was this?

"Come on now."

"But I *didn't*."

"We both know you know how to lie, Eric."

He sighed again. "Fine. I had fun playing with you today."

Holly's pretty face scrunched into a bewildered expression at that. "Huh?"

"Happy?" he growled.

"Delighted," replied Ford. "Go to Main Street. Start in front of that barber shop. The compass will do the rest."

"That's it?"

"That's it! Good luck out there. Oh, and you might consider taking some backup. Things might get hairy once you're inside."

The line went dead and Eric lowered the phone. "I really hate that guy."

"What was that about?" asked Holly. "And where did he get my number?"

"Did he say what we should do next?" asked Paul.

Eric nodded and stood up. "Yeah. He did."

"Something about sticking his dildo in his pucker hole, wasn't it?" said Ally.

"Can you seriously not stop?" exclaimed Holly, exasperated.

"I seriously can't," she replied without a hint of apology in her voice. She glanced over at Eric and said, "By the way, Aunt Karen says have fun with your new toy." Then she turned and looked at Justin, a wicked grin tugging at the corners of her mouth. "Hey! So now you have a *dildo* in your man hole. It just keeps getting better, doesn't it?"

Justin shook his head, frustrated. "*Evil* girl. Just…just *evil*."

"Depraved," agreed Greg.

"Totally uncalled for," grunted Adam.

"Awe," she said, pouting at them, "you guys feel left out? Want one for *your* man holes, too?"

"Demonic," decided Greg.

"She-devil," agreed Adam.

Chapter Thirty-Six

The gloomy day was already sinking toward nightfall when Justin parked his pickup in front of Zegler's Barber Shop just east of the Main Street bridge. Soon, they'd be searching in the dark in addition to avoiding skinwalkers. And to make matters even worse, the temperature was dropping.

"What're we looking for?" asked Paul from the back seat.

"You know as much as I do," Eric told him. He was studying the compass, trying to wrap his head around how the thing worked. Did you just hold it by the stick part? Which way was supposed to point forward?

Black World tech, he thought, looking it over. Ford called it a compass. A tool for finding your way, just like a map. A *black* map... "I see," he muttered under his breath. That was what that meant. A black map and a black key. All the clues were coming together. This was the endgame.

Which meant it probably wasn't going to get any easier from here on out.

"Here's a better question for you," said Adam, who was squeezed into the back seat with Greg and Paul. His voice squeaking more than was strictly necessary for a man his size, he said, "Why am *I* here?"

"We're here to watch Eric's back so he can do whatever it is he has to do to keep this town from being overrun by those skinwalkers," replied Justin. He met the chubby coward's frightened gaze in the mirror. "Unless you think you'd rather take your chances with the skinwalkers, instead?"

"No thank you!" he croaked.

"Man up," grunted Greg. "You'll be fine. I've done this kind of thing millions of times." Although the tremble in his voice and the sickly, terrified look on his face strongly suggested otherwise.

While the four of them crowded into Justin's truck and headed off to Main Street, Holly drove Paige and Ally to the museum to help Mrs. Balm hold the containment spell that was rapidly failing against Yenaldlooshi's growing consciousness. He couldn't help but think, then, that they would undoubtedly be the monster's first victims if he were to fail, followed quickly by everyone else he cared about.

He was used to racing the clock when it came to the weird. It was just as Cordelia had said. Although a great many of the tragedies he was tasked with preventing had been in motion for a while, sometimes building up over *decades* to reach such a perilous boiling point, he only ever seemed to show up for some strange reason at the very last minute, as if the universe delighted in dropping him right in the middle of the action in the eleventh hour, only to rush around like a clueless madman. This time, however, felt particularly unnerving. Even after all these hours, his stomach was still twisted into knots and his jaw ached because he couldn't seem to stop clenching his teeth.

If he ever found himself face-to-face with whatever "greater power" kept putting him in these situations, he was going to have a few choice words to say to it and he didn't care *who* it was.

"Well, we're at Zegler's shop," said Justin, looking out at the faded and motionless colors of the barber pole. "Is it going to be a problem that he's already closed up for the night?"

"We're not here for haircuts," grumbled Eric. He gripped the handle with the wires at the top of the device so that they curved backward over his hand and frowned at it. That seemed like the only real way to hold it that he could surmise. Any other way just didn't make sense. "Unless what we're looking for turns out to be in his waiting room, I guess."

"Then what?" asked Greg.

"Then I guess we'll have to break in."

Adam raised his hand as if he were crammed into an elementary school desk instead of the back seat of Justin's truck. "Um... I can't go to jail. If that's a problem, I can leave."

Eric held the device closer to his face and examined the

back of his hand. The hair there was standing up. It felt like a buildup of static electricity, like when you held a balloon over your head and it lifted up your hair. Was that a part of the function, or a perfectly natural thing to happen while holding an inside-out kitchen whisk with the wire bristles hovering over your hand?

He opened the door and stepped out into the fading light. "The compass'll do the rest..." he mumbled. "Sure..."

At least traffic was light. There weren't a lot of people driving by to gawk at him as he wandered around looking lost, covered from head to toe in ash and waving his backward kitchen gadget in the air like some escaped lunatic.

All four of them were covered in ash. After his experience in the woods with those four skinwalkers, Eric had insisted that everyone take maximum precautions. That had included the girls, as well. Holly, Paige and Ally had all doused themselves in white ash and he'd sent word to Karen for her, Diane and Perri to do the same at home and Mr. Iverley and Mrs. Balm at the museum.

The skinwalkers *really* didn't like that stuff, and he was going to use that to his advantage. Unfortunately, it also meant that everyone sort of stood out like a sore thumb. As the seven of them left the Man Hole and set off in Justin's truck and Holly's Prius, they'd discovered precisely why Paige had seen "white people" in the divination. Because that was the best way to describe just how they'd all looked in the growing gloom of the wooded driveway. And standing out put them at a disadvantage. After all, they'd be in serious trouble if they had the misfortune of catching the attention of a curious passing cop, especially since all of them except Eric were carrying guns loaded with ash-coated bullets under their coats. Even if they weren't technically breaking any laws, they'd probably be plenty suspicious enough to detain for questioning, and the city simply didn't have that kind of time left.

"Well this is nostalgic..." grumbled Paul.

Eric glanced over at him, distracted, then followed his gaze to the buildings. "That's right...this was..."

"Where that Steampunk Monk weirdo blinded Kevin." He

gestured at the alleyway between the barber shop and the tobacco store on the corner. "Right in there."

Against Eric's better judgement, Paul and his son had been following the agent as he explored Main Street, trying to keep an eye on him. Naturally, he noticed the two tailing him and ducked into this alley, where he dropped one of his homemade devices, some kind of little plastic egg that spewed noxious black smoke when Kevin stepped on it.

"Coincidence?" wondered Eric.

"You don't really still believe in those anymore, do you?"

"Right. Good point." He turned his attention to the alleyway, holding the strange device out in front of him.

"We lost Steampunk after that," recalled Paul. "He just sort of disappeared. I always figured he darted around the back and got away while we were distracted, but..."

Eric stepped into the alleyway and looked down at the device. "The first time I met that guy, he was carrying a strange device, too." Though it looked nothing like this one. It was just a little black box with a gauge and a single, long needle sticking out of it, waving back and forth. "Pointed it at me and said I was collecting psychic energy or something."

Paul nodded. "I'm thinking now that he didn't run away. He went to whatever place we're looking for, didn't he?"

It made sense. Steampunk Monk was looking for something with that device. Looking back now, it seemed like he was mapping the city's weird features. He'd even possessed a shard of the looking glass, allowing him access to all of the unseen. If there was something here to be found, there was a good chance he knew about it.

That strange, static-like sensation was stronger here. It felt crackly, like when he took laundry out of the dryer and it was stuck together. Was this how the device worked? He was supposed to follow the increasing charge in the air? How did it know what it was looking for? What kind of energy was it utilizing?

With his free hand, he took his phone from his pocket and glanced at the screen.

I'M NOT FEELING ANYTHING, reported Isabelle.

"I should probably stay and guard the truck, don't you think?" whimpered Adam.

"Don't make me tell Ally you were being a little bitch," replied Justin.

"We don't care what you tell that she-demon," declared Greg.

"Don't care," agreed Adam.

"She only *thinks* she scares people," Greg went on.

"Not scared of her," agreed Adam.

And yet Eric noticed that neither of them dared to stay behind as he led the way into the gloomy alleyway.

The static feeling in his hand continued to grow more intense as he moved toward the back of the buildings, where a small parking area separated the property from those surrounding it, eerily similar to the one behind the bookshop, he realized with some dread.

Fortunately, he didn't see any skinwalkers creeping around.

Not yet, anyway.

Eric stood there for a moment, scanning his surroundings, wondering which way to go first.

"This is a lot like Albuquerque," announced Greg, "when the SWAT team hired me to help hunt down a satanic cult that was kidnapping children all over the city."

"Don't wanna talk about that kinda thing right now," croaked Adam.

"Back in 'ninety-six, that was."

Eric wondered if he was really trying to impress anyone or if he was merely trying to make himself feel braver. Or if he truly believed that he'd actually done these fanciful things. Whatever the reason, he wasn't convincing anyone. He had the wide, terrified eyes of a child wandering alone in a Halloween spook house, just waiting for something to jump out at him.

He turned right and walked back behind the tobacco store. Was the signal getting weaker now? Or was he just getting used to that weird, staticky feeling in his hand?

Or was it that he didn't have a clue how this thing worked and was only imagining things? That was probably just as likely.

He stopped short of the back door and went back the other way.

"That was big news for a while," Greg went on.

"Big news," muttered Adam.

"'Course, the government covered it up pretty quickly. You can't hardly find anything about it now."

"Cover ups," agreed Adam.

Somewhere nearby a truck's air brakes sounded and both Greg and Adam jumped as if something had just grabbed them from behind.

"You guys are seriously wimping things up," grumbled Justin. "You know that, right?"

"People don't realize it," Greg informed him, "but it's perfectly normal for people who've been trained in the art of assassination to be jumpy."

"Reflexes," said Adam, nodding in agreement even while he looked as if he might pass out at any second.

"Right," said Justin. "If you say so."

That crackly sensation on his hand was definitely getting more intense now.

He walked past Zegler's back door, past the dumpster enclosure and another unnecessarily narrow alleyway, his eyes peeled the entire time for deceptive faces peering out from impossible places. It was eerie how familiar the setting was. He felt as if he'd circled right back around to where he started. This lot was bigger. And it wasn't fenced in. But it was darker than it was when he was in that first lot, which somehow made it feel smaller and more claustrophobic.

He made his way past the next building and around a concrete porch, following the growing crackle of the otherworldly compass until it suddenly seemed to weaken.

He paused, confused, and turned back again. For a moment, he fumbled around with the device, unsure if he was even doing it right.

"Seems like it's somewhere in this area," he concluded.

Everyone turned and surveyed their surroundings, but there wasn't anything here.

There was a single doorway leading into the back of the building, which if Eric remembered right was a little drug store. And there was another concrete stairwell leading down to a basement entrance, just like the one back at Tubby's. But a quick check by Paul and Justin revealed both to be tightly locked.

"Now what?" wondered Greg.

"We tried," reasoned Adam. "We should probably head back to the Man Hole."

Eric turned and paced around the area, feeling the change in that strange, static energy against his hand. It was strongest near the building.

He *really* didn't want to break into a drug store. A place like that was going to have plenty of security.

"Do we try the key right here?" wondered Paul.

Eric reached into his pocket and took out the other device. But it only took a moment to realize that there was nowhere to use it. There was no keyhole to match the key.

"Do you think Steampunk took whatever it was when he was here?"

Eric shook his head and held up the key. "Even if he *was* able to find it, he didn't have this."

"Maybe it's unseen?" tried Paul, and was immediately answered by his ringing phone, which he took from his pocket and set to speaker.

"I don't feel any unseen energy," replied Isabelle.

"Hey," called Greg, who'd wandered on past the drug store. "There's another door over here. A *suspicious* one."

Eric walked over to where he was standing and peered around the corner of the building. It wasn't an alley at all, he saw. It only went back a few yards. Another set of concrete steps led down to a pair of heavy, iron doors with an ominous looking "KEEP OUT" sign bolted to it. A heavy chain had been looped through the handles and secured with a padlock, but now the chain and lock lay strewn on the concrete in front of the door. Even more encouraging—or perhaps *less* encouraging would be a more appropriate description—he felt the compass react as he descended the steps. "Yep," he decided as he tucked the key back into his jacket pocket. "That looks like the right sort of place."

Greg nodded. "Experienced eyes can just tell, am I right?"

"Something like that," he muttered.

"Awesome…" groaned Adam in a voice that made it perfectly clear that he didn't think it was awesome in the least. "I was worried we wouldn't find it…"

"Creek Bend Public Works…" read Paul as they drew closer to the sign. "You don't think they're involved in this, do you? Like, do the agents have people planted in the city government or something?"

"Hard to say what they're capable of," grumbled Eric. It *did* seem like those freaks had the run of the place sometimes.

He withdrew the flashlight from his pocket, then pushed open the door and shined it into the creepy hallway that waited on the other side.

"Just like when I flushed out those terrorists hiding in the sewers of Boston back in two thousand three…" said Greg, his voice trembling audibly now. "I wasn't afraid at all… Just charged right in there and…" But that bravado didn't seem to have carried over because his voice choked away completely as he stepped into the darkness and looked around.

"Can't wait to go in the scary dark place," agreed Adam, his own voice little more than a high-pitched whisper by now.

"Those guys are *so* going to get eaten first if monsters show up," decided Isabelle. "You know that right?"

Chapter Thirty-Seven

"What is this place?" asked Justin.

"No idea," replied Paul. "Never knew this was here. Maybe it's like the municipal tunnels that run under the courthouse and police station?" He glanced over at Eric. "You remember those, don't you? That's where that kid left you wire-tied to the bars with your pants around your ankles."

"I remember just fine. Thanks."

"Hey, is that picture Kevin took still the background on Karen's phone?"

"No. Can we stay on track please?"

"I think Diane might still have it on hers, though," volunteered Isabelle.

Eric glared at Paul's phone.

"Those are *not* nice words you're thinking," she told him.

"Just shut it," he snapped. "Both of you."

The passage was bricked off a short distance to the right, leaving left the only option. Fortunately, that was also the way the static crackle of the compass was telling him to go.

Brushing aside the cobwebs, he led the way through the spider-infested darkness.

This certainly wasn't the team he would've put together if given the choice. Paul was one thing. Even Justin seemed rather competent when it came down to it. But between Greg's constant stream of fairy tales and Adam's spineless whimpering, he could think of *lots* of people he would've chosen besides the two of them. But this was the team he had. And it was considerably more than he usually had when things started getting hairy.

There were no lights installed down here. The walls were grimy and covered with cobwebs. The floor was muddy, packed earth. Every sound they made seemed to echo back and forth, making it sound as if there were more people here than they'd brought.

"Okay, *this* place is definitely haunted," decided Justin. "Any second now, we're going to hear footsteps and chains rattling and people screaming."

"Definitely," agreed Greg. "I've seen my fair share of ghosts. They're here. I'm sure of it."

"Right now?" whimpered Adam. "Like, *now* now?"

"I'm not feeling any spiritual energy in that place," reported Isabelle. "Those guys are just stupid."

"Ghosts are the least of my concerns," decided Eric as he frowned at the compass. His hand was really buzzing now. It felt like his skin was going numb.

"I seriously feel like I can hear a little girl crying right now," whispered Greg.

"Sorry..." whimpered Adam.

"Jesus, man!" hissed Justin.

"I can't help it!" he whined. "You guys know I have a thing about spiders!"

"You have a thing about *everything!*"

"I can't help it!"

Ahead of them, the tunnel opened up, revealing an empty room about twelve feet wide that stretched off into the darkness to the right.

Eric switched the compass to his other hand, cursing at the crackle and pop of the static electricity. He could even see it now. Little sparks of electricity flashed in the darkness, arcing between the wires and his skin. Did that mean they were getting close? Was it inside this room?

"Seems like just old infrastructure under the newer buildings," observed Paul as he swept his light around the empty room. "There're a lot of places like this around. Sometimes when places would flood, they'd just raise the ground up around it, burying the original floors."

"I can't count the times I've cleaned out huge drug stashes from places just like this," boasted Greg.

"Drugs," agreed Adam. "Yeah. That's probably it."

"You'd be surprised how many millions of dollars' worth of cocaine can be carted out of a room this size," Greg went on.

"Millions," agreed Adam.

Eric tightened his grip on the device and pushed deeper into the gloom. "God, just listening to those two is dragging down my IQ."

"You get used to it," said Paul.

"*You* probably do," countered Isabelle. "Yours isn't that much higher than theirs."

"Don't make me kick you out of my phone again."

"I'm just saying what Eric was thinking."

"She is," admitted Eric.

"You're both shitheads. You know that right?"

"You know what bugs me about this whole thing?" said Justin as he shined his light back the way they came. "Who cut that chain back there? Was someone here already? I mean, you don't think someone took what we were looking for, do you?"

"Not if this thing is leading us there," replied Eric. It was getting less and less fun to be holding the stupid thing. His hand was starting to throb.

It wasn't going to give him cancer or something, was it?

"I don't think anyone's been in here in some time," deduced Paul as he raked the cobwebs from his path.

Finally, the far wall came into view, revealing an empty doorway curtained with thick layers of dusty spiderwebs.

"Is that the doorway Poppy saw in her divination?" asked Isabelle.

Eric thought that was probably pretty likely. He pressed the compass into it and felt the wires sparking over his skin, flashing and strobing in the darkness.

"Be careful," she warned him.

He used the device to clear the cobwebs and then stepped through the doorway, only to find that there was nothing there.

The room here was empty. There was nothing here and nowhere left to go.

"Okay…" said Paul. "Now what?"

Eric didn't get the chance to reply that he had no idea. As

he crossed the small, empty room, the compass gave off a blinding flash and a loud pop and he cursed and threw it onto the floor.

"Was that a good thing or a bad thing?" asked Justin.

Eric stood there, rubbing at his stinging hand. He wasn't sure yet. One way or another, this was the end of the line. The compass lay on the ground, sparking and crackling like a live power line. Tendrils of smoke were rising off of it and those thin wires were starting to glow with heat in the gloom. The only thing he knew for certain was that he wasn't going to be picking it back up in that state.

Paul walked around the device and kicked it back through the open doorway. "I guess we'll pick that up on our way out," he decided, scratching at his ashy beard.

Eric wasn't paying attention to him. He stepped up to the wall and brushed away the cobwebs, revealing a strange, concave metal disk set into the stone. "The compass leads us there..." he recalled. "Then the key opens the way..."

"So that's the keyhole?" wondered Paul.

"It's the only thing here," reasoned Eric, glancing around at the rest of the room.

Justin leaned closer, shining his own light onto the disk. "Uh...that's not a hole."

"Black World tech..." sighed Eric, pulling the key from his jacket pocket and examining it. "It's not just advanced," he recalled, "it works on completely different physics." He turned it around and pressed the tip of the small end against the curved disk.

"I'm just saying it don't look like it's going to fit," said Justin.

Paul snorted. Then he coughed and stifled the grin on his face when Eric glared at him.

Justin wasn't wrong. By all accounts, the concave disk in the wall was *not* a hole and the key shouldn't fit. But he found that as he pushed the key against the disk, it somehow gave, allowing the key to slide into it.

"Huh..." said Justin, leaning over his shoulder. "Look at

that. It just opens right up, doesn't it?"

Again, Paul snorted.

"Seriously?" growled Eric.

"Sorry."

"I just didn't think it'd take the whole thing like that," said Justin.

"Oh my god, will you shut up already!" shouted Eric.

Paul didn't even try to stifle the laughter this time.

"What's so funny?" asked Greg.

"Don't get it," agreed Adam.

"Everyone just shut up!" snapped Eric. He turned his attention back to the key, grumbling about Paul's horrid parenting skills. In all seriousness, the key fit the keyhole. It was obvious that this was where they were meant to be. But nothing had happened. Not yet. You didn't just insert a key to unlock a door. You also had to turn it. So he took hold of the flared end and gave it a twist. It rotated easily, as if the mechanism were brand new, circling all the way around inside the hole.

What happened next was weird. With a great gust of air and popping of ears, as if the room had suddenly depressurized, the wall sort of *unwound itself*. Watching it happen, it was as if it were nothing more than a tightly stretched sheet of rubber. It snapped outward from around the device in his hand, which had now transformed into a single, spiraling, metallic disk a little smaller than a Frisbee that dropped from his hand and clattered to the ground at his feet.

The room was now twice as long as it was a moment ago and another open doorway waited on the far side of the room, looking out over more darkness between two dingy windows.

Ford had called it a "pucker point," and now that he'd seen it, he thought he could almost grasp the concept. It was as if the device had "puckered" the physical space around it, sort of like tying off the end of a bread bag. Reality here was scrunched together, making it impossible to pass unless you used the key to un-scrunch it.

"Well *that* was weird…" said Justin.

"I knew that was going to happen," said Greg.

Chapter Thirty-Eight

Eric walked through the newly discovered half of the room, sweeping the area with his light, taking in the differences between the two sides. The air had completely changed. It wasn't as stuffy as it was before. And it smelled different. That dank, underground smell of the basement had suddenly been replaced with something dryer and subtler. It was also colder. But the most alarming difference was the cobwebs. They stopped precisely where the wall used to be, leaving the newly revealed half covered in years of accumulated dust and grime, but not a single strand of webbing, as if even the spiders had no way of reaching this place.

The idea of being somewhere that even spiders wouldn't tread seemed especially ominous.

"Something's different," said Isabelle.

"No shit," grumbled Paul, looking down at his screen.

"No, like *really* different. The energy's completely changed. Check your compass."

"I broke it," said Eric, glancing back toward the doorway where Paul kicked the overheating contraption.

"No, your *other* compass," she said, exasperated.

"Oh, right!" He withdrew the pocket watch and opened it. The second hand was whirling like a fan blade.

Paul whistled. "That's probably not good, is it?"

"What's that mean?" asked Justin. "Are we time traveling or something?"

"Not *time*," explained Eric, snapping it shut and returning it to his pocket. "It's *distance*." And a *considerable* distance, at that. It was moving much faster now than when he was in Cordelia's woods.

"Distance to *what*?" pushed Justin.

"To *the known universe*," replied Isabelle. "You've crossed into another dimension."

"What?" gasped Adam. "Is that bad? Are we in trouble?"

"Dimensional travel…" croaked Greg. "I've done it before, of course…" But he didn't sound like he'd ever done *anything* like this before, because all the strength had left his voice. He sounded as if he could barely breathe. "Not necessarily to *this* dimension…"

"I should go back now," whimpered Adam. "I don't think my passport's up to date."

Justin, however, only took off his hat and scratched his head. "Seriously? We're really in another world right now?"

"Welcome to the club," grunted Eric. He stepped through the newly revealed doorway and found himself on an old dirt street with several buildings lined up on either side, all of them badly burned.

"Are we *outside*?" asked Justin. "This really is real, isn't it? We're really in another world." He shook his head and added, as if he couldn't quite make himself believe it, "I'm in another world."

Eric turned and followed the street, shining his light over the charred storefronts. There appeared to be a much larger building just beyond these.

"Sky's even different," observed Justin, peering up into the empty, endless darkness above. It wasn't merely that it was dark. The sky they left in Creek Bend was overcast. There were no clouds up there. There was only blackness.

"The sky's not supposed to change," groaned Adam, his neck craned as he turned in a circle, scanning the endless void above him. "The sky's the sky. Anywhere you go the sky's the one thing that's supposed to stay the same. What kind of awful place doesn't have the *sky*?"

Eric walked on. Why did this look familiar? He was pretty sure he'd never been here before.

"Yeah, where'd the stars go?" wondered Justin.

"Bordering worlds like these are usually finite," explained Isabelle. "They're not very big. Wander too far and you can cross the hazy boundaries and get lost forever. Naturally, they don't reach all the way to other stars."

"Huh…" said Justin.

"So if this isn't our world," wondered Paul, "then where did these buildings come from? Someone obviously had to build them. Where *are* we?"

"We're in Creek Bend," replied Eric. He was standing in front of the larger building now, his light fixed on the remains of the old sign.

Paul stepped toward him, curious. "What do you mean, Creek Bend?"

"It's the Gudenhaus Inn," he explained, still staring at the remaining letters on the sign. Only the first four letters were visible, but he didn't need to read the whole thing. He recognized this sign. He'd seen pictures of it just that morning, during the book signing. "This was one of the places that was supposed to have burned to the ground in the Fire of 1881."

"You're telling me this is some kind of *alternate Creek Bend*?" said Justin.

"Bet it's a secret government project," decided Greg. Some of the shock of finding himself in another world seemed to have eased a little, because we was telling his lies with a bit more confidence again. "Like the Philadelphia Experiment. I was involved in a few of those. Can't talk about it, though."

"Some serious *Stranger Things* shit right here…" whimpered Adam. He was looking around, expecting to be attacked by a monster at any second.

As he stood staring at the old, forgotten inn, Eric began to put the pieces together at last. It was the book, he realized. It all started there. Not just because he was reading it shortly before that first run-in with a skinwalker. Ford told him that it was Voskstern's book that brought him to Creek Bend. He teased him about it, telling him that there were *secrets* inside it.

And then there were the things Cordelia and Naida told him, too. *Take a closer look at the past*, he recalled. *Find what's lost.* She was talking about this place. Nadia had even advised him to, "Turn back the pages," literally referring, he now realized, to the pages of the book.

Paul turned and looked back at the other buildings. "So all these places were just *assumed* to have burned up in the fire? But in reality, they just...*came here?*"

"Wouldn't someone have been able to tell the difference?" wondered Justin.

"People never noticed that the old high school just disappeared," Isabelle explained. "And the old asylum in the hospital parking lot."

"Fair point," admitted Paul.

"Okay..." said Justin. "But I mean, something just picked up this whole street and dropped it here?"

"More likely," reasoned Isabelle, "something made the entire area shift into this neighboring dimension."

"She's right, you know," said a voice from Eric's pocket.

Surprised, he pulled out his own cell phone and looked at the screen. It hadn't rung and he hadn't accepted any calls, but the screen was lit and the line was open. "Ford?"

"The night of that fire, something tore the fabric of the universe," explained Ford, "causing a large chunk of land to fall into *this* dimension. To compensate, the physical space surrounding the newly created void compressed and stitched itself back together. Creek Bend, and in fact the entire universe, *shrank* by a few acres that day."

"That makes no sense," said Justin. "Wouldn't people notice if the world was suddenly smaller? I mean wouldn't all the maps be off?"

"If the space depicted on a map were to change within the greater scope of reality," explained Ford, "then the space depicted on a map would have to change as well. It's just not possible for a map to depict an impossibility. I'm betting *you* can't think of a way to draw a map of a space that doesn't exist."

Justin frowned. "Uh...?"

"The universe has a way of self-correcting itself," Ford went on. "It has to. These kinds of things simply aren't that uncommon. I mean, what did you think would have happened if the Conqueror Worm in Hedge Lake had succeeded in chewing a hole through the fabric of reality. Chances are good that all of Hedge Lake would've been sucked into the physical space of the worm's dimension, leaving behind only a stitch in your world."

"It sort of makes sense," said Isabelle.

"Does it?" wondered Justin.

"I mean, you didn't really think you'd saved the *entire world* that day, did you?" asked Ford.

Eric ran his hand through his hair, sending a cloud of ash and dust raining down onto his shoulders. "Maybe a little..." he muttered.

"That's cute."

"Where are you?" demanded Eric.

"Not far away. Come find me. I'll bet Izzy there knows the way."

He glanced over at Paul's phone.

"I *do* feel something," she said. "Some kind of faint energy. Not far away."

"See there," said Ford. "Now come find me. Boy, have I got a surprise for you!"

Before Eric could tell him that he wasn't interested in surprises, the line went dead.

"I don't think I like that guy," said Adam.

"He's not wrong, though," said Greg. "I could've told you about that whole 'stitch' thing. If you'd asked."

"Just shut up," said Eric.

Chapter Thirty-Nine

In addition to the Gudenhaus Inn, Eric soon discovered that the Allendar Mansion still existed and, furthermore, had mostly escaped the blaze. It was no wonder Emanuel Voskstern had so much trouble piecing together what the city would look like today. The city *had* changed over the years. Streets were raised to prevent flooding, old structures were torn down and replaced, businesses had popped up where farm fields once stood. But a large portion of the city simply wasn't there anymore.

It was difficult to imagine all these places simply vanishing one night without anyone even noticing. But Isabelle was right about it being no different from the unseen. Perhaps they *did* notice it and then they all forgot. Something about these sorts of places seemed to cause them to be erased from people's memories as well as from their perception. He wondered if perhaps the physical world and the minds of people were linked. He wondered if there was some truth to that old thought that one's perceptions of the world shaped and altered it. Then he wondered why he was bothering to wonder all these things as if he possessed the mental fortitude to even understand any of it.

A part of him really wanted to poke around in these old buildings. History was lingering inside them, as Voskstern had so passionately written in his book. There was no telling what treasures had been sitting in these dark buildings all this time, both historical *and* literal, given the rumors about the Allendar family wealth. But time was short. And it was growing shorter with each passing second.

How long did they have before Yenaldlooshi awoke from his slumber? And what would happen once he did? Would the rest of Creek Bend be plunged into this eternal, starless darkness?

They followed the dirt street past the Allendar Mansion gate and through a grove of dead trees. Time seemed to have slowed to a stop here, even the decay. All that was living was long dead, but the earth at their feet still bore the remarkably well-preserved ruts of bygone boot prints, wagon wheels and horseshoe tracks.

Eric couldn't decide if he was more impressed with the preservation of this place or horrified by the lifelessness of it. But by the time he reached the gave yard, he was definitely leaning toward the latter.

Without a single blade of grass, the extra-dead cemetery was exactly as Cierra had described it. And looming beyond it was the crumbling form of the very church Holly and Paige described.

Was there anything left, he wondered? Had he missed anything? Because he was tired of surprises.

It was waiting for them there on the steps of the church. A small lump of vaguely doll-shaped clay with strands of rotten straw protruding from the lumps that made up its head, arms and legs.

Eric didn't waste time pondering the possibility of a trap. At this point, he was too tired to overthink anything. He walked up to the steps and picked up the idol.

This was it? This was the thing that had kept Yenaldlooshi docile for more than thirteen decades? An ugly hunk of clay and straw?

"I knew you could do it," said a voice that echoed ominously from the depths of the church.

Eric said nothing. He tucked the idol under his arm and looked up as the strange little man in the colorful scarf stepped from the shadows and stood just inside the doorway, just within the glow of their flashlights.

"After all, you're Eric Fortrell! The great shining knight!"

"I'm just an English teacher," said Eric. He was getting tired of telling people that. Why did everyone want to shove this "hero" nonsense onto him. He only wanted to be normal.

Ford took a step forward. It was an odd sort of step. Exaggerated and strangely stiff. Eric found himself taking a step backward, expecting some nasty surprise. "I wonder though... Have you really pieced it all together yet? Do you really know anything at all?"

"I know that it can't be this easy."

"No?"

"Just take the idol and walk back out of here? You expect me to believe that?"

He took another of those stiff steps forward. "Why not? That was our agreement, wasn't it? You do the legwork? Find the compass and the key? Retrieve the idol? Save the city? What more could there be?"

"That's the question, isn't it?" said Eric. "What more is there? What are you *really* after?"

Ford thrust his arms out to his sides and dramatically threw back his head. "Whatever could you possibly mean?"

"Uh...Eric?" whispered Paul.

"I know," he whispered back. There was something wrong about this situation. He could feel it. It was gnawing at him. Raising his voice, he said, "You got here before us. You knew right where it was. You've known everything all along. What to do. Where to go. Where to find me. How to threaten me. You never needed me in the first place."

He was still standing there with his arms out at his sides and his head back, as if he'd been hung on an invisible crucifix.

"You even interfered in the divination, didn't you? That's why it was so specific that we go to Ternheart. *You* were the one who told us to go to Furnanter Park."

"That was *him*?" grunted Paul.

"That was him," affirmed Eric.

"Son of a..."

"You hid the device in the fireplace," he went on. "You put those starved spirits there. Everything that's happened here was you. *You* stole the idol. That was *your* voice speaking to me in Yenaldlooshi's head during the spell."

Finally, Ford lowered his arms and slowly rolled his head to the side, glaring at him with those creepy, sunken eyes. In that gloom, they looked utterly black. "You're disappointing me, Eric.

I thought you'd have put more of it together by now."

"You mean like *why* you stole the idol and then put me to work finding it for you? That's a question I'd like the answer to."

"No…" he replied. "I mean, like *why did Ezra Joval bring Yee Naaldlooshii to Creek Bend in the first place?*"

This caught Eric off guard. He blinked, confused. That *was* a good question, but it wasn't at the top of his list at the moment.

Ford took another step forward, his head still tilted dramatically to one side. As he approached the flashlights, more of his pale face came into view. He looked even paler than he did before. "The answer? Because *I* told him to."

"Ezra Joval's been dead for at least a hundred years," said Paul.

He lifted his head from one shoulder and tipped it all the way over to the other. "Your point?"

"Ah…" said Paul, his breath seemingly sapped away. "Right… I get it…"

"He's a lot older than he looks, huh?" said Justin.

"Too old…" croaked Greg.

Adam tried to add his usual agreement but only succeeded in producing a terrified, high-pitched squeak.

"Exactly," said Eric. "You're no agent. You never were. What are you?"

The *thing* calling itself Ford staggered toward them two more steps, wobbling his head and flapping his arms wildly in the process and making a loop of his colorful scarf slip over his shoulder. "Oh, but you're wrong. I *was* an agent. It was exactly as I told you. I saw the ad for the book signing. I read Vosktern's fascinating book. I saw the pictures inside. The Gudenhaus Inn. The Allendar Mansion. This church. I *recognized* those places. They were described in certain *research files* accumulated by teams who exploited this area's peculiar physical properties before a series of disasters shut down the project. I did what no one has ever done before." Again, he lifted his head and tipped it to the other side, flashing him an insane grin as he did so. "I found the source of Creek Bend's anomaly!"

Eric backed up as the madman staggered down the steps, swaying madly.

When he stopped, Ford's mad grin was gone. Instead, he had his lower lip pushed out in a childish pout, those strange, black eyes glistening in the flashlight's glare. "But no sooner had I arrived in this town when something terrible happened to me."

"And what was that?" dared Eric.

"Yeah," gasped Adam. "What happened?"

"Well..." Ford leaned closer, holding his hands out at his sides in a strange pose as he did so. At the same time, his scarf finally slid off his shoulder, revealing the brutal bruises and twisted flesh of his strangled neck. "I was murdered," he explained.

Behind him, Paul, Justin and Greg all cursed and backed farther away. Adam, on the other hand, only made another of those terrified squeaking noises.

"And now..." said Ford as that blackness drained from his eyes and revealed the glazed corpse stare hidden beneath them. One of those outstretched arms dropped, as if suspended by a wire that had just but cut. "...I'm just..." Then his head drooped, too and he slouched over, seemingly hanging by just the one upraised hand. "...a puppet." As he said this last word Ford's lifeless corpse dropped into a silent heap on the ground at Eric's feet.

Paul cursed again.

Justin was mumbling something that might've been a prayer.

And from the sound of it, Adam was hyperventilating.

Eric stared at the strangled corpse, confused. A puppet? Meaning someone had been controlling this lifeless carcass this whole time? Then who...?

A strangely ominous giggle drew his attention up to the roof of the church where a man was suddenly sitting, watching them all. He was wearing an old, green sport coat, sloppy, brown pants, a black hat and an all-too familiar goofy-looking tie. His face was a ghastly white, with a wide, red smear for a mouth and dark circles around his eyes.

"Long time no see, *bestie*," said the clown.

Before Eric could think of anything to say to the ghoulish thing lounging on the rotting eaves of the church, Adam finally bolted and fled back down the dirt road, stumbling over wagon ruts and screaming, "No one said there'd be a clown!"

"Wait for me!" shouted Greg, taking off through the darkness after him.

"Get back here, you cowards!" shouted Justin.

But the two men kept going, their darting flashlight beams receding into the distance.

The clown watched them flee, his painted face scrunched into a puzzled expression. "What *is* it with you people being so afraid of these clown things, anyway?" he wondered.

"I'm not afraid," said Eric, standing his ground. "I just don't like you."

The clown… The very *same* clown that caused all that chaos with the rat demon at the play park, putting all those children in danger before making his escape…

"You can't possibly be *that* surprised," said the clown. "I mean I told you my name was Wilford Lafayette. I mean how dense can you be? Will Laff?"

Eric stared at him. "That's just stupid."

The pasty-faced weirdo managed to look indignant. "Well obviously *you* didn't get it. Even though that was supposed to be the easy part."

"What are you doing here?" he demanded.

"I'm just here for a playdate with my best buddy."

"I'm not your friend."

"But like it or not," said the clown through an evil grin, "You're *mine*."

Eric stared at him. This thing looked like a man, but he was no such thing. This was a monster. A *powerful* monster.

"And like the totally awesome friend that I am," Ford, went on, "I've been looking out for you. I even took care of our agent friend here when he came nosing around three days ago." He glanced down at the lifeless heap on the ground. "That guy was *no fun at all*, by the way. All dark and gloomy and serious. No sense of humor whatsoever. I made a *way* better agent, if I do say so myself."

"Just tell me what you want," growled Eric.

"I already told you," sighed the clown. "I want to *play with you.*" He stood up, crossed his arms behind his back and began tiptoeing along the edge of the roof as if he weren't precariously balanced on the edge of a two story drop that was probably ready to fall apart at the slightest touch. "Specifically speaking, I'm fascinated by your role in all these exciting new changes that are going on in the universe."

"What changes?"

"See?" said the clown. "That's the best part. You don't even know what's going on, yet you're right smack in the middle of it all."

"In the middle of what?" he demanded. He was growing impatient. He hated this back-and-forth nonsense.

The clown twirled around and started back the other way. "The machine, of course. The great *prophecy.* The long-foretold *end of the cycle.* And how you're a pivotal part of the gears turning inside it." He twirled again, this time facing Eric. He even bent forward and propped his hands on his knees, letting that stupid tie dangle over the precarious drop beneath him. "I had a theory, you see. That no matter what I did to throw a wrench in that enormous contraption, someone would be there to keep the wheels turning. And so I thought I'd test it with a little game. I stole the idol, putting you and the entire city in imminent peril, and made it unlikely that you'd be able to put things right in time."

"So you were setting me up," said Eric.

"Not very sporting," grumbled Paul.

"Dick move," agreed Justin.

But the clown gave them all a dismissive wave. "You were *fine.* They weren't going to let anything happen to you. And they didn't, did they? What happened every time you found your back against the wall? Something happened to save your neck. Just like something *always* happens."

"The universe loves you," muttered Paul.

"Quiet," grumbled Eric.

"No, no!" said the clown, holding up a finger. "He's *right*. He's *absolutely* right. Except the *universe* tends to be run by these *pretentious busybodies* who can't keep their noses out of other people's business." He turned and started tiptoeing along the edge of the roof again. "Call themselves the 'Caretakers,' like they're some kind of high and mighty *neighborhood association* or something."

"I don't understand any of this," said Eric.

"Sounds to me like he's describing pagan gods," said Justin.

Eric and Paul both glanced back at him, surprised.

"Precisely!" exclaimed the clown. "Humans don't really possess the ability to comprehend the personalities of these higher entities, much less possess the concepts necessary to *identify* them. It's not possible. Their minds are *universes* apart. They lump them into simple categories like gods and demons and angels and faeries. But those old religions might've come closer than most to understanding how things actually work between them. Bickering, scheming, plotting, raging, jealous, pompous things infinitely more concerned with their own petty issues than the world they're trampling beneath their filthy feet."

Eric shook his head. "Gods? Really?" *Why* did things keep circling back to *gods* of all things?

The clown shrugged. "It's a loose interpretation, really. I mean some of them like to call themselves gods, but *those* aren't nearly as impressive as some that are much more 'godlike' but modest enough not to say so. And then there's the upper echelon where the ones that could actually be described as the *real* gods are believed to be watching over *everything*... And then there's just *God*. Way up at the very top of it all where nobody can see Him and can't even agree on whether He even really exists. It's complicated. You probably shouldn't worry too much about it all."

Was this guy being serious? Or was he just yanking them around. That stupid tie strongly suggested the latter. "And what about you?" he asked. "You said when we first met that only a god could've stolen the idol. Is that how you see yourself?"

He grinned an especially slimy sort of grin and replied,

"Let's just say I qualify much more than some who lay claim to the title." Then he twirled around again and tiptoed back the other way. "I've been watching you since our last meeting," he said, changing the subject. "The way you handled my pet was *intriguing*, to say the least."

"Pet?" grumbled Paul. "Is he talking about that *rat demon*?"

"It got me curious," the clown went on, ignoring him. "So I kept an eye on you. I watched how you handled yourself against those karmic sinners and that infernal machine. And I did my research, too. Learned all I could about you. I could tell that you were someone special, but I never imagined that I was playing with someone of such *cosmic importance*."

"What's your point?" growled Eric. "Why are you telling me all this?"

"Only because you deserve to know the truth. Those...*things* out there...*pretending* to help you... They're just *using* you. You're a pawn. And you're at their mercy. They're not protecting *you*. They're protecting the machines they're building with you. And when you're all used up, they'll throw you away."

"Fine," he replied. "Maybe then I'll finally be able to get some goddamn peace and quiet."

The clown threw his head back and cackled. "You are, hands down, my absolute *favorite* human. Do you know that?"

"What was the point in all this?" demanded Eric. "Why go through all this trouble if you already knew the 'universe' was going to protect me?"

He looked shocked to be asked such a question. "Because it was *fun*. Duh."

But Eric shook his head. "No. There had to be something else to it all. You were after something."

That evil grin spread across the painted lunatic's face. "Perhaps... But then again, perhaps not. Maybe I just like screwing with people."

"What do you really want?" pressed Eric.

"I'd like to tell you. I really would. But do you really have time to listen? I mean there's still the matter of that slumbering evil I mentioned earlier. Remember that? The one that's due to wake up any moment now?"

Eric tightened his grip on the idol. He was right. As much as he wanted answers, he needed to get back to the museum as soon as possible.

"Oh, that's right," said the clown, "and there's also the matter of Yee Naaldlooshii. He'll be a problem, too, won't he?"

He blinked, confused. "What?"

"Or didn't you realize yet that the 'evil' I kept talking about wasn't that silly elder skinwalker of yours?"

He looked back at Paul and Justin, who only returned his look of bewilderment and shrugged.

"Do you want to know what really happened that night in eighteen eighty-one? The reason I led Ezra Joval to believe that Creek Bend was the ideal place to hide the monster? It's because there was *already* something slumbering beneath this city. Something was here long before the first buildings were raised. Something that has fed on cities erected on these grounds for *millennia*. The very cause of the dimensional crossroads that subconsciously lures people to this place to build those cities, so that it may awaken and *devour* them."

Eric couldn't quite suppress a shudder. What was this guy talking about?

"And right now," the clown went on, spreading his arms and gesturing out at the darkness all around them, "we're all standing in *his* world." Then he dropped his arms to his side. That mad smile melted from his face. "Or can't you feel it?" He turned and looked off into the distance.

Eric followed his gaze. Was it only his imagination, or *did* he feel something out there somewhere?

"It's not your imagination," Isabelle said, speaking up from Paul's phone for the first time since arriving at the church. "I've been feeling it all along. There's something over there. And I think it's slowly getting stronger."

"When Ezra Joval brought Yee Naaldlooshii to this place all those years ago," the clown said, "even so subdued by magic that he was unable to claw his way out of a wooden crate, his power was strong enough to be felt from here. The moment they arrived in this city it began to stir. And that night, it opened its eyes."

"What was it?" croaked Justin.

"Something *incredible*," sighed the clown. "An entity of such terrible power that it would tear open the very world and swallow all of Creek Bend whole."

"Another demon?" wondered Eric, none too happy at the thought of dealing with another of those.

"No, no. Not a demon. A *devil*. There's a difference. They're both extremely powerful and extremely rare, but only a *devil* actually originates from hell."

"Right…" said Eric, confused. Now that he was thinking about it, didn't a fairy once tell him something about demons not really being from hell?

"But not just any devil. A *shayatin*. Terrible beyond imagining. It woke up that night. And it was *hungry*." He sighed and shook his head. "It was going to be a spectacle to behold."

"You *wanted* it to happen?" marveled Eric. "A whole city *devoured* by some cosmic hellspawn and you treated it like a show?"

The clown looked indignant. "I'm old as shit, Eric. You get bored after you've been around for a few cycles."

He shook his head, bewildered at the very idea of it all.

"But the city *didn't* get devoured, did it?" said the clown. "For some reason a *jinn*, of all things, showed up out of thin air." He shook his head. "*That* I didn't see coming. It just sort of popped in, riding some blazing tower, breathing hellfire through the streets like an angry god…which I suppose it sort of was, really… Shayatin and jinn are natural enemies. They'll seek each other out across time and space. That night, the shayatin was outmatched. It withdrew back into its lair and returned to sleep. The world stitched itself back together. The jinn vanished as quickly as it appeared. And the rest of the city burned."

It was a lot to take in, but Eric found that it did at least explain a few things. If this creep was telling the truth, then the cause of the fire really was the jinn, who must've been drawn to the past because that was the nearest point in both space and time when the shayatin was awake…which happened because of the presence of Yenadlooshi…who was only here because the *clown* sent him here…

His headache was getting worse.

"But I mean a *jinn* of all things?" the clown went on, shaking his head. "What were the odds? It was maddening. I couldn't wrap my head around it. Not then, anyway. I had no way of knowing what the future would hold." Now he turned and flashed Eric that eerily mad grin. "Not until I started following *you* around."

"Did you follow all that?" whispered Justin.

"Nope," Paul whispered back.

"Just checking."

"Well now," announced the clown. He faced the three of them and then gave them all a deep bow, as if he'd just finished a rousing performance on stage. "Talky time is over. Yee Naaldlooshii will be waking up any minute now. *And* his brood of freaks should be finding their way through the gate you opened."

Somewhere in the distance, they heard gunshots and screams.

"Right on time," said the clown, grinning. "By my calculations, there's no way you'll have time to get back to the museum and complete the binding spell. I wonder how your 'godly' friends will keep you alive now. Especially if you don't want that shayatin waking up before you can even leave here."

"Wait…" said Justin. "What?"

That grin spread almost from ear to ear. It looked monstrous. "Wakey, wakey!" he laughed.

Behind him, the church bell sounded, its clanging deafening in the perfect silence of the forsaken acres.

Eric felt a terrible dread spreading through his already-burning belly. Would that noise really wake a shayatin?

"Good luck with that!" laughed the clown. Then he vanished into thin air.

"Get back here!" shouted Eric as the bell clanged over and over again. "You still owe me for that drink!"

Chapter Forty

Well this was a hell of a mess. That deafening din sounded like it could wake the dead in the surrounding cemetery, much less a devil already on the verge of waking up. The three of them raced into the church and up the charred staircase, uncertain with each frantic step they took if the long-rotten lumber would even hold their weight.

Eric didn't know what was happening with Greg and Adam back on the old Main Street. The clown told them the skinwalkers had found their way through the doorway into this world, and he couldn't think of what else the sounds of gunfire and shouting in the distance could mean. They needed to get out there and help the two of them, but first they needed to silence this damned bell.

Make sure what's sleeping doesn't wake up, he thought, remembering Cordelia's dire warning. At the time, he'd assumed she was talking about Yenaldlooshi, but now it seemed that she, like Ford, had been talking about a completely different slumbering evil this whole time. Nadia had even specifically warned him to "hit the snooze button," strongly suggesting that she already knew he'd find himself scrambling to shut off the world's largest alarm clock.

Why they couldn't just tell him these things directly, he simply couldn't understand.

One thing was certain, though. He now knew precisely why Poppy and her sisters heard an ominous bell while peering into the divination water.

The top of the tower was a narrow space, barely big enough for the three of them to crowd into. And the swinging bell only made it that much smaller.

It wasn't as big as Eric expected it to be, but it looked

heavy. And it was swinging with such force that it looked like it might snap the rotten lumber and go flying out over the roof at any moment.

"How do we turn it off?" shouted Paul.

"How is it even *on*?" Justin shouted back. "There's no rope!"

He was right. As Eric circled around the thing, his hands clasped over his ears, he could see that the rope operating the swinging mechanism was long gone, yet it swung back and forth, clanging away, seemingly under its own power.

Justin reached out and grabbed the bell, intending to stop its motion, but it swung back with such force that it practically dragged him off his feet.

Whatever was making it move was too strong for such a basic tactic. They were going to need to use their heads.

"Grab the clacker!" cried Justin.

Paul and Eric both ducked down and peered up inside the bell. That little metal ball was the source of the sound and it looked much easier to stop than the much heavier frame around it. But when Paul reached up and grabbed it to stop its motion, he only ended up getting his hand mashed between the ball and the inner wall of the bell. The sound was muffled a little bit, but Paul's cursing more than made up for it as he snatched his hand back and cradled it against his chest.

"That's messed up!" shouted Justin as he clasped his hands over his ringing ears. "What're we supposed to do?"

It was a good question. At this rate, they were all going to go deaf in addition to being devoured by a devil.

Eric turned and looked out across the darkness, wondering how much time they had to figure this out. Was it only his imagination, or did he feel something out there in the distance?

"Try this!" shouted Justin. He shrugged out of his jacket and knelt down next to the bell. Then, careful not to get his own hand mashed between the two parts, he shoved the jacket up inside it. The sound was immediately stifled to a much more hollow series of thuds, but not silenced. "Yours too!" shouted Justin.

As Paul took off his own jacket, Eric found himself staring out into that darkness, distracted. Something was out there. Something dreadful beyond imagining. Small and distant, but slowly getting bigger and closer.

Paul knelt down and shoved his jacket up into the bell with Justin's.

"Try to wedge it up in there," grunted Justin. "Knot it around th—" But the bell clanged hard against his head, cutting him off and knocking him backward.

"Careful!" shouted Paul.

It was waking up, Eric realized. That little pinpoint blossoming in the distance was a monstrous consciousness. It was already stirring, but it was waking faster now. And merely feeling it out there was filling him with such an intense and overwhelming dread that he could barely stand it.

He closed his eyes, but it didn't go away. If anything, it only made it worse. Now everything was gone *except* for that little pinpoint in the distance. It shined in the darkness, growing brighter with every passing second, ebbing and waning as if with the slow pounding of a great, beating heart, looking like a…

He opened his eyes. "Lighthouse…" he sighed. It was like a lighthouse shining in the dark in the distance. Just like Perri described. This was what she saw.

"Eric!"

He turned around, dazed.

The deafening clanging was now a deep, reverberating *thumping* noise now that the clacker inside the bell was padded, but they were still struggling to knot the fabric while the bell swung back and forth, seemingly trying to shake them off.

He pushed back that crippling dread and shrugged out of his jacket.

Patience was what was called for here. Though time was desperately short, there was no way around it. He reached under the bell, careful to keep his hands clear of the apparently unstoppable clacker and his head clear of the swinging bell, and carefully knotted the sleeves of his tattered jacket around the other two. Then, when everything was lined up right, he pulled it tight, knotting it and binding it all in place.

As soon as the job was done, the bell abruptly quit swinging and slowed to a stop, as if surrendering.

"Well that was a pain," said Justin, his voice considerably louder than necessary now that the noise had stopped.

"What?" shouted Paul, still shaking his smashed hand. It was already starting to bruise.

Eric turned and gazed out over the darkness again. That blossoming consciousness was still there. He could still feel it. But was it growing a little slower now?

"I think you silenced that bell just in time," observed Isabelle. "But it's not over. It's still waking up. You've got to get back to the museum. Right now."

"Right," he said, snatching the idol off the floor and cradling it under his arm. "You heard the lady."

"Not as well as I *used* to hear her," grumbled Paul.

The three of them made their way back down from the bell tower, the rickety steps groaning and creaking beneath their feet, and then raced back out into the starless darkness, where they found Adam and Greg running through the cemetery toward them with a pack of upright, doglike monstrosities close on their heels.

"Get 'em off me!" shrieked Adam.

Paul and Justin both drew their guns and fired. The closest members of the pack dropped and thrashed around on the ground.

"This way!" shouted Eric, retreating back into the church.

Adam and Greg raced in after him. Paul and Justin backed in last. Then Eric slammed the door shut and threw his weight into it.

"Now what?" gasped Justin.

It was a good question. They'd stopped the bell from tolling, but now they were trapped inside the church, unable to get back to Creek Bend and the museum.

Paul cursed and clutched at his hand. Firing his gun had been difficult. He was probably going to need X-rays when this was over. Assuming he lived through it. "This is exactly what that clown freak wanted to happen, wasn't it?"

It did seem so.

"We have to get past them, though, don't we?" reasoned Justin. "We have to get back to the real Creek Bend."

"Not happening," grunted Greg. "Gate we came through's gone. The building it was in collapsed when those monsters came pouring out of it."

"What?" gasped Justin.

"Gone…" affirmed Adam, panting. "Fell down… Big cloud of dust…"

Justin turned and looked at Eric. "Please tell me that wasn't our only way out of here!"

But Eric could tell him no such thing. He cursed. The way back was blocked?

"Probably the clown's work, too," guessed Paul.

"Probably," agreed Eric.

"Not good," said Isabelle.

"What do we do, then?" asked Justin.

"Guuuuuuys!" shrieked Adam.

Eric turned to see several pairs of eyes shining back at him from the oppressive darkness hanging over the rotting pews.

"I'm guessing no one checked the back door…" wheezed Justin.

"No shit…" replied Paul.

There were more circling around the outsides of the pews on either side of the room, cutting off any possible routes of escape. All around them, hungry eyes shined back at them.

Adam let out a blubbery, terrified whimper and tripped himself backing away from the beasts.

Greg had no stories to share. He was only uttering the same swear word over and over again.

Justin and Paul fired at the glowing eyes, hitting several of the monsters, which dropped to the floor like the ones outside, thrashing and howling with pain, but there were just too many of them. Soon they were out of bullets and the pack was still closing in around them.

"This would be a good time for the universe to save your

ass!" groaned Paul.

"It would, wouldn't it?" agreed Eric.

But the universe didn't seem to have noticed that he needed help just yet. The skinwalkers were closing in around them as they cowered back against the door.

"You think they're mad about what happened to that bitch you mind raped back in the Man Hole?" wondered Justin.

"Can we not call it 'mind rape' please?" grumbled Eric. "That is *not* one of the last things I want to hear before I die."

"*I'd rather not die at all!*" cried Adam. He was still on the floor, scooting his sizeable posterior across the splintered floorboards as the monsters approached.

"Any time now…" growled Paul.

"I don't have any control over it!" Eric informed him.

"I know none of you ever believe any of my bullshit…" croaked Greg, his face pale in the reflected glow of the flashlights, "…I know I'm just a pathetic loser…but for what it's worth…thanks for listening all those times."

"Ah, hell…" said Justin. "Why you gotta go and say shit like that?"

"Aaaaaaany time…" croaked Paul, panic welling up in his voice.

But time was up.

The skinwalkers pounced.

Screams and snarls filled the silent church.

Eric raised his arms to shield his face.

And the entire world slowed to a terrifying stop.

Chapter Forty-One

The world literally stopped around them.

When Eric dared a peek between his upraised arms, the skinwalkers were frozen in mid-air, as if time, itself, had come to a screeching halt.

Paul was gasping for breath beside him. Greg was still uttering that same swear word under his breath. Justin was praying. And Adam was sobbing on the floor, inches from the toothy maw of a frozen skinwalker.

"What just happened?" panted Paul.

Eric wasn't sure. The universe again? Cordelia, perhaps? The gas station attendant? Maybe even the Lady of the Murk?

But it was none of those.

"Have you reconsidered yet?" hissed the voice of the Woman of the Hoard.

"*Whossat?*" blubbered Adam as he scooted himself backward, away from the monstrous jaws of that skinwalker. "What's happening?"

"Mamma?" squeaked Greg, his wide, delirious eyes fixed on the monster floating before his face.

"Shall we strike a deal *now?*" asked the Woman of the Hoard.

"I said no," Eric told her, standing his ground even though a part of him could barely believe he was saying it.

"Are you sure about that," she laughed. The sound of that laugh was terrible. "There's nothing you desperately need right now? Because it seems to me that you're not in a position to be choosy."

"What's going on?" gasped Justin. "Why're we in *The Matrix?*"

"I always have a choice," Eric told her.

"You don't really believe that."

No, he didn't. In fact, at this point in time, he didn't seem to have any choice in anything at all. But Cordelia warned him not to be tempted to bargain for anything except the key. She was adamant about that.

But...maybe *this* wasn't what she had in mind? What would she have him do if she were here? He could certainly use some advice right about now. But he was on his own.

"I can save you all, you know. Isn't that worth a measly little price?"

"No," insisted Eric.

"What're you doing?" hissed Justin. "Let the nice lady with the scary voice save us!"

"*I wanna go home now,*" hiccupped Adam.

"Don't listen to her," said Eric. "You don't want to pay her price. Trust me."

"*I'm* open to negotiation," whimpered Adam.

"No, you're not! Besides, she can't let anything happen to me. Isn't that right? I still owe you a favor, remember? The Skies of Esepthal? Let me die and you lose. I've already used the key. You'll get *nothing.*"

"Perhaps..." she hissed. "But *they* don't owe me *anything.*"

Eric glanced around. The four of them were staring back at him.

"What do I care if *they* die?"

He wasn't sure how to get out of this one.

Around them, time began to start up again. The skinwalkers began to creep forward, their jaws opening wider and wider.

Greg thrust his arm up in the air, "I vote for a deal!"

"No you don't!" snapped Eric.

"I'm with Greg on this one..." said Justin.

"Stop it!"

"Time's running out," the Woman of the Hoard informed him. "How much are their lives worth to you?"

"Just for the record," blubbered Adam, "I always liked you way better than your brother!"

"Shithead!" snapped Paul.

"*I just really don't want my face ripped off, okay?*"

Eric clenched his jaw, frustrated. Cordelia warned him not to make bargains with this…*thing*…but what was he supposed to do?

The world around them continued to pick up speed. The skinwalkers crept forward a little faster. He could see shining droplets of drool oozing from their teeth in slow motion.

"Last chance…" sighed the Woman of the Hoard. "Make me a deal for their lives. Or let them all die. It's your choice."

Paul stared at him, his eyes wide. "Just give her something already!"

"It's not that easy! It's not like she's accepting *cash!*"

"That's true…" she sighed. "I'll take what I want. Beggars can't be choosers, after all."

The world sped up a little more.

The skinwalkers were moving more quickly now.

Adam let out a shrill scream and covered his face.

"*I'll* do it!" blurted Paul.

"No!" shouted Eric.

"*I'll* make the deal!"

"Stop!"

"Just get us out of here!"

The Woman of the Hoard laughed a delighted and, Eric thought, a very *evil* sort of laugh. "Pleasure doing business with you."

The world sped up again.

The skinwalkers pounced.

A cold wind whistled through the church.

And in another instant, the four of them were in the dim glow of an electric security light, surrounded by antique farm machinery.

"What just happened?" gasped Justin.

Greg was whimpering the same vulgar word over and over again.

Adam was curled up on the floor, blubbering in a high-pitched voice.

"Where are we?" said Paul.

"The museum..." sighed Eric, looking around. The basement. But he was having a hard time feeling relieved. He turned on Paul, furious. "*What did you do?*"

"I saved us?"

"No, you didn't!"

"We're out of there, aren't we?"

"You made a deal with her!"

"Yes, I did."

"Without even settling on her price!"

"We'll deal with it later! Like always!"

"There might not *be* a later! Do you remember that conversation we had about fates *worse* than dying? About how I didn't just *die* in Evancurt, but *ceased to exist?*"

Paul stared at him, his mouth half open.

"That *thing* can take whatever it wants from you! *Anything!*" He stepped closer, glaring at him. "And you can bet that it won't take anything short of *everything.*"

Paul swallowed hard, but he didn't avert his eyes. "Well... It's too late now, isn't it?"

"*Stupid!*"

"Do you really think all of us were getting out of there alive otherwise?"

He shook his head and turned away. The truth was that he didn't know. Maybe he was right. Maybe dealing with the Woman of the Hoard was the only way to bring them all back alive.

But it didn't feel that way.

It felt like they'd just made a terrible mistake.

Distracted by the sound of approaching footsteps, he turned to find Ally hurrying toward them, her hair and clothes white with ash.

"You guys're finally back! You need to get in here. Things are getting *really* freaky."

Eric clutched at the idol under his arm. Yenaldlooshi! He'd almost forgotten!

Then Ally turned her gaze on Adam as he struggled to his feet. "Did you piss your pants?"

"*Don't start with me, demon girl!*" he shrieked at her.

Chapter Forty-Two

Even as he ran past the plexiglass-topped casket of the fake Monster of Creek Bend and through the previously hidden doorway, he could feel the evil aura of the real monster waiting at the far end of the tunnel.

It seemed like weeks ago that he was last here, though it had only been hours. Thinking about all that had happened in such a short time was almost disorienting.

But he couldn't let himself be distracted by that. He had to hurry. He was holding in his hands the only thing that could finally end this madness. Was the clown only messing with his head when he said that time was up? Or did he mean it when he said they wouldn't have time to get back here with the idol? And if he did mean it, did the unfortunate deal Paul made with the Woman of the Hoard save them enough time to still save everyone?

So many questions.

Up ahead, he could see the harsh glare of the flood lights. Mrs. Balm and Holly were standing on either side of the barred door, their backs turned to him. Paige was sitting cross-legged on the floor behind them with her back against the tunnel wall, cradling Ghede in her lap, her eyes closed, muttering quiet prayers. An ashen sheet of folded paper lay smoking on a silver tray in front of her, the remains of one of her poems. Mr. Iverley was standing over her, leaning on his cane and nervously flexing his arthritic hands over and over again on the handle. All of them were covered in white ash and glowed like spirits in the harsh, reflected glow of the flood lights, making the whole scene appear eerily surreal, even after all he'd been through.

As he approached, the old man looked up at him, then stood up straight. "Thank God! You've found it!" Then he turned and opened the iron gate. "Quickly now!"

Inside his cage, Yenaldlooshi was *writhing*. Its head thrashed from one side to the other, its monstrous hands clutching the bars.

"Put it back on its pedestal!" gasped Mrs. Balm. She sounded exhausted. How long had they been at this? "Hurry!"

But as Eric stepped through the gate and into the room where no one had set foot in almost fourteen decades, the hideous, cloth-wrapped face inside the box peeled its cracked lips back from its bristling teeth and howled in a monstrous, nightmarish voice, "*Fortrell!*"

Eric froze. The sound of the thing uttering his name like that was just as petrifyingly terrifying as it was when he watched Paul's video. It took every ounce of willpower he had to force himself to take those next few steps closer to the thing.

But running away wasn't an option. Any second now Yenaldlooshi was going to be free of the spell that had kept him bound to this place for the past one hundred thirty-seven years. Struggling to keep moving against the paralyzing fear that weighted down his weary legs, he managed those last few steps and placed the idol on the copper pedestal.

As soon as the two touched, a strange gust of wild energy seemed to pulse outward from it and the clay cracked violently in his hands.

It was like dropping an ice cube into a glass of water. It split right down the middle, almost completely in half. Eric stared at it as he held it there, his eyes wide with disbelief. Then, slowly, he turned and looked back at the others.

Mr. Iverley was still standing by the gate. Mrs. Balm and Holly stood on either side of him. Behind them, Paul, Justin and Ally were crowded in the dark corridor behind Paige. There was no sign of Greg or Adam. After the fright they'd had, they were probably still back in the farm machinery room. But everyone else was there, and they were staring at him with the same wide-eyed horror that he imagined was painted on his own face.

This wasn't part of the plan. Had he done something wrong? Or had the clown perhaps done something to sabotage it?

"Don't let go!" gasped Mrs. Balm. "Whatever you do, don't let go of it!"

He looked back down at the broken idol clasped between his hands, then up at the horror writhing in its iron bindings only a few feet away. Don't let go of it? That wasn't the deal. That wasn't what he signed up for. He was supposed to put the stupid thing on the pedestal and then turn around and haul ass back out of this terrifying room!

Why was nothing going right today?

"*Fortrell!*" howled the terror in the box, the voice sending another icy chill racing through his veins.

"I really don't want to be in here!" he cried, his quivering voice somewhat less than manly.

"Just hang in there a little longer!" shouted Mr. Iverley. "You can do this! I know you can!"

Why did he have the overwhelming feeling that the old man knew *no such thing*?

He could hear Holly and Mrs. Balm behind him. They weren't exactly chanting. It was more like a soft prayer. And it didn't sound like any language he'd ever heard before, which wasn't that uncommon when it came to magic. After all, most of the really scary magic he'd encountered seemed to come from a time and place long gone, far older than any of the languages that English had even evolved from.

Yenaldlooshi's body jerked violently inside the box, rocking it hard to one side.

"Hurry up back there!" he gasped.

"It's not like a thrust!" Holly informed him. "It's not something you can exactly fire off on a whim!"

"Focus!" snapped Mrs. Balm.

Again, the monster convulsed. Again, the box rocked back and forth.

What happened if the thing managed to knock itself over?

Mrs. Balm and Holly raised their voices together. An odd, warm wind gusted at Eric's back. Was that it? Had they finally gotten a grip on the monster with their magic?

But the monster let out a furious, blood-curdling shriek that made his knees go weak and his legs tremble, and a much colder and fouler gust pushed back, seemingly originating from the iron box in front of him. And with this festering chill came a series of strange images that flashed through his head in rapid succession. Images of alien skies and shadowy creatures and blood-soaked earth. Images of pain and desperation and death.

He'd seen many of these things before, while using the forbidden spell in the Man Hole to probe the monster's mind through the filter of the captured female skinwalker. He witnessed the sweltering, sunless depths of its foul, bottomless lair. And he saw glimpses of a far earlier time as well, and a far more alien world.

These were the ancient memories of Yenaldlooshi, himself.

He stared at the wrapped face thrashing and writhing within the iron bars of the box in front of him. What were these alien places he saw in its memories? Where did this monster come from? And how long had it been alive?

And one memory in particular seemed to dominate the thing's unfathomable lifespan. A bold burglary. A quest deep inside a blistering chasm. A mysterious treasure of unimaginable value. A desperate flight across a hellish wasteland from furious, godlike figures.

It was like a scene from ancient mythology, a tale of the time before the great Greek gods, far back in the age of the titans. It was like watching Prometheus steal fire from the Olympians and give it to mankind to usher in the first civilization.

The idea was somehow both terrifying and intriguing. He felt certain somehow that this ancient memory was of vast significance. This was an event that changed *everything*. But he didn't get the chance to ponder it. He became distracted by an odd, numbing sensation in his hands where he was holding the idol.

"Something's wrong…" he heard Paige say behind him.

"We're out of alignment," gasped Mrs. Balm. "The broken idol…"

"What's happening back there?" demanded Eric.

"I think we should get out of here!" groaned Justin.

"And go where?" snapped Paul. "You saw where this city's going if that thing gets loose."

There was a flare of yellow light as Paige ignited another poem from her notebook and let it burn. He could smell the smoke. He could hear her muttering to the spirits, likely asking for protection and aid in the casting of the sealing spell.

The first time he watched her use her magic, he found himself face to face with the powerful Papa Ghede, himself, after whom her stuffed bunny had been named. He was an imposing figure, even while wearing the body of a young girl, radiating power and wisdom. It was Papa Ghede who insisted that Paige remain at his side that night and tasked him with keeping her safe, a promise he very nearly died keeping.

"We can't let up," said Mrs. Balm, though she sounded out of breath. "We can do this."

Eric could feel that icy numbness slowly enveloping his hands and creeping up his wrists. "Something's happening in here…" he informed them. "This doesn't feel right…"

"Keep holding onto it, Eric," said Mrs. Balm.

"I can feel something…" said Holly, "…but…?"

"Just keep going," she told her. "We can't stop. For everyone's sake, we can't stop."

"Something's *way* wrong…" said Paige. She sounded on the verge of tears.

The monster was thrashing harder now. The box was rocking back and forth, a shower of white ash and dust raining down around it. Terrifying moans and growls were echoing off the walls of the tunnel, seeming to come from every direction at once.

And as that numb sensation crept up to his elbows, Eric began to realize what was happening.

"Wait!" shouted Holly.

"We can't!" scolded Mrs. Balm. "We don't have a choice!"

"What's happening?" demanded Paul.

Eric looked back over his shoulder and met Holly's terrified gaze. "I'm not going to be able to leave this room."

She shook her head. "No…"

"He's right," said Mrs. Balm. "He's the idol now. He's the only thing that can hold the spell."

"You can't!" cried Holly. "We need you!"

"Stop this!" shouted Paul.

"What's happening?" said Justin. "I don't understand any of this."

"We don't have a choice," said Mrs. Balm. "I'm sorry."

But Holly was adamant. "We just need more magic. We can do this."

"We don't *have* any more magic! We're all we have! And this is our only chance!"

"Just do what has to be done!" shouted Eric. "Don't worry about me!"

"No!" shouted Paul. "Put me in there instead!"

"It doesn't work that way," shouted Mrs. Balm.

"I can't!" whimpered Holly.

"You have to!" insisted Eric. "You have to protect everyone else!"

"But…"

Again, the monster howled that terrifying howl. A gnarled and twisted hand reached out through the bars of the box, stretching toward Eric. "Fortreeeeeeellllllllllll…"

"*Do it now!*" he shouted. "*Whatever it takes! Just do it!*"

Mrs. Balm began again. He could hear her voice behind him, speaking softly, as if uttering a quiet prayer but in that strange, unfamiliar language.

He didn't think Holly would. He wasn't sure she could. And he wouldn't have blamed her. He wasn't sure *he* could make such a decision, either, if he were to be honest. If their places were switched, he simply didn't think he could do it. But after a moment, he heard her voice, too.

The numbness spread throughout his entire body, chilling him deep inside.

He stared at that awful, outstretched hand and took a long, ragged breath that came back out in a cloud of cold steam when he let it go.

This was the power of the idol, he realized. Whatever was

inside it, whatever gave it the power necessary to bind Yenaldlooshi, was no longer contained within the clay. But the doll was broken and it was now leeching into *him*.

He was never again going to leave this terrible room. His corpse would keep the Monster of Creek Bend sleeping here from now on.

No… The universe would protect him. Everyone kept saying so.

Right?

He could hear Paul shouting behind him. He probably thought it should be him. After all, there was still a lot of work to be done.

What was going to happen now, he wondered? The karmic sin. The favor he owed the Woman of the Hoard. And what about that promise he made to the toll collector? And what about Isabelle? That was a lot of things left to do. He wondered who was going to take care of all those things once he was gone.

Yenaldlooshi thrashed violently to the side. This time, the iron box tipped too far. It teetered there on the edge of balance for a few seconds. Then it fell.

And yet, amazingly, it stopped again.

A shadowy figure appeared and stood it upright again. A second shadow appeared on the other side of it. Then a third grasped it from the back, all of them holding the monster down.

"Finish casting the spell," said Paige in a strange and oddly familiar voice.

He looked back at her over his shoulder and found not Paige's eyes looking back at him, but the dingy, ancient eyes of Papa Ghede.

"We'll hold him. *You* focus on feeding the power back into the idol."

Eric blinked at her (at *him?*) for a moment, then looked down at the broken doll in his hands again. "How…?"

But then someone else was there, too. Cold, soft hands closed around his.

A broken, warbling voice in his ear said, "Imagine the cold leaving your body and seeping back into the clay."

"Tessa…" he gasped. He couldn't see her, but he could hear her. And he could feel her. She was with him.

Mrs. Balm was wrong. They *did* have more magic.

The Creek Man let out a furious howl and thrashed inside his box, but the loa held him down as Tessa began chanting the mysterious words of the spell over his shoulder.

The atmosphere changed. A charge filled the air. And Yenaldlooshi didn't like it one bit. He shrieked at them like a cornered animal, snarling and snapping at the bars of his tiny prison.

Eric tore his eyes off the incredible scene before him and focused on the broken idol. *Feed the power back into it*, he thought. *Imagine the cold leaving your body and seeping back into the clay.*

That sounded simple enough.

He forced every other thought from his head and tried to imagine just that. Almost immediately, he felt that icy feeling reverse direction. It unwound itself from his bones. It slithered back out of his veins. It crept back down his arms.

"Fortreeeeeeeeeellllllllll!" shrieked Yenaldlooshi.

His hands began to warm.

A layer of frost crackled over the surface of the doll.

Almost there…

Then, with a final, furious shriek, the relic in the box went silent.

The shadowy figures winked out like candles in the dark.

Tessa's cold hands faded away.

Eric finally let go of the idol and turned around. He felt as if he'd been awake for a week straight. He could barely hold his head up. He stumbled back through the gate and dropped to his knees on the damp floor.

Holly and Paige were there in an instant, kneeling over him, checking on him.

"It's over," said Mrs. Balm, sounding as if she barely believed it herself.

"Don't ever do that again!" gasped Holly, clinging to his arm.

"Papa Ghede said you weren't allowed to die," Paige informed him. "He says not until you finish cleaning up all your messes."

Eric nodded. "Sounds reasonable," he gasped.

"Are we done?" asked Paul, still looking around the room.

"I think we're done," affirmed Mr. Iverley, sounding as cheerful as ever. "Well done, everyone."

Then Ally blurted out, "What the fuck did I just witness?"

Chapter Forty-Three

Eric sat slumped in one of the chairs in Mr. Iverley's office, waiting for his head to clear. That intense, initial weariness had receded a little, but he was still exhausted. And it was no wonder, really. Stairway City, by itself, was probably the most intense workout of his life. His feet and legs were still aching. He wasn't confident he was going to be able to get out of bed in the morning.

"Paige says Yenaldlooshi still hasn't moved," reported Isabelle. "It really does seem to be asleep again. Which I guess means the skinwalkers should be slinking back off to wherever it was they came from."

"I sure hope so," he grumbled.

"And I guess that shayatin thing won't be waking up tonight, either."

"God willing..."

Holly drove Justin to pick up his truck, which was still parked on Main Street in front of the barber shop. As soon as they were back, Justin would take Paul, Ally and the two morons back to the Man Hole to retrieve their own vehicles and Holly and Paige would drop him off before returning home themselves. In the meantime, all there was for him to do was sit and rest. But rest was difficult with so many fresh thoughts circling through his mind.

He owed the Woman of the Hoard something called the Skies of Esepthal...whatever the hell that was. He had no idea what retrieving such a thing might entail, but if Cordelia said for him to offer it, then he had to believe that he could get it. That didn't mean, however, that it would be easy. On the contrary, there wasn't a doubt in his mind that when the time came it was going to be a *huge* pain in his ass.

More importantly, what would she end up demanding from Paul after his ill-informed dealings in the old church? Not that he really blamed him, deep down. He didn't know what *else* could have been done in that terrifying moment. After all, the universe didn't send a friendly, bloody-eyed ghost or a freaky cat or any other beacons of hope to save them under that black sky. All it sent them was *her*. And while he still didn't think she would've let him die in there, not while he still owed her something, he was also quite sure that she had no reason whatsoever to save Paul and the others. In the end, he knew that he wouldn't have been capable of just letting them die. If Paul hadn't spoken up when he did…if just another second or two had passed…the truth was that he probably would have made the very same decision. But that didn't change the fact that he felt as if they'd made a very grave mistake.

And then there was the clown. *That* freak was still out there. And he was taking a very concerning interest in Eric's life. He was going to continue to be a problem, that much was obvious.

Should he have realized who he was dealing with from the start? In hindsight, Ford *had* behaved rather clownish, he supposed. But he'd only assumed the man was a little on the insane side. That seemed to be common when it came to agents.

More importantly, where was he now? What was he up to? And when would he show his creepy face again?

And what about the shayatin sleeping in that black remnant of Creek Bend's past? How long did they have before something else came along and decided to wake it up? And what horrors would this city endure when it finally did?

"Do you remember Hedge Lake?" asked Isabelle.

He glanced down at the phone, distracted. "How could I forget?"

"That little ghost girl. Jordan. Remember what she told you before she moved on?"

Eric frowned at the memory. It wasn't one of his favorites. She wasn't supposed to be dead. She was supposed to be one of the ones he'd saved. But he *did* remember her. Vividly. And he remembered those mysterious words she'd said to him as if it were only yesterday.

"She said there was a secret in Creek Bend. And that you'd have to stop it, just like you stopped the worm that night."

He nodded. And it *was* like Hedge Lake, wasn't it? Something terrible was trying to break the borders holding the worlds apart.

"I was thinking earlier that she must've been talking about Yenaldlooshi, but she was talking about the *bigger* monster. The shayatin sleeping in the forsaken acres. Eventually it's going to wake up again. I could feel it when you were down there. It wasn't quite time today, but sometime soon, it'll wake up on its own. You're going to have to stop it."

"Yeah…"

"But not yet. Because she said you'd have to find somebody first, remember?"

"Euphemia Blue," recalled Eric.

"Right. Her. If she was right about that, then you can't stop the shayatin until you find Euphemia Blue."

"I guess we'll have to start looking for her," he reasoned. But where did you begin looking for one person in an entire world? He tried looking it up online when he first returned from Hedge Lake, but searching that name had turned up no results.

Still, that was a long time ago. He could try again. But he didn't think he'd find anything. Whoever Euphemia Blue was, she was doubtlessly a part of the weird. And the weird never failed to find him When the time came, he was certain that he'd find her. In fact, *she* would probably end up finding *him*.

Just like Perri and Evancurt.

The weird always found him…

The screen cut to an incoming call and his phone began to ring. It was Karen. He accepted the call and lifted it to his ear. "Hey," he answered.

"Isabelle says it's over," said Karen.

"Yeah. Monsters are sleeping again."

"She said it was the clown."

"Yep."

"You okay? I know how you are with clowns."

"I'm not afraid of them," he grumbled.

"I know. You just don't like them. I can't believe he's been stalking you like that."

"Creeper," said Diane in the background.

"*Total* creeper," agreed Karen. "Do you think he'll come back again?"

"I'm certain of it."

"Well…on the plus side, doesn't that mean the agents probably don't know everything about you that he said they did?"

He cocked his head to one side, considering it. "It's possible…" After all, the clown said he murdered the agent shortly after he arrived. That meant that the agent he met was *always* the clown in disguise.

"The clown is scary, but I feel like I'll sleep a little better knowing there's not a whole army of superpowered freaks out there who know my address."

"That's true," agreed Eric. "Silver lining, I guess."

"Yeah."

He stared off into the distance for a moment, exhausted, wondering how long it would be before Holly came back to drive him home.

And how long would he have before the weird came back to ruin his life some more?

He really hoped it wasn't for a very long time. He needed a good, long break.

"So you're coming home soon?" asked Karen.

"Pretty soon, yeah."

"Everything's done?"

"Yep."

"So…did you put the dildo in your pucker hole?"

"Not you, too," growled Eric.

He could already hear Diane laughing hysterically in the background.

"Was it hard? Or did it just slide right in there?"

"Stop."

"Did you have to pause for a breath when it was halfway in?"

"*Shut it.*"

"OH GOD!" gasped Diane. "I CAN'T BREATHE!"

"That's what *he* said!" exclaimed Karen before bursting into side-splitting laughter herself.

Eric rubbed his aching temples. "I'm hanging up now."

"*Wait-wait-wait!*" gasped Karen. "*Don't go!* Seriously, though… *Seriously.*"

"Yes?" he sighed.

"Did you call it 'daddy'?"

Eric disconnected the call, cutting off Karen's snorting laughter, only to have it replaced with a text from Isabelle that filled the screen with, AHAHAHAHAHAHAHAHAHA

"I hate all of you," he grumbled.

ABOUT THE AUTHOR

Brian Harmon grew up in rural Missouri and now lives in Southern Wisconsin with his wife, Guinevere, and their three children.

For more about Brian Harmon and his work, visit
www.HarmonUniverse.com